WHITEROCK

BOOK ONE OF THE AVIAN AGE

HAL AETUS

aetusart.com

WHITEROCK - BOOK ONE OF THE AVIAN AGE

Soft Cover ISBN-13: 979-8-9898252-3-3
Electronic Edition ISBN-13: 979-8-9898252-5-7

Special Adult Edition also available to readers 18 years and older.

Published by:
Aetus Art
PO Box 44236
Milwaukee, Wisconsin, 53214, USA
aetusart.com

Cover art and design by Hal Aetus. All interior art, except where mentioned is by Hal Aetus. Additional art, as labeled herein, provided by Silver Arts (silvergriffin21@gmail.com).

 **No AI Pledge:** No artificial intelligence (AI), generative or otherwise, was used in the creation of the story, artwork, or cover.

Dedication

Thank you, Colin, for enduring my art and authoring obsession. I love you, husbird. My eternal gratitude to Buddy, a real bald eagle who bonded with me and taught me how eagles experience the world and care for each other. I only hope I can pass on some of what he gifted me.

Thanks to Silver and Trisha, friends who inspired me early on to write the first short story and build off their characters (Nyx and Silver from Silver, and Tristan, later renamed to Sashya, from Trisha).

Many thanks to Joshua Essoe for his editing services of an early version of the manuscript. He not only gave me an honest and thorough analysis of what I had, but also showed me what it could be, and gave me the resources to improve my writing on my own.

Thank you to Megasploot for their map-making tool, Wonderdraft. It's what I used to create the maps of Volatus and Galinta. I highly recommend checking them out if you are an author, fantasy gamer, or dreamer who likes to build new worlds.

Thank you to the awesome troupe of beta-readers and friends that provided much-needed input and grounding: Aquiliqex, Astor, B-York, Barnibu, Dilong, Eric Malves, McFan, Pteri Grus, Silver, and Trisha. I also appreciate the significant financial backing of my many Patreon patrons, particularly the stellar supporters Barnibu and WorldsBestEagle.

And thank you to all the friends and fans who have shared their mutual desire to be birds in a fresh new world. I look forward to seeing what others can create based upon this world I've only started to build.

Contents

Introduction

By Hal Aetus of the Anthropocene Age

Thank you for joining me in an avian adventure. If you've desired to be a bird, this book was written for you, because that's been my dream my whole life and has influenced pretty much every aspect of my career and life. You are not alone and there are many of us that hold on to that fantasy well into our adult lives. I invite you to feed that fantasy, draw inspiration from it to care about the natural world, to strive for something better in our society, drawing inspiration from nature, and to care for each other.

With that, feel free to read on into the book and maybe come back to this if you have questions. Otherwise, what follows might help you fly higher and farther into the Avian Age. Let's do this in the style of Frequently Asked Questions:

Why do the birds in Whiterock talk and express emotions like people?

It's pretty easy to see that birds are vastly different from us. And, yet, deep down we still share the same basic needs, share some common physiology and anatomy, and have the same drives. I've built on those similarities to make the characters more relatable while hopefully maintaining their bird-ness. But ultimately, this book is intended for people so I had to make some difficult artistic choices. These compromises were not easy for my vision of immersing you in the mind and body of a bird in this world, so I only did them where I felt it was absolutely necessary.

Also, you'll soon learn that the characters are not exactly normal birds. They were imbued, or "Awakened," by enterprising people looking for cheap, but smart, laborers back before society destroyed itself in the late 21st century. This included giving birds human qualities such as speech, the ability to read, and the ability to reason about the world and theorize alternative solutions to problems. I am reluctant to say that humans are alone in these capabilities as science is continually refining our understanding of avian intelligence, teaching us that they already have a surprising degree of communication, empathy, and reasoning abilities.

How do real birds express emotions?

Avian body language is different from ours, yet understandable to those familiar with birds. Birds lack most of the facial muscles we enjoy so while they may not smile like us, they can subtly adjust their facial feathers, the shape of their eyelids, the diameter of their pupils, and the height of their head plumage to indicate their emotional state. I wanted to write something completely immersed in such a world and attempted this through experimental writings ("An Eagle's Life" being one of the first), but I found these exercises impeded by continuous infodumps to the reader to translate the meanings of the character's actions, which resulted in stories that read more like entries in a textbook. I've compromised in Whiterock by mixing birdisms with human conventions, so that when I say a bird smiles, you may choose to envision that in a human sense with the beak corners turning up slightly, or you can see it in a species-appropriate sense of eyes narrowing, pupils contracting, and facial plumage erecting. For those of us that have lived our lives imagining ourselves as birds, this exercise won't be difficult. For others, give it a try. Consider this story a Rosetta stone for experiencing the world from a bird's perspective.

Why is Whiterock written in first-person point-of-view?

Each chapter is written from the first-person perspective of one of four characters. I chose this with the hope it would connect the reader more naturally with the emotions of the characters, regardless of how they express them, and the world as they perceive it, rather than how we might experience it as mere humans. It also negated the need for infodumping since the birds already understand their world and you can learn what you need from their internal monologue as the story progresses. If that's not enough, there's a glossary in the back of the book.

What is the source of your avian knowledge for Whiterock?

I created the Avian Age based on what I know from our current bird world and years of experience working directly with birds and those that study them. In my professional career, I'm a board-certified avian veterinarian who has attended birds in a veterinary capacity for twenty-seven years.

Why are mundane behaviors like preening, rousing, and pooping mentioned?

First, to remind you that this is a bird story, not a human one. Birds live an active life centered around flight, meaning they are in a daily (or hourly) race to fuel their bodies, maintain their feathers, and watch out for danger and opportunity. In some ways, it's not dissimilar from our lives in that they seek opportunities to sate their desires and needs as conveniently as possible, only that their wants and needs are much more acutely felt, particularly at scarce times of the year. Where we may be hungry enough to heat up leftovers from the fridge that didn't seem appetizing earlier in the day, a raven surviving winter can be hungry enough to relish tallow from the bones of a month-old carcass or fresh canine excrement (no, I'm not making that up). Thankfully the birds of the Avian Age are generally not that desperate.

Being able to fly also means sparing as much weight as possible. Their anatomy reflects this in the fusion of many bones to reduce the need for muscles to support their body in flight, as well as the more well-known feature of hollow, pneumatized bones. Liquids and solid wastes are also heavy, which is why birds eliminate them frequently, especially just before flight.

Why are the birds in Whiterock so horny?

No joke, my editor actually asked this of one of my early versions of Whiterock. It was a good reminder that I'm writing for a human audience from a society with different views on sex than birds may have.

First of all, the book opens in March in the northern hemisphere, a period when a majority of birds are experiencing spring mating drive. For birds, sex only comes to the forefront of their mind for a brief period once a year. Taking cues from the abundance of food, the presence of mates, nest sites, and courtship songs around them, their brains secrete hormones that prepare them for breeding. In response, their gonads, which exist in lightweight, shriveled forms for most of the year, enlarge to hundreds of times their usual mass. The chemical juicing that follows fuels an all-consuming fire of territoriality, nesting, and mating desire. After the springtime "mating fever" ends, they resume their primary tasks of self-care. There are instances where non-procreative copulation is observed though, indicating that they still have the drive and take advantage of it when opportunities arise. It's a cool reminder that birds are not biological automatons. They probably have emotions and desires, perhaps similar to us, but not always expressed in ways we easily recognize.

I've dampened down the sexuality (a little bit) because the birds of the Avian Age, generally speaking, have an appreciation for civility, personal boundaries, and order. Through cooperation and laws, and revulsion of an aristocratic past that stole the personal liberties of undervalued species, they've managed to improve quality of life for most birds, and have made competition for food, shelter, and mates, less cutthroat. The extra time and energy this creates has allowed Volatian citizens more time for creative arts and scientific advancement, particularly in the times of year outside breeding season.

Civilized birds still value a highly sex-positive society with few moral objections to sex between consenting adult birds, regardless of species or sex. Prostitution is legal and considered a necessary social enterprise in springtime as it allows the release of biological tension that may otherwise drive birds to criminal behavior. The system is by no means perfect, and requires policing to protect the vulnerable. As with real birds, the trade-off to all of this mating frenzy is that for the rest of the year, hormones wane and most birds are more rational. They still have desire and can mate, but the drive is much more manageable.

Wouldn't a bird world have no streets, sidewalks, or stairs?

Yes, and neither does the Avian Age... mostly. Birds live in three dimensions, frequently viewing the world in a top-down perspective, with no borders and few obstacles. Yet, consider that for civilized birds, there might be times when heavy items might need to be moved. If they're too heavy to lift in flight, they only have a few practical choices: Move it by air in little pieces, move it by air in an apparatus of some kind, move it over the ground using wheels or greased skids perhaps, or simply build around and leave it in place. You'll see all of these strategies used in Volatus.

Also, what do you do if you can't fly? Say you need to get to a hospital for care of a broken wing? You might need paths or stairs or ramps to get yourself to help. You'll see some of this within towns but, as of yet, there are no roadways connecting population centers. As you read, you'll encounter wind and wing-powered craft, but for the most part, birds can fly fast and efficiently enough to take themselves all over Volatus.

What do these bird terms mean?

I would've loved going full bird with this series, but in earlier test readings, it was clear that this would alienate readers who were new to birds and bird lingo. Not only that, but using familiar human terms for things sometimes seems silly, particularly those that are based on proper nouns. A good example is the species name Steller's sea eagle. I would hope that in a few hundred years of sapience, birds would have come up with their own terms for themselves, hence why I dubbed them as "crowned eagles" or simply "crownies."

I hope I've struck a good balance between immersing the reader, and not drowning the less bird-familiar with the need to look up words constantly. In most cases, I have tried to introduce technical terms and invented Jargon in such a way that you can infer their meaning from the context of their use. Just in case that doesn't work, **there is a glossary and anatomy diagrams in the back of the book**, should you require it.

How do I keep track of all these characters?

As the Avian Age world grew, so did the cast of characters, some of whom play minor roles now but may be critical to events later in the series. If you're like me, it's hard to keep track of names without a face or a few other facts, and it's helpful to have a "yearbook" of sorts to fall back on. If you need that too, **there's a character biography section at the back of the book** with sketches and notes.

Where can I learn more about the Avian Age?

There is a large amount of additional lore that couldn't be easily dispensed in these pages. Because of this, I started a wiki (wiki.aetusart. com) that contains cool world-building stuff like calendars, historical timelines, maps, sketches of avian tools, and characters from history. The wiki is not essential to enjoying the books but if you can't get enough of the world from the stories, check it out and keep checking as it is likely to grow. If you have ideas on what to add, please contact me as I'm interested in having additional contributors.

Maps

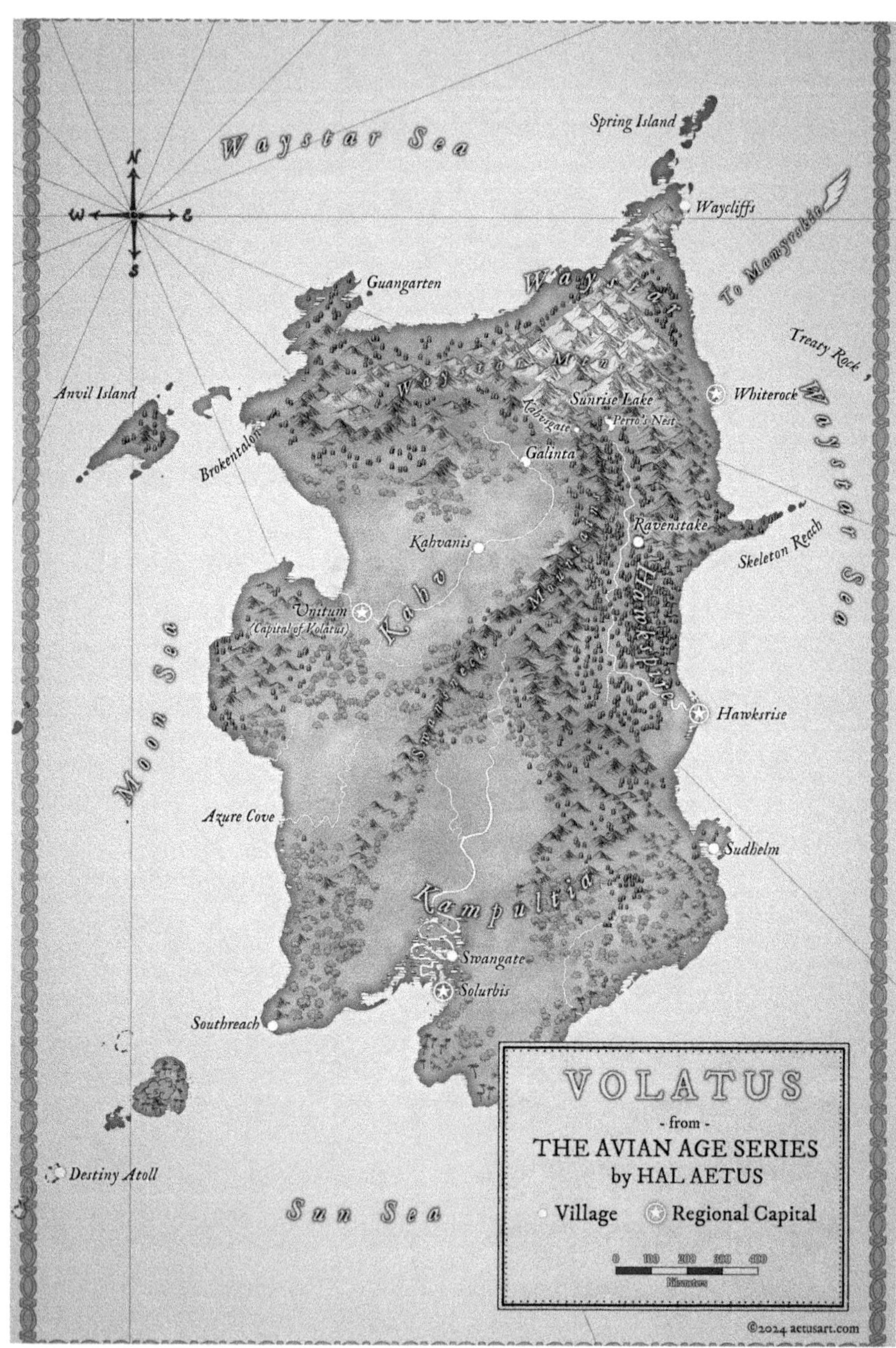
Waystar Sea
Spring Island
Waycliffs
To Mamyrokia
Guangarten
Treaty Rock
Waystar Mtn
Anvil Island
Sunrise Lake
Whiterock
Kahvigate
Perro's Nest
Brokentalon
Galinta
Ravenstake
Skeleton Reach
Kahvanis
Waystar Sea
Unitum
(Capital of Volatus)
Kabo
Hawkspire
Moon Sea
Hawksrise
Azure Cove
Sudhelm
Kampultia
Swangate
Solurbis
Southreach
Destiny Atoll
Sun Sea
VOLATUS
- from -
THE AVIAN AGE SERIES
by HAL AETUS
Village   Regional Capital
0   100   200   300   400
Kilometres
©2024 aetusart.com

GALINTA
Northern Kahv, Volatus
from the
Avian Age Series
By Hal Aetus
©2024 aetusart.com
Kor's Forge
Galinta River
Amphitheater
Blackbeak's Pub
Tailwind Inn
Watchtower
Broody's Parlor
Suvork's Smeltery
Tumbling Creek
Galinta Midden
0 200 400 600 800 1000
Meters

Chapter 1

The Commission

By Sashya of Kahvanis

It was the end of a cool, wet day when four stately eagles floated down out of the gray rain and alighted at the gate to Kor's Forge. I had never seen a crowny before, or Steller's sea eagle as the Featherless had named them, though I had been taught about their kind and how they had once held dominion over our country, Volatus. I wondered if I was reliving a moment from a few lifetimes past, when crowny lords dropped in to exert authority over their subjects. But I was only approaching my third hatchday and had just read of such things in the pages of our history.

The crownies were magnificently plumed in slaty brown with crisp, snow-white legs, tail, and wrists. A forehead patch formed a white crown above a beak the color of the setting sun on a winter day. Three wore leather armor and helmets and a lead bird wore only a blue sash with a white star.

They carried their heads high as they roused the rain from their feathers and folded their wings. The lead bird stood a meter tall, and although not the largest of the group, he carried himself with the most authority. He strode proudly through the mud towards me with his gleaming tail swishing behind his broad thighs and his eyes fixed on me like two gold coins. I froze and dropped my pail of ashes.

He stopped, only a wingspan away, and bowed his head as rain dripped from his sharp beak. "Do not fear, fine owl," he said. "We come as customers. Is Master Kor in today?" His voice groaned like an oak in a stiff breeze, and consonants clonked like the stir of wooden wind chimes with vowels as their reverberations. Though different from our casual local dialect, it was understandable Apterian, or English, as the Featherless had termed the language.

The eagle straightened from his courteous bow, blinked, and cocked his head. "Do you understand me?" he asked.

I snapped out of my awestruck state. "Yes, sir. Sorry, who may I say is calling?"

A warm smile spread across the corners of his beak, "I am King Vasili of Mamyrskit." He turned and directed his eyes to the others. "This is my daughter, Princess Vouli. Beside her is my Wingwarden, Tulivor, and Second-Talon, Ruusch."

The three subordinates each tipped their beaks solemnly as their names were spoken. Their leather helmets gleamed with steel points that projected above the eyes and beak. Their feet were clad in jointed leather armor with fearsome steel scimitars that overlapped their already capable talons. I recognized the high craftsbirdship of their battle claws as they lacked the serrations that so many less capable blacksmiths tended to employ in compensation for lower quality steel. The leather plates on their backs and breasts were painted blue and bore a white, eight-pointed star. Princess Vouli's armor and helmet were edged in glittering gold.

My heart pounded as I made eye contact and tipped my beak to each bird. Vouli eyed me with impatience barely disguised by the courteous smile the circumstances demanded. The left side of Tulivor's face bore a deep yellow scar that crossed through a cloudy eye and trailed off into white, scraggly feathers below. I wondered what sobering story explained Tulivor's scar, but I found Vouli's haughty gaze more chilling.

I bowed and said, "I'm Sashya, apprentice to Master Kor. Pleased to meet you."

The town bell rang rapidly five times, announcing the arrival of dignitaries. Perhaps the delay was due to the inclement weather, but it was equally likely that old Kassir, the red-tailed hawk on watch that day, had dozed off in her cupola. Curious beaks poked out from nearby dwellings and Haymir, the constable swan, waddled out of the village pub to stare at us from across the square.

The King smiled broadly and chuckled, "Young master, might we go inside out of the rain?"

"Yes, of course, Your Majesty! Please come this way."

I turned and led them through the stone arch that separated Kor's shop yard from the village square. From the arch projected a hanging

sign with Kor's insignia: A silhouetted raven head with an onyx stone for the eye. The outer wall and arch were the remains of an iron and brick Apterian building that once stood there. Kor and his father had constructed a spacious blacksmith and jewelry shop out the rest of the ruin. Metal scraps, wood for handles, firewood, and coal were organized in neat piles in the yard and a massive oak spread out above the back of the shop.

We entered the warmth of the shop through a wide, arched doorway, and the eagles shook the rain from their feathers. A stone and iron hearth dominated the center of the shop. Above this, in the rafters, a waterwheel's axle turned slowly, providing power to pulleys and belts to drive our forge hammer, bellows, sharpening wheel, and lathe. Above this, a mosaic of multicolored glass fragments, carefully fitted together with frames of hammered iron and wood, served as roof and source of illumination. The lively glasswork curved and flowed, in contrast with the few remaining square glass panes of Apterian origin. In the right rear corner of the workshop, a doorway led to the colorful windowed bubble of Kor's parlor where he sketched and crafted jewelry.

Pepro, sat perched at an anvil on the hearth, striking glowing hot steel with a forging hammer in his foot. He bore the white head and tail of an adult bald eagle approaching their sixth hatchday. He had been Kor's apprentice for nearly a year and was my tutor and constant companion since I arrived the previous fall.

Orange sparks flew with each clank of his hammer and reflected off the glass lenses of his leather hood as acrid metallic smoke swirled about his head. Between the dazzling flicker and noise, he didn't notice us until he paused and thrust the steel back into the coals. His head snapped around when he realized he wasn't alone, then he cocked his beak curiously. For a moment, all stood still except the whoosh of the bellows, the creaks of wood and leather machinery, and the pattering of rain on the colorful windows above.

Vasili broke the silence: "What an impressive shop! It's so colorful and bright, even on so dark a day as today! And who is this fine eagle? Please introduce me."

His warm manners melted away formal barriers between us, but the gravity of interacting with a king, perhaps the most important bird I would ever meet, had not been erased.

I nervously stammered, "Y-your Majesty, sir, this is Pepro, senior apprentice to Master Kor. Pepro, this is King Vasili from *Mammerskit.*"

Vasili laughed, "Let me help you with pronouncing that. Maa-MIR-skit! Mamyrskit!"

My beak blushed with embarrassment. "Sorry, sir. It's the first I've heard the name spoken in such an accent."

"Ha ha, don't fear, young owl. We may be the first crowned eagles you've ever even met! And Mamyrskit is a long way away from these fair lands." He leaned closer and spread a wing out as though directing my eyes towards a distant horizon and said, "It's far across the Waystar Sea, in a stormy and cold place. A place teaming with bird-kind in summer, but sparse, and lonely, most of the year. So, when we meet friends, old or new, we greet warmly, like this..."

He held out his wings wide as he stepped closer to me, much closer than I normally allow strangers. But he was a king, so I closed my eyes and cringed as he wrapped me in a warm, soft embrace. He towered twice as tall as myself, so that my head met his broad breast. My acute ears heard every whisper of breath and surge of blood in his chest. His outer feathers were damp, but his down was deep, soft, and dry, and his muscles noticeably firm. His plumage carried a faintly salty scent that I couldn't place. This was my first sampling of ocean spray, an odor that puzzled me at the time, but which would soon become as common to me as the charred aroma of the forge.

As he released me, he tapped his beak softly to mine and left me speechless with the conviction that no stranger had ever hugged me so genuinely. In that moment, my fear melted away as though the eagle had a magic spell that erased the gulf between our class and culture.

My gaze stayed fixed on his smiling face as he backed away and I said, "That's an amazing greeting, sir. I shall have to remember that custom."

The king amiably turned to Pepro and beckoned with his wings, "Please, Pepro, come here and let me embrace you, so that we may be done with formalities."

Pepro snagged off his hood with a talon and laid it down on the

hearth. He hopped down to the floor with a thud and bowed his head before Vasili, then said, "Sir, I'm filthy from work."

"And I'm wet from the rain. Don't worry about it! I am pleased to meet a fellow, handsome eagle, Pepro. Thank you for receiving us." The king repeated his stately hug on Pepro, who glanced over at me with a nervous smile on his beak as they released.

I said, "Sir, I'll just go and get Kor for you now." But as I spun on one foot and spread my wings, Kor was already approaching, and I stumbled into him.

Kor glowered at me and flashed his white nictitating membranes in annoyance, then shook his feathers back into place. He was a soot-black raven with singed nasal bristles above a beak worn with scrapes and scratches. His plumage was almost always peppered with ash, and he bore manners as callused as his tool-hardened feet, yet he was never disingenuous. He was firm, and demanding of our best efforts, but ultimately fair and when recognizing a job well done, his heart glowed as warmly as his forge.

I apologized, and he croaked in reply, "I see we have guests! Why don't you introduce us?"

"You must be Master Kor!" Vasili bowed low and stared at his feet a moment, a mannerism that I had learned from Pepro common among sea eagles when showing respect or, as was often the case with Pepro, lost in thought. He lifted his head and stated, "I am King Vasili of Mamyrskit. Your reputation as the finest crafter of metals is unmatched in Volatus and so, I am here to humbly request your services. Please, allow me to greet you in our manner."

Kor held up his wings to halt the king's advance, "Sorry, sir, but I'm not one for embraces, though I am deeply honored, by your offer."

Vasili laughed, "You're exactly as I was told to expect. Excuse my levity, but I'm so pleased to find you that I can scarce contain my joy."

Kor nodded and asked, "How can I be of service?"

Vasili smiled broadly and his piercing gold eyes lifted to the sky windows as though he were admiring a distant and glorious star. As if on cue, the sky brightened momentarily as the sun attempted to burn through the rain clouds. "I would be honored if you would craft a pair of rings for the forthcoming bonding of myself and Volatus's finest eagle, my love and future queen, Miss Tuliann of Whiterock!"

A renowned and respected healer, I had heard Tuliann's name before, as had most any Awakened bird with ears to hear the gossip of the land. A short time before I hatched, she helped Mamyrskit bring an end to a plague. She saved hundreds, perhaps thousands, and became a hero honored by both nations.

Kor ignored the theatrics. "And when will this take place?"

Vasili's beak blushed, and he sheepishly replied, "Uh, yes, well, I'm embarrassed to say we are very late in our preparations. The new moon. The First of Ovum."

Kor gawked and flashed his third eyelids. He growled, "The new year? But, your Majesty, today's the 34th of Nidum. It's a cast year, so we have an extra day, but that still only gives us twelve days to make and get them to you in Whiterock!"

The King shrugged apologetically. "I may be a capable warrior, but I am not a capable bonding-planner I'm afraid."

Kor snapped his beak thoughtfully and his eyes flicked about. "Gold, I presume?"

Vasili nodded.

Kor asked, "Do you have any with you?"

Vasili shook his beak and shrugged, "I'm afraid we traveled hastily on this journey. Also, my treasurer has not yet made the journey to Whiterock. To make up for this, I will pay double whatever you ask but it will have to be at the ceremony."

Kor's facial feathers bristled with concern, "I don't doubt your credit, Your Majesty. But I am out of gold myself. It would take a few days just to--"

"Four times normal rate!" Vasili declared excitedly.

My heart fluttered at the king's casualness with so much money at stake. What he offered would be a years' wages for a flock of laborers. We hung on Kor's sooty expression and muffled grumbling for a moment. His corvid mental gears turned as relentlessly as the groaning axle above our heads. Patrons never haggled the price upwards, so to pause and cogitate so earnestly could only mean he knew the job would be extremely challenging.

The kind king lowered his head and pleaded, "Sir, I am begging you, do not refuse. It is my error for waiting this long and I will pay anything you ask."

The princess scoffed quietly, though not loudly enough for anyone but an owl's to hear. When I looked towards her, she immediately turned away.

At last, Kor's beak corners turned up in a smile and he croaked, "Very well, we have a bargain!"

Vasili lifted his face and exclaimed, "Splendid!" He laughed heartily and declared, "And when it is done, I want you to come to the ceremony as my special guests. All of you!"

The invitation stunned me. I had roamed scarcely a day's journey from where I hatched in Kahvanis, and had never seen the sea. Pepro wore a grin a wingspan wide. Yet, even as we trembled with excitement, the rest of the eagle entourage stood stalwart and disinterested by the doorway.

Vasili chuckled, "Yes! Yes! I want you to be as happy as I." He turned to Ruusch and Tulivor, who snapped to attention. "Bring out the food and drink. Let us toast to the occasion!"

The two birds reached their beaks into their breast satchels and unloaded a leathery bladder, bulging with liquid, and a linen-wrapped package. Princess Vouli presented the gifts and lifted them with her beak to the low table where we negotiated with customers. When she unwrapped the package and revealed a stack of shiny fish, Pepro's head feathers flared, and his eyes twinkled with delight.

Vasili noticed, and laughed, "It's been some time since you've seen capelin like these, no?"

Pepro replied, "Sir, I haven't been to the sea in two years." He whispered to me, "See their fat bellies? They're full of roe!"

Vasili proudly declared, "The finest and freshest from Whiterock yesterday. Please, eat!"

Pepro picked a fish up by the head and tipped it down his throat. As it sank slowly out of sight, small white eggs escaped and filled his beak corners. He swallowed them all with eyes creased closed in rapture. "Mmm... incredible. Thank you, Sir." He beckoned to me, "Sashya, you have to try it."

I had tasted local trout before, caught by a crow family that operated a fish weir in Galinta River. As I latched on to one of the smallest fish, the scent was saltier and fishier than I anticipated, and I wasn't convinced I would enjoy it. But with so many expectant eyes upon me, I didn't dare show hesitation, so I gulped it down. An explosion of salty fluid with notes of iron, welled up in my throat and I nearly gagged. But through watery eyes, I continued swallowing and faked a smile. "Yum!" I lied.

"Ha!" Vasili exclaimed. "You are being polite, but a king hears many flatteries, and I can tell when they are false."

"I'm sorry, Your Majesty."

"Tsk, tsk, not to worry. It is clearly not a moon owl's delight, but you were brave to try it." He patted my head with an apologetic wingtip. "Perhaps some deer instead? Ruusch, share some of today's quarry."

Ruusch pulled open another package containing a lump of dark red meat peppered here and there with deer hair. He stepped one of his thick orange feet onto the fleshy wad, grasped the center with his beak tip, ripped away a thick strip of the flesh, and tossed it at my feet.

I wasn't sure if Ruusch's intense smile expressed hunger for the deer flesh, or my own, but I gingerly nodded and thanked him before I nervously gulped the savory meat.

Vasili footed the flask, yanked the cork off with his beak, and tossed it over his shoulder as though its useful days were over. "May all the drink land in our bellies and not a drop on the floor!"

Kor flapped up to the table and grasped a sooty clay jar, his familiar drinking vessel, with his beak. He chucked the last of his day's tea on the floor and set the cup down, ready for Vasili to fill it. He nodded to Pepro and I, and growled, "Don't wait for a written invitation, boys."

Pepro and I fetched our wooden drinking cups and set them down. Vasili expertly poured the alcohol and filled the jars of his entourage too. At last, the king looked us all over, flask held high in his foot. "To the master craftsman and his students, savior of the ceremonies, and our new friends. Good health and wealth to you!"

The eagles chirped their affirmation, Kor bowed politely, and we all tipped our vessels and drank.

The pungent drink had a vegetal scent that made my stomach clench around the heavy wad of deer meat. I tipped my cup back too quickly, and a mouthful of the burning fluid filled my throat. I sampled elderberry wine the previous autumn and enjoyed it, but instead of sweetness, this drink struck with metallic bitterness like bile. My eyes watered, and I wanted to spew it out, but I couldn't violate the king's oath to not spill a drop. I swallowed with a loud gulp and gaped, drinking in fresh air to soothe the violation of my tongue and throat.

As Pepro rubbed my shoulders with a wing, warmth spread through me from my gut to my wingtips, raised the feathers on my nape, and tingled to a flame on the tip of my beak and claws. Pepro's touch grounded me, but when I gazed into his eyes, I couldn't focus.

"How ya doin', Sashya?" Pepro's eyes sparkled like a stream in the noonday sun. His voice seemed distant, an odd sensation for me since an owl's hearing is the best of any creature. He turned to the others and declared, "I think he likes it!"

As the sound of rushing blood subsided from my ears, the unpleasant flavor faded to a hazy memory, and I decided to take another taste.

"Huzzah! He does like it!" Declared Vasili.

Kor grumbled, "Pepro, you know what this is, right?"

Pepro replied cheerily, "Yes sir, seashine!"

Kor nodded, "Mm-hmm, brewed from seaweed, and stronger than even my nest-sister Ral makes out in Skeleton Reach. You boys shut down the shop now before you drink much more. Get the hearth ready for tomorrow, then you're free to do as you will. Tomorrow will be a big day for the both of you, so get your rest, understand?"

Kor's face tilted slowly, until I realized I was leaning, and snapped back straight again.

Kor chuckled. "Looks like Master Sashya is tipsy already. Pepro, make sure he doesn't overdo it, all right? Now get on with it!"

Vasili and Kor drank and discussed the details of the rings while Pepro and I did our chores. Vasili dismissed his cohort, and they gathered outside the door, singing and laughing. We shoveled out the hearth, restocked it with fresh kindling and coal, closed the waterwheel sluice, and put away the tools.

As I worked, I sang along quietly to the boisterous eagles in the background, and the warmth of the drink brought out memories of old songs from home. The abstract history I learned in school came alive in my ears, for though the words they uttered were different, the tune and emotion were the same.

My home village, Kahvanis, lay in the heart of Kahv, a broad plain of gentle hills and waving grass, broken by leafy forests. It had been prized territory to several kingdoms in the three centuries since the Featherless perished. I was taught that Volatian culture had its roots in Talaamiolar, the last kingdom of the crownies, which ended in a bloody rebellion barely fifty-five winters before. Now, in the songs of the eagles, I felt those teachings confirmed.

I wondered how many other things we had in common, but the guards' demeanor did not invite me to attempt academic conversation with them. Indeed, I had a cold feeling that I wouldn't like what they had to say about our common past. Perhaps someday, I concluded, I would meet other, warmer Mamyrskins like Vasili, and I could learn more.

Pepro flew up to the rafters to close the ventilation hatches. The warmed stones of the hearth kept the shop, and our roosts in the rafters, warm and dry throughout the night.

I returned to our cups and found that Kor had set aside a pile of capelin and deer meat. I ate a strip of the venison, tipped back another swallow of the harsh seashine, and alcoholic warmth spilled through me again.

Vasili had moved to the sketching parlor, where Kor sat on his drafter's saddle, an elevated pedestal for his breast that left his feet free to sketch. He held a shaft of charcoal in each foot, drawing with each simultaneously, while the king admired a delicate five-petaled pink flower he had set on the table.

Vasili tenderly spoke, as if his usual voice were too harsh to intone the name of the sacred flower. "We call this summerstar. It blooms in the moss that lines our oldest nests. This one I saved from my dear departed Queen Meri's nest. I would like it to be carved on the ring of my new mate."

Kor replied, "It's lovely. I can put it here, between the clasped talons."

"Yes, oh yes! Perfect." the King replied.

Pepro floated down from above and landed next to me. He brusquely gulped down one capelin after the other, then took a noisy draft of his cup of seashine. I reshaped my facial disk feathers forward to focus on the creative conversation in the next room, but Pepro's gulping and slurping made it impossible. When he belched a soggy rip, I gave up listening and glared at him instead.

Pepro stopped rubbing his beak on the feaking post and asked sheepishly, "Am I being too noisy?"

The round earnestness of his eyes melted my heart. They were a toasty gold with flecks and edges of brown, the last vestiges of his subadult colors. While we birds may not be able to smile much with our beak corners, our eyes show our expression well, and Peppy's were creased with happiness.

"It's all right, Peppy. You really love that fish, don't you?"

He replied with a smile, "Mm-hmm. Sorry it doesn't agree with you."

"It's okay. The deer was a rare treat. What do you say we take our cups down to the stream and take a bath?"

He sighed and smiled, "That's the best idea I've heard all day."

We walked to the door with our mugs in our beaks, but found our path blocked by the back of Princess Vouli.

Pepro muttered around the cup handle in his beak, "Pardon our passage."

The Princess swiveled her head around and shot Pepro a narrow, piercing stare that could have sent a goshawk fleeing.

Pepro muttered, "Oh crap."

Since before the Awakening, male eagles afforded females more

latitude and respect, when they met on equal footing. Female birds of prey were more aggressive by nature but, too, they required more space to move since they were bulkier. It wasn't law, at least not in Volatus, and in a case like this, would normally be a mild breech of social courtesy, hardly worth mentioning. But these eagles were not from Volatus, and their icy stares told of more formal expectations, despite the incredible informality of their king.

Pepro set down his cup and compressed his feathers, a sign of submission, as he bowed. "Forgive me, Lady Vouli. No disrespect intended. May we please pass?"

She strained a smile, "That's better. Clearly you are not accustomed to our protocols. Yes, of course, you may pass." Her dismissive tone hinted that a social debt was being silently tallied behind her haughty gaze. Her battle claws scraped as she turned her body to the side and gestured into open space with a wing that wafted the scent of clean feathers and leather. The two other crownies parted and stood on each side of the courtyard path.

"Pepro, is it? And Sashya?" The Princess's smile faded, and her indignant stare pressed down. I averted my eyes and bowed as I hurried past. Pepro picked up his cup and followed, and the eagles closed in behind us as we passed.

I sighed in relief as we reached the courtyard arch, glad to be clear of their intimidating stares. But Vouli stopped us in our tracks when she asked, "Did you enjoy the meal?"

We were obliged to turn and meet her eyes again, but my syrinx froze, and I had no words. Thankfully, Pepro took the initiative, and chirped graciously, "It was wonderful. Thank you, Your Grace. It's been a long time since I last enjoyed such a treat."

Vouli smugly replied, "I'm sure."

Pepro tentatively asked, "How was your journey?"

The eagles blinked with flat expressions and Tulivor yawned, then said in a tone dripping with boredom, "Long."

Ruusch grunted, "And wet."

After a brief and awkward pause under Vouli's frowning countenance, she fluffed her hackles and looked away, "You must be eager to rest from your toils. You may go."

Pepro nodded, "Yes, my Lady, thank you."

After a few paces, we hastened into the air, happy to increase our distance from the stalwart eagles. I wobbled in flight and found it diffi-cult to stay level. I tried to glance back at the eagles and nearly crashed into Pepro, spilling some of the content of my cup in the process.

The clouds had broken up so that the late afternoon sun warmed our feathers. The tall elm and oak trees below us bristled with newly budded leaves, and the meadowy slopes glistened from the day's rain. I closed my eyes momentarily and inhaled the clean, cool air, then let out a long sigh of relief.

When I opened my eyes, the world had gone sideways again and Pepro was staring at me. The warm sky reflected in his peppered gold-en eyes.

"You all right?" Pepro chirped around the cup in his beak.

I straightened up and mumbled an affirmative.

Pepro said, "Those eagles were none too friendly. Except Vasili. Though anyone can be gracious when they're desperate."

I mentally reviewed my interaction with Vasili. "I don't know Pe-pro. He seemed genuinely friendly to me."

Pepro disagreed, "Well practiced, I expect. He's probably used to having his talons licked so I'm sure he's a good actor at licking back when he has to."

I chuckled, "Since when would a king need to 'lick talons?' I've never met one before, but from the old stories, our past crowny kings would just command whatever they wanted, and you'd die if you didn't do it."

"Maybe," he conceded. "But those stories sound exaggerated, ya know. If you were a champion warrior, or rich, or, you know, someone popular, a king might need to kiss your tail to get your allegiance, right?"

We set our wings and spiraled down over a gap in the trees to land at our favorite bath spot: a bend in the river with a gently sloping beach of small round rocks. We were alone today except for an Un-awakened skylark singing cheerily on the hillside.

We set our cups down, and I replied to Pepro's question, "You might be right, Peppy, but he had me convinced. I don't think I've ever been hugged that way before. Not even by my own parents. That's it! It felt like the hug my father would give me as an owlet. Like he's strong enough to protect, and kind enough to care."

Pepro cocked his head with a smile. "Well, yeah, when you put it that way, I see what you mean. It was a good hug. But, just sayin', could be a good actor, right?"

"All right, big beak, see if you can give me a convincing hug then." In my drunkenness, I blurted those words without thinking. I had bumped into Pepro many times in the shop, and we were best friends to be sure, but we never hugged before.

Pepro looked called out for a moment, as though he may prefer to lose the argument than do something awkward. I second-guessed whether I should have just let the matter drop too, but to my surprise, he stepped closer and put out his wings.

Elated to see where this would go, not to mention drunk, I goaded him on. "No, no, no, Peppy. Do it like you're a king. Or at least like one of the actors we see at the flockplace. See if your hug can convince me to protect your kingdom with my life."

Pepro's feathers roused, and his wings swung wider. He lifted his beak like royalty, but his smile stayed wide and silly. He mimicked Vasili's accent, "Come, young one! Let me greet you like we do in Mammaryskat!"

I cackled with laughter, "Silly beak! It's Mamyrskit!"

Undaunted, Pepro stiffly moved forward with his wings out and beak open in an unnatural smile. "Come! I will hug you into believing me!"

My laughter ceased when Pepro's wings wrapped around and pulled me into a soft, warm embrace. I pressed my face under his left wing and listened to his heart thump, and the air move in his chest. His wings tightened and held me moments longer than the eagle king had earlier, and I relaxed as though I were arriving home from a long and lonely journey. I realized I didn't want the hug to end, and I wondered if Pepro felt something too, for his heart skipped a beat right before he relaxed his wings.

I swiveled my beak from under his wing, and looked up into his face. The grin had vanished, replaced by a mellow expression and glistening, attentive eyes. He studied my face as though fascinated with every detail. I had never enjoyed such close attention from him before, and I basked in it like a tulip in the first warm sun of spring. He leaned down a little, as though to touch beaks, and hesitated as his pupils rippled with conflicting impulses. Then he withdrew slowly, swallowed, and transitioned back to a grin.

"How was that?" Pepro asked in a strained voice.

I tilted my head sideways. *Did Pepro almost kiss me? Was it a genuine impulse or was he just playing with me?* The safest reaction was to play along. "That was really good, Peppy." My beak felt warm, and my heart fluttered. "But I think I need more convincing. Maybe you'd better try again."

Pepro blushed along the sides of his beak, and he chuckled nervously, "Ha ha, no, I don't think so. I, uh, think we can let it go." He released me and added, "I guess I'm not such a good actor after all. Doesn't mean Vasili isn't though."

Pepro turned away and marched off toward the water. I wanted to stop him and tell him that he had more than convinced me, but he was uncomfortable, so I let it go. Honestly, the feelings that stirred within me were new, and needed time to incubate. *Or were they new? Had I not actually yearned subconsciously, for weeks, to be closer to Pepro?*

The feathers on the back of my neck prickled as I looked upon Pepro with new eyes. He was attractive, and that acknowledgment felt right and good. No one would question my choice, and yet I hesitated. He was my best friend, and I didn't want to threaten that with awkwardness. We owls reach maturity in only a year, so I was no stranger to feelings of passions in springtime. Even so, I was inexperienced in matters of love, but somehow I knew I should let Pepro express himself in due time. But I've never forgotten how the tingle of that almost-kiss lingered, delicious and tantalizingly close, on my beak and in my mind for the rest of that night and well into the next day.

Chapter 2

The Mission

By Sashya

We stayed out in the pleasant evening air, preening our feathers and talking, far longer than planned, enjoying our intoxication and each other's company. We returned to Kor's Forge under a sky sprinkled with stars. The crownies had gone and Kor was alone in his parlor scribbling away. He told us the Mamyrskins were keen to continue their journey, so they departed to take advantage of the break in the weather. Then he gruffly bade us "Good roosting," and sent us off.

Our roosts were in a private corner of the attic. We had two perches next to each other with our personal belongings nestled on shelves and hooks by each one. I was living in a society addicted to functioning by day, so I had forced myself to adjust to a diurnal schedule too. We were both so tired that we said little as we settled in for the night, but the thought of Pepro's hug filled my dreams and before I knew it, I was awake, and the morning star perched high in the east.

We shook the sleep from our feathers and hopped down to the the shop to start the day. I rekindled the fire using an ember saved in an ember case from the previous night. Pepro stomped on a foot-operated bellows that drove a stream of fresh air to the heart of the forge to get it started. Its glowing embers cast throbbing orange light on his white head and focused eyes.

Once the fire crackled strongly, he shoveled in coal while I fetched materials from the shelves, lining them up on the workbench for the day's projects. There was the blade Pepro was forging and an elm branch for the handle. I had a copper cup that I planned to inscribe for a great horned owl customer.

It was then that we heard the approach of Kor's whistling wings as he landed outside and waddled in. He had a private space in the rafters but on clear nights, such as last night, he chose to sleep outdoors in the tree above the shop.

"Pepro! Sashya! Stop what you're doing and follow me."

We followed behind as Kor flapped into his parlor and perched on the ledge in front of the colorful windows. When satisfied that we were paying attention, he said, "I have an important assignment for you two. As you know, King Vasili is commissioning us to make his bonding rings."

I blurted out excitedly, "It's an amazing honor, Master!"

Kor lifted his beak, "Indeed it is! The highest sort of honor for a jeweler. So, we're not going to let him down. Now the design isn't very complicated and there's only one jewel. You two noticed how Vasili didn't cloak himself in finery, right?"

Pepro chirped, "Truly, Master."

Kor nodded, "Some birds cover themselves with glittery objects to impress while others glow from the inside out. Vasili is the latter, wouldn't you agree?"

"I sensed it too, Master. The others faked their politeness, but I wanted to get away from them. Vasili was completely the opposite."

"A fine judge of character, Sashya. And between us, if you cross paths with those birds again, you best stay clear. I've seen that look before. They have no regard for us 'lesser folk' as they would call us. They'd kill you and take your valuables with hardly more thought than snapping an insect from the air. They know full well that their status, and a little bribe, would absolve them of any crime where they're from."

Pepro replied with a sad note, "I think you're right, Master. It even happens here in Volatus sometimes."

Kor grunted in agreement, "True, but this is different, Pepro. Those younger warriors remind me of the old Foley Aristocracy. Fifty-five winters they've been banished, their crimes near forgotten, but it chilled me to my gizzard to see the spark of prejudice alive and well in their eyes. Vasili was genuine and he gives me hope, but he is one bird out of thousands." Kor shrugged, "Maybe joining our two societies in this bonding will be the beginning of something great for us all. Can't hurt. But make no mistake, those slave-masters didn't leave willingly, and their poison lingers still in the hearts of many. We would do well to not forget it!"

Pepro and I agreed, "Yes, Master Kor."

Kor continued, "Now as I was saying, these rings are simple because two classy eagles don't need a lot of glitz. There's only one jewel, and some fine etching. They will be worn in court, but probably won't be knocked around all day, every day. So, Pepro, what alloy do you think we should use?"

I was surprised Kor had asked Pepro, since I had the keen interest in jewelry-making and Pepro preferred working with steel. But his smiling wink to me, as Pepro studied his feet for the proper response, told me he was counting on me for the answer, and I could hardly wait to give it.

"Um, maybe nine parts gold to two parts silver?" Pepro replied.

Kor shrugged, "Close, Pepro, but I think that would be too soft. How about you, Sashya?"

"I think fifteen parts gold with three parts silver and two parts copper would be right. It would look nice against an eagle's complexion too and be easy to carve and polish."

Kor smiled, "Almost exactly my thought. Maybe just a touch more copper to contrast better with the orange in Vasili's toes. Take a look at the drawing board. That's what we'll be making."

Below Kor's drafting saddle lay several sketches of a ring with talons clasped on one side and a central ornamentation area between them. Two separate sketches, one labeled for Vasili and the other for Tuliann, detailed what would go within this area. Tuliann's featured a carved summerstar flower, just like the one Vasili had laid on the table. Vasili's ring featured an eight-pointed star with a sapphire in its center.

As Pepro and I studied the drawings, Kor continued, "From the sizing cords Vasili provided, we'll need about ten grams of gold. We have plenty silver and copper but there's not a single fleck of gold. But I have something we can trade for all the gold we'll need."

"Where will we get so much gold?" I asked.

Kor flashed his white nictitating membranes, "I'm sending you two to Whiterock for it."

Pepro's eyes brightened, and he declared, "Hey, Sash, what do you think of that? I'm taking you on an adventure!"

"It's gonna be great Pepro!" I said with excitement, even though I had reservations. Galinta had been my home since the 45th of Messis, right after the final fall harvest in my home village of Kahvanis. It had been a day-long flight, and my longest journey till then. The thought of roaming days away intimidated me, particularly by day since nocturnal species like me are universally targeted by the Unawakened in the daylight. But it would be a chance to meet new birds, see the ocean, the mountains, and perhaps some fantastic Apterian ruins. Perhaps I would even have a chance to go to the Whiterock Institute, a place of knowledge dedicated to the study of Apterian technology, which was a fascination of mine.

Kor walked to a corner of the room and poked his beak into a knothole, probed around, and then made a quick stabbing motion and swallowed something. The he picked up two folded letters from the table, each closed with red wax and his embossed seal: A raven with a sparkling eye. He set them down before Pepro.

"Pepro, keep those dry. Is your satchel in good repair for a long trip?" Kor asked.

Pepro replied, "Yes sir, she's dry and waxed."

"Good. One is addressed to Miss Penelope. She's a dear acquaintance of mine." Kor gave a smiling wink. "She's a rather upscale magpie that owns an inn. It's near the center of town in a tower built by the Featherless. Her banner is an oak tree with a crescent moon. It's called the Avian Haven. That letter will be your meal ticket, if I'm still in her favor. Treat her like the lovely flower that she is, and you'll be fine."

I asked Kor, "Sir, Is she our gold supplier?"

"Ah, no. But she hears a lot of news, so if you need something, she can help you find it." Kor's eyes narrowed. "The gold supplier is a big, salty bag of feathers by the name of Perry. He'll probably be in Low Town in one of the brothels. It's down by the cliffs where birds with low standards can find most anything they desire. He won't be hard to find, provided he hasn't drunken or copulated himself to death. He's a smudgie albatross. He's a huge bird, but harmless unless you stand in the way of his drink or the tails he's chasing. And unless you're offering your own tail to him, you'll have trouble keeping his attention. That is, unless you show him this!"

Kor jerked his head and brought something up from his gullet into his beak. He extended his tongue and on it sat a glittering, transparent, pea-sized crystal. The gem caught the light from the rising sun outside and threw small rainbows around the floor. I had never seen any gem with such clarity and sparkle before, even though we had worked with many precious stones.

I looked at Pepro and his pupils were tiny from the dazzling spectacle. He asked with awe in his voice, "What is it, Master? It's shinier than glass or metal."

Kor carefully set the crystal on the sunlit table and his raven eyes sparkled as much as the gem. "The Featherless called it a diamond and they went to great lengths to cut them from deep in the ground and carve them into this shape. This one was removed from a piece of Apterian jewelry. They're very rare now, particularly gems of this quality. But as pretty as it is, it will get Perry's attention for a different reason. Once you have his attention, give him the letter marked for him and make sure he reads it. And brace yourselves for a river of tears."

Pepro asked, "Why will he be sad, Master?"

"I can't tell ya that. I'll leave that to him. Just don't be surprised by it. He's an emotional sort."

Kor dropped the diamond into a small leather pouch. He pulled out a beakful of copper coins from a drawer and dropped those into

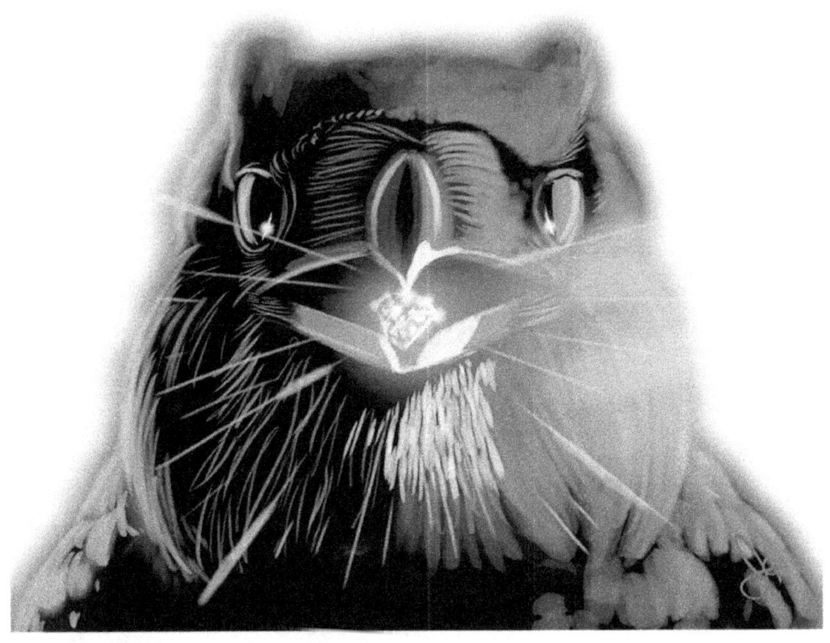

the bag, then stepped on it and pulled the thong snug with his beak. He slipped the loop of the closed bag over my head like a necklace.

"Preen your neck feathers over this and hide it well. Use the money wisely, just getting what you need. You should be able to hunt your own food on the way there and back. And I suggest that you get going soon. Pepro, you know your way to Sunrise Lake, right?"

"Of course, Master, I know it well. It's my uncle Perro's territory. He raised me there after my father died."

"Ah yes, that's right. Well, it will take you all day to get there and another day to catch thermals and cross the coastal mountains to get to Whiterock. So, travel light and get going, right away."

Chapter 3

Journey to Sunrise Lake

By Sashya

We thanked Kor again and as soon as I helped Pepro on with his satchel and harness, we were off into the morning sky.

Galinta sat at the confluence of Galinta River from the west and Tumbling Creek from the south. Galinta Valley was broad and gentle with forest concentrated on the steeper north-facing slopes and meadows on the southern exposures. Conifers dominated the tops of the ridges and alder, willow, ash, and oaks dominated the river bottoms. Songbirds sang with springtime vigor from practically every bush and branch as we rose above the village.

Pepro was far more experienced a traveler than I, so he took the lead. He traced a wide, ascending circle over town, climbing to get his bearings from sighting distant landmarks.

Galinta was a quiet, mid-sized village of around 500 Awakened birds. It was a common stopover for travelers in the midlands, especially those flying between Whiterock and Unitum, our nation's capital to the southwest.

As with many places in Volatus, Galinta sat atop the ruins of an Apterian settlement. Only foundations of brick, and the gray stone known as concrete, remained. Kor's grandfather founded the village some fifty summers prior and established a mining service, smeltery, foundry, and forge to make use of the wealth of metals buried in the nearby Apterian midden.

As we soared upwards, the midden came into view to the south of town as an ugly orange and brown scar that spilled ocher rivulets down the hillside. It was a grimy, unpleasant place that smelled of pungent rot and ferrous earth. Layers of crushed metal, glass, and all manner of strange Apterian materials were exposed by the relentless corvid pickers, or when hard rains deepened the wound. The Apterians buried it long ago, deeming the contents too useless and unsightly to be tolerated above ground.

Pepro and I were often sent there to fetch scraps of metal. During these visits, excited pickers showed us their latest finds, be it bits of mirror glass, porcelain cups, and tools made of a type of steel alloy that didn't rust. One of the oddest materials they unearthed in abundance was a brittle translucent substance that we could not categorize as glass, mineral, or metal. Attempts to smelt the strange stuff only resulted in acrid, sputtering flames, thick smoke, and drooling blobs of sticky black filth. I was told that it was plentiful throughout Volatus, just under the surface, but how the Apterians made it was a mystery, and it resisted all our efforts to reforge it into anything useful.

In the middle of town was a wide area, paved in flat stones, and circled in fruit trees. This was where most birds lived and sold their goods. Around this were some of the largest remains of Apterian structures, decayed into ghostly rectangles of concrete and brick with glassless openings, and heaps of rubble and brush within. Some of the walls were higher than the poplar and elm that surrounded town and provided relaxing spots to perch and take in the valley below. Pepro and I frequented them when drying our feathers after our baths. It was also where the village council stationed watchbirds that heralded the town when important visitors approached.

Atop some of these walls and ledges, locals had added homes of wood, metal scraps, and accrement, a cement commonly used in avian dwellings and inspired by Apterian concrete. Many chose to enhance it with bits of shell, glass, and bone to make it stronger and more attractive. The round bubbles of their abodes were stacked atop each other and shared by extended families. Most of Galinta's inhabitants were ravens and crows, but there were also owls, hawks, swans, and woodpeckers who took part in society.

I took a longing look at my favorite place in town, the flock-place. It stood just to the east of the town market, set before a curved brick wall above a bend in Galinta River. It was built early on after Galinta's founding, and the carefully crafted wooden perches were worn smooth, and the blue and red decorative dyes from local berries had faded wherever the sun touched them. In the center sat a concrete plinth, perfectly placed for amplifying the sounds of whomever perched there and addressed the gathered flock. Locals gathered there to hear news from traveling oracles, participate in council meetings, or be entertained. My favorites were the plays and music, sometimes performed by locals but often by traveling troupes. As our shadows passed over the empty flockplace, I thought of the last performance we saw there together, music played by a band of local crows.

And then our shadows passed a bit further to the east and crossed our favorite bathing spot. A flock of crows splashed in the bright sun while some of their companions conversed and preened on the rocks.

In moments, that disappeared behind the trees too as we soared over the ridge line north of town. Pepro flattened his wings and glided eastward toward sun-warmed rocks on another distant ridge. He had spotted rising pollen and insects, the telltale signs of a column of rising air, or thermal, that would lift us higher. Moon owls are not adept at soaring or using thermals, but fortunately I flew with an expert soarer. I stayed close behind Pepro as we circled in the bubble of warmth and rose hundreds of wingspans above Galinta Valley. By the time the thermal dissipated, the sun was ten degrees above the horizon, and we had drifted so far east that Galinta became a faint patch of trees that blended into the background of hazy blue forests and meadows.

A wide, new world spread out before me, and it frightened me. The dizzying heights and the vast, emptiness around me, made me feel as insignificant as a downy feather floating in an ocean of air. Pepro was my raft of security, so I stayed close to him to ease my panic. But with a wingspan only half as wide as his, I struggled to keep up, and I soon became tired.

Pepro sensed my unease and chirped, "Get in behind me, just a bit to the right and a little above."

I tilted my wings and made for the position Pepro recommended. But a sudden gust of wind buffeted me and jolted me out of position. When I finally slipped into the proper position, flying became much easier. Air spilled off his outermost primary feathers, those thin blades on the edge of an eagle's wings, in undulating swirls, like water washing over smooth rocks in a river. By riding in the upwash, I was pulled along with less effort. I relaxed and shouted, "Thanks, Peppy, it's working!"

He shouted over the moving air, "When I swing around in the thermals, always ride the wing that's on the downwind side. You'll get a better boost."

We flattened into a long, straight glide, and headed for another rippling thermal on a ridge a couple kilometers away, and slowly lost altitude until we caught the rising air just above a cluster of weathered gray boulders. We gradually rode it up until we were even higher than the previous thermal. My heart raced, and I laughed euphorically, staving off panic as we topped out and my gizzard dropped.

Pepro smiled, "Great, isn't it? I love this high flying. Don't be scared! Yell past your fear. Tell the world below that you are not afraid!"

I thought I had lost my mind, for moon owls never fly so high. I pressed myself to scream, but my first attempt was pathetic.

"Kek! Kek! Kek! Kekekekekekkkkkkk!" Pepro cackled in his rarely used, Unawakened bald eagle voice. He did it for me, so I tried harder to scream too.

"Screeeeeeeeaaaaaah!" I screeched. My cry was rough and unpracticed, but familiar, like exercising a muscle that you rarely had reason to use.

"Yes! That's it! Again! Kekekekekekkkkkk!"

I screeched again and again, my chest relaxing further with each yell, until the screams burned in my syrinx, and my wings buzzed from self-actualization. I swirled from side to side around Pepro playfully, feeling confidence grow from within and without, and his smiles were warmer to me than the blazing sun on our backs. Then we settled into a long sinking glide toward the next distant ridge.

As the day progressed though, and temperature gradients doubled, even Pepro got tossed about violently at times. The air was rougher than I had ever encountered in flight, and I feared my slender body would be ripped apart if the sky suddenly changed its mood for anything worse.

Pepro must've seen the fear in my face. He said, "You're doing great! Don't worry. I'm right here with you. And you know what? You're doing much better than I did the first time I flew this high."

"Really? I must have a better teacher."

"At that point, I had no teacher, except the sky itself."

A sharp blast of wind rocked me, and I closed my eyes and screeched. My wings were getting numb from the cold and the strain.

"Aww, Sashya, it's all right. Here, ride on my back for a while."

Pepro dropped his toes to slow himself and slide under me. "Come onboard, let me help ya."

I lowered my feet and relaxed my wings to settle my toes into the warm feathers above his satchel.

"Ah! That tickles!" Pepro chuckled and staggered in flight.

I fumbled and slid off, flapped to catch up, and then tried again. I curled my toes this time and settled my hocks down on each side of his body. I buried my chilled feet into his feathers and relaxed into his warmth, keeping my wings extended to ease the burden of my weight. I rubbed my feet in the depths of Pepro's warm tail fluff and churred appreciatively, "Thank you Peppy."

His mention of his first high flight reminded me of what he told me about his Wander, the ritualistic departure of sea eagles from their natal territory when they drifted far and wide until adulthood. Pepro had always discussed it with awe but also sadness, as though it were a time of great testing but also great loneliness. It fascinated me, but I hesitated to bring it up because of the melancholy feelings it stirred within him. But he seemed happy to open up about it now, so I asked, "Was it scary when you left home on your Wander?"

He kept his eyes on the horizon and nodded, "Oh, yes, it was tough."

"How did you do it?"

"My Uncle Perro prepared me. He taught me to fish and hunt, and I had friends to encourage me too. So, when I finally went off on my own, sure it was scary, but I had built up my confidence with lots of practice. I remembered my loved ones, their words of encouragement, and then took one challenge at a time." Pepro cocked an eye toward me and said with a smile, "And I'll do the same for you."

"We moon owls don't normally go far from our home roost. Skies! This might be the highest any member of my family has ever dared fly. Why do eagles go on Wanders?"

"In the old days, before our families stayed closer together, it might have helped more of us survive. Ya know, in case there was scarcity of prey back in one spot. Some say it's so we learn everything we need to know to be good parents. Others say it's so you can decide whether you want to live the feral life or be a part of Volatus's Awakened society. But we don't really know. It's just something we do and so do Unawakened eagles."

"What did it mean to you?"

Pepro went quiet for a moment, but his voice was thoughtful and warm when he finally replied, "I learned a lot about myself I guess. What I was capable of. Places I liked, or hated, what I want to do in life. You know, Sash, you're the first to ask me that."

I worried I may have asked too much. "I'm sorry, Peppy. We can talk about something else."

"No. You're my best friend, Sash. I like telling you about it."

"The bits you tell me are fascinating, Pep. But I worry because it seems to make you sad to talk about it very much."

Pepro's neck plumage fluffed and he closed his eyes and dipped his head. I regretted pressing him.

But before I could retract my words, he smiled back at me and said, "We've reached Kahvsgate. What do you say we take a break?"

I followed Pepro's lead and cheerily replied, "Sure!"

Pepro chirped affirmatively, so I spread my wings wider and lifted off his back.

The sun arced into the last quarter of daylight as we passed through Kahvsgate, a narrow pass in the Swansneck Mountains, a range that ran the entire length of Volatus from north to south. I had seen the place on maps but had never visited. It was the easiest route for moving between the east and west halves of northern Volatus, and it had once served as a border gate between the old western kingdom of Kahv, and the eastern kingdom of Hawkspire. A smattering of Apterian ruins dotted the pass and offered temporary refuge for travelers during storms, but as far as I could tell, no permanent village remained.

Kahv fell behind us with all her waters flowing west to the Moon Sea. The cracked granite crowns around us were bare and rugged, dotted occasionally with clusters of storm-twisted spruce. To the north, in the distant haze, the Swansnecks merged into the Waystar Mountains; tall, jagged peaks that stabbed against the sky. The land before us sank east into Hawkspire, a broad river valley blanketed in evergreens. All her waters flowed into the Waystar Sea on the eastern shores of Volatus. Farther in the emerald haze on the east side of Hawkspire Valley, the jagged peaks of the Hawkspire Mountains marched down from the north. Nestled at their base lay a pale blue sliver of water.

We circled down toward the top of a prominent dead spruce standing next to a field of boulders and stone ruins. The tree was stripped

of most of its branches, leaving a twisted, white skeleton, tortured by years of winter gales.

Pepro dropped his legs, pulled his wings in, and lifted his head. It turned him into a wall of ruffling feathers, bringing him down swiftly and smoothly without picking up speed. He dropped below the ridge than snapped his wings open, and used up the last of his momentum to swoop up to a gentle landing with only one lazy wing stroke.

I took longer to float down. My fluffy body was meant for stealth, not fancy flying. As I descended, I quietly decided to not say anything more about Pepro's Wander unless he brought it up. I soon fluttered to a silent stop on a branch beside him.

"You put the 'pro' in 'Pepro!' You landed almost as quietly as me!"

"Thanks! that's a big compliment, coming from an owl. Good thing I don't need to be quiet to sneak up on fish though." Pepro's gizzard growled. "I could use some fish right now. You see that lake in the distance? That's Sunrise Lake. We're almost there. We'll stay at my Uncle Perro's nest."

"I'm excited to meet him and see where you learned to fish!"

Pepro replied, "I don't think he's there now. When his mate died, he went back to Unitum to fish for the capital. But the territory is still his and he's never been averse to travelers, particularly family, staying there. And I can catch us some nice, fresh supper. We'll sleep with full bellies tonight!"

My gizzard shuddered at the thought of more oily fish. "Don't be offended, Pepro, but I'm hoping that I can find something less fishy for dinner. Maybe I can catch some voles along the shore."

"Ah, yes, there should be plenty." Pepro preened a wing feather and then stared back out toward the distant sliver of blue. His voice sounded as gentle as a soft breeze when he spoke again.

"You know, Sash, I meant what I said. I like telling you about my Wander. It's a personal thing that I don't tell everyone, at least not the deeper stuff. But I think I'm ready to tell you."

A pleasant rush of blood filled my beak with warmth. "Are you sure? I don't want to make you sad."

Pepro sighed, "You couldn't make me sad."

His words were like sunshine to my soul, and I puffed my breast to soak in their warmth.

Pepro continued, "And, you know you can tell me anything too. Best friends, right?"

When happy, Pepro's eyes smiled more than his beak corners. The back corners crinkled, and the lower lids drew up a little. He gave me that look just then.

I moved closer to him and placed my foot gently on his, "We are, Peppy. And I'm so glad to say so."

Pepro wrapped a wing over my shoulders, and I thrilled to be close to him again while not being distracted by a thousand spans of empty space below me. I wanted to be nowhere else but wrapped in his soft feathers and feel his living, breathing body against mine.

Pepro asked, "How are your wings holding up?"

"Not bad, thanks to you. That screaming trick helped. But my wings were getting pretty stiff from the cold until you let me ride on your back."

Pepro gave a chirpy eagle chuckle, "I saw! Like I said, it's no small thing to swim so high in the sky and be at the mercy of those currents. Even at my size I must respect the wind, read it, know when to bend it to my will and when to let it bend me."

"I see what you mean. My wings are best for gliding through

meadows on moonless nights. But I'm having fun trying something new."

Pepro squeezed me and said, "You're doing great, Sash. And I love your wings just the way they are."

I closed my eyes and leaned my head against Pepro's side and listened to his heart beating. His wing tightened briefly around me, so I knew he enjoyed the closeness too.

It had been quite a day. I had explored new horizons, both in flight and in my friendship with Pepro. I didn't know where the journey might lead, but I could scarcely wait to find out.

A breeze broke the stillness, and the old tree creaked under us. A pileated woodpecker drummed out his springtime love song on a tree in the forest below. Pepro stayed snuggled up to me, but I felt his body shift and tense from the sway of the tree. I wanted to stay wrapped in his embrace, but we had to move on.

Pepro broke the silence and said, "Hey, I've got an idea. I'll get you something special for dinner tonight. There are rocks high above the lake, rife with marmots. I would have to hurry to get one before dark, so we'd have to separate for a while. Is that all right with you?"

I'm certain he saw the nervousness in my eyes. I was in unfamiliar territory in broad daylight. Many birds, Awakened or not, would see me as an enemy or target for plunder. Pepro's expression curved from joy to concern. But I didn't want to crush his plans.

"Sure!" I replied. "I just have to head for that lake, right?"

Pepro's smile returned, "Yes! When you get to the lake, you'll see an island with a big spruce and an eagle's nest. It should be empty but if Perro's there, he'll be quite friendly, I assure you. Just let him know I'll be along shortly. If I see anything unusual on my way, I'll intercept you and we'll go in together, all right?"

It sounded like a solid plan, and I relaxed. "Sounds good. I'll stay low to the tree tops and weave my way down."

"Owl style!" Pepro said. "Follow that creek down to that confluence, then cross that ridge and even at treetop level, you'll see the lake. You're a good flier. You might just beat me to the nest."

Pepro's optimism was contagious, and I looked forward to seeing the surprise he had in store. In preparation for flight, he arched his wings up over his back and stretched his breast muscles.

"All right, Sash, see you at sunset!" Pepro cried as he pushed off.

"Good luck, Peppy! Be careful!"

Pepro circled a few times and drifted away as he sang a traveling tune. He had a wonderful voice, yet I never convinced him to sing at the flockplace on talent nights.

I likewise prepared for flight, pushed off from the tree, and glided down through the spruce tops below. The sunny spring day had pumped sweet sap up to the tips of their budding branches and the scent warmed my lungs. With my heart aglow and mountain springtime bursting all around, I hummed a tune and made my way toward Sunrise Lake.

The time went quickly, as it always does when the journey is varied and interesting, and I found plenty along the way to keep my interest. The stream I followed began as a bubbling brook, joined others, and soon swelled into a rumbling creek. I glided past a black bear as it snuffed around in the black mud dotted with the yellow flowers of skunk cabbage. Further down, on the edge of the creek, a white-tailed doe, her belly heavy with a fawn, browsed on budding salmonberry bushes. When I startled a chubby chipmunk, I remembered the fat marmot that Pepro had promised and salivated reflexively. My growing hunger sharpened my senses, so I pressed on eagerly toward the goal of dinner and hard-earned rest.

Soon I reached the confluence we had spotted from the mountaintop, and I zig-zagged my way up the face of the adjacent ridge. As I topped out over the forest canopy, I took a moment to survey the area around Sunrise Lake again.

The broad valley had steep sides blanketed with spruce and larch, interrupted here and there with slides of granite boulders. Sharp white peaks glared down from above like rows of teeth. The lake stretched three or four kilometers long but only about a kilometer wide. The water along the shores shown brilliant green, dropping away swiftly to deep blue in the center. The nest island stood at the north end a couple of kilometers away. Rather than fly straight down to the shoreline, where I would be more visible, I decided on a secretive route through the forest to approach closer at the upper end of the lake.

As I descended through the forest, I passed into cooler evening shadows. I scared up a flock of migrating crossbills and a goshawk flashed past to grab one out of the air. The hapless songbird screamed its last as the hawk lighted on a branch to eat her prize. Her red eyes watched me intently, but she said nothing. The wild look in her eyes told me she was Unawakened, and I was glad she had a meal to distract her.

Just before I approached the shore of the lake, I stopped and rested briefly to survey the area. Milky-green ribbons of icy water spilled from the snowfields above and merged into a creek that entered the north end of the lake. The creek was framed in naked brambles of wild rose, interspersed with fluffy clusters of last year's cattails and yellow heads of erupting skunk cabbage. Judging by the flattened grasses, winter's snows had only recently left the valley.

The nest island was a small, humped backbone of granite, barely a dozen wingbeats across. A massive old spruce grew from the center, surrounded by smaller saplings reaching up like eager children. Around its shore, alders clamored for a foothold on the sparse soil and bent out over the water in a competition for the sun. The dominating spruce tree had three crowns that split apart two-thirds up its full height. One of the trunks was dead and its pale, twisted heartwood reached up like skeletal talons above the green tops of the other two. An enormous nest rested in the crook formed by the branching tops.

Pepro had told me how eagles used the same nest year after year, piling them up with branches until they grew massive. This one was wide and thick, as though it must be generations old. But no one appeared to be home. The white heads of adult bald eagles normally glow brilliantly to my eyes, and I saw none. Also, there were no fresh branches in the nest, so I felt certain Pepro's uncle was not there.

The spooky encounter with the goshawk lingered with me. I felt those cold, red eyes piercing the back of my head as though she could materialize again at any moment. It would be rare for a hawk to attack an owl, particularly with game so abundant nearby. But goshawks were notoriously unpredictable. Though we were closely matched, it might not deter her if she were crazed with desire to protect a nest.

I decided to press onward to the island, as from there I would be able to keep a watch on all approaches. But first I would have to cross the water. I would be easy to spot against a background of dark waters and spruce. But the safety of the nest beckoned, and I couldn't resist.

Varied thrushes broke their evening trills as I broke out of the forest and entered the empty space over the lake. But my timing could not have been worse. As I crossed the shoreline, I startled a pair of ravens that were picking at carrion on the water's edge.

Aggressive caws exploded in stereo behind me, and I knew, without looking, they were giving chase. I didn't think I could outpace a raven, but I had to try. Perhaps they would just give up and return to their meal.

My heart sank as one of them cawed, "There's something around his neck!"

Fear tingled in my breast as I realized they were thieves and would not likely give up easily. They gained on me quickly while still far from the island. For the first time in my life, I knew the sinking sensation of prey when they know they are about to die. Dread closed around my thoughts with clammy talons, so I pushed myself harder to keep beyond its clutches.

I kept my eyes on the island as the ravens' whooshing wings approached, and a beak stabbed my tail. I screeched, and the raven cackled. The sharp pain of a plucked tail feather was quickly replaced by the cool ache of an empty follicle.

"How many feathers do you want to lose? Give us the shinies and we may let you live!"

Negotiation was not an option, for any raven bold enough to attack would surely not leave me alive to tell of their thievery.

"Give it to us!" The raven grated. It jerked another of my tail feathers with a snap of its powerful beak. The yank on my tail slowed me down, and I knew I wouldn't make it. My vision blurred, my heart faltered, and my wings cramped. The long day of flying, combined with panic, meant I didn't have any strength left. But, if I was going to die, it wouldn't be without a fight.

The other raven swooped in and sank its claws into my back. I flipped over and flashed my talons.

The raven luffed up and out of reach easily, and laughed to its companion, "Look at those puny talons! Even yours are bigger than his!"

"Shut up, and grab his neck pouch!" the other croaked.

As they jabbered, I made a bold move. I feinted a descent and dropped back, spun around, and ripped a patch of feathers out of the raven behind me. His cocky grin turned to an angry scowl. That's when he nailed me with his beak, right between my eyes, so hard that my whole body buzzed like a numb limb. I had watched Kor hammer his massive beak against stubborn tools to dislodge them, and the force impressed me. Now I learned what the tools experienced. My vision went dark, and as I faltered into blackness, a foot clutched my chest, and the necklace was yanked away. The last thing I remembered of them was their cackling glee, and I thought to myself, *Damn those fucking ravens.*

Hal Aetus

Chapter 4

The Close Caw

By Pepro of Waycliffs

The day's travel from Galinta to Sunrise Lake had been glorious. It was the first truly warm day since the snows melted, and when I slowed my thoughts and listened to the world, it sang that spring had finally arrived.

The thermals were plentiful, so we made amazing progress. Sashya flew in the River Winds for the first time, and his wonder and fear reminded me of my first experience. With his delicate wings, he had a tough time when the wind gusted, so I let him ride on my back for part of the journey. But I enjoyed his company so much that I hardly noticed the extra weight.

We split up after resting at Kahvsgate, where I thought up the idea to go hunting for a marmot for Sashya. After all, he had endured my fish, which I knew he didn't like, and I knew he would love the fat marmots that live easy on the mountainsides above Sunrise Lake.

I had just scored a marmot and was flying back when a shadow crossed my back. A falcon ripped past and surprised me so badly that I almost dropped my quarry. She recovered from the stoop and circled back toward me.

It was Nyx, a friendly peregrine falcon who had hatched, like me, in Waycliffs. But I hadn't gotten to know her until I was living at Sunrise Lake with my Uncle Perro. My father had died, and my mother disappeared, so he took over my education, and taught me how to hunt. He encouraged me to practice catching a variety of prey so I wouldn't have to rely only on fish and carrion, and so I sometimes soared to the alpine to practice hunting marmots.

Nyx had been hunting her way south, on a sort of Wander of her own, when we crossed paths high on the mountainside. I convinced her to stay with us for half a moon, until encroaching mountain snows pushed her to continue her trip. Those were happy days full of challenge and fun as we pushed each other to excellence in flying, hunting, and teasing my uncle's fledglings.

The reunion was warm, and I wanted to hear all of Nyx's adventures, but I had to hurry back down to meet Sashya before dark. So, I invited her to dine and spend the night with us.

We casually chatted as we descended, until I saw Sashya fall under attack by raven bandits.

I shouted to Nyx, "My friend Sashya's in trouble!"

I folded my wings and dropped as fast as I could, but no sooner was I free-falling than a feathered blue blur shot past me, like a spear, directly toward the lake.

The ravens pulled at Sashya's tail feathers and slowed him down. I compressed my body to slip faster, but I couldn't touch Nyx's speed. When Sashya fought his attackers, I shouted to distract them, but I was still too far away to be a threat. My shouts turned to violent screams when one of them clutched Sashya's limp body, ripped the pouch from his neck, and cast him off like a sour carcass. Sashya tumbled head over tail toward the water, and I strained myself toward the dark waters to save him.

When the companion raven saw Nyx falling toward them, he turned away in a flurry of caws. His triumphant friend, still clutching Sashya's leather necklace, looked up just in time to be slammed by Nyx's talons.

The thief spun in a glorious cloud of his own wretched feathers, and lost bowel control along with his precious bag of shinies. Nyx let the raven go and flipped her body through an incredible outside roll to fetch the falling bag of coins before it touched the water. The raven, meanwhile, sprinkled the lake with its blood, leveled out, and beat a retreat with its companion toward the western shore, cawing and cursing all the way to safety.

Sashya's moth-like wings eased his fall so that he struck the water with only a modest splash. I lowered my legs, opened my wings just enough for control without sacrificing speed, and plucked him from the lake before his feathers were soaked through.

"Sashya! Sashya!" I chirped, but he appeared lifeless. I hauled

him to Uncle Perro's nest as quickly as possible and laid him in the soft moss. Nyx landed a moment later.

I shook from panic, and my vision blurred from guilty tears. "Nyx! Help Sashya! Is he alive? Damn me and pushing him to go on his own!"

Nyx calmly opened Sashya's beak. We spotted a fresh smear of blood coating the roof of his mouth, and he inhaled sharply. "He's breathing. He's alive."

"Oh great skies!" I gasped.

"Breathing is clear so the blood is from his head, not his lungs." Nyx rolled him onto his breast and propped his head up on a pillow of lichen. She gently opened his eyes, one at a time, with a knuckle of her closed toes. It was always hard to see Sashya's pupils against his black irises, but there was just enough light left to make them out. They constricted and his third eyelid blinked slowly. "Good. His eyes are responding so his brain's not scrambled. But he's got one hell of a bruise on his cere. The bastards brained him good. Gonna be a killer of a headache. We should tuck him in to keep warm and quiet. Need to put some wet moss on his forehead too to ease the swelling. Pepro?"

My ears went numb at Nyx's affirmation that Sashya was alive, and I cried grateful tears. I had seen birds get hurt or die, but this time was different. When I looked at his wound, I almost felt the sharp pain in my own skull. When I thought he might be dead, an empty chasm opened in my chest. I knew, then, that Sashya was more than a flock-friend. He was a part of my life, as important as a wing or foot. I had lived alone most of my life, with only myself to care for. Now there was someone else that meant as much, or more, to me as myself.

Nyx poked her beak into my face and chirped loudly to snap me out of my pit of worry.

"Are you all right, Pepro?" Her dark eyes flitted over my face, and I turned away in tears. She touched me with her wing and said, "Did you hear me? He's going to be fine. And, hey, it's not your fault. Sashya just had the bad luck of jumping these particular ventsores."

"I sent him into danger and failed to protect him."

Nyx softened her demeanor, "You didn't know. And, as careful as we can be, we can't protect our friends from everything." She cocked her head and added with a knowing smile, "Or even the ones we love."

Love? I thought. *Is that why I feel this way?* She was right about the rest, perhaps, but seeing Sashya laid out unconscious did nothing to assuage my guilt or quell the shaky feeling that I had almost lost the best thing in my life.

Nyx knew how to deal with emergencies. She learned these skills from her parents, who were leaders in the community and lent helping talons to anyone in need. They had been there helping ma and me when my father died, until Uncle Perro came to fetch me. Nyx grew up a no-nonsense northerner, or starthener as the locals said, and knew when to be tough. She fixed me in her obsidian stare and commanded me with the sharp chups of a falcon in charge, and it was just what I needed.

"Look!" she ordered. "You can shit all over yourself later, but right now we have work to do. Now get me some moss to tuck him in. The nice, fluffy green stuff. Also, get some of the dense clumpy moss for that shiner. While you're at it, grab the marmot you dropped in the water when you fetched Sashya. He'll be hungry eventually. And if you see any pussy willow, grab a few branches. It'll help his headache. I'm gonna start scooping out the nest for him so get going!"

By the time we had Sashya set up in a fluffy, cozy nest, the sky had turned dark and full of stars. We spoke quietly in the starlight while Sashya snoozed. I was dead tired from the long day, but I wanted to be awake in case he needed anything and since it had been a few years since I last saw Nyx, we had a lot of catching up to do.

Nyx's ruffled feathers had smoothed out and she spoke in the soft voice of a caring mother. "Why don't you eat some fish now. Nothing better for snoozing than a crop full of food, am I right?"

She was referring to a trout I had caught while gathering willow. "Yeah, I am hungry. Please, have some of Sashya's marmot too. He won't be able to eat it all."

"I'm doing all right, but I should probably eat before continuing on tomorrow. I'll have some nibbles while we chat."

I crunched into the head of the fish, wolfed it down, and then bit into the collar meat. It was juicy and sweet. "I had almost forgotten how good these springtime trout taste. Have some."

I offered Nyx a bit of the tender pink meat on my beak. She grinned and took it with hers. She smiled and savored it a moment in her gullet and then swallowed it down. "Oh yeah, that is good! This marmot you caught is nice too."

"Yeah? Let me have a taste."

Nyx offered a bite of the dark red shoulder meat from her beak. As our beaks touched, she held on to the meat for just a second, before releasing it. I caught the peculiar aroma of game and weathered granite that was a common feature of falcon aeries. The meat was soft and rich, the wholesome sort that restores energy quickly. "Hmm, yes, that'll be real nice for Sashya when he wakes up."

When I glanced back at Nyx she grinned broadly and stared at me. "What?"

"Oh, nothing."

"That's a big smile for being nothing."

"So how long have you and Sashya been together?"

"He came to Kor's six months ago, matched up as part of the National Apprenticeship Program. He's quite the artist and..."

Nyx interrupted, "No, marmot-brain. *Together?*"

"Oh! Uh, well. We're best friends."

"Come on, Peppy. There may be some years between us seeing each other, but I know you're as queer as a flock of mallard drakes before the hens show up."

I choked on a fin and chuckled. "Damn, Nyx. You really know how to cut the crap."

"We're a bit like nest siblings, you and I. I can tell you have no romantic interest in females now, not even a gorgeous bird like me."

I chuckled, "You are gorgeous."

"You know nobody would care if you're gay. Or that you're an eagle and he's an owl. It happens. I think you're a hell of a catch and Sashya's lucky."

"Well, I'm still sorting it out. I've not had any mates yet."

"Uh-huh. Meanwhile every other tiercel hunk your age has flung their seed into every willing hen from Waycliffs to Sudhelm."

I laughed out loud and nodded, "True, very true."

"But, hey, I know how it is. The heart wants what it wants. You've got standards. And while it may be accepted that some birds love differently, we're so spread out that it's hard to find the 'right one.' Consider yourself fortunate."

I nodded, and my beak warmed from blushing as I thought over her words. I glanced at Sashya, aglow in silvery light. The waning three-quarter moon had risen above the peaks and reflected off the alpine snowfields, casting the entire valley in ethereal light. I didn't have words to say what I felt, but Nyx read my thoughts anyway.

"I think your parents would be proud, Pep. Proud of you and how you've turned out. And whomever you choose to love."

Feeble memories of my parents crowded my thoughts as I replied,

"Thank you, Nyx. I hope so. I often wonder if they would have preferred me following the feral life. They wanted me to try it so badly. So, I flew my Wander. I lived off the land and sea. I watched a thousand sunrises while I flew the whole perimeter of Volatus. I watched the sand dry on hundreds of beaches, slept in the rain through long winter nights, and bathed in sandy streams while the sunset lit the sky on fire."

"Do you think you found the meaning of the Wander then?"

I nodded, "Funny you should ask that, Nyx. Sashya asked me that very same thing today and it's the perfect question. And I'm thinking that you never stop asking that question. The Wander prepares one for life in practical terms, but the memories never stop teaching their own lessons. It changed the way I think. I kept asking myself what I should be learning, and that led me to wonder what the purpose of learning was, why I exist, and whether having purpose is better than just living in the present."

Nyx nodded solemnly as she wiped blood from her beak. "Perhaps the Wander is never really over."

"Yes! I don't have much of my mom's advice to go on, but I have a good memory of her explaining what a gift it was to be Awakened, but that I should know what it means to live with nature too. When she brooded me, she sang about an eagle's chest beating in tune with the bubbling of a creek or rising and falling with the surge of the ocean. On my Wander, my life was bound, completely, to the rhythm of land and sea, and it was a peaceful existence. Heck, sometimes it felt as though it connected me back to them, and the generations before them, and they were all there with me in the dance of life. I was alone most of the time but not completely lonely. It kept me going."

Nyx smiled attentively; her dark silhouette outlined in alabaster moonlight. She falcon-whined, "Aw, That's beautiful Pepro. She would be so proud of you. So why did you come back to society? How did you end up at Galinta?"

"After four years of drifting around, I realized that if a Wander is exploration, it should include all the possibilities. I decided to give civilization a try too. We baldies are nothing if great at making the most of any opportunity, after all."

"You're an amazingly resourceful lot." Nyx agreed.

"Aunt Star had taught me the basics while I lived here. How to write, read, some history, and math. But I was only here for little more than a year. So, I checked into the school in Brokentalon for a winter and fished for the town to make some coppers. It was quite a change to hunt for money rather than survival. It felt, I don't know..."

"Joyless?"

"Yeah. I ate carrion to sustain myself, but it was only the freshest, fattest fish that fetched good money. I know not every bird can hunt in society and it's necessary, but after being so reliant on the creatures I was killing, I didn't like the feeling of taking life for anything short of sustaining my own, or those close to me. A stranger eating my catch wouldn't have the connection and satisfaction."

Nyx sighed, "I know what you mean. I've done it some too, when I needed money. My clutch-brother, Kerul, makes a good living hunting for Waycliffs, and I respect that. Every pretty pebble on the beach has a gritty side to it. Hunting for pay is the dirtier side of being a civilized predator I suppose."

"So what do you do now?" I asked.

"I'm taking on the mantle of my folks. I'm their aide to Whiterock. I take messages back and forth, escort officials, sometimes even go to Unitum on business. I'm on my way to Whiterock on business now but took the scenic route."

"Look at you!" I exclaimed. "Quite the responsibility. But no letter bag?"

"I prefer traveling light. If I have books to carry, I bring along an assistant. But I'm a proxy, so my word and my lovely face are usually enough."

I hadn't heard the term "proxy" before, and it showed in my expression.

Nyx chuckled, "You bumpkin! Proxy means I've been formally introduced and pledged so my words are as good as the bird sending them."

"Oh! Damn, that's amazing, Nyx. You're moving up!"

"Yeah, I'm doing all right. It's tough, and I'm learning, but if I keep going, I guess it puts me in line to be a politician if I ever want to go that way."

I smiled. "Incredible, Nyx. I can see you being a great one. Tough as talons but as caring as a brooding mother. And not in it for yourself."

"Thank you, Pep." She replied. "Despite its rough edges, Volatus is pretty special. So many different birds working together. We've achieved so much, and I know there's nothing we can't do if we do it together. We just have to make sure everyone has the opportunity to play a part."

"Yeah? What sorts of problems do you run across?"

Nyx cocked her head in thought, "I suppose it's less obvious in the rural places where you live, since everyone has to pull together more anyway. But in the big towns, there are problems with sanitation, thievery, making sure everyone has enough to eat. Corruption of power too. And the old species prejudices sometimes rear their head."

"We were talking about that this morning. We met some crownies yesterday that were none too friendly."

Nyx replied stiffly, "Watch yourself around them, Pep. In the past, most I met were aloof, quiet, but trustworthy. It's like they bore cultural guilt for their past crimes. But this past year, there's been more showing up in groups of two or three, sometimes more, being rude and pushy and thwarting our social code. The local constables are at a loss to push back because they're not exactly breaking laws, they're just sowing discontent and scaring citizens. Rural peacekeepers are outnumbered and not equipped to deal with them."

"What's being done?" I asked.

"The capital has been recruiting larger species, like mottles and you bad-ass baldies, to send out as marshals, but training them takes time."

"What do the malcontents want?"

"So far, they don't seem organized, so it's hard to know. Mamyrskit's population has soared, so we think they're just looking for easier hunting and more space, which is understandable. But given their country's less-than-stellar history with democracy, it's unsettling when they don't respect our system of governance. It's like they don't care about the war and the lives their past prejudice cost. It nearly wiped them out."

"I didn't have much chance to study history. I mostly learned from stories Uncle told me. But I know being born one species or another shouldn't make us better or worse than others. Sure, we eagles might be good fishers or strong fighters, but a cunning little owl, like Sashya, could best any bird with his brains. Like you said, we all deserve a chance to be our best."

Nyx nodded. "Did you finish your winter term?"

"Oh! Yes! Well, I tried my talons at tool making. That's when I heard of the trade apprenticeship program. Master Kor in Galinta needed a new steelsmith, and I was the strongest bird that applied. I've been with him almost a year now and Sashya showed up last fall."

"Do you like it?" she asked.

"Very much! The work is hard, but it's satisfying to create something new and put my mark on it. And Kor is good to us. There's plenty of business, so we keep warm and well fed."

"What a journey! You know, speaking of learning, since you're going to Whiterock, you have to check out the Institute. It's amazing!" Nyx gesticulated with her wings to imply scale. "They've built machines that run on sparks. They have torches that give light with no fire or smoke. Their healers cure diseases, fix broken bones, sew up wounds. Miss Tuliann runs it all now and they love her so much. You've got to see it when you're in town. I'm sure I could get us a tour."

"Sure!" I replied. "I've only seen Whiterock from a distance. I stayed clear as I wasn't too social on my Wander. But I'm different now. I'm looking forward to it. I'm sure Sashya will love it too. He's from Kahvanis and studied there for two years. He loves all things Apterian."

"Oh, I've heard about their work in Kahvanis to make food portable. They dry it or pack it in skins and fire it so it lasts longer. He'll have to see the cold rooms at the Institute. They have a big machine that can freeze food and make ice!"

I shook my head, "Torches without fire? Making ice? You're pulling my tail."

She chuckled, "It's crazy, I know. But you'll see. If you don't mind me asking, what's your business in Whiterock?"

"You know about Tuliann's bonding, right?"

Nyx nodded, "Mm-hmm, part of my business in Whiterock involves the ceremony, and I'm to stay in town to attend it with my folks. Will you be attending too?"

"We've been invited by King Vasili himself. He's commissioned us to make the bonding rings. We're going to Whiterock to fetch gold for the job."

Nyx inhaled sharply with delight. "What an honor! But you don't have much time."

"Yeah, I know. Gotta get the gold from a contact there and hightail it back to Kor. Sashya will probably help him craft the rings. He's a fantastic artist with precious metals. Let me show you."

I leaned my neck forward and preened open my feathers above my crop to expose a small copper pendant on a leather string. Nyx leaned closer to inspect it.

I lowered my voice to a whisper, "I don't think he knows I have it as it was just a practice bit that he didn't much care for. But I love it. See the tree and the eagle? And the ocean? I think it's me."

Nyx's dark eyes focused intently on it in the moonlight and she said, "It *is* you. How lovely. How special." She looked up at me. "He likes you too. You need to tell him how you feel. You two belong together."

I tucked the pendant back in under my feathers and nodded. "I'm getting there. I think I'm ready. I was planning on telling him here tonight over that special dinner but, well, plans changed."

A sleepy mumble arose from Sashya. He weakly asked, "What were you planning to tell me?"

"Sashya!" I exclaimed and spun my head around. I walked over and leaned down over him. "How are you feeling?"

He winced and opened his eyes narrowly. His cere was dark and swollen and he spoke with a stronger nasal tone than usual. "Easy, easy, big fella. Roosting voice."

"Oh, sorry." I whispered.

Sashya's eyes widened upon noticing Nyx standing close by. "Who are you?" he rasped with concern.

"It's fine, Sash. This is Nyx. She's an old friend. She saved your tail from the thieves."

Nyx smiled and added quietly, "With help, of course." She nudged my wing. She examined Sashya's face closely and whispered, "Head hurting?"

Sashya nodded slowly.

Nyx added, "You best keep this moss on your forehead. It'll keep that swelling down. I'm going to chew up some willow bark for you too. It'll stop that throbbing in your skull." She moved away to strip and pick apart the bark of the willow branches.

I picked up the lump of moss and moistened it with cool lake water in a copper cup we'd found hanging by the nest. I placed the wet poultice on Sashya's forehead and gently preened the feathers up around it to keep it there.

"Thanks, Peppy." Sashya whispered. He sobbed, "I'm sorry. I lost the money and the diamond! What are we gonna do?"

My vision blurred from happy tears. "Shh there Sash. Don't worry, we got it back. Everything's all right."

Sashya sighed with relief, "Oh skies! Really? I've had the worst dreams about it."

I gently laid down beside him and covered him with my wing as though brooding a precious eaglet. "You can dream easy now. It's all right. I'm here. Nyx is here. You're safe and the money is safe."

Nyx came back with bitter breath and a wad of chewed bark. She looked at me and gestured to Sashya. She wanted me to give it to him. I nodded and took the bolus from her beak.

She smiled and faked a yawn before saying, "Well, you two boys keep it down, all right. I'm gonna go over there and get some winks in." She walked away to the other side of the nest, facing away. *Thanks, Nyx*, I thought to myself.

"Sash, I have some medicine here. It's not bad, if you don't let it sit in your beak too long."

"All right, I'll take it." he replied.

I leaned my face down closer to Sashya's than ever before. His beak was warm, and his dark eyes reflected the moon and the pale outline of my face. He smiled and touched my tongue with his as I released the bark. He pulled his tongue in and swallowed it loudly. Then his eyes narrowed, and his beak corners frowned.

"Oh that's foul!" he gagged.

I chuckled, and beaked the cup closer to him so he could drink. He dipped his face in and tipped back a big swallow of water, then another, then nodded that he had finished.

I moved the cup away, and he snuggled closer.

"Can we try that again?" he asked.

"What?" I asked.

"You know. Touching tongues?"

I knew what he meant and I happily obliged. He could have eaten a whole tree's worth of willow bark, and that first kiss would still have tasted sweeter than all the freshest capelin in Whiterock.

Chapter 5

Uncle Perro

By Sashya

By the time I awoke, the sun had already peeked over the Hawkspires and I lay in a glorious pool of warm sunshine. Somehow Pepro had managed to get up without waking me, which was amazing considering how lightly I normally sleep. Basking felt so good that I wanted to just stay right there all morning, but I knew we had to get going soon.

Through the night, Pepro and I snuggled and beaked together. That's as far as it went, but it was the most satisfying, and erotic, time of my life spent close to another. I realized I needn't have worried about hurting our friendship, nor questioned my attraction to him. Our closeness had an allure beyond physical pleasure. I felt at home in his wings and tantalizingly close to the potential of having a companion for life. I tasted a new reality, and I wanted to go on exploring it.

I squinted into the bright sunlight and swiveled my head around to look for the others. I didn't see Pepro anywhere but heard him talking quietly somewhere below. I rose slowly, sorely, and a dull ache throbbed behind my eyes and a fullness pressed at my backside. I made my way slowly to the nest's edge and relieved myself, then chewed some of the willow bark Nyx had left nearby and quickly drank some water to wash down the bitterness.

The face of last night's meal grinned at me from under a loose covering of spruce boughs. I smiled as I recalled how tenderly Pepro had beaked little bits of the marmot to me in the night, just as if I were a newly hatched eaglet. His salty saliva moistened each piece, just as a dutiful parent would do. It was achingly cute to recall, and I glowed with the feeling that he loved me.

By the light of day, the advanced disrepair of the nest was plain. The lighter sticks and spruce needles had rotted into a thick layer of soil-scented duff with moss growing on top. Spruce cones filled the center in various stages of decomposition. Except for the fresh greenery retrieved by Nyx and Pepro the previous night, everything else hinted at years of disuse.

I noticed an oval plaque of tarnished brass embedded in the bark of the tree. It depicted a large star at the top and four others arranged below it. A nest with an egg was inscribed at the bottom and the name "Perro" took up the center.

I preened my feathers, stretched my legs and tail, then my wings, and it felt good to flex and move. I flew up from the nest, circled the tree, and spotted Pepro and Nyx in the branches further down the nest tree. They appeared to be looking through some of Perro's belongings.

"Hey, sleepy head!" Pepro chirped out to me.

I banked in and landed next to him.

"Good morning, Sashya." Pepro said as he reached his beak down for a kiss. I eagerly engaged beak tips with him and churred happily. Neither of us hesitated, as if nothing were more natural. I smiled broadly in the knowledge that last night was no dream. Pepro loved me.

Nyx asked cheerily, "Feeling better, Sashya?"

"Much better. Headache is almost gone, thanks to you."

"Good!" Nyx replied. "You'll want to chew a bit more of that pussy willow bark before we go."

Pepro added, "I can put some in my bag for later too, Sash."

"Thanks, Pep." I looked over the scene more closely. There was a writing desk consisting of a cabinet of thin wood planks fitted tightly together with a slanted, hinged top. Expert craftsmanship was evident, although years of weather and lack of regular oiling were taking their toll and turned the wood gray and rough. It stood in front of a branch at just the right height for perching on one foot and writing with the other. Pepro was perched in the writer's position with a sharpened bit of charcoal in his foot poised above the open pages of a tattered journal.

Pepro noticed my curiosity and said, "We're leaving a note."

I snuggled closer and looked over the half page of writing. It was remarkably uniform and neat, undoubtedly the scribe of a learned and patient bird.

"Is Perro a teacher?" I asked.

Pepro nodded, "He taught at Unitum, at the Presidential College."

Nyx asked, "What subjects?"

Pepro replied as he scribbled, "Hmm, history for sure and rhetoric I believe, but mostly ichthyology."

I chuckled, "The way you speak of him, he probably knows everything about fish."

Pepro replied, "He does. He said it wasn't enough for us to know how to catch them. We had to care for them too."

"What? Like feed them?" I asked.

"No, more like paying attention to what they need. Keeping water clean, making sure the lakes and rivers and sea can support them."

We birds were so few, and the world was so big, it was hard to imagine that ever being a problem. And yet, I had seen the signs of the Featherless everywhere, including the staggering layers of their refuse in the Galinta Midden.

Pepro went on, "He called it stewardship, like how lords of old took care of a master's aerie, only in this case, it's for future generations. I guess it was something the Featherless tried to do, but failed."

I watched Pepro writing and said quietly, "Sounds wise. And who better to care about fish than eagles?"

Pepro nodded, "Yes, Uncle Perro thinks so."

Nyx chimed in, "He's quite the fisher. When I was here four years ago, I saw him catch one fish in one foot and another in the other foot and bring both back without stopping in between. It was incredible."

"He's the best. That's why he was the Volatus Champion Fisher six summers in a row. He was in the fishing service of the capital for ten winters before retiring and nesting here some ten years ago."

"Oh, is that what the plaque in the nest was for?" I asked.

"Yep! That gives Uncle Perro title to this nest and territory in thanks for his years of service to Volatus."

"What did he say in the book?" I asked.

"His last entry was three autumns ago. Looks like no one bothered recording a visit since, not even his kids."

"Is that unusual?"

Pepro shrugged, "I don't really know. His fledges might have their own territories and families that keep them busy now. Chala and See-angela were the two I helped raised, and I've completely lost track of them."

I smiled at the names, "I guess your uncle likes historical names."

Pepro chuckled. "That's Uncle Perro for sure. He loves the great characters of history. He knows everything there is to know about the Rebellion. His dad, my grandpa, had served in it. He told me that he had even met Seeangela when she was quite old."

"Great Awakening!" Nyx declared.

"That's amazing, Pep!" I added. "I hope to meet Perro some day and ask him about his experiences."

"You will! And he would love to meet you too, Sash."

A thrill rose in my throat and blushed my beak. It wasn't just the excitement of meeting a legendary bird who had met our heroes of old, it was the way Pepro spoke as though I were already part of his family. I touched his foot with mine and wrapped my toes around his.

Pepro smiled at me, then finished the note to Perro. It said he was here with me and Nyx, that all was well, and invited him to visit us in Galinta. He signed it 'Love Pepro' and closed the book. I helped him open the desk and he put the book and pencil back inside.

A warm breeze riffled the surface of the lake, and the nest tree creaked.

Pepro looked at me and said, "Are you feeling strong enough to continue?"

"I'm ready. I'm glad you fed me last night because those mountains would be tough to cross on a full gizzard."

Nyx's dark eyes changed shape as the lenses flexed to focus on distant ripples of air. "There are some great thermals building over those sunny rocks there. Looks like a good time to go."

We quickly tidied the nest, fetched the willow bark, and it wasn't long before we were winging our way toward the thermal that Nyx had spotted.

On the way, Pepro said to me, "If you feel tired or sore, you just climb on my back, all right? It's no burden at all."

I replied, "I will, Peppy. Thanks for being so good to me." His beak beamed with a smile that made his lower eyelids crease. He liked having me close and caring for me and that made me feel bigger and more complete than ever. Ironically, the energy it inspired in me made it less likely that I would need help, but I would gladly accept it all the same. As we circled up through the thermal, I thought on how letting Pepro help me was, in a sense, a way of giving back. Birds of prey seldom show weakness or need so being open to another's care,

I realized, is an act of love on its own. If it made Pepro happy, it made me happy, and I felt the reverse was true too.

We climbed until we were higher than the snowy peaks, and the valley became a hazy ribbon below. The smoother, warmer air and the closeness of the peaks made me feel less vulnerable than our more exposed flights the day before. And far to the east, I saw a blue sliver across the pale horizon.

I screeched with glee, "Peppy! I see the ocean!"

Pepro chirped back, "Yes! Can't wait to show you up close!"

A team of six swans pulling a cloud-white sky sled passed below us heading west. A seventh swan flapped close behind and honked out a traveling tune in time to the wingbeats of the team, who joined in singing the refrains. The sled's long, slender wings and v-shaped tail resembled the shape of a seabird, but its nose bore orange and black livery that resembled the face of the imperial swans that pulled it.

We exited the thermal and made a long glide to the next row of foothills. Nyx and I took stations on either side, just behind Pepro's wings, riding his wingtip vortices. We rode thermal after thermal and by the third quarter of daylight, we crossed the last forested ridge.

Among the spruce trees and granite cliffs, I spotted a pair of ravens and a mottle keeping watch from a crumbled tower of stones and rusted steel. We passed low over them, and they called out greetings to us, which we returned in kind.

And then we began a long, final glide toward a distant smudge of birds and ruins clinging to white cliffs at the edge of the sea.

Chapter 6

Whiterock

By Sashya

As we drew closer to town, distant birds swirled in the sky like white flakes of hoarfrost. A little closer and the specks became swarms, and the city appeared as a beehive. Closer still, and the "bees" sharpened into birds of diverse colors, shapes, and sizes that darted and swirled between the ruins. An entire busy bird city spread before us.

As with other Apterian city ruins I had seen, healing scars criss-crossed the land, breaking it up into a checkerboard of ruins, rubble, trees, and meadows. Decayed buildings had collapsed into heaps of concrete, stone, and rusted iron that were grown over with vegetation, but many still rose above the trees. Most of these were not more than ten or twenty wingspans tall, or just a bit higher than the spruce and aspen trees, but a few soared much higher and were the tallest and least decayed artificial structures I have ever seen.

Each crumbling ruin was covered in birds and bird dwellings. As in Galinta, they were made of wood, accrement, or scraps of metal and whatever else could be gleaned from Apterian ruins. Most were curved and built with tiered landing platforms that overlapped their neighbors, more like a colony of nesting cliff swallows than the angled, rigid block shapes of the crumbled Apterian homes.

The cacophony of the screaming seabirds, who were the most abundant species, deafened my sensitive ears. It was exhilarating, though, and transmitted the energy of the city straight to my brain until my whole body vibrated with it.

Although I grew up within a day's hard flight of our capital, Unitum, I had never actually visited it. But even if I had, it would be completely outdone by Whiterock, which was twice as populous and known to be the largest city in all Volatus. I had simply never been prepared to see so many Awakened birds concentrated in one place at one time.

As we approached the center of the city, the cliffside ruins became close enough to study. The land had split and sent buildings tumbling into the sea so that only tall facades remained with empty windows full of sky. In the cliffs, round caves of concrete gaped, draped by a myriad of rusted iron tubes and dark vines that were too stiff to be natural. Below, a jumble of rusted metal bones and massive boulders of concrete surged in a chaos of foamy green water, teaming with plunging gannets, razorbills, and puffins. As with the ruins above, the cliffs and caves were likewise caked with bird-built structures of accrement, partitioning off the caverns into hosts of lively establishments.

On the sea in front of the cliffs, a row of three gannets tugged a narrow craft, three wingspans long and one wide, while two others worked ropes to raise a set of billowing sails. They were setting north out of a crowd of similar boats set in a small cove at the south end of the bluffs.

As we crossed the brow of the cliffs, the wind shifted and washed a briny waft of fishy guano vapors upwards through my feathers. I gagged and staggered in midair.

Nyx saw my stricken expression and watering eyes, and chuckled, "What's the matter, landbird? Never smelled the ocean before?"

I winced, "Somehow I thought it wouldn't be quite so spicy."

Pepro laughed and said, "It's not, when you're not flying over thousands of shitting seabirds. But still, somehow, that smell makes my mouth water. So many good things down there to eat."

I replied sarcastically, "Makes my mouth water too. Like right before I'm gonna cast a pellet!"

Pepro called to Nyx, "Is that the Avian Haven there?" He pointed his beak toward a white tower whose top had an emblem, constructed of a mosaic of colored stones, shaped like a branching tree with a crescent moon.

Nyx chupped in reply, "Yep. Miss Penelope's place. It's the best roostery in Whiterock."

"That's where we were instructed to stay." replied Pepro.

Nyx said, "My goodness! Kor's a real generous bird to put you up there."

Pepro said, "I guess he knows Miss Penelope. Kor said to treat her extra nicely. What's she like?"

Nyx answered, "Fancy and rich, but she's a good egg. She's well-connected and knows all the gossip, so everyone treats her well, and she expects it. You'll see."

I followed as Pepro and Nyx banked and descended toward the tower. It was made of Apterian concrete with tall window openings, each filled by a wall of accrement. The accrement walls each had an entrance archway or bird-sized windows with hinged doors and shutters. In front of each entrance hung a wooden landing platform. Unlike most ruins, this one's concrete had been meticulously restored and maintained. Rust-stained cracks were few and larger gaps had been filled with accrement. The whole structure was coated in fresh white paint.

One of the platforms, near the top of the tower, had a flag hanging from it that lofted in the gentle sea breeze. It was blue with a white star, just like the ones I had seen on the armor of King Vasili's companions. Additionally, two crownies stood on each side of the doorway, wearing similar armor. I thrilled to think I might see King Vasili again, but I would have foregone the pleasure if it also meant crossing paths with the Princess.

The tile mosaic on the top of the tower was even more splendid up close. Shades of blue and violet rimmed the perimeter of a square on the east half of the rooftop and the black silhouette of the tree and moon were in the center. Slate was stacked into warm basking tables along the north side and a shallow, circular, tiled pond took up the south.

The western half of the rooftop had been remodeled with accrement and other avian touches to create a reception hall and adjoining rooms. A dome of multicolored glass was the centerpiece of the hall. The front of the structure faced east, and a trail of blue tiles led from the emblem to the entrance.

We fluttered to a stop on the edge of the terrace where an immaculate ring-billed gull sat loafing on one of the slate stacks. It regarded us lazily before closing its golden eyes. A crow hopped about and stabbed up stray feathers to keep the rooftop spotless. She hopped to the edge of the rooftop and dropped a beakful of debris over the side as I watched.

Soft curtains of silky blue fabric hung down on either side of the arched entranceway. Nyx nodded toward the opening and Pepro and I walked ahead of her into the reception area.

Inside, columns of white stone stood tall around a circular floor of similarly white stone. It was shiny and clean and furnished with perches of polished wood and blue fabric. Round tables were placed between semicircular perches and the dome overhead cast a colored light over everything. Below the dome was an elaborate brass oil lantern dangling with chains of crystals that transformed light into miniature rainbows all around the floor.

Around the central dome, the ceiling was covered in a tile mosaic of light blue with white clouds. The square perimeter of the room was likewise rimmed by columns, each with a curious brass fixture attached. The fixture resembled a lantern, but in place of a candle or lamp wick, there was only a bulb of glass with a metal bristle within.

The openings between the columns offered sweeping views of the city to the north, east, and south and the western wall was covered with mirror glass, the largest such panes I had ever seen in one piece. The entire ballroom was bright and fresh with sea air and sunshine, blurring my impression of where the room ended and the sky began.

"Pepro?" I asked. "On your Wander, did you ever see anything like this?"

He shook his head in silence.

Nyx snickered, "It is amazing, but you rubes really need to get out more."

A crow stalked our way, side-eyeing us carefully. He cawed qui-

etly, "May I help you?" His accent was even more nasal than most crows.

Pepro turned to him with his beak still open in wonder. "Uh, yes. We're here on business from Galinta."

"Galinta? Do you need a room?"

"Well, our master instructed us to talk with Miss Penelope. Is she in?"

"I'm afraid Miss Penelope is occupied at the moment."

"Can you let her know we're here?"

"Perhaps. Whom may I say sent you?"

"Master Kor."

"Kor?" the crow repeated.

"Kory?! From Galinta?" said a smooth metallic magpie voice from an adjacent room.

We looked toward the voice and a plump-breasted magpie swaggered gracefully in through a doorway. Her beak shined as though rubbed with fine emollient, and her black head and nape feathers shimmered from metallic green and purple hues, perfectly preened to enhance their colors. Her dark eyelash quills beckoned out and swept back as if each one had been crafted to send a classy greeting of its own. A gold chain swept from her nape and connected on each side of her beak to a gold nasal ring. Dangling on the chain were two pearls on the left side and a silver bead on the right. Her black and white wingtips and long tail swept the floor below her puffed-out plumes.

She studied us with sparkling eyes and asked excitedly, "Did you say Kor of Galinta?"

The crow replied, "Miss Penelope, I have three guests to see you, sent by Kor of Galinta. Allow me to introduce—"

"Relax, Aank." Miss Penelope admonished. "Kor is a dear friend. Please have Miss Schreider fetch tea and treats for us in the parlor."

Aank bowed and stalked into a backroom. Miss Penelope turned to Nyx and cheerfully spoke, "Now you, I know. Miss Nyx of Waycliffs, is it?"

"That's right!" Nyx said with a respectful nod. "Your memory is impeccable, Miss Penelope."

"Thank you, dear. So nice to see you again. I hope your lovely parents are well."

"Yes, ma'am. A hard winter, but we weathered it out."

"Splendid. The Northerners prevail again!" She turned to Pepro and me and asked, "And who are your fine companions from Galinta?"

Pepro bowed and said, "I'm Pepro, ma'am, apprentice to Master Kor."

"Oh yes! Kory has mentioned you in his letters. A strapping and handsome one you are. And who is this?" Penelope asked as she cast her dark eyes upon me.

"I'm Sashya, ma'am," I said as I bowed. "I'm second apprentice to Master Kor."

"Oh my, dear, what happened to your beak?" She crood. She turned her beak and leaned closer to study my face.

"Some raven bandit, ma'am, out at Sunrise Lake."

"Tsk, tsk, terrible!" she sympathized. "Did they steal anything?"

Pepro replied, "We stopped 'em just in time, ma'am."

Nyx chimed in with a lowered voice, "I kicked their asses."

I was surprised Nyx would use such crass language, but Miss Penelope nodded and growled, "Good for you, dear." She said to me, "I can arrange for you to see my healer, if you like? You have willow bark at least?"

"Yes ma'am, it hardly hurts now."

"All right, you just let me know if you need anything for that." She bowed politely, "Welcome, dears, to the Avian Haven. Now, please, won't you join me for tea and snacks? You must be hungry after your long journey."

Nyx took the lead and said, "Oh yes, ma'am, how gracious of you."

Miss Penelope smiled with beak held straight and proud, "But of course! But there is a price. You must tell me everything you can about dear Kory and your life with him in Galinta. Now come along!"

Miss Penelope turned and waltzed her way toward a back hallway. Pepro stifled a chuckle, and so did I, for neither of us had ever heard Kor referred to as *Kory* before.

Miss Penelope led us down a short, wide passage to a modestly sized reception room in the northwest corner of the building, decorated with dark-stained wood panels and colorful shells on the ceiling. There more of the multi-paned, multi-hued windows of Kor's favorite design, one on each outside wall of the room, and a round table filled the corner. As with the tables in the hall, a perch encircled it, this time upholstered in red. Matching red nesting pillows were stacked in the corner, and I surmised that the room could be rearranged for all manner of small gatherings. I had never seen such lavish comforts before.

Miss Penelope said, "Please come inside, lay down your burdens, and relax."

We filed into the cozy room, and I helped Pepro slip off his satchel and hang it up, and then we took our perches around the table. A slim magpie entered the room carrying a basket in her beak and another strapped to her back. She stopped at the table and set out four round platters and a small cup on each one. I was fascinated by the construction of the cups as they were exceptionally thin and light. The stone was smooth as glass, whiter than bone, and painted with delicate floral patterns of robin's egg blue.

From a pot in the beak basket, the magpie filled each of our cups with tea and then laid out a golden cake beside each one. As she finished her task, Miss Penelope said, "Thank you, Miss Schreider."

"Yes, ma'am." the waiting magpie replied. "Will there be anything else?"

"Yes!" Penelope said with a smile. "Please close the door and don't let anyone disturb us."

Miss Schreider nodded, left the room, and slid the door shut behind her.

Miss Penelope reminded me of my grandmother. She surrounded herself with rare and pretty things and loved to show them off. It wasn't merely to brag, but to stimulate lively conversation. I surmised Miss Penelope might be the same, so I inquired about the cups.

"Miss Penelope, these cups are incredible. Are they Apterian?"

She flashed her nictitating membranes and nodded. "You use the scholarly term. You've surely had some schooling. How delightful!"

"Yes, ma'am. Two years at the owl school in Kahvanis."

"Impressive! And, yes, you are correct. These are porcelain cups, over five hundred years old."

"They must be priceless," I said, afraid to touch them, much less eat from them, for fear of breaking one.

Miss Penelope added, "Oh they had a price, and believe me it wasn't easy, rare as they are in such complete condition and of appropriate size. Most Apterian dishes are too unwieldy and large for us birds to use, but these were made as playthings for their young offspring. Perfect for our use, so no matter the cost, I just had to have them. I'm glad you appreciate them."

Pepro changed the subject, "Kor sends his best, ma'am. He spoke highly of you, and I can see why."

Penelope fanned her tail and shivered her wings with delight. "Ohh myyy! He always makes me melt like a hen pie in her first spring! Now, please enjoy your tea and bug bread while you tell me everything."

I watched Miss Penelope bite off a bit of her bread, dip it into the tea, and swallow it daintily, and so I did likewise. The light, sweet bread dissolved quickly in my mouth, leaving bits of softened grubs and dried fruit on my tongue, while the minty tea washed and refreshed my palate.

Miss Penelope noticed my thoughtful smile. "Do you like it?"

I nodded and replied, "It's amazing! It reminds me of the bread my grandmother makes, though this is much lighter and spongy by comparison. She would love to know how you make this."

"I can have Miss Schreider write down her recipe for you." Miss Penelope said.

"Oh ma'am, I wouldn't want to trouble you."

"Tsk! No trouble at all," she cheerfully replied. "Miss Schreider is ever so protective of her recipes, but as I tell her, there's no better way to win customers than through their gizzard. Soon, all the owls of Kahvanis will want to come stay at the Avian Haven, just to have a taste of her original bug bread!"

Miss Penelope's eyes twinkled, and she punctuated her words with flips of her beak that jostled the attached chains. I saw why Kor liked her. Her gay and generous demeanor would make anyone feel like a friend.

"Now come, no more delay. How is Kory? Does he eat well? Most importantly, is he still single?" She nibbled her cake and eyed me expectantly.

I cleared my throat as I thought of what to say about Kor's love life. His eyes sparkled when a particular maiden crow would drop by to deliver kindling. Her visits never failed to raise the feathers on the sides of his head and distract him from his work. As she departed, he would stare dreamily up at her underfluffies until she flew out of sight. And on more than one occasion, he came to work casually with a skip in his step and his feathers disheveled and smelling of grass. We never asked, but we were sure he didn't roll in the meadow by himself.

But, of course, my response to Miss Penelope was exactly what she wanted to hear. "Oh yes, ma'am, he's single, all right. And yes, he eats well. He takes good care of us too."

Miss Penelope chuckled and then stared at me blandly, "Now relax, dears. There's no judgment, and we speak only the truth inside these walls."

I feared she would press further on Kor's faithfulness and my gizzard froze.

To my relief, Pepro came to the rescue. He casually said, "Kor is mostly business around us, ma'am. You know how he is. Married to the forge and no time for messing around."

The sparkle returned to Miss Penelope's eyes, and she said, "Yes, that sounds like Kory all right. It's a challenge, even here, far from his forge, to get him to relax. But he is such a sweet-talker, and a warm-hearted soul underneath those sooty feathers. I tell him he should sell that old forge and move here to Whiterock. He could set up a shop in the Institute and keep teaching, and we would have such a fabulous life together."

I sympathized with Miss Penelope, for now that I had Pepro, I hated to imagine being days apart from his warmth. I smiled at him, and he returned it, confirming he felt the same.

I said to Miss Penelope, "It must be painful when the one you love is so far away."

She paused in mid-gulp and nodded. "Indeed, Sashya. I would do anything for that grizzled old raven. He makes me so happy, and I know he's happy with me. The separation is unbearable."

Pepro said, "Sash and I will work on him, Miss Penelope. We'll convince him to let us tend the shop more so he can come see you. Before long, he'll realize he has everything he needs right here."

It wasn't an empty promise. Pepro and I were more than capable of managing the day-to-day work on our own. And the thought of working and living alone with Pepro stirred nesting instincts deep within me and filled me with warmth.

Miss Penelope fluffed her feathers and fluttered her nictitating membranes. "That would be wonderful. You'll make an old hen so happy!"

"Oh, Pep, the letter!" I exclaimed.

"Ah, right!" Pepro said. He rummaged in his satchel and pulled out Kor's letter with his beak, then offered it to Miss Penelope.

The portly magpie excitedly snatched the letter and inhaled. "Mmm, I still smell his smoky scent!" She hopped indelicately onto the table, broke the wax seal, and spread the page out with her feet.

Penelope beaked the words silently to herself smiling all the while. She nodded after a moment and said, "You must stay here and be my guests, please!"

Pepro replied, "But Ma'am, we have money."

Miss Penelope shook her beak. "No sir, your money's no good here. I won't hear of it! You're on an important mission for Kory, and I'm happy to help. Besides, I know what an adventure this is for you two, and how you must work so hard all the time. You deserve to have the best time while you're here, and I shall provide it!"

She resumed reading the letter and then rolled her eyes with a sharp inhale. "I can't believe he's sending you to find Perry." She clicked her beak with concern, "You're in luck, I guess, if you can call it that." Her voice hardened to flinty edge. "I heard he's in town. I can point you in the right direction, but he hasn't been welcome in my place for a year or so. So don't bring him around here." She dipped her beak in her tea curtly, her head feathers bristling.

Nyx cocked her head and asked, "Not welcome? Is there something we should know?"

Penelope erupted into a breathless torrent of terse words, "We kicked that low life out after he brought his louse-ridden hennies here and wrecked one of my rooms! It took days of scrubbing to get rid of the bugs, the stench, and those stains! On the floor, on the walls, on the ceil--" She closed her eyes a moment and reigned in her temper.

I should have been mortified, but instead I exercised my best owl stoicism to keep from laughing.

In a moment, Miss Penelope gathered her wits and resumed, more calmly, "Sorry, that was more than you wanted to hear, I'm sure. Just, please be careful associating with that worthless waste of feathers."

Pepro nodded, "Of course, ma'am."

I asked, "Can you tell us more about him, ma'am? Anything at all would help since I have to negotiate for gold, and I don't know him."

Miss Penelope dipped the last morsel of her bug bread in her tea and swallowed it down. "He's well known around here and was once a respected member of the community. He's been all over the three seas and carried messages to far off lands, even to Mamyrskit. He was regarded as the best finder of treasure. I bought some of my finest gems from him. He had all the trappings to be a successful trader."

She cocked her head in thought, "But something happened ten winters ago, and he's been worthless ever since. The polite gossip is he had a secret love, someone of high position, that ultimately rejected him. But those stories are probably just leavings. Whatever the cause, now he comes to town weighed down with jewels and gold and blows it all in the breeding parlors on loose hens and strong drink."

Pepro asked, "Where do you think we can find him?"

Miss Penelope chuckled, "He'll be where his gold goes farthest. Follow the stink to the dingiest sewer in Low Town. If you don't find him there, he'll be locked up in the peacekeeper citadel. You can't miss it. It's the red and white tower on the big white rock at the north end of town. But be careful down there. You can't trust the drunks and the peacekeepers aren't much nicer."

I nodded appreciatively and said, "Thank you for the warning, Miss Penelope."

She grimaced, and touched her forehead with a fisted foot, as though she had a headache growing right between her eyes. "I hate to send you down to that dreadful, dirty place. Can I recommend another source for your gold? Or can I give you some of my gold jewelry?"

Pepro replied, "Oh no, ma'am, we won't hear of it. You're very generous but Kor would be upset if we overstepped. He was very specific about us finding Perry. We have a private message for him too."

"Well, if you must," Miss Penelope replied. "I suppose Kory knows what he's sending you into." She stopped talking then and sighed.

I didn't want the conversation to end so sourly, so I said, "Thanks, Miss Penelope. Master Kor said that you're a good friend and someone we can trust. He was right."

The sparkle returned to her eyes again. "That's my sweet Kory. Wait! I didn't finish the letter, did I?"

She resumed reading and broke with a broad smile. She trilled with delight, "Kory's coming here! You've all been invited to the Royal Bonding!" She pattered her feet on the table and covered her beak with her wings. "I have rooms now, but the place is booked up tight as a nest of swallows for the days around the Royal Bonding. But we'll make room for you all, somehow, even if I must put you up in my own residence!"

"Thank you, ma'am! We won't be any trouble to you."

Nyx chimed in, "Ma'am, my folks have already made arrangements for us, so no need to make room for me."

"Of course, dear." Miss Penelope replied.

Pepro spoke. "Ma'am, speaking of the Bonding, we noticed crownies standing guard in front of one of the rooms. Is King Vasili staying here?"

"Indeed, he is. He returned this morning, probably from his trip to see Kory. He's here with some of his nobles and the princess."

Pepro's eyes lit up. "We met him when he visited. He sure was warm and friendly. Do you think he would mind visitors?"

Penelope closed her beak in thought. "You can try, dear. You can check with his staff. They'll let you know if he's available. I know his dinner plans include meeting Governor P'tilo in his suite tonight, and he's been dreadfully busy with his bonding plans. I think trying tomorrow would be best, dear."

"Yes, ma'am, thank you." Pepro replied.

Miss Penelope went on, "Anyway, you must all need a rest from your trip. Let's get you into your room. Miss Schreider!" Penelope cried out with her eyes fixed on the door.

"Yes, ma'am?" came Miss Schreider's muffled voice from the other side.

Miss Penelope replied, "I knew you were listening in, you old gossip! But I'm in too good a mood to care. Hurry, now, fetch up a room for these special visitors. One of the family suites should do. And please let the kitchen know that we'll be having a falcon, a moon owl, and a bald eagle as dinner guests."

"Yes, ma'am!" she replied, followed by a scurrying of claws on the floor.

Miss Penelope turned to us and said, "Schreider is quite the stealthy listener. Every gossip in town envies her. But she knows how to keep her beak shut most of the time."

Miss Penelope escorted us back to the ballroom and, to my surprise, Princess Vouli was there, exchanging terse words with Aank.

The crow kept his beak up, but his tight plumage and flashing nictitating membranes belied his discomfort.

"I am truly sorry, Your Grace," Aank said apologetically. "I'll have a word with the cleaning staff and see that the toilet chute is repaired."

"See to it, before I return," Vouli said with lifted hackles and tight pupils.

Aank bowed, "Of course, Your Grace. Please excuse me."

As Aank turned away, Vouli noticed us. Her irritated expression relaxed, and she smiled unconvincingly, "The apprentices from Galinta. My, my, that's a ghastly bruise on your cere, little owl. Did you fly into a tree?"

"No m'Lady. Bandits at Sunrise Lake."

"Oh my, how did you survive such a terrible attack?" Vouli asked.

Nyx clenched a fist and responded, "I kicked their butt, Your Grace."

Vouli's smile faded to a smirk, "Such a fierce falcon. And you are?"

"Miss Nyx of Waycliffs. Pleased to meet you, Lady Vouli. You must be excited about your father's bonding."

Princess Vouli yawned long and loud with flared plumage and pupils pinned. "What was that? Oh, the bonding. Yes, most excited," she said with the enthusiasm of dropping a rancid mouse.

She turned to me and Pepro with steel in her eyes. "Aren't you two working on the bonding rings for my father?"

"Yes, Lady Vouli, we're here to buy the gold."

"Mm-hmm, I see," she said with chagrin. "Finest jewelers in Volatus and yet you don't have enough gold for two rings. Tsk, tsk."

Pepro replied, "M'Lady, we had just used up all our—"

The princess flared her head feathers and seethed, "Excuses already? My father is paying you a ransom. Now I want to know: Will the rings be done on time?" She annunciated the last statement slowly as though chastising naughty eaglets.

I was scared, but I didn't like our integrity being questioned by someone who barely knew us, whatever their station in life. I met her intense gaze, and said, "Lady Vouli, your father made the contract with Kor because he knows of his good reputation. And Kor charged us with getting the gold because he trusts us. We won't let Kor down, and he won't let King Vasili down. If you question any of this, please take it up with your father, m'Lady, for he's the one who made the contract." I bowed respectfully.

The Princess pulled her head high and blinked in disbelief. I had affronted her, but I did it with such respect that she had no proper retort. Her eyes burned with contempt, and it shook me. Pepro placed a reassuring wing on my shoulders.

Miss Penelope scolded, "You, Miss Vouli, are quite out of line! I dare say Master Kor's name carries more respect here than yours. Now stop harassing my guests, or I will be forced to have words with your father!"

The crowny's pupils pinned and her hackles lifted higher. Her claws grated on the floor as her feet tensed. She surveyed us with vengeful eyes, then turned and growled, "Such insolence! It will not be forgotten." Then briskly exited and flew away.

Nyx asked Pepro, "Is that the cold crowny you told me about?"

Pepro replied, "One of them."

I trembled. I was elated for successfully defending Kor, but also afraid she would not soon forget my "insolence".

Pepro tugged me into a hug, "I'm proud of you, Sash. That was intense." His soft embrace melted away my fear.

Miss Penelope added, "Well done, young owl. You have a good instinct for knowing how to tell off a princess."

Nyx added, "I agree. But I don't like those last words of hers. What was up with that?"

Miss Penelope replied, "Nothing dear. Just the empty threats of a royally spoiled brat."

Moments later, Aank escorted us to our suite. It was spacious and clean, with a table, perches, and an oil lantern up front, and two big nests in the back corners, separated by a wall between them and curtains at their front.

Aank pointed his beak to a couple of large jars in the corner. "The blue one has fresh water; the red one is for food waste. If you need to relieve yourself, please do not use the platforms or the windows."

I looked around and saw no alternative. "So, uh, what do we use?"

Aank dryly pointed his beak at a slanted metal tube in the corner fitted with a wooden lid. "Be sure to replace the lid each time or you'll regret it."

"Thanks!" I said. "We'll figure it out."

Aank continued with a bored tone, "Dinner is at three bells."

When Aank didn't leave right away, Nyx beaked a copper from her neck purse and offered it to him. Without a thank you, he took the coin, stalked out the door, and fluttered away.

I shook my head, "You have to pay for answers to questions?"

Nyx chuckled, "It's the big city, Sashya. Everything runs on money."

Chapter 7

Reunion

By Nyx of Waycliffs

I left Sashya and Pepro at the Avian Haven. They didn't say it, but I knew they were anxious to have some quiet time together, and I was happy to give them space. Besides, I had my message to deliver, so I flew north to the Government Quarter.

The territorial and city offices were within a massive old ruin of gleaming marble. Like many stone buildings, it had weathered the ages better than most Apterian structures. It had four wings, pointing to the cardinal directions, and a dome over the center. The dome had cracked and partially collapsed, along with a good portion of the southern wing's backbone. In the center of the rotunda under the dome, vines and trees grew high up from within, seeking sunlight.

I descended toward the opening in the dome and landed on the precariously perched cupola. A ferruginous hawk stood watch duty, charged with the important tasks of measuring noon, ringing the bell to announce the quarters of the day, and keeping track of birds coming and going.

"Name?" She asked. Hers was an unfamiliar, young face. Her brown barred wings and tail lacked the deep ocher of adults.

I replied, "I'm Nyx, Proxy for Waycliffs."

"Regional council?" she asked.

"Yes."

The hawk nodded and scribbled on a logbook. "Busy times, eh? Staying for the Bonding?"

"Oh yes! Whole family is coming down. Will you be there?"

"I'm new so, no, I'll be on duty here."

"Oh, that's unfortunate. Hopefully someone can bring you treats from the feast."

"Indeed. You know your way?" the hawk asked.

"Yes, of course. What's your name?"

"Garnet, of Azure Cove," she replied with a smile.

"You've come a long way north."

"Indeed," she nodded, "But there's little opportunity out there, at least for what I want to do."

"Studying?" I asked.

Garnet's face lit up, "Yes, Aerodynamics, at the Institute."

"Aero-whats?"

"The study of how flight works," she replied with a smile.

"Tsk, tsk, we're birds. What more is there to know?"

Garnet chuckled, "Yes, ma'am, but we're making sky sleds."

"Oh, interesting! Well, good luck to you in your studies. Build 'em strong and fast."

"I will, ma'am. Good day to you!"

I bid my farewell and descended through the hole into the rotunda below. Three floors of white marble and Apterian concrete mezzanines surrounded the space, and a tall spruce grew up through the center. Great gilded statues of perched eagles, left over from the Folegalian Dynasty, solemnly held massive lanterns in their beaks to illuminate the center of the hall. Smaller lanterns dotted the mezzanines, casting a warm glow on the columns and statues. A cool resinous scent mingled with the mustiness of old documents, rose up through the rotunda.

I spiraled downward around the great, two-hundred-year-old tree to a corridor on the north side of the first floor and glided into the paneled anteroom of the council chambers. A great horned owl straddled a scribe's saddle, writing with a quill pen in her right foot. It was Hemlock, an affable veteran of Star Talons, a unit of the Waystar militia. She served for thirty years, an extraordinarily long career. She finally retired to serve with the council when her wings were too stiff to keep up with the recruits she loved to train. But her experience was invaluable in government. She lent a continuity back to the days when the last of the Rebellion's warriors shared their wisdom before passing away into history. When she heard my wings whistle in through the door, she looked up and smiled.

"Nyx!" she hooted.

"Greetings from Waycliffs, Hemlock! How are you?"

"Very well for an old soldier of thirty-three."

"Is that all?" I lied as I noted the appearance of new gray in her plumicorns.

She hooted, "Kind of you to say. How was your journey?"

"Smooth. The weather treated me well all the way."

"I bet it was splendid, with spring bursting everywhere across Waystar. I miss those flights."

"Yes, quite lovely. Mom and dad send their best to all here. I can report that things are going well, mostly. I have a verbal report for the council."

"Shall I transcribe it for you, or will you attend?"

"It's an entry for the agenda. But, yes, I'll be with my folks at the next session, the day after the royal bonding, right?"

"Yes, that's right."

"Good, well the message is that Waycliffs formally submits a request for two peacekeepers. We raised the necessary village levy, so we're requesting matching regional and national assets."

Hemlock swapped parchments on the tilted desk plane below her saddle and scribbled a note. "Splendid. The request has been entered into the agenda."

"Thank you."

"Are you having trouble with muddies too?"

I cringed. My folks and I were sensitive to the use of species slurs, even ones as mild as this. After all, it was less than sixty springs prior that crownies had ruled and labeled us all with their hateful slurs. My grandfather, Anatolia, who was a slave for a Folegalian crowny lord, told me how he was cursed repeatedly with the label "putrefactor" for allegedly fetching only the most frounce-rotted pigeons to poison his master's family with disease. Each rejection meant no pay and he would have to repeat his hunt. "Mudhead" wasn't as bad, but it carried implications of inferiority and was not befitting a member of government.

I did not stifle my irritation, "If you mean mottles, yes dear."

Hemlock replied, "Sorry, ma'am. Of course. It's just that we've had so many similar reports. I apologize for the unprofessional language."

I nodded, "Just remember the labels put on us too, Hemlock. Anyway, mottles, yes, but crownies too. They've been coming over from Mamyrskit the past few years. We welcome them, but a few are stirring up unrest. We've met with them, tried to address their concerns. My folks will deliver a complete report at the meeting."

"Very good," she said as she finished scribbling. "Your sister Mano came by recently looking for you. She left a note."

Hemlock hopped down from her saddle, stretched her legs, and fluttered her tail. "Oh it feels good to get off that thing sometimes," she said. "The Good Mother made us for flying all night, not breasted at a desk all day." She beaked open a drawer and rummaged around. "Ah! Here it is."

She presented me with a folded scrap of parchment. I flipped it open with my toes and read it.

> *To Nyx. When you return to Whiterock, seek me out at the Lusty Loon.*
> *—Mano*

"When did Mano leave this?" I asked.

"The back has the date, ma'am," Hemlock said.

The scrawl read, *28 Nidum*. I smiled, "Eight days ago." My nest-sister had reached out to me, and it was the first anyone had heard from her in four years. We were hatched a year apart but as is common in our family, she stayed for a year to attend school in Waycliffs and assist mom and dad with raising the next year's clutch.

She often read to me from the writings of Hanu and Millay, philosophers from the days of the Folegalian Dynasty, whose forbidden writings fueled Seeangela's fiery passion for a free society. She eschewed use of our family's reputation, even for the good things it accomplished. As she put it, she wanted to know the depths of Volatian society before she took on the privileges of its heights.

This vexed our parents greatly. After all, if life granted you connections and a higher station, why not use that to do as much good as possible? *Was there no higher calling than the benevolence possible from wealth and political power?*

Our folks disagreed with her loose plans to make her own life and reputation in Whiterock, but she was determined to live among the poor and write of her experiences. They pleaded for her to stay in touch, and come back to them if she needed anything, but she never did. We weren't even sure if she was still alive. I loved her and missed her dearly.

I nodded to Hemlock, "Thank you. Do you know where the Lusty Loon is?"

Hemlock churred a hootish laugh that made the white crescent feathers of her throat vibrate. "Not anywhere a lady like you wants to go."

"A brothel?" I asked.

"One of the worst. It's on the Promenade in Low Town."

I cocked my head and smiled, "And just how do you know?"

"Ha! You just keep wondering, Miss Nyx."

I thanked her again and walked back to the rotunda. My mind swirled with questions that darted about like nighthawks in an evening sky. *If she was looking to shun our name and dive into Whiterock's depths, sounds like she's succeeded. I just hope she's all right.* I flew up past the great tree and out of the dome. I tipped my beak to Garnet and set out for the leaning facades and seaside cliffs that marked Low Town.

Above the frothy rocks and twisted iron of Whiterock's shore stood a slate-paved ledge in the cliffs that varied from three to five wingspans wide. In some places, where too much earth had washed away, the pavers were replaced by rough planks. As dusk approached, two herons strode the promenade lighting oil lanterns that hung from wood poles along the walkway.

Many of the tunnels, tubes, and arcades of brick work and Apterian cement were exposed, and the less precarious examples were adapted for avian businesses and dwellings. The establishments bore signs above their entrances, with pictograms and text to let fliers know at a glance what they offered. I glided south until I saw a wooden sign with a loon wearing a frisky grin. I dropped and fluttered to a stop under the sign and rolled my eyes at the crude attempt to mimic a loon's backside. Pink-painted concrete filled a narrow horizontal crack in the pale rock and dark paint marked off the outline of a loon's posterior. As a final touch, a canopy of black planks jutted out overhead, painted to resemble a loon's fanned tail.

I strolled into a dark, stuffy anteroom where two serious-looking male mottles parted to let me enter.

I said to one, "I'm looking for my nest-sister Mano. Is this the right place?"

The mottle nodded, "See Premaden Elbee, the swan that runs the place."

I pressed in through a curtain of cloaca-pink fabric, and entered a large interior space with a red, curved ceiling supported on red brick arches. The place reeked of alcohol, damp feathers, and smoldering kinnikinnick. Five round, shallow drinking troughs were spaced around the room, each one surrounded by circular perches clad in red leather. Above the troughs were platforms of woven reeds supported by poles clad in black leather. Their purpose was obvious, even without the show that a duo of female sandhill cranes was putting on. They intertwined necks and caressed each other's bills, while their shapely posteriors solicited to a rapt audience below. Three male mottles, a female baldy, and a male great gray owl fluffed with arousal and uttered their species' unique copulatory notes.

A plump imperial swan, wearing a detached expression, watched the entertainment from a wide cushion on a dais at the back. Her white plumage had been preened to a high fluff, and her bill oiled to enhance its deep, earthy orange color. Her cheeks were subtly powdered with umber and her neck dotted with carefully applied flecks of black, concentrated most densely around the back of her cheeks and nape, and peppered more sparsely as my eye progressed downward, until they discontinued at the base of her neck. She wore a pearl stud through her nares with a silver toggle. She was a masterpiece of makeup, too perfect to be natural, or to have been applied by herself.

A male mottle stood attentively behind her; his eyes fixed ahead. I approached her platform as she nibbled from a silver pail of greens, but she did not acknowledge me. She chewed the greens, dipped her bill in her water, and swallowed, moving delicately while making the most indelicate sounds. It culminated in her closing her eyes, grunting, and voiding into a bucket behind her. She wagged her tail, and to my amazement, the mottled eagle picked up the silver excrement bucket in their beak and removed it, then delicately preened her underfluffies back into place, and placed a fresh, polished bucket back under her posterior.

I had never seen such casual opulence and entitlement, and it troubled me to the core. Worse, the eagle's submissive gaze communicated lack of worth, except in the context of their singular job to a "worthy" master. They might have been polishing a gilded foot goblet

for a royal crowny, fearful of brutal reprisal if one grain of dust was carelessly missed.

Who the fuck is this fat princess and what the hell is my nest-sister doing working for her? I kept my indignation to myself, but the swan read my face.

"You disapprove?" she asked without making eye contact.

"Is my approval necessary?" I asked.

She dabbled in her water pail and nodded. The mottle broke from his spell and marched around the nest toward me. I skipped back from his aggressive advance, my heart in my throat.

The mottle scowled, "This is Premaden Elbee, direct descendant of Premaden Zeschau, the last caretaker of Queen Tulis, the last of Talaamiolar's Royals. You will always address her respectfully as Stewardess or Premaden or Premaden Elbee."

I was in over my head. *Stewardess of what?* I recognized the name Tulis and Talaamiolar, references to the long-gone royalty and title for the nation that ended with a bloody war at the founding of Volatus. Beyond that, I had no idea what premadens were or why they required an extra measure of respect. She lived in a fantasy of entitlement, and this mottle was surely just playing along, albeit quite convincingly.

"Mm-hmm," I said. I didn't want to fight over something as trivial as a made-up title, so I obeyed. "Miss Premaden Elbee, I am Nyx of Waycliffs, proxy and daughter of Anja, perchleader for Waycliffs." I fought back a sarcastic chuckle as I concocted these barely legitimate titles. "Would her Grace please grant my request of an audience with my nest-sister, Mano."

The swan softly nodded. "Very nice manners. I compliment you. What is your business with Miss Mano?"

I thought, *What an oddly formal question.* "Premaden, she's my beloved nest-sister. She is my blood. Is that not enough?"

Premaden Elbee cocked her head and tilted her head in a half nod, half shrug. "I suppose it is. I knew you must be related as soon as you entered. Were it not for your bewildered, unawakened appearance, I might have even believed you were her."

Nice one. She insulted me while complimenting my sister. I was in the presence of a master of haughty sarcasm. It sickened me to smile, but I forced it and said, "I'll take that as a compliment, Premaden."

"As you should. Your nest-sister is a lovely creature. She is even lovelier when perched in her hood and jesses." The Premaden nibbled another leaf and swung her eyes upwards.

I followed her gaze to a trapeze high above the center table.

The swan went on, "Her best act is to lift her tail, and push out her eggs onto the platform. My most honored patrons pay a royal ransom to watch. She hides the pain well. Not a tremble, not a peep, even if she bleeds. And if she does it perfectly, and she almost always has, the egg breaks when it hits the platform. The eagles go absolutely ravenous for her golden yolks. Their beaks snap all around her drooling cloaca as they feast." She smiled and casually snapped her bill in the air to mimic the hungry eagles.

My sister may be steady as a rock, but I trembled with indignation, and my vision blurred with restrained fury. The swan had painted an indelible mental image of my poor sister suffering as she dropped her eggs, our family's future, as mere snacks for depraved maniacs. All for the profit of this bloated, fake princess. My heart raced, and my talons clenched the stony floor, eager to rip the smile from the premaden's face.

Premaden Elbee smiled and grunted to the shit-bucket attendant, "Rasha, see Miss Nyx to Mano's chamber. And inform her that for this interruption, she'll need to perform an extra show tonight at four bells."

I winced but didn't dare protest, for fear of making my sister's sentence worse. I followed the mottle around a corner, and we flew up a short Apterian stairway to a long passage. Former Apterian doorways were plastered over with accrement and fitted with smaller doors more suited to birds. A baldy wearing a war helmet stood guard at the end of the hall. The mottle landed before a door with a broken, brown-speckled egg painted on it.

I frowned at the sign and said, "Thank you, sir. Please, can you tell me, how long has Miss Mano been working here?"

The stern eagle grumped, "She's your sister. Ask the whore yourself."

I lifted my hackles and clenched my beak. "You need to learn some manners!"

He flicked his wing, and I jumped back but still took a stinging blow to the beak from his primaries. He smiled but his eyes burned with contempt. Shocked by the attack, I had no immediate retort.

"I teach the manners here, Miss, and it would be my *pleasure* to give you *a nice, hard lesson.*" The words he emphasized were uttered slow and filthily. I stepped back further for fear of being violated. He banged the door with his carpus and shouted, "You have a visitor! And The Premaden wants a show at four bells!" A sick smile clung to his beak as he turned and flapped back the way we had come, laughing all the way.

I collapsed to the floor in fits of panicked breaths, feeling as though the walls were closing in. I needed air. The door creaked opened, and my nest-sister poked her head out.

"Nyx! Are you all right?" She covered me in her wings and my heart broke.

"Mano? What are you doing in this awful place?" I sobbed. "Are you in trouble? I have money. I can get you out!"

"Shh, shh, Nyx. Don't talk about money out here. Come." Mano begged as she tugged me into her room.

She shut the door, but there was no latch. There was also no other exit, and only a small, barred window high above. Despite being made of cold concrete, there were efforts made to make it welcome, probably for the sake of horny patrons more than for my sister. A deep, pebbly nest scrape occupied one corner, opposite a thick nest of fragrant cedar bows, lined with a rabbit skin rug. An upholstered leather block perch stood in the middle of the room with a chamber pot poised below, and a clay pot nearby for water. A large mirror covered the wall by the nest and a black leather hood, jesses, wing restraints, and bells hung on pegs in the wall. The cedar and stone smelled like home, but only barely abated my discomfort.

"Mano, we've got to get out of here!" I chupped.

"Easy, Nyx, eeeeasy. Breathe, dear. Here, have some water."

She opened the lid of the water vessel and eased me towards it. I dipped my beak and tipped back several dabbles of water before my breathing slowed to normal and my tears ceased.

I hugged her tight and felt scars on her breast. "My skies, you've been mistreated!" My tears returned, "Please tell me what's wrong, my sweet sister. What trouble are you in?"

She whispered, "Shh, now. None. Not for real, at least."

I shook my head and struggled to keep my voice low, "No, you're mistaken. Or they've done something to make you forget, poor dear."

"No, no. I'm here on purpose, but they don't know that."

"I don't understand."

"And I can't explain. Not all of it at least."

I rocked her in my wings, my beloved big sister. She fed me tiny bits of food when I could barely open my eyes. She taught me letters and how to read. She shared her dreams and ideals with me as we played together on the black cliffs of home. I couldn't stand to see her like that. There had to be a reasonable explanation.

"Oh, sweet Mano, you're working on your book, aren't you? Please tell me you're doing this for some noble reason."

Mano nodded, "Yes, sis."

"But, how? There's no scribe's saddle." I shuddered at her lack of privacy and the prison-like conditions.

"They let me out every day to exercise and go to the bathhouse. I use some of that time to go to the Archives and write. They keep my notes safe there. I can only rest and entertain here."

"You mean fuck clients," I sniffled.

Her voice faded to a wisp, "Yes."

"I wanted to tear out that fat swan's lying tongue. She said that you lay eggs and let the eagles eat them. Please tell me the truth."

Her silent swallow, felt against my neck, confirmed my fear. I clung to her and sank to my breast, crying. "That's our future! And those eagles hurt you while they rub out their lust? It's degrading! And it's not worth your health. Nor the dishonor to our family."

She breasted down beside me and laid a wing over my back. "Some things are," she said with calm sureness.

"What things? Please tell me!"

"I can't say."

"Why?"

She pressed her beak to my left ear and whispered, "Shh, if you love me, you won't keep asking."

"Then why did you bring me here?"

"I wanted to tell you that I love you dearly. I wanted you to know that I'm safe, even here. And I also need you to do something for me that nobody else can do. It will be very difficult."

"Anything for you, nest-sister."

"Tell our parents that I'm formally leaving the family."

I sobbed, "What? I—"

"Shh, I'm leaving the family. Tell them I'm a prostitute, but don't tell them where I am. Promise me you'll convince them. And tell no one, *no one,* the truth, if you value my life."

"What does this have to do with writing a book?"

"And I need you to make a big scene as you leave. We need to fight. You need to hurt me. And you need to dis-name me."

My eyes burned with tears as I shook my head, "I can't. It would be a lie that none would believe."

"Please. Do this for me and I will love you forever. And someday I'll explain." She pressed her beak to my cheek and closed her eyes as she kissed me.

"I'll try," I whimpered.

She backed away, but her dark eyes stirred with love, and regret, for what she was about to do. Then she straightened her body, spread her wings, and flew straight at me with fisted feet.

I reared instinctively, and she tackled me backward.

"Get out, you self-righteous squab!" she yelled. "Go back to mommy and daddy and tell them I'm a big girl now."

She used to call me a squab when I was just a knee-high lumpy blob of feathers, but it was a term of endearment, not an insult. She stung my face with a slap of one wing, then the other, back and forth. The more I resisted hurting her, the harder she pushed me.

"Fine, lie there and take it! You always were a helpless little squab, sitting in your own filth!" she jeered.

I hurt more inside than out, as she turned our precious terms of endearment into weapons. But I had to fight, if I loved her.

As the blows accumulated, I found what I needed. I loathed the bloated whore-mistress who thought she owned my nest-sister, and I turned that rage at Mano. I kicked her away and she tripped over the chamber pot, skidding in the excrement. She flipped up to her feet and kicked the pot back at me. As I dodged the sailing missile, she flew at me with talons out.

Her feet pounded my chest and sent me to the wall. It shocked me, just as Rasha's slap had earlier, and indignation blazed as I recalled his filthy peppery eyes and horrible intents. I seized her chest in my talons and ripped out a wad of feathers.

She shrieked and kicked me hard in the gut.

Stunned, I let her go and she flung the door open screeching, "Get out! Get the hell out of here!" Then she grabbed my throat with a foot and flapped her wings to drag me into the hallway.

The bald eagle guard startled and broke his stoic pose.

I kicked my sister again and again until she released my throat, and I fell back against the floor. Blood dripped from my sister's breast and my eyes filled with tears.

The guard swaggered toward us, "What is this? Stop at once!"

Mano's eyes were as steady as two spheres of polished obsidian. She hissed, "Leave me. Tell our parents I'm no longer theirs."

"Fine!" I snapped. "You want to leave us and be a worthless whore, so be it! You want to drop our name and be a nack, so be it." I choked on my words, then spat them out like distasteful entrails, "No more Miss Mano of Waycliffs. Now you're just Whore Mano of Low Town!"

The guard's armor scraped as he approached within a wingspan, "You there! Get out!"

For an instant, I saw hurt in her eyes. Then I turned and flew away, my eyes blurred with fury and tears. I barely remember the trip, but somehow, I made it out without killing anyone.

I flew down to a rock on the edge of the sea and found the solitude

I needed to dry my eyes. My heart had torn in half, but I had to patch it back together and act like it was whole. Mano was incredibly tough, if she could serve such vile masters and do the unspeakable things she did. As I preened my feathers into place and licked my wounds, I contemplated what she risked. She trusted me with secrets that she implied could be deadly if revealed.

I looked to the horizon, and cursed Whiterock for swallowing my sister. It was a bony lump of sadness to swallow, much less put over and eliminate. I had no choice but to try, and to hope the future brought answers.

Chapter 8

Promise

By Pepro

Sashya and I enjoyed a peaceful afternoon napping together in our nest at the Avian Haven. We tasted each other's beaks, snuggled and preened each other, and little was said. It was enough to just be alone together. When Sashya fell asleep, I let him rest under my wing as I studied the small details of his face: His pink beak, the delicate white feathers of his closed eyelids, the soft bristles that guided sounds into his ears, and the toasty freckles that bordered his face. I treasured it all.

At one point, when Sashya was using the toilet chute in the corner, we learned that it conducted not just excrement, but sound too. We were treated to the arduous chirps and ruffling feathers of two mating eagles. Sashya and I smirked at each other as their voices climaxed into copulatory cries. My tail stiffened with arousal when I heard the eagles grunting at the peak of their passion, and the thought crossed my mind of how compatible Sashya and I might be for mating, but I was not ready to push our courtship that far yet.

As I was contemplating this, Sashya suddenly compressed his plumage, and his eyes widened. He hastily replaced the lid to the toilet chute and walked back to me, his beak paler than usual.

I chuckled, "Too ripe?"

"No. Well, yes. But I heard something scary."

He told me that his fine ears recognized the voices of Princess Vouli and Tulivor, speaking delicately to each other of bond-pledges and siring royal eggs. Sashya returned to the nest, and I held him tight until he dozed off, but I couldn't sleep anymore with the thought of those two unfriendly birds within earshot. We were privy to a danger-ous secret, one they would surely protect, and that terrified me.

Nyx returned at dusk, tense and distraught. I tried to coax her to talk about it, but she sternly refused to open up. Instead, she swore she was just sore and hungry from the journey, but I knew better.

I let the matter drop, though, and about that time, the town bell rang three. I woke Sashya and the three of us flew up to the top floor to join Miss Penelope again in her private dining room. On our way in, we found that the glass spheres in the ballroom were aglow. They produced a soft, warm light that was unsteady, brightening and dimming collectively.

Sashya was fascinated.

I chuckled, "Nyx told me of flameless torches, but I had no idea what she meant. Now I've seen everything."

Nyx coolly observed the glowing orbs but didn't respond to my comment. I nudged her and she startled.

I asked her, "So what do you think of these things?"

Nyx put on a forced smile and scoffed, "You haven't seen anything yet, village boys. I'll take you to the Whiterock Institute and show you stuff that'll knock your feathers off."

"I would like that," Sashya said.

"Yeah, it's just a glide away." Nyx replied, "See those strings on all the bulbs? Those feed the lights here with sparks created by contraptions over at the Institute. I've got a friend there that can show us everything."

"Sparks?" Sashya asked. "How does that work?"

Nyx shrugged, "Heck if I know. You'll have to ask Barnibu when we take a tour."

Nyx put on a good act, but a slight limp and flecks of dry blood under one of her talons said otherwise. I worried most about the emotional scars that were harder to see. Later, after our social obligations, I would sit on her if that's what it took to get her to open up about it.

Aside from the bug bread, I hadn't eaten all day. I was served a side of fresh salmon, Sashya had a tree squirrel, and Nyx was served a hen green-winged teal. All were carefully prepared with the skin sliced and peeled back so that the prey could be eaten with no struggle or plucking. It made it possible to politely talk while we feasted, though I was so famished, I found it hard to resist gobbling the fish right away.

Miss Penelope had many more questions about Kor and our life with him. She also told us the story about how she had met him five years before when he was in town on business.

"He attended a gathering here, in my ballroom, with P'tilo, General Rys, and a flock of other officials."

Nyx marveled, "Everyone but the President was there by the sound of it. That's a swanky party."

"Indeed, my dear," Miss Penelope replied. "Kory was commissioned to design new armor and weapons for the militia. So, as part of that, he came to oversee the local blacksmiths who were learning to make them."

I said, "Oh! He told me about that. He's been teaching me to make those too."

Miss Penelope proudly responded, "He's the best. That's why they had him here. But he looked so out of place in that soirée, let me tell you. His grizzled beak and singed feathers stood out from the fluff and finery of those bureaucrats and officers. After eating and dipping wine with the others for a while, he withdrew to the side. I had seen that out-of-place look before."

I commented, "Master Kor is a doer, not much of a talker."

Miss Penelope went on, "Very much so. Well, dear, after fulfilling my social duties as hostess, I joined him. I had to get to know this mysterious corvid in the corner. As it turned out, he was the most interesting bird in a room full of billowing airsacs."

The conversation went on and I grew anxious to continue our mission, but I couldn't leave our gracious host abruptly. Miss Penelope had a keen knowledge of many officials and well-known families in Volatus and Waystar. When I mentioned that I was from Waycliffs, and that we had stopped at my uncle's nest at Sunrise Lake, she gasped and dropped one of her berries.

"Is Perro, the famous fisherbird, your uncle?" she asked.

Her urgent concern, to near the point of tears, made my skin prickle with anxiety.

"Yes, ma'am. He's my uncle, on my father's side. He taught me how to fish after my father died and my mother disappeared. Is something wrong?"

"Oh, goodness!" Penelope crooed. Her soft beak corners drooped, and her fluffy feathers sagged. "Oh, you poor dear... I'm so sorry."

I took courage that perhaps her sadness was at the loss of my folks. "Oh, ma'am, I appreciate the sentiment. But that was a long time ago."

"Young sir, it's sad that your father died, but I was referring to your uncle!"

My airsacs collapsed and my body tensed. "What's happened to Uncle Perro?"

"Don't you know?"

My heart raced, "No! What happened?"

"I'm so sorry to be the one to tell you. He's dead, dear. It happened while on official business."

I blinked to hold back my tears. I couldn't accept the news for a moment and looked at my feet for consolation. "What happened?" I asked.

"I'm afraid I don't have the details. Just a half-moon ago, Regional Governor P'tilo hosted a gathering here. We were having dinner, right here in this room, when an official courier pigeon arrived with an urgent message. The Governor wouldn't divulge the particulars at the time, but one of our hostesses, er," Miss Penelope fluttered her third eyelids in embarrassment. "She spent some private time with him that evening and overheard that Perro had been on a mission and perished. A few days later, after the story was confirmed, I suppose, an official announcement was made. How could you know, I suppose, since it just happened."

"Was there a releasing?" I asked somberly.

Miss Penelope replied, "No, I don't think so dear. The announcement said he was lost with no remains, but there would be a memorial in Unitum at the next full moon."

Sashya stepped closer and wrapped a wing around my back. He swiveled his white face to meet my downcast eyes. "Peppy?" he said. "I'm so sorry. I'm here for you." He clasped my talons in his delicate foot.

My world had just collapsed, and not even Sashya could piece it back together at that moment. My beak quivered and my emotions verged on slipping from control. I needed solitude and open air.

I broke our foot embrace and stepped back from my perch. I blurted, "Sash, everyone, I'm sorry... I need to be alone." I hurried off on the wing, whooshed through the lobby, out the portico of the ballroom, and landed on the edge of the building under the star-filled sky.

Once alone, I let go, and sorrowful tears flowed down my face. Uncle Perro, the legendary fisherbird, and my loving, surrogate father, was dead. Died on a mission. *But what mission? Since when is fishing considered a dangerous mission?*

I cried bitterly, until my neck feathers were wet. My last connection to my parents and the entire rest of my family was gone. I was alone. The only things I had left of my folks were my mother's songs, and the painful memory of my father sacrificing his life. I envied the Unawakened who moved through the wilderness with little regard to others, and no anguish or expectations of fairness in life.

Amidst the sadness, I thought of Perro and his sweet mate, Lily, doing their best to fill the holes in my childhood that my parents had left behind. Now even that connection was gone. Frustration built inside, and I clenched the stony edge of the tower so tightly that the tips of my talons frayed. I screamed into the darkness, hoping it would clear my head as it did when I pushed the limits of fear in flight.

As my cry faded, I heard another voice, the whisper of Sashya at my back. I turned to find him there, tears in his sweet eyes, and sadness on his beak.

"Peppy," he said, "I love you, and I won't let you mourn alone."

His timing was perfect. *He said he loved me.* All my anger drained away, and I turned and hugged him tight. Ironically, comforting him comforted me. I sobbed out my sadness on his shoulder, until I felt strong enough to speak.

I said, "You wanted to know about my Wander, and thought it too painful for me to talk about?"

"Yes." Sashya replied.

"The Wander was special, but the reason I always seem sad when the subject comes up is because it reminds me of my parents. I've never told you about them, have I?"

"No, just that they were gone," he said.

I gathered my courage, and told him the story. "My father's name was Sol. We lost him just before I fledged. I was the only eaglet hatched that year. A long winter made for late herring returns and they were scarce when they finally showed. Mergansers had a poor time nesting too, so ducklings, which are usually an abundant and critical source of food for northern eaglets, were hard to come by. The North is tough but that spring was the worst. Fortunately for me, Te, my mother, was a tough bird, and Pa was a good hunter. Between Ma skipping meals, and Pa ranging way out to hunt seal pups on the coastal islands, often going overnight, they managed to keep me fed. But, about a half-moon before I could fly, a fire destroyed our nest tree."

"How terrible! Were you hurt?"

"I only got a little bruised when I fell, but the fire was all around me. Pa wouldn't leave me. He heaped green boughs and damp moss on me, and when that wasn't enough, he covered me with his wings, even when the fire..." I choked on my emotions, but Sashya met my eyes and gave me the courage to continue. "The fire burned most of his flight feathers off. He couldn't fly and, worse, he couldn't breathe well. Me and Ma took care of him, and the village healer tried too, but he got worse and died a couple days later. We could do nothing but watch."

Sashya's eyes glistened, "How terrible. Did your mom die in the fire too?"

"No, she was okay. She was busy helping others fight the fire and escaped getting hurt. Nyx's folks lent mom a wing with hunting and helped us with Pa's releasing. His was the only releasing I've ever attended. We burned his body where he died, there at the foot of our beloved nest tree, and Ma and I dropped his semiplumes into the wind, so he could rejoin the sky and the sea. And that was the last time I saw Ma. She sent a courier to Uncle Perro and as soon as he arrived, she disappeared. She was anxious to go, and Perro told me she went after those that caused the fire."

"What?" Sashya exclaimed. "Someone started the fire on purpose?"

"I don't really know, Sash. The only one I ever heard say that was Uncle Perro. The fire was odd since there was no lightning or likely sources around. Our nest was on the far side of the cove away from the village."

Sashya slid a wing under mine and up over my back and pressed close. Feeling his warmth against me recharged my hope.

"Sashya, I love you too. I had hoped it would be better circumstances when I finally told you."

Sashya smiled up at me, his face stained from the genuine tears that had fallen.

I added, "You shared my pain. That's true love, Sash. I'll never forget it, and I'll share in your sorrows too, when you need it."

Sashya solemnly nodded and said, "By the way, I know why you screamed."

"You do?"

"Yeah. You're frustrated because you don't have answers."

Sashya's empathy amazed me, and he was dead right. "There are no answers, Sash. I try to put the losses out of my mind so I can bear them."

Sashya moved his face closer to mine and quietly said, "There are answers out there, somewhere. When this is all done, after the bonding, we'll find the answers you deserve."

It seemed impossible to me. "It's been so long and now I don't even have Uncle Perro to ask. I'm not sure where to even start."

Sashya's eyes brimmed with confidence. "Don't worry about that, Pep. You're not alone on your Wander anymore. Look at all the new friends we've got who know birds in high places. Plus, you've got me. We'll figure it out together."

I touched my beak to his and chortled a tiercel eagle's heartfelt purr of affection. My heart that had been cold and empty only moments before, beat stronger with the love Sashya had breathed into my soul. I leaned into him with a tender kiss, caressed his back, and cherished his love. I had been working and living among friends but not intertwining my destiny with theirs. No more. Sashya and I needed each other. From then on, whatever plans I made, whatever dreams I had, Sashya would be in them.

Chapter 9

Low Town

By Sashya

A short time later, Nyx joined Sashya and me outside. She grumped about being left alone with Miss Penelope who was as relentless, and adept, at stealing secrets as a starling is at picking pockets.

The three of us glided into the night to find Perry. I took the lead and used my better night vision to hunt for an albatross.

Upper Whiterock had darkened from a lively dance of towers and flocks into a ghostly landscape of moonlit spires. Soft points of candlelight from thousands of avian homes dotted the ruins and dark canyons. The surf roared against the nearby cliffs, filling the cool air with a briny bouquet.

The atmosphere changed as we approached Low Town. As we approached what Nyx called the "Promenade," we found a lively world of colorful glass lanterns and throngs of seabirds enjoying the night life. Along the Promenade were portals of brick and cement, many containing brightly lit caverns full of raucous flocks jumping and flapping to energetic music. There were strings, drums, bellows fitted with reeds, peck bells, and all octaves of bird song. The salty air reeked of excrement, fish, and alcohol.

In Galinta, Taka, a pileated woodpecker, played a stringed instrument and chimes with his bill. Accompanied by Daanuk, a bard crow, it was a dreamy combination. Outside of that, it was rare for visitors to bring their own instruments as it was costly to hire swans to transport them to such a remote place. But there were no such limitations in a big town like Whiterock. Instead of a crow serenade that made my heart soar, the pounding instruments beckoned my wings to flap, my tail to sway, and my feet to stomp, and I reveled in the new sensations.

I was so distracted with the fresh sounds that I nearly collided with a gull. I saw the flailing mass of feathers just in time to roll under as he swept past.

The gull made an exaggerated recovery, and slurred back "Hey, watch it ya crazy drunk!"

I screeched back, "Look who's squawkin'!"

Our laughter carried us all the way to the north end of Low Town. There were no albatrosses obvious among the thousands of partying seabirds, so we decided on starting with the peacekeepers at the Citadel to see if they were holding Perry.

The closer we drew to the Citadel, the quieter the atmosphere became until, for the last kilometer, there were just a few hollows that bore the crescent moon pictogram of a roostery. Others were shuttered or dark inside, and small flocks of gulls napped on the rocks.

The peacekeeper citadel was built in an Apterian tower about twenty wingspans tall and five wide at the base, with many shapes and sizes of openings along its sides. It bore faded red and white markings, and the broken top was bridged with a flat platform. Above this fluttered the standard of Volatus, a white flag with five stars in a circle and a nest and egg within. The tower sat atop a white sea-stack, the source of the town's name. A rope-and-plank bridge connected a path from the Promenade to the Citadel.

In front of the tower lay a circular memorial, paved in small flat stones. Surrounding this were eight plinths, each capped by copper—plated statues of birds holding glass-encased oil lanterns in their beaks. Each bird was a different species, but all bore the same stern expression. At the center stood a massive statue of a gull, its face looking to the west and its graceful wings soaring above the paved circle. From its beak a bronze censure hung with a multitude of burning wicks, flicking shadows across its face and illuminating the circle of solemn vigils. Two storm gulls, or black-backed gulls as the Apterians knew them, stood at the front of the monument guarding the approach to the tower so we landed on the bridge a respectable distance away from the monument and its guards. The atmosphere was reverent and still.

Nyx cautioned, "You two realize that the peacekeepers are non-nonsense ventsores, right? See how quiet it is over here? Nobody messes around under their beaks."

"Let me go talk to them. I'm small and polite, not like the drunks they deal with all day."

Nyx shrugged, "Give it a try, Sash, but don't say any more than you have to, or they might poke their beaks further into our business than we want."

I walked down the stone-paved path and approached the two gull guards. They wore red sashes, but one had golden thread along the borders and a silver shell pinned over the breast. His jaw was wide, his head thick, and his back markings dark and crisp, all suggesting he was a male. Because of the sash decorations, I presumed he was in charge, so I approached him first.

The peacekeeper surveyed me sternly as I approached. He was my height but easily twice as heavy. His chiseled beak was longer than mine and sharp enough to pluck an eye out.

He squawked abruptly "What's your business?"

I gathered my courage. "Sir, I'm looking for Perry, an albatross."

He cocked his head and studied me with a narrow, suspicious eye, "What's your business with him?" he asked.

"Well, sir, it's private business," I said.

"Then what concern is it of mine?" He leaned forward and sniffed the air.

I had to change tactics. I fluffed my feathers to look undaunted and struck a more relaxed tone. "It's important business, and it'll probably keep him out of trouble for a while."

The gull cried a hearty laugh, "That bird is nothing *but* trouble. What you say isn't possible."

"Sir, it's important. Please, is he here or shall we keep looking elsewhere?"

He sighed. "No, lad, Perry isn't here, not yet anyway. No doubt before sunrise we'll have to drag him in and deal with his stinking carcass. You best be looking for him in the bordellos yonder." The gull motioned with his beak toward the busier part of Low Town. "He's been around for half a moon, so he's bound to be running low on treasure. That means he'll be in the less pleasant places."

"I see." I bowed slightly, "Thank you, sir."

As soon as I straightened up, like thrusting a staff, the gull jabbed my chest. I wasn't prepared for the assault, so it knocked me back a step.

Brant growled, "I see that shiner on your cere. You been gettin' in scraps!"

"No sir! Bandits attacked me at Sunrise Lake," I exclaimed.

He pinned his pupils and screed, "Hmmf, sounds like droppings to me. You and your friends best stay out of trouble, you hear? You smell like you came from Miss Penelope's. Stay close to the likes of her instead of getting robbed down here. As for that waste of fish guts, Perry, you best bank clear of 'im. Cuz if you fly in his wake, you'll all be seeing me in much a less pleasant mood. You got that?"

"Yes sir," I replied as I started back up the path, nursing my bruised keel bone.

I had only taken a few steps when the gull said, "Wait!"

I faced him again and his expression softened. He said, "Son, try the Musky Murre. It's cheaper and it's one of his favorites."

I nodded and flew back to the others and told them what happened.

Pepro asked, "Did he peck you?"

"Yeah, pretty hard too. Worse than the schoolmaster in Kahvanis. You weren't kidding about their attitude, Nyx. And he warned me to stay away from Perry."

Nyx shook her head, "This guy sounds like a total loser. You sure you want to bother? I might be able to stir up another source for you."

I nodded, "Appreciate it, Nyx, but Kor seemed pretty adamant about doing business with Perry, so we'll try that first."

With that, we lifted off and flew back towards Low Town.

Chapter 10

The Dance

By Sashya

We glided down the rows of cliff-side hollows, dodging birds that were flying every which way. Halfway down, among a thick crowd, we found an establishment displaying a wooden sign bearing the slim, pointed silhouette of a murre's face with a winking eye and squiggly lines above it.

"Look!" I gestured and shouted. "Looks like a musky murre to me."

The others followed me, and we landed on the edge of the tumult. A row of brick arches created an arcade with a spacious brick-lined cavern beyond. From openings above the entrance, the slim black faces of murres poked out. They called with wispy whistles and piercing titters that drew the lusty gaze of passersby, even above the raucous crowd and pounding music.

"This place is crazy!" I screeched. "Pepro! Maybe you can push your way in, and we can follow behind?"

We pressed into the flock with Pepro at point, and the throng parted before us. The music felt good, so I let my beak weave and bob to the beat.

Nyx's mood lightened too, and soon she swayed her tail and hips to the music. Her head bobbed and her wingtips flicked in time with the dancing crowd, and at one point she fluffed her belly feathers and fluttered her tail at a high point of a song, raising a small cheer from the birds around us.

Pepro cocked his head to see what we were doing. He smiled and said to Nyx, "Good to see you feeling better."

Nyx chupped agreeably, "I'm getting there. Music helps. Come on, Pep! Let your wings down."

"How?" asked Pepro, in a fluster.

Nyx shook her head in disbelief. "Even the Unawakened know how to dance. Listen to the music and let it move you. Watch me."

We swayed, slid our feet, bobbed our heads, and fanned our tails. The crowd was so tight that we frequently bumped into each other and the birds around us, but nobody cared. As the crowd tightened in the doorway, I wrapped my wings around Pepro's middle from behind, and we moved as one bird with four feet. His thick muscles and musky plumage were warm and arousing. His eyes locked on mine and his pale irises pinned. He felt it too. I buried my face in his breast fluff, and he hugged me tight as we moved into the center of the dance hall.

The whole place reverberated with the slaps of feet, most of them webbed, and the band played louder in response. The noise hurt my sensitive ears, but it felt too good, rubbing up against Pepro, to stop dancing. We intertwined our wings and spun as the tempo increased, spinning in a swirl of feathers. We turned one way, then the other, laughing and improvising as the music moved us. As we sensed the song coming to an end, we followed the crowd's lead and raised our wings, then called out in one mighty shout as the music ceased. The whole flock cheered the band in a cacophony of calls, and then the noise died to a murmur.

"Not bad, for a pair of rubes," Nyx chuckled, her chest heaving from the energetic dancing.

I touched my beak to Pepro's, and he nibbled the tip. I felt intoxicated and hadn't even touched the wine troughs yet.

"You think every day is like this in Low Town?" I asked.

"I hope so," Pepro said as he kissed my beak again.

The band, a quintet of crows, played a slower, gentler piece. One of the birds pecked a rack of flashy metal plates, another stroked a standing bass, the third and fourth softly brushed skin drums with their wings, and the fifth warbled out a tune of youth and sweet summer courtship.

The cavern hosted the band on a dais at one end and had raised bronze troughs with perches around them at the other. Birds were dipping their beaks into the troughs and gulping down strong-smelling brews. At the back of the cavern stood a ledge and a circular brick tunnel leading back into the earth. Steps rose from the dance floor to meet the ledge and tunnel, and on either side of this, along the base of the ledge, was a toilet trench, a narrow slit in the floor where birds discretely relieved themselves.

As the song played, many birds paired up and preened or billed each other under the romantic influence. Other pairs drifted up the tunnel at the back, though I noticed that usually one of the pair had a black cord around one leg.

To the side of the mysterious tunnel stood a buxom white owl with black speckles on her wings, nape, back, and tail. I recognized these as the markings of a female snowy owl. Because of her prominent position, and scrutiny of all who entered the tunnel, I assumed she was in charge.

Birds soon filled the dance floor again and pressed us to the back of the room.

Nyx said, "That snowy owl there must be the head hen. She'll know if Perry is here."

"Head hen?" I asked.

Pepro chuckled, "I think she means to say that this is a brothel, and that owl runs the place."

"You don't have brothels in Galinta?" Nyx asked.

Pepro replied, "Oh, there's a mating parlor, but I've never been inside."

Nyx said, "It's big business here, especially in springtime. Lots of birds come through Whiterock from all over. The farther from home, the lonelier they get." Nyx's eyes pinned and her plumage compressed as though a cloud had passed through her thoughts.

"You all right, Nyx?" I asked.

She shook her head, "It's nothing, Pep. Say, Sashya, why don't you go and ask her about Perry?"

"Me? Why me?"

"Well, you're an owl," she said. "And like you said before, you're small and polite. She'll warm right up to a sweet, young morsel like you."

My beak warmed, "Are you forgetting I'm gay?"

Nyx sighed, "I didn't say to mate with her, just conversation. Relax, have fun, and I bet she'll open up to you."

I looked at Pepro, "You fine with this?"

Pepro laughed and nodded, "Are you kidding? I *gotta* see this."

Nyx chupped, "Come on, Pep. I need a drink. Let's watch from over there."

As Nyx and Pepro drifted toward the drinking troughs, I gathered my courage and strutted casually toward the great white owl.

As I climbed the steps, the snowy's broad white face swiveled to meet my eyes. She pleasantly churred, "You're a handsome young owl. Looking for some special fun?"

Her smile formed a delicious pink seam across her fluffy cloud of a face. Her sultry yellow eyes shone down like two half-moons upon me. Leaning forward, she delicately teased my face bristles hers and wrapped a wing around my shoulders. The warm scent of sweet grass and lavender wafted from her feathers.

I didn't expect such a warm welcome, so at first I tried to back away. But her deep, soft hug pulled me in, and I floated weightlessly in a white void of fluff.

She whispered to me, "That's it. Relax, dear, and let Miss Snowdrift take away your cares."

I closed my eyes as her feathers swallowed me until our hot skin touched. Her beak locked onto mine and her tongue slid inside. Just as that invasion happened, a wing feather penetrated my underfluffies and brushed across my posterior.

I shuddered and whimpered from the new sensation. Nobody had ever touched me that intimately before. It felt nice, though I would have preferred to have Pepro doing it. As she pulled her beak back a little, her clean taste lingered on my tongue.

The magical effect took my speech away for a moment.

"You're a virgin." she said. It wasn't a question. She read me as plainly as the pictograms on the signs outside. She stroked a wing down my back, and I reflexively arched my spine and bobbed my tail in unison with a spasm of my cloaca.

"Ah! Oh!" I chirped.

Miss Snowdrift's throat vibrated with a deep laugh. "I delight in making you fresh young things squirm. Especially the ones that don't fancy females."

I opened my eyes partway.

"How do I know?" She laughed again. "I've been a pleasure hen for fifteen years. I know all there is to know about pleasing males of most any species, including moonies. I can teach you plenty on how to please your dashing tiercel eagle over there too."

I glanced at Pepro and Nyx, and they smiled back and laughed.

Miss Snowdrift probed behind the right edge of my facial disk with her beak, and gave a slow, warm sigh into my ear canal that tingled my brain with arousal.

"I'll give you my special introductory price, little owl."

I mumbled blissfully, "I'm, ah, loving this, Miss Snowdrift, but I—"

"Looking for someone?"

I nodded sheepishly. "Too obvious?"

"Only to me. Tell ya what, give me another of your innocent, virgin kisses, and I'll see what I can do to help you."

I churred, "That's a deal." I pressed my beak to hers and mimicked what she did to me. I probed her sweet, succulent maw with my tongue and swirled it across the back of her throat as my wings stroked her sides and our breasts rubbed together.

She softly moaned and set my feet back on the floor as our beaks parted.

"Nice kiss," she said. "Do that with your mate next time and see what he thinks. What's your name, handsome?"

"Sashya."

"And your friends?" she asked.

"Pepro and Nyx."

"And who are you looking for?"

"Perry the albatross, ma'am."

Her eyelids raised, "Ah, I see." Her throat throbbed with a chuckle. "Well, he's a regular here for sure." She wrapped her wings around me again and tipped my head back. This time she parted the left edge of my facial disk, and my knees shook as she stimulated deep inside my ear.

I moaned and groaned as my powers to resist crumbled.

Miss Snowdrift whispered, "You don't fit the mold of a peacekeeper, but maybe they're getting smarter." Acid crept into her voice. "Before I tell you anything about Perry, you have to convince me I can trust you. Who sent you?" She said casually as her sharp claws scraped against my tender thigh.

"Oh! No ma'am, I'm not with the constabulary." Her claws tightened, and while it didn't hurt, the taste of her strength alarmed me. "Ah! We were sent by Master Kor, a raven blacksmith in Galinta. P-perhaps you've heard of him. We were sent to buy gold for bonding rings from Perry. A-and we have a private message for him."

Her foot relaxed and she whispered, "Kor is a name I know. I've done business with him, and I don't just mean ironwork, hon." She set me on the floor and waved a wing to Pepro and Nyx. "You birds need to hurry."

I nodded, "I know! The new moon is only ten days away."

Snowy shook her head, "No, it's worse than you think. Perry's just about out of gold!"

Pepro and Nyx arrived, and Miss Snowdrift said, "Your friend here is marvelous. But I think he prefers tall, handsome eagles. Pepro is it?"

"Yes ma'am," Pepro nodded.

Miss Snowdrift nodded, "You can call me Snowy, dear."

I excitedly told them, "She knows where Perry is."

"Yes, Perry is here," Miss Snowdrift added, "But getting you to him is complicated."

Nyx snapped her beak. "What's so complicated about kicking a bum out of a nest?"

Snowy's smile dropped and she replied sarcastically, "Well, Miss Nyx, you've got peacekeepers tailing you for starters. They know you're lookin' for Perry and he ain't supposed to be here. They find out he's here— they'll flip this place upside down lookin' for him. And that's bad for business, get it?"

Nyx glanced around.

"Stop!" hissed Miss Snowdrift. "Don't look, but there's a toothy at the wine trough. He's your tail."

I recollected seeing him perched next to Pepro and Nyx moments before. He was a squat black-and-white puffin, no taller than a crow. His round cheeks and dark, tooth-shaped eye markings gave him a sad expression. He had been dipping his orange and yellow beak into the brew and bobbing to the music.

Miss Snowdrift continued, "That's Ano. He's a creepy admirer of Lara, one of my working hens, and general snitch for the peacekeepers. Did you visit the peacekeepers?"

"Yeah. This big grumpy gull told me to come here." I said.

Snowy asked, "Did his red sash have a silver shell on it?"

I nodded.

Snowy rolled her head back. "Ugh, great. That's Brant. Sure as shit he knows Perry's here."

I felt played. "And he set me up to come here so they could locate him too. I'm sorry, Snowy."

She replied, "Forget it, dear. No way you could've known."

"What should we do?"

A mischievous grin grew on Miss Snowdrift's face. "I've got just the distraction for that pudgy snitch. And we'll use the crowd to lose any other tails. Then we'll get you back to see Perry."

Pepro cocked his head and asked, "How do we stir up the crowd?"

"Dance!" she hooted.

Pepro wrapped a wing around my shoulders and drew me away from Snowy's embrace. "Excuse me, sir, may I have this dance?" he asked.

Miss Snowdrift's smile faded a little as she said to Nyx softly, "I don't know what bad news you got today, hon, but you need to dance with me, darling."

Nyx's eyes flashed uncertainty, "No, I—"

"Come on, dear. You don't gotta say what it is. Just loosen up and have a dance with me."

Nyx smiled and nodded.

Miss Snowdrift beckoned to a white falcon with dark eyes and blue-gray beak. He sported a black leather collar around his neck with rings attached to it and black cuffs around each of his tarsi. He stalked over to Miss Snowdrift who whispered something in his ear. He nodded and walked off toward the tunnel.

Miss Snowdrift boomed a wavering hoot that killed the music. The lead singer looked to her for a cue, and she shouted, "Hey, Ree! Play me 'Fire Dance!'"

Ree turned to the players and lifted his wings. The percussionists poised their beak sticks over the drums. The bassist picked up his bow and pushed a foot against the strings. The singer tapped his foot rhythmically and the players bobbed their beaks until all were in sync. Then the drums exploded with an energetic introduction and the band lurched into a galloping tune that put the crowd into an uproar of dance and cheers.

Pepro pulled me close, and we swayed in place until we found the beat. Then we pressed our bodies together and stepped back and forth in unison.

Snowy pulled Nyx close, and the two spun in a whirl of light and dark feathers.

Someone squawked, "Snowy's dancing!"

The crowd cheered and opened into a circle around us to watch. In all the times I watched other performers, I hadn't imagined myself as one. But there I was at the center of the crowd's attention, its emotions at my command. If we shook our tails, they cheered. If Pepro dipped me back for a beak kiss, they called their approval. The party atmosphere, and Pepro's strong body against mine, melted away all my inhibitions. I swung and laughed; giddy as the day I had flown to new heights on Pepro's back.

Pepro must have felt the power too, because he leaned into me until I arched back into a dip, and his tail flipped high in the air. The crowd cheered, and I knew why, for I often stared at the deep fluff under Pepro's tail and cheered inside too. He was my best friend first, but I had always adored his deep downy underfluffies.

I took a bold chance, and followed Pepro's dip down until my back touched the floor, and I slid through his widely-placed legs. I continued the slide until my head pressed up through the fluff under his tail, and I came to my knees again and flashed my wings open. The crowd roared approval and tossed coppers on the floor.

Miss Snowdrift and Nyx had locked wings together, side by side, and teased the crowd with their shaking tails. Nyx fumbled and laughed as Snowy pulled her one direction, then swung the other way, stepping dramatically to the beat and showing off her fluffy white legs. The crowd tossed coppers around her high-kicking legs as they cheered.

As Pepro and I rejoined our wings, we rested our beaks on each other's backs, and swung our tails back and forth, high and low, churning our hips to the swaying rhythm. His muscles rippled and tensed, and his warm breath bathed my shoulders. It took a lot of my consciousness to coordinate our moves, yet the sensuality of the moment was far from lost. I didn't have to pretend to be turned on for the crowd because I was on fire. *Perhaps tonight,* I told myself. *We would have the gold, and Nyx could give us the room to ourselves to take things to the next level.*

At last, the music hit a fever pitch and ended with the whole flock vibrating as one. The shrill seabird cries and clattering drums vibrated in my head, rivaled only by the throbbing under my tail. As I hugged Pepro amidst the cheers, I blushed and confessed, "You're amazing, Pep. I love you."

He said back, "Love you too, Sash."

We turned to find Nyx and Miss Snowdrift locked together in a hug.

"Nyx?" Pepro asked.

The two girls pulled apart and Nyx shyly glanced our way. Miss Snowdrift churred, "That was verrrry good, hon. You feel better?"

Nyx nodded dreamily and delicately pecked Snowy on the cheek. I couldn't hear the words, but I'm certain she whispered a warm *thank you.*

I glanced about for Ano, but he was gone. "Where'd the puffin go?" I asked.

Miss Snowdrift roused her plumage, "Yes, right. He's having a little fun on the house. I had Shock pair him up with Silver, one of my working owls. But I don't think she'll keep him busy for long, so gather the coppers and come along, dears."

We tossed all the coins into an open cinch-cloth Snowy dropped on the floor. When it was loaded, she pulled the cinch-cord and closed it up. The pendulous load of coins swayed in her beak as we followed her up the steps and into the tunnel beyond.

The crowd's echoes faded behind us as we made our way up the gentle incline. Candles along the walls lit our way and there were doorways along the sides that led into rooms and junctions with other tunnels. Some rooms were open, and some closed off by curtains or wooden doors.

Most of the open rooms were furnished with soft nests of moss and downy feathers, drinking basins, and clusters of fragrant cedar bows or flowers. One room contained a bow perch with thongs and bells dangling from it, and a leather hood hanging on the wall. As we passed one of the closed rooms, low puffin groans accompanied the lusty chitters of a hen owl, and I wondered if it was Ano having his free fun.

Miss Snowdrift poked open a double doorway at the end of the tunnel and beckoned us through. Inside, the right side of the tube's wall had been hollowed out into a spacious burrow lined with bleached driftwood panels painted with bright flowers. Bundles of dried lavender hung on the walls and filled the room with their sweet aroma. A nest took up the center of the room and a shiny copper basin of water stood nearby. An oil lamp hung by a cord overhead. Miss Snowdrift dropped the sack of coins, swung the doors shut behind us, and latched them with her beak.

I saw no other door, nor an albatross, in the room. I held my curiosity about this as Miss Snowdrift counted out ten coppers and stacked them at my feet.

She said, "Here ya go, young owl. You divvy it up amongst yourselves, and I don't want no humble, gullshit refusal either. I always share thirty percent with my dance partners, and you earned it."

"Thank you, ma'am," I replied. "Pep, you mind carrying those?"

"No problem," he said, and beaked the coppers into his satchel.

Miss Snowdrift walked to one of the planks in the wall and pushed against it with her forehead. It creaked and swung outward revealing a pitch-dark tunnel beyond. She stepped into the darkness and came back with a small candle lantern. She nodded to Nyx and said, "Lower the lamp dear."

Nyx stepped to the wall where the overhead lamp's cord was looped around a cleat. She unhooked the loop, carefully lowered it, and Snowy ignited the lantern's candle from the lamp's flame.

She put the candle into the lantern and closed the front glass while Nyx raised the lamp back up and secured the loop again.

Snowy glanced into the dark passage, "You seen those flameless torches yet? We sure can use those down here, but I'll be dead and released before those Uppers gift us with anything but vent gleet and their rank shitwater."

As if to punctuate her words, a breath of cold rot wafted in from the tunnel beyond. It was no wonder she stuffed her room with flowers and cedar.

Miss Snowdrift offered the candle lantern to Pepro, "Here, stud. You and Sashya go on up. Go ten paces and take a right. Don't go straight too far. A sinkhole opened up in a rain shower last year, so there's a nasty drop now. When you go up to the right, you'll come to a door with a bell. Ring it once, pause, then twice more."

Pepro nodded.

Miss Snowdrift said to Nyx, "Girl, you stay here with me. We bought some time, but there's bound to be some more peacekeepers coming soon. If I'm here, engaged with a lovely falcon, it'll slow 'em down."

Nyx blushed, but didn't refuse.

Snowy said to Pepro and I, "You two get Perry on his feet, and I mean quick."

I was touched by Snowy's concern. She had a business to run and didn't need to go to all this trouble for us. I hugged her and gave her beak a gentle kiss. "Thank you, Snowy, for everything."

She churred and licked her beak. "That, my dear, is the best payment I've had all day." She winked at Pepro, "You take good care of this special owl."

Pepro smiled at me and then said to Miss Snowdrift, "I will, Snowy. Thank you."

We stepped off into the dark and began our way up the tunnel as the door creaked shut behind us.

Chapter 11

Perry

by Pepro

The smell of decay intensified as we penetrated deeper up the tunnel. We came to the side passage and saw the hole in the brick floor that Miss Snowdrift had warned us about. A thin stream of liquid drained steadily down the floor of the tunnel on the opposite side and disappeared into the hole. I leaned over the edge, but couldn't see the bottom, though water splashed somewhere deep down in the blackness.

"I wouldn't want to fall down there," I said.

A silent wave of stink greeted my nares, and I recoiled.

Sashya wrinkled his face and gagged. "Pepro, let's go! I'm gonna be sick."

We turned up the branching tunnel and soon found a sturdy wall of accrement blocking our path. It had a small arched door on the right side. The borders of the door were dimly lit by light leaking around the edges of its rough-cut planks. As we approached, I heard chirps and moans coming from the other side. I nodded at Sashya, and he tugged on the bell string with the prescribed sequence of pulls.

The voices on the other side hushed with the first ding, then erupted into relaxed laughter after the second pair of dings. Feathers ruffled and webbed feet slapped across the floor toward us. A small slit slid open in the door and a murre's black face and shiny eye scrutinized us from the other side.

"Who's there?" came a high-pitched city accent.

I held the lantern in my beak, so Sashya answered for me. "Ma'am, Miss Snowdrift let us in to see Perry. A mutual friend sent us."

A wooden latch clunked, and the door swung open. Before Sashya said another word, the murre wrapped her wings around him, dragged him in, and I followed along.

In a high, thin voice, she piped out, "Woo, aren't you a fresh, clean face. Come on in out of the stink."

The chamber was warm and humid, and smelled heavily of moist feathers and sex. Rough wooden planks had been laid to cover the grimy, cold stone of the tunnel. As with Snowy's chamber, a big nest filled the middle of the room. In the nest, a huge smudgie albatross, or Laysan as Sashya said the Featherless called them, lie on their back on a thick bed of moss, cedar bows, and downy feathers. Their white breast and ample white belly were framed by charcoal-colored wings folded at his sides and pink, webbed feet jutting into the air. The bird's massive, pink-and-orange bill ended in a dark, hooked tip. Around their obsidian eyes were smudges of dark feathers, as though he had rubbed them with soot. The bird had to be Perry.

A murre straddled his belly, sitting vertically with her posterior planted against Perry's, rubbing in circles as he paddled his feet and moaned. Her beak pointed upwards, and she filled the air with a sweet song laced with thin, whistling cries. I didn't recognize the tune, but it was smooth and relaxing. Another murre straddled his breast with her tail in his face.

The murre that greeted us wrapped a dark wing around Sashya's neck and said playfully, "I'm Sora. And who are you, dear?"

Sashya's eyes stayed fixed on the carnal spectacle before us, and he didn't answer immediately.

Sora glanced at the others, then said nonchalantly, "He's almost done, then he'll talk."

I had seen a lot of things on my Wander, but never a trio of fornication like this. The scent and the steamy action affected me on a gut level. Despite our differences, every bird species feels the effects of spring powerfully, and seeing others have sex only inflames our lust. Over the past moon, I'd felt my testes, deep in my belly, grow heavier with the lengthening days. Too, my vent softened in preparation for mating, and my belly feathers thinned in preparation for brooding eggs. These seasonal changes were stronger than previous years, and I knew what it meant. I had managed to work around the strongest urges, but the past couple of days of being heart to heart, as well as body to body, with Sashya had stoked my sexual tension.

Sashya pressed close and his touch made me tremble. He asked, "Are you all right, Pep?"

I gulped and uttered a muffled chirp.

"Oh!" he said and smiled coyly. "Spring fever?"

I nodded. "This place isn't helping it." I closed my eyes a moment to regain control.

Sashya chuckled and whispered, "I feel it too, especially when I'm close to you. Maybe tonight we can have some special time alone."

I nodded emphatically. "Let's get this done quick."

Sashya nodded, turned to Perry, and said firmly, "We've come a long way to see you, Perry. Master Kor of Galinta sent us."

Perry's voice grated and creaked like rusty iron, and his speech slurred from intoxication. "Be with you in a moment, boysssss."

As Perry dug his tongue deeper into the rump at his beak and the murre whistled higher, I turned away with Pepro and waited until the shrieks and moans had died down. After some sighs and ruffling feathers, Perry purred his appreciation, "Thank you girlsss. That was the bessst yet."

We turned back to them as the hens dismounted.

"You bet, Perry," said the ass-rider.

The one who received Perry's beaking said to me, "I'm Lara."

"I'm Pepro and this is Sashya," I replied.

"Enjoy the show?" she asked.

I shook my stiff tail. "Yeah, I guess I did."

She chuckled and asked, "So who sent ya?"

"Kor, master blacksmith of Galinta."

"Huh." she said. "Don't know any blacksmiths."

We stepped closer to Perry, avoiding the smears of questionable fluids on the floor. Perry's beak danced rhythmically to the left and right. He was dizzy drunk. His eyelids were swollen, and salt-crusted secretions dripped from his nares. His flakey beak and face feathers were smeared with brown, greasy stains. He did not look healthy. He coughed, retched, and flicked a blob of oily fluid to the floor. An invisible cloud of rotten krill slammed my face like a forge hammer, and I staggered backward.

Perry laughed heartily, blowing the stench farther into the tight room. Sashya retreated toward the door, preferring the sewer air to Perry's festering stomach oils. My eyes watered, and I felt cured of any springtime lust for the moment.

The fat seabird bellowed, "Well, out with it! What's so important that you tracked me down here? Or are you here for a little fun?" He winked and cast his twitching eyes down my body and back up to my face. "Wouldn't be the first time with an eagle, ya know."

Whether serious or not, the offer did not tempt me. "Kor sent us with an important message."

Perry shook with effort as he raised his upper body. He weaved his head back and forth wildly, threatening to tumble out of the nest.

"Korrr?" he slurred. "Korrrrr?" Then he crossed his eyes, wilted back into the nest, and passed out with a gurgling belch.

Perry lay so still that Sashya and I crept closer to check if he had died. When he snored loudly, it startled us both.

The three murres collectively sighed in relief. The one that had been riding Perry's rear squatted down and rubbed her butt on a wad of moss. She said to Sashya with a nasally sneer, "Thanks, hon, for knocking him out cold with your news. I thought he'd never quit! Finally, I can go wash up." She nodded to one of the others and whined with all the passion of a worn-out waitress, "It's your turn to coddle him, Lara."

Lara whined back, "Aww, no way!"

"You know damn well it is! I cleaned his sorry tail last night."

Lara sighed, "Dammit! Well, I'm gonna get some fresh water first." The three murres continued gabbing as they picked up our candle lantern and waddled down the passage.

Sashya looked defeated. "Kor, Miss Penelope, that Peacekeeper Brant, they weren't kidding. He's a total wreck!"

I nodded in agreement. "I've never seen someone so rough. Looks like he's damn near dead."

Sashya sighed and shoved Perry with his foot. "Perry! Perry! Wake up!"

"No use, dear. Best to just leave him lay." Lara said as returned with a pail of water. She set the bucket down and pulled out a sopping sea sponge, squeezed it with her bill, then wiped it back and forth on Perry's sticky belly. He chuckled in drunken delirium while wiggling his tail and paddling his feet. She avoided his flailing webs, and once he had settled down, she pushed him onto his side so that his snoring lessened. Then she turned to scrubbing the floor and spoke to us while she worked.

"So how you fellas know Perry?" she asked.

"We have a common friend, ma'am," Pepro replied.

"Oh?" Lara asked, "This Kor you mentioned? I didn't think Perry had any friends. Leastways not any real friends."

Sashya replied confidently, "Well, ma'am, he does. From what I've heard, he wasn't always like this."

Lara stopped working and smirked at Sashya. "Humph! Hon, you're young and sweet, but you've got a lot to learn. Those rumors about Perry having some secret love and losing her? What a load of droppings!" She dipped the sponge in the bucket, flopped it wetly on the floor, and squished it with her toes before rubbing it around some more. "He's lotsa fun, far as tricks go, and can be real sweet to me. But I ain't never seen a serious feather on his body. He's a joke! Half the town is disgusted by 'im, and the rest just plays along if it means gettin' his gold."

Sashya looked down at Perry's wrecked carcass and sagged. It was his first time seeing someone so broken, and it hurt him. I put a wing around his shoulders.

"What's on your mind, Sash?" I asked.

He looked at me with eyes that glistened with sadness.

Lara saw the sympathy in his eyes too and said, "It's real sweet that you care. He's a pitiful mess. But listen, hon, he's a lost cause. You should find someone else to do your business with."

"Maybe you're right," I muttered.

Sashya wouldn't have any of it though. He stiffened up and said firmly, "Everyone keeps saying that. But I think Master Kor knew what he was doing when he sent us to Perry. If he believed in Perry, then we've got to at least try."

I rubbed Sashya's shoulders. His determination inspired me. "All right, Sash. Let's do this."

Lara shook her head and went back to scrubbing. "Your faith is admirable. Naïve but admirable. Well, what can I do to help ya's?"

"Wake him up!" I exclaimed.

"Believe me, hon, I would like nothin' better than to get him outta my feathers but there ain't no waking him up until he's slept this off."

"How long does that take?" Sashya asked.

"Midday maybe."

Sashya exclaimed, "Midday! We can't wait that long. The peace-keepers figured out he's here. We had to ditch a puffin officer in the dance hall. Snowy said they'd be busting down the door to arrest him soon."

Lara snickered. "Good Cod, deary, they just might. They've been plenty grumpy with him since he trashed the Lusty Loon and crapped on one of their deputies." She snickered. "It wasn't like he meant to, and there was lotsa birds around watchin' so they couldn't rough him up. But they told him to get the hell outta town for a month. I suppose they'll haul him away if they catch 'im."

I nodded, "And if he's arrested, we won't get the gold, we won't be able to make the bonding rings, and the bonding ceremony will have to be delayed."

Lara gawked, "Seriously?"

I nodded again, "Seriously."

Lara cocked her head, and a mischievous smile grew on her face. She stood and latched the door again, then picked up her pail of water and emptied it on Perry's face. He flailed, sputtered, and knocked her over accidentally.

"Whaaat's the big ideeeaaa?" he shouted.

Sashya jumped on Perry's chest and cried, "Perry! Wake up! The peacekeepers are on their way!"

Lara got back up on her feet and shook her feathers back into place.

"Peacekeeperssss? Oh shhhiiit!" Perry moaned. "Get offff meee!" Sashya fluttered off as Perry tossed. His stomach gurgled ominously, and he urgently rolled onto his belly. His body lurched as he retched over the side of the nest. A liquid splash on the floor confirmed the success of his purge, and he repeated it a few more times. The room filled with a burning gas of seabird stomach oils, rancid sea creatures, and fermented seaweed brew.

Lara and I reeled from the olfactory assault, but Sashya surprised me by stepping forward through the unspeakable vapors and placing a wing on the massive bird's back as he spasmed his last heave of oily filth.

Sashya spoked comfortingly, "Good bird, Perry, get rid of all that garbage. Get it all out. We gotta get you outta here and sober you up."

Perry panted a few moments, then licked his beak. "What? Where?" He belched.

I urged him, "The deputies are on to you, Perry. If we don't get out of here, right now, they're going to lock you up."

Perry huffed and spit to clear his beak. "Oh damn. Gotta get myself together." His tired bill dropped toward the messy floor, and he murmured, "Did you say something about Kor?" He turned his face toward Sashya and a great blob of brown mucus dangled from the tip.

Sashya picked up a wad of moss and dabbed the filth away, then gagged, dropped the soiled mass, and fanned his beak with his wing. Then he continued, "Yes, Perry, we're Kor's apprentices! He gave us this letter. It'll explain everything."

I pulled the letter out of my satchel and spread it on the floor. Sashya stepped back, shrugged off his coin purse, and opened it up. He plucked out the diamond Kor had entrusted to him and held it up for Perry to see.

Perry's swollen eyes quivered as tears pooled in the corners. Rainbows of refracted candlelight danced across Perry's face, and Lara gasped at the spectacle.

"Could that be?" Perry muttered through his tears. "Oh, dear Tuliann." He wiped his beak with a wing and shakily took the diamond from Sashya and laid back. He set the diamond on his chest and watched it sparkle. "Son, I can barely hold my eyes steady, much less read anything right now. Please, read the letter to me."

I nodded and read it aloud:

> *Dear Perry,*
> *Sorry, my salty friend, that I cannot deliver this message to you personally. I've been commissioned to create two gold rings for the bonding of King Vasili with Miss Tuliann. I need ten grams of gold, right away, and I trust this diamond will be payment enough. I wager you thought you'd never see it again after you sold it for a flask of wine when we last drank together. I retrieved it from the buyer, and I've kept it safe since. It's yours now, to remind you of who you once were. Your old flame needs your help now. You'll be happy to know that I had a long conversation with Vasili, and he's a good mate. He loves her and will take good care of her. They both deserve your help. So, pull yourself out of the gutter, old friend, and save the day. I have faith that you can flip the crest-wind and*

carry this mission through.
— Kor

PS: Keep your eyes out for flotsam. The king's guard was
surly and cool. Don't trust any of them Mamyrskins but
Vasili.

The familiarity that Kor expressed for Perry intrigued me. It showed previously unknown parts of Kor's personality and hinted to a colorful past.

Perry sobbed bitterly, and the diamond rolled off his breast and bounced across the floor. "I don't have that much gold."

Sashya's expression, which had lifted with hope, sank again.

"There's nothing I can do!" Perry squawked. "Leave me alone and get out before the peacekeepers get here. Tuliann didn't want me before. She's forgotten I exist, and I can't help you anyway. I'm hopeless!"

I placed a wing gently on Sashya's back, "Maybe we should just leave before the peacekeepers get here."

Sashya steadfastly shook his head, "I'm not done." He clenched his beak and hopped onto Perry's broad chest again. He clamped his feet deep into Perry's feathers and seized the bird's undivided attention.

Perry yelped and writhed. "Ow! What the hell?"

Sashya flapped to stay atop the bucking seabird. I helped by clutching Perry's beak shut with my thick foot. After a moment, his squirming stopped, as did his cussing.

Sashya exclaimed, "You are worth something, Perry. Kor doesn't make friends with just anybody. He believes in you. He sent us all the way here, halfway across Volatus. Don't you fucking let him down!"

Perry huffed through my clenched toes while his gaze remained fixed on Sashya.

Sashya laid it on more, "You must have more someplace, right? Some stash or source?"

Perry nodded his beak in my grasp and mumbled affirmatively.

Sashya added, "Then you're going to help us. You *have* to help us."

Perry sagged submissively, so I released his beak. "You don't understand!" he groaned as he covered his face with his wings and cried. "Long ago, I Tuliann and I were in love."

I said, "So that's why Kor knew you'd help us!"

Lara's eyes widened, "Great Awakening," she gasped.

Perry closed his eyes. "The diamond our bond-seal. I offered my pledge to her." He laid his head back in the nest as his body shook with spasms of sorrow. "She returned this diamond to me with a message that said that we could never be together. That it was impossible. It destroyed me." Tears flowed down his cheeks. "She didn't say it, but I know she was pressured to break our engagement. It was so sudden. We were an unlikely pair, and we knew it, but we didn't care. We were in love. We made each other happy."

Perry's condition made more sense now. I was on the cusp of my first pair bond. I had been strong and content on my own, but for the first time, there was something stronger, and better, I could be part of. Intertwining my life, and my dreams, with Sashya's felt like weaving together threads in a rope. We would be stronger as one, joys would be higher, and lows would be bearable. The only risk was that if that rope were cut, as with Perry and Tuliann, both our lives might unravel forever. I shuddered to consider it.

Sashya relaxed his grip on Perry's chest, and spoke softly, "You've lost so much. I understand. It must feel like there's nothing left to hope for. But you still love Miss Tuliann, don't you?"

Perry moaned, "More than anything."

Sashya smiled, "Others would be bitter and angry, and for good reason. But you're not. You just want her to be happy. It's beautiful, isn't it Peppy?"

I nodded with misty eyes, as the hope and redemption that Sashya visualized came into focus for myself. His heart contained wisdom beyond his years. I replied with solemn pride, "You're absolutely right, Sash. It *is* beautiful."

Sashya went on, "You can't be her mate maybe, but if you still truly love her and just want her to be happy, now's your chance. And helping her might just heal your heart too."

A flicker of understanding lit Perry's eyes. "You're a mean lil guy, but very persssuasive. Wass your name again?"

"I'm Sashya."

"Ah, yeah, Kor's apprentissss." Perry slurred.

"Sash, where can we hide him?" I asked.

Sashya replied, "We've got to take him back to the Avian Haven with us."

Perry chuckled, "Miss Penelope will make fancy steaksss outta me if I go there. And then she'll kick you out too."

I nodded.

Unswayed, Sashya said, "It'll only be for a little while. Just don't make a mess."

"Can you fly?" I asked.

Perry cleared his throat and flicked another blob on the floor. "I think so." He rolled to his feet and stood shakily.

I folded up the letter and tucked it back in my satchel. As I did this, I asked Perry, "What did Kor mean by 'flotsam' and 'flip the crest-wind?'"

"Flotsam is debris on the ocean. We pelagic birds also use it to mean debris in conversation. Things that are said to cover truth. Wreckage that points toward trouble. And 'flipping the crest-wind' is something that we albatrosses do better than anyone. When we rise behind an ocean swell and come above the crest, we catch a boost by the wind that speeds up over the face. We twist our long wings to catch it and up we go." Perry's eyes twinkled. "It's ol' Kor's way of saying that I should use this situation as my boost and change my direction for the better."

Lara held out a soft bundle of wet moss in her beak and Perry wiped his face and nares upon it. He winked and said, "Thank you, sweetie." Then he turned to me and added, "I think Kor is worried that Tuliann's in trouble and wants me to look out for her."

Perry took a shaky step, his leg gave way, and he fell on his face.

Lara said to Sashya, "Deary, he can't even walk yet, much less fly."

A gull cry echoed up the tunnel behind the door.

"Shit!" I cursed, "That must be the peacekeepers."

Lara nodded, "Able to fly or not, you guys best skedaddle."

"How?" I asked, "I don't see any other way out."

Lara nodded at the lantern cord attached to the planks in the back wall. "Unhook that, and push on the wall."

I followed her instruction and a well-disguised door, which had been held shut by the pull of the lantern cord, swung open.

"Wait!" Perry exclaimed as he stumbled over to the corner of the nest and pecked through his vomit. "One, two, three..."

Sashya bristled in disgust. "What in the skies are you doing?"

Lara said, "Hon, he's gathering his money."

I shrugged, "Hmm, I guess he can't digest it. That's one way to hide it."

Perry swallowed six small gold nuggets and the diamond, and said, "Found 'em all." He set a seventh nugget on the edge of the nest and said to Lara, "Here, Lara, a little extra for the mess."

"Aww! What's new, hon?" She picked stray bits of moss and straw from Perry's ruffled plumage. "Gee, Perry, I always wondered if the rumors were true." She looked into his eyes sweetly, "Sorry I didn't believe 'em till now."

Perry replied, "Do me a favor, darlin', and keep that secret un-hatched."

Lara pecked him gently on the beak. "Good luck, dear. You've got some real gems for friends. Don't let 'em down."

Beyond the doorway angry gull voices grew closer, cursing the stench and the darkness. The webbed feet stopped, and a beak rapped viciously on the door. "Open up! I can smell that worthless sack of gullshit! His ugly, gold-pukin' ass is mine now!"

Lara shouted to the impatient constable, "I'll be with ya in a minute, Brant! Give me a chance to clean up!" She supported one of Perry's wings and worked with Sashya to push him through the secret door into the back tunnel.

Lara whispered to me, "You should stay, hon. He'll never buy that I was alone. And Snowy doesn't want 'em finding out about the back entrance neither. They know too much as it is."

I felt torn. The last time I sent Sashya off on his own, he almost got killed. "I can't let him go alone."

Another set of heavy pecks bashed against the door. "Who are you whisperin' with? Open this gull-damn door or we'll break it down!"

Sashya whispered, "I'll be fine. It's best this way. Slow those guys down as much as you can cuz it's gonna be slow going."

I rubbed my beak to Sashya's white cheek and said, "Be careful. I'll meet you back at the Haven."

"See you soon, Pep." Sashya licked my beak and disappeared into the darkness beyond. My heart went with him, but I had no time to think about it. I shut the door, rehooked the lantern cord, then dove into the nasty nest and sprawled on my back.

Lara whispered, "Roll over and act sick."

I flipped over and hung my head over the edge of the nest, my beak pointed at the oily vomit left by Perry. *Wait, bad idea,* I thought as I choked in disgust.

Brant slammed the door with his body. "This is your last chance!"

I watched from the corner of my vision as Lara lifted the latch, and the door violently burst open. A large storm gull with a decorated red sash, the same one Sashya had spoken with earlier, stomped into the room.

"Hey!" Lara shrilled as she was indelicately shoved aside.

Another storm gull, Ano, Nyx, and Miss Snowdrift, all filed in a few steps behind Brant. I feigned sickness by coughing and retching in the corner.

Brant lifted his beak and shook his head, "Great Gull! What a stench!" The gull blinked his watering eyes. "Sure smells like Perry. I've cleaned up his messes enough times." His eyes wandered the room and settled on the glint of Perry's gold nugget on the edge of the nest box. "Where is he?" Brant demanded.

When the smell hit the rest of them, all backed up except Nyx. She hurried closer with concern on her beak. She whined and asked, "What happened to you, Pep?"

I winked and gave her a secret little smile.

Nyx noticed but gave no hint as she played along. "Oh, dear! I told you not to eat that stinkfish! And you drank too much seaberry wine again!" She stroked the back of my head with her wing. "When will you ever learn?"

I moaned and retched, barely having to fake it, as my face hovered uncomfortably close to Perry's multicolored spoils.

Brant marched closer and sternly gruffed, "Go ahead and puke your guts out. But then you're coming with me to answer some questions."

Miss Snowdrift intervened, "Oh, honestly, Brant, why can't you just leave the poor soul alone? Like I said, Perry's not here. These birds had business with him, but when they learned he wasn't here, they decided to stick around for some fun."

Brant spun around, knocking Lara brusquely across the face with his tail.

"That's it!" Lara screeched. "I'm tired of gettin' knocked around!" She bit down on one of his small, crisp, white tail feathers, and yanked it out.

"Ah!" Brant squawked and jumped forward. "Why you!" he cocked his wing back to slap her, but Nyx's raised hackles checked his aggression.

Miss Snowdrift shook her head, "You just try it, Brant. Even you aren't immune to the penalty of harming a working hen. If not an angry falcon, or me, it'll be an angry mob that rips you apart."

Brant's clenched beak and vicious yellow stare relaxed as he lowered his wing. He spat a question at Nyx, "Where's your owl friend, falcon?"

Nyx relaxed her hackles and replied, "I don't know. I lost track of him a while ago. When we couldn't find Perry, I hooked up with Snowy. I hope he's living it up in one of the other chambers."

"Gullshit!" Brant exclaimed.

Nyx lifted her hackles again and emitted a falcon's warning chup. "Nobody calls me a liar!"

She matched the gull's height but was less than half his weight. That barely mattered, though, as I knew Nyx's reflexes were fast as

Art by Silver Griffin

lightning, and she could easily rip Brant's throat out before he reacted.

The gull spread his wings wide and grinned, "You don't know what trouble is, lady, until you mess with a peacekeeper." The deputy gull took up position by Brant's side, beak sharp and ready. Ano sidled close to Lara and tried to protect her with his tiny wings, but Snowy shoved him aside, and wrapped her own around her instead.

Nyx clenched a foot and cracked her knuckles. "I guess you've never *messed* with a falcon from Waycliffs before."

The sour air stood still.

"Waycliffs, eh?" The gull's stony stare faltered, and he lowered his wings.

I let out my bated breath.

Brant squawked out a raucous gull laugh. "I'll beak it to ya, girl, you come from good stock. But what would your folks, and their Upper-friends, think of you down here mashing tails with common whores?"

Snowy hissed, "Watch your beak you bag of guts!"

"You best be watchin' yours, Snowy, and mind who you let into this joint. Your lies ain't foolin' me. Perry's been here. Might still be here. We're gonna turn this shithole inside out to see. But if you see him first, tell him to keep his stench out of my nares until the next full moon. The Royal Bonding is headache enough, and I don't need to be cleaning up after 'im." Brant turned to Nyx and me and said, "That goes for you too. Stay clear of Perry and stay out of trouble!"

Brant turned back to his deputies and squawked, "C'mon, let's get to searchin'" The gulls stomped out of the room, but Ano stayed behind.

Ano said in a groaning, anxious voice, "Miss Lara, might I have some time with you?"

The tired expression on her face told me this would not go well.

"Sure," Lara replied. She picked up a filthy sponge and stuffed it in his bill. "Here. Help me scrub the floor."

The puffin gagged and dropped the sponge then flicked the muddy water from his beak.

I stifled a chuckle. Served him right.

Miss Snowdrift ran out of patience and glowered at him. "Get out, Ano!" she boomed as she pointed a wing toward the door.

Ano scurried to the door and Miss Snowdrift slammed it against his ass, sending him stumbling into the darkness. She promptly latched it and turned back to us.

I withdrew from the puke puddle and smiled at Nyx. "Wonderful performance. You should join an acting guild."

Nyx asked, "Did you make that mess?"

I chuckled, "No, that's Perry's. But I almost added to it. Sashya lit out the back with him. Hopefully they made it back to the room by now. There's a lot more to tell but, phew! I need fresh air." I asked Snowy, "All right if go out the back?"

Snowy nodded, "Yeah, those idiots won't know which way you took."

I anxiously wanted to catch up to Sashya and make sure he was safe. I opened the back door and beckoned for Nyx, then nodded to Snowy and said, "Thanks for the help, ma'am."

She replied, "Anything for a cute couple like you and Sashya. Give him a peck for me."

"Mind if I borrow the lantern?"

She nodded, "You're gonna need it, hon. Go to the end, kill the lantern, and leave it hanging inside the door on the hook. Follow the fresh air to the left." She gave Nyx a robust, lingering hug, and Nyx hugged back with equal affection.

Nyx chupped softly, "You are such a dear. Thank you for the help, and the heart-to-heart."

Miss Snowdrift emitted a guttural chur that vibrated her fluffy throat. "I had a good time too. You be sure to come back again."

Nyx locked beaks with Snowy in a final warm kiss, we said goodbye to Lara and made our way into the darkness.

When we exited the brick tunnel, we found ourselves in a spacious Apterian arcade with starlight visible through a gaping exit to our left. A flow of glorious fresh air poured past us. The outside of the door had been decorated with broken masonry so that, once closed, it looked like any another crack in walls of imperfection and decay. I drank the predawn air like cool water and spread my tail and wings to let the breeze carry away the stink that clung to my feathers.

Nyx whispered, "Still smells like shit, but anything beats the reek of that pleasure suite."

We walked silently up a slope, hop-flapped over a heap of rubble, and emerged in the canyon between rows of ruined buildings, still and quiet in predawn sleep. The sky was a shade lighter than black, and the Morning Star had risen. A cluster of rats spooked and squeaked away into the crevices. A red fox sniffed the air then skittered away, his claws scraping on the rusted shell of a crumpled, half-buried Apterian relic.

It felt so good to be out of the catacombs that we took a moment to stretch and preen in silence. After hours of noise, the stillness of the night was a gift. But, as attested by the creatures we stirred, and the yips that followed, it would have been dangerous to linger.

While we flew back to the Avian Haven, I filled Nyx in on what happened in the pleasure suite. I tried to describe Perry kindly, but I knew her patience would be tested by someone so crude and depleted of ambition. I asked her what she had talked with Snowy about, but she blew if off as "hen-talk." I figured it might be more, but I decided to change the subject for the last few minutes and praised her instead for her amazing talent for exotic dancing. That's when she threatened to knock my head off and use my skull for a helmet if I ever told anyone about it.

My urgency to see Sashya grew as we approached the Avian Haven. I knew he could make it back to the Haven on his own, but the trauma of seeing him nearly killed at Sunrise Lake still haunted me, and I couldn't relax until I saw him safe and sound.

We alighted quietly on the landing platform, I eagerly pushed open the doors, and there he stood, smiling back at me. We locked beaks together and embraced in what I'm convinced was the most wholesome greeting I had yet experienced.

I chirped quietly, "Sounds silly, I know, but I missed you, Sash."

Sashya sighed, "Missed you too, Pep."

As he nibbled my beak, I noticed a faint odor haunting the room, like stale blubber, and loud snores resounding from one of the nests in the back.

"Perry made it?" I asked.

Sashya nodded, "He's asleep. How did it go with the peacekeepers?"

"Brant lived down to his reputation, but Nyx stood up to him. I guess he decided she was too much trouble and let us go."

Nyx shook her fisted foot in the air, "Sometimes you gotta persuade with more than just words."

Sashya said, "He knows we're staying here. When we chatted at the Citadel, he mentioned that I smelled like Miss Penelope's parlor."

Nyx said, "That might be a problem. But I'll wager letting us go means they have bigger concerns, so maybe we've got a bit of time."

Sashya said, "I hope so. It's going to be daylight soon and then we won't be able to move Perry anywhere without being seen."

Nyx wore a sickened expression and waved a wing before her nares. "Too bad we can't risk escorting him to the public baths."

"Did he say anything else about gold?"

Sashya shook his head, "Not much. Says it's not in town though."

It had been a long trip followed by a long night, and I was exhausted. Weariness outweighed all other concerns. I wrapped a wing around Sashya, and he looked at me with equally tired eyes. "How about we take the other roost? There's a perch for you too, Nyx."

She yawned, "Thanks, Pep."

I guided Sashya towards the nest and muttered, "Maybe we can get out of town before the peacekeepers find us." I hoped that would be the case as I soberly counted only nine days left before the Royal Bonding.

Chapter 12

A Bloody Mess

By Scrivener Ebel, as told by Brant

An orange-blue slash marked the sea's horizon as dawn approached. The promenade outside The Musky Murre had all but been abandoned. A few drunken seabirds lay wrecked against the cliff face, snoring loudly, while the earliest of the Unawakened gulls pecked at food scraps among them. Sometimes I envied the Unawakened. They ate whatever, shit wherever, and didn't have the stress of holding this town together.

Sharpstone glided out from the Musky and stopped a wingspan from me. He shook his head and said, "Nothin', Cap'. Perry's long gone. Turned the place upside down and searched every crack and nack."

"Every nack, eh? Very thorough."

"I learned from the best," he replied.

Sharpstone followed close as I made my way through the dance hall toward Snowy's chamber to wrap up our business. The fun was over, partly because first bell approached but also because we had kicked everyone out. Some stragglers, too drunk to crawl outside, snoozed amid strewn feathers and trash as the staff cleaned up. Two rats gnawed at discarded bones in a corner. An Unawakened herring gull walked about warily, looking for scraps. I charged and sent him fleeing out the door.

I chased away the gull because I had a soft spot for Loy, a well-known, half-blind crow beggar that lived on the promenade. He meandered around the hall pecking up bits of food, some disgorged by drunk patrons, and stuffed them into a sack for later. It would be nutritious and stave off his alcohol-dependent shakes for a while.

We climbed the steps and entered the back tunnel.

"Fuc-king hell!" I squawked to Sharpstone. "Nine days to go and this Royal Bonding gullshit is making everybody crazy. We're gonna be falling asleep on the wing before this is through. How ya holdin' up? Stayin' *sharp,* Sharpstone?"

He mumbled, "Could use a break, Cap, but so could any of us. I'll have to settle for drowning in a cup of waybrew instead."

"I'm sure Luu's keeping it hot."

He asked, "When are reinforcements comin' from Unitum?"

I shook my beak, "Not soon enough. You know how it is, though. No reason for them to hurry when the need is far, far away."

Sharpstone hummed a bar of "Far, Far Away," and we both squawked the last chorus:

> *It's a gulldamn disgrace*
> *With perps shittin' in your face*
> *And the Council's in no race*
> *Cuz they're far, far awaaaaay!*

We had sung it so often that we harmonized smartly.

Sharpstone said, "Damn, Cap, this filthy hole makes even you sound good."

"Ha! I'll keep my day job."

We passed into Snowy's chamber just as Sora came busting in from the back door. "Brant! You gots ta come back in here!"

"What now?" I asked. "We were just there!"

"It's Lara. She's been—" Sora trembled and tears spilled from her dark eyes..

"What? Unpaid? Shit on? Spit it out!"

"Ripped apart. Eaten." Sora sobbed.

I scowled, "Shit." I regretted my words a little bit. The mating parlors were a constant source of drama, but murder wasn't the usual.

"Sora, stay back here." Skrank stood guard at the back doorway. I turned to him and said, "Lad, Make yourself useful. Grab that lantern and come along."

We shoved through the back door and slapped our feet up the tunnel with Skrank in the lead.

"Hold!" I squawked. Something red had caught my gaze. "Shine the light by that hole."

A few drops of bright blood lay by the hole along with a small white feather. I peered into the darkness but couldn't see the bottom.

I said to Sharpstone, "We'll need Bluewing over here. Tell 'im there's a deep, dark hole to explore, and I don't mean the working hens."

"You got it, Cap."

We continued to the pleasure suite and found a rare mess. It looked like the work of a feral predator. Feathers fucking everywhere, guts and bloody bits on the wall, and the sleek severed head of Lara staring into the beyond. Snowy sat perched on the nest, disheveled and bawlin' her eyes out. Fortunately, Silver was there to console her.

"Sharpy, cover up Lara's face," I said quietly. I moved over to Snowy to ask some questions. She wasn't usually inclined to trust me, and I wasn't usually inclined to be soft on those that lied to me, but I extended a wing of support.

Snowy slapped it away and cursed, "Fuck off! You were nothing but evil to her. I don't want your pity. I want you to figure out who did this to my sweet Lara." She sobbed into Silver's feathers.

My eyes met Silver's. What a beauty! Of all Snowy's hennies, she's the only one that drew me in. Her plumage was the gray-brown pattern of spruce bark, her eyes a delicious shade of orange like yolks of auklet eggs, and her dark plumicorns rose tall and proud. A silver stud, a secret gift from myself, pierced her cere, and added the touch of class she deserved. Sadness softened her eyes, but didn't blunt the dangerous point of her beak. I hated to admit it, but grief really worked on her.

But it was more than good looks that attracted me. She was a tough bird, with a taste for other tough birds. It felt dangerous to be close to her, and foolish when I teased her to the limits of her lust. With a voluntary spasm of my irises from across the room, I could remind her of those steamy moments when she went unhinged in the nest chamber, and her pupils would pin with sexual excitement. She enjoyed the control and I, of course, loved exercising it.

I didn't give her those eyes now, though. She had her head on Snowy's back, gently rocking with her as she cried.

"Snowy," I said gently, "you're right. We'll do our best, hon. Just help me out. Tell me what you know."

Snowy told me between snivels that she had come back to check on Lara and found this mess. As far as she knew, the last birds there had been Pepro, Sashya, and Nyx, but they left shortly before Snowy did.

"How?" I asked. "We never saw 'em leave out the front."

She was conspicuously quiet.

"Cap!" said Sharpstone. "You should see this."

I stepped lightly over to the center of the carnage. "See the blood trail?"

Smears of blood stopped abruptly at the wall's bottom edge. I pushed on the wall with my breast, and it swung open like a door. "Looks like they normally keep this shut with the lantern stay, but the perp must've taken it with 'em. This how they left, Snowy?"

She nodded with swollen eyes and white cheeks stained with tears.

"Sharpy, take Skrank and get on up that tunnel. Each of ya take a lantern and look for evidence. Step lightly and if you see any good tracks, get Foamy to make a casting."

Sharpstone took one of the other lanterns in the room and left with the deputy.

Turning back to the distraught Snowy, I asked, "You sure those strangers didn't come back and do this?"

Snowy stared at me with genuine horror, "I. No way. I know my customers. There's not a cruel feather on those birds." Her shock told me it wasn't impossible.

"You sure?" I asked. "That lying falcon..." I let out a thin whistle to emphasize my words, "She sure has a fiery temper. And she said the moon owl was off having fun. We couldn't find him in your rooms. Now you tell me he was here after all. And that puking eagle. He looked more than capable. So, you mind telling me the truth?"

Snowy sighed, "Perry was here. They came to get some gold from him. They were sent by Kor, the master blacksmith in Galinta, to get it so he can make the Royal Bonding rings. They're his apprentices."

"Humf! That so hard? Why the fuck didn't ya just tell me that to begin with?"

"Cuz you're a flaming ventsore, Brant! Especially when it comes to Perry."

I couldn't argue with that. "Yeah, well he deserves it. I clean up after him constantly when he's in town. But this sounds like a damned valid excuse, so I might've given 'im a pass. Even a ventsore like me has to let filth pass through now and then."

Snowy nodded and wiped her face with her wings.

My eyes weren't picking up much else. Lara had done an amazing job cleaning the place up in a short time before the killer did their worst.

I asked Snowy, "You see anything else? Move anything around?"

She shook her head.

"How about any unsavories that might've wanted Lara?"

Snowy's poisonous yellow eyes scowled back, "Just your creepy puffin snitch."

"Well, yeah, he's not much, but he has his uses. We'll be asking him some questions too." I pressed, "How about anybody asking for Perry."

She replied, "Just you guys and those apprentices. Everyone else just ignores him, you know that."

"Hmm, yeah." Pretty much what I would expect. Perry may have been an idiot, but few would mess with that big bill of his. How 'bout that blood in the tunnel junction? Down by the pit?"

Snowy perked up, "What? I didn't see it. But it's been a long night."

I sighed and adjusted my sash. "Look, Snowy, we got a lot o' work to do. It'd be best if you were out 'the way. And we're gonna be traipsing in and out through your room too, so why don't you rest up in one of the others? We'll wake ya up if we got any more questions."

Snowy nodded and hopped off the edge of the nest. That's when I noticed the nugget of gold resting there.

"Well looky there. Hello." I reached down and tapped the glinting pebble with my foot. "That was there when I checked the room earlier. Some generous payment to your hennies, I presume." I sighed, "Very generous. And it means whoever did this wasn't after gold."

Silver asked, "Then what did they want?"

I mused, "I think we might have ourselves a real, deal, cold-blooded killer here."

Silver gently laid a wing on Snowy and said, "Use my room, dear. I'm too freaked out to sleep anyway, so I think I'll just get these flat-foots some waybrew and see what I can do to help."

Snowy, slumped and heart-torn, took one last look at Lara's destroyed body, and touched the covered head with a gentle claw. She spoke softly, "Fly free, sweetie," then left the room.

When Snowy had left, I approached Silver and asked, "How you doin'?"

"Stupid question. I've seen shit like this before but not involving anyone I knew and loved." Her plumicorns hung low and her plumage, normally fluffed and robust, lay deflated. "Lara was a good girl. Felt like a sister I never knew."

"You got any idea who might've done this?" I asked.

Silver shook her head, but I wondered if she'd made up her mind yet. "You got anything for me on anything else? How 'bout that mudhead with the weird ear tattoo?"

"Yeah, he came in yesterday and asked around for Ano. Speaking of which, I had to give him a fling last night." She winced like she had eaten a bad rodent, "He was really demanding and in a damn hurry, ordering me around like a pimp in charge. Snowy wanted him distracted."

"You fucked Ano?"

"Dear, I'm a prostitute. I fuck whoever they tell me to fuck."

I pinned my pupils, and jealousy curled my beak corners. "Sendin' that jerk down here was a mistake. Contaminated my girl. You can fuck a hundred other puffins, but that little shit stain? Have some standards. I'm reassignin' his ass."

Silver shook her head. "If it weren't that we were standing in my friend's guts right now, I might give a shit." She turned away toward the door.

"Just remember, whore, your ass is mine. Bought and paid for with secrets that go way down. You go too far outta line and it'll take more than the occasional hot fuck to keep you out my jail."

Silver laughed sarcastically and paused at the doorway, still facing ahead into the darkness. "Let me know when you're done, and I'll take care of Lara." Then she spun her head around, looked at me with those gorgeous grief-torn eyes, and said, "And be careful."

I grinned to myself as she disappeared down the dark passage. I couldn't admit it to anyone, not even her, but my threats were empty. I loved that hen too much.

Chapter 13

Torn

By Sashya

Despite Perry's snoring, Nyx, Pepro, and I had fallen right to sleep back at our room. I felt as though I'd spent all night hunting on the wing, so I collapsed face-down in the nest, and Pepro had settled at my side and wrapped me up in his soft wings.

I awoke first and tried to hide from the day by pressing my face deeper into Pepro's fluff. He chortled softly and wiggled his beak in his back feathers, but didn't wake up. I listened to his heartbeat, felt his breathing against me, and basked in the warmth from his hot skin. I yearned to explore his body and coax him into a steamy fulfillment of last night's admitted desires, but Nyx snoozed on a perch nearby, and I doubted she wanted to watch.

I would have stayed snuggled there all day, but my cloaca felt close to bursting. I reluctantly, carefully, extricated myself from Pepro's brooding body, and stalked quietly to the front room. Nyx shuffled and peered sleepily at me, then stuffed her head back in her scapular feathers and dozed off again. I peeked around the wall between roost chambers, and found Perry sprawled out on his belly. His head dangled over the edge of the nest and drool hung from his open bill.

I shuffled over to the toilet chute and lifted the cover. The reek drove me to hurry with my business and recap it as Aank had advised. But the acrid odor persisted, so I opened the shutters of the nearby window.

Sunlight blazed into the room along with a breeze that tossed open the opposite window's shutters with a bang. Pepro roused his feathers, and Nyx cussed in mid-yawn. In a few moments, both wearily emerged from the roost chamber.

I regretted disturbing their sleep. "Good morning. Sorry, the breeze just—"

Nyx grumbled, "It's fine, Sash. It's probably time we get moving anyway."

They both took turns using the chute too, and we all set about preening and chatting.

"Some night, wasn't it?" Nyx reminisced.

Pepro nodded, "I loved it. I still feel like I'm bouncing to the music."

I smiled, "Me too." Pepro smiled back. "Damn, that was a close one getting Perry outta there."

Perry coughed and groaned in his roost chamber. "Waybrew. Waybreeeew! I need it!" he demanded.

Nyx shouted back, "This look like the Musky Murre? Do I sound like a henny? Wait, don't answer that. Just get off your tail and get it yourself."

I felt more charitable. I hopped down and checked out the clay pots. One of them contained dark fibrous lumps, and the tannic aroma told me it must be pressed black tea.

I picked up a large cup with my beak, filled it from the water jar, then dropped one of the tea lumps in. I poked and stirred the dissolving blob with a wooden rod, until the scent was stiff and pleasing. With the cup in my beak, I prepared to take it to Perry, but a glare from Nyx froze me in place.

She chupped, "Sash, he probably needs that, but the worst way to help a user like that is to substitute yourself for the thing that addicts them."

I nodded, "Maybe I'll meet him halfway then." I shouted to Perry, "Got some tea for ya, Perry."

When the albatross didn't stir for a minute, Nyx shouted, "Get your ass out here or I'm gonna drink it!"

In a moment, Perry's feet scuffed slowly across the floor toward us. His steps were straighter than the previous night, but his face and plumage were still a disaster of vomit stains, crusted secretions, and unkempt feathers. He paused in front of the cup of tea and dropped his face into it. He bubbled for a moment, then lifted his head and swallowed. He repeated this again, then picked up the whole cup and tipped the contents down his gullet in one heavy, wet gulp. He dropped the cup noisily, emitted a gurgling belch, and shuffled to the relief chute.

The sounds that followed were a treat to no one, nor was the sickening aroma that emanated from the chute he carelessly left uncapped.

Nyx huffed, hopped off her perch, and stomped outside to the landing platform, leaving the doors open.

"Whassa matter with her?" Perry asked.

Pepro chuckled, "I'd not press her to answer that right now if I were you."

"Feel better?" I asked Perry.

Perry yawned and waved away a fly that landed on his beak. "Are you kidding? Shaky, hungry, thirsty. Drinkin' keeps all that away. Speakin' of which, that flask of wine there might just do the trick."

Perry reached for the flask hanging on a wall peg but Pepro hopped off his perch, charged over, and slapped it out of his beak.

"Hey! What's the big idea?" Perry protested.

His hackles up and his jaw firm, Pepro marched to the window and flung the flask out.

"No!" Perry cried as he ran toward the door to go after it. But Pepro blocked his path and Nyx joined him.

Perry reared up briefly with a contemptuous look, then rolled his eyes in resignation, and sank to his breast on the floor. "You don't have to say it! I get the point! You guys are gonna clean me up you think."

Nyx stepped up. "You can't help us if you're drunk."

Perry wagged his head and repeated her words mockingly.

Nyx's foot shot out and clamped around his massive pink bill.

"Mff!" he exclaimed through the seams of his beak, his eyes as wide as eggs.

Nyx shook his beak to the cadence of her words, "We need you clean, so we can help the love of your life. Remember?"

Perry nodded. Nyx released him and he moaned, "You're gonna have your wings full keeping me sober."

Nyx glared, "You can go right back to drinking and humping yourself to death in those stinking caves if you want, *after* you pay your debt to Kor. I presume you've got more gold stashed somewhere?"

Perry nodded sheepishly like a naughty nestling.

Nyx added, "We don't have time to tend you like a nestling, so I'm only going to say this once. You fuck this up and these talons will make you pay. Not just that, I'll turn you over to Brant and he'll have his way with you. After that, the whole town will finish you off. You understand?"

Perry sulked in silence a moment. I'll wager that no friend, had ever stood up to him quite like this before when it came to the subject of his lifestyle.

I ended the tense moment by saying, "Perry? You want some more tea?"

Perry swallowed and contritely replied, "Yes, please."

"Anyone else?" I asked.

Pepro smiled and nodded. I think he was glad I changed the mood to a kinder note. As I prepared the tea, he asked Perry about where he kept his treasure.

"Most of the gold I find comes from waaay down south where I go in the winter. I keep the spot secret, and I make a few trips a year. I got several stashes, the closest one's at Treaty Island, about a day's journey east from here."

"East?" Pepro asked. "Across Waystar Sea?"

Perry nodded.

Pepro looked at his feet in thought and remarked, "So that's two days to go there and back. Whew, we are cutting it close. Still gotta get back to Kor and make the rings, and bring them back, all in nine days."

"How much gold I got left, anyway?" Perry asked. "My memory's pretty hazy. I better check." His stomach growled, and he stretched open his maw to empty it.

Nyx's foot clamped onto his beak again. "Six pebbles," she said menacingly. "That's what Pepro said you counted last night. Six! Don't make a mess in here!"

The albatross's eyes bulged, and he swallowed, then sat back down.

Nyx released his bill and waved invisible contamination from her toes. "You don't have any here in town?"

I brought the fresh cups to Pepro and Perry and they dabbled and drank.

Perry said between sips. "Nope. What makes it here, gets spent. But, hey, I can go get the gold for ya. About time to go get some more anyway."

Nyx shook her head. "No way. You're not leaving our sight until we have that gold in our talons."

The thought of flying an entire day over open water terrified me. I had barely been able to hold it together flying high in the River Winds over land.

Nyx read my mind, "That's a hell of a long flight over ocean. No offense, Sashya, but I don't think you're built for that."

Pepro agreed, "Yeah, and there's no reason for all of us to risk it. I'll go."

I knew it would be no picnic for Pepro either, so I asked, "You sure there's no other way to get the gold? Something closer and safer? Couldn't we just sell the diamond for gold?"

Perry coughed and spat. "Son, ain't no seller gonna want to pay what this diamond is worth. 'Sides, Kor gave this to me for a different purpose."

Pepro replied, "It's for Tuliann, isn't it?"

Perry nodded, "She's the real gem. If I'm lucky, I'll have the chance to give it to her. A token of my love, no rings attached, to treasure. Like a releasing feather that will lay our past dreams to rest."

Nyx jarred me when she shook her head contemptuously and blurted, "I can't believe a bum like you and that intelligent, beautiful eagle ever courted."

"Nyx!" I hissed. It was the most insensitive thing I had heard her say yet, and it was too far.

Tears glistened in Perry's eyes, and his beak sagged in dejection. "I know I'm worthless, and I can't have her. But I still want her to be happy."

Perry walked outside and Nyx let him pass, a self-ashamed frown on her beak. She said to Pepro and me, "I can't believe I said that."

Pepro replied, "That was a doozy, Nyx. You gotta give that guy some slack. You weren't there last night."

I added, "He really does love her. He lost the best thing in his whole life when she said 'no.'"

Pepro hugged me and preened the top of my head. Our relationship was new, but I sensed that I would be as broken as Perry if Pepro ever rejected me.

Nyx said, "I think I'll try to apologize," and walked out the door.

Pepro said quietly to me, "Sorry we didn't have a chance to get frisky last night. Maybe we should've just done it there in the pleasure suite." He chuckled and dipped his beak in his cup.

I laughed, "Right there in that smelly room?"

He chuckled, "Well, maybe not there."

I flicked my tail playfully and Pepro's pupils pinned. He grinned and tugged me close with a wing. We kissed again, and his tongue tasted as sweet as ever.

He whispered, "I hate leaving you again. I wish I could take you with me."

I fished my beak into his breast feathers and pulled out the secret pendant.

Pepro asked with blushed beak, "You knew? How?"

"I saw you pick it out of the scrap pail."

"Why didn't you say anything?" he asked.

"The perfected one was going to be a hatchday gift for you, but, well, as you might guess, it meant more. You meant more. And the longer you kept quiet about finding it, the more I wondered if you felt the same. I didn't want to embarrass you by asking. I figured you'd let me know when you were ready."

Pepro fluffed his head plumage, and his eyes glistened with overflowing affection. "You knew all along."

I chuckled and nibbled his beak, "I hoped. But, hey, I'm glad you have it. It'll remind you of how much I love you."

"I don't need a pendant for that, Sash. I think about you all the time anyway."

We hugged tight and Pepro said, "Promise me you'll keep your beak out of trouble?"

I rubbed my face in his throat feathers, "I'll wait right here for you, Peppy. You keep your feathers dry and hurry back."

We walked outside and found Nyx finishing her apology to Perry. Nyx finished by saying, "Thanks, Perry. You keep a stiff beak out there and take good care of yourself. Take good care of Peppy too." She turned to Pepro and me, and chirped plaintively, "I'm a stuck up, rotten egg sometimes. I'm trying to be better. Sorry guys."

Perry looked at Pepro and said sarcastically, "Is that true, Pepro? Just 'sometimes?'"

Pepro and I suppressed our laughs.

Nyx rolled her eyes, and matched Perry's sarcasm, "Maybe you'd best empty your cargo, Gold Guts. Go in and use the cup like a civilized bird. Go now. Go!" She shooed him along with her wings.

Nyx gave Pepro a hug and pecked his beak. "You be careful. Weather gets rough or anything, don't push your luck. Just stick tight there and wait out the storm, Bonding be damned."

I hugged Pepro and stole one last kiss, the warmth of which challenged all the others. "I love you, Peppy."

"Love you too, Sash. See you soon." he replied as we broke away from each other.

Perry stepped back outside, stretched his legs and tail, and then his neck with an audible crack. "Cargo off-loaded. Nice westerly wind. Yellow sunrise, so the weather should be good to the east. Yep, we are ready for departure."

Pepro asked, "We'll get back by three bells tomorrow, right?"

"Yes, maybe sooner if we fly by the moon and winds are following."

"Let's get this over with." Pepro muttered. He gazed adoringly into my eyes once more, and I returned it, both of us wishing to avoid the painful moment of parting. Then he turned and dropped off the platform on spread wings.

Perry made a running start, and his fat body fell steeply over the edge. But he quickly caught the breeze and lifted on his long, narrow wings back into view and joined Pepro. In a few moments they blended into the clouds of busy birds over the sea, and I lost track of them.

After the past few days of Pepro's near-continuous companionship, the world felt larger and emptier as I watched my mate disappear. Despite the sun, I shivered. Despite Nyx's affable company, I felt alone. Despite Pepro's strength, I feared he would never return. It would be a long two days.

Hal Aetus

Chapter 14

The Institute

By Nyx

With Pepro and that stinking albatross gone, Sashya and I were left alone with only our worries to gnaw at us. I hate idle time, and there was just no use in pacing around, so I begged Sashya to join me on a trip to the Whiterock Institute.

"Look, Sash, would Peppy want you to sulk in the room all day, or go explore the town and have some fun? How often do you get a whole day to yourself?"

Sashya replied with a sad note, "He would want me to have fun."

"There's no amount of worrying that's gonna help him get back faster. I mean, if wishing were all it took to get what we want, what use would we have for wings and talons?"

"I know. You're right, I need the distraction."

He was still sluggish, but we entrusted our valuables to Miss Penelope for safe keeping, then set off for the marble porticos and masonry of the Institute, just a short glide away.

As we descended, I attempted to infect Sashya with excitement. "I took a course here a couple of years ago, and I always make it for the annual Technology Exposition. There's something new and amazing every time I visit."

He sounded more like his usual cheerful self when he said, "I've heard bits and pieces about it from news oracles. Never thought I'd see it for myself though. Can we see how they make the flameless torches?"

I had him hooked. "Barnibu, my teacher for the course, will tell you all you want to know!" Actuality, I knew Barnibu would tell us more than we wanted to know. Once you got him started, he could go on all day and night about all things Apterian.

We landed at the front of a white building with cornices and columns that rose ten wingspans. In front of this lay a large square where ruins had been painstakingly cleared away, bit by bit, and the ground leveled and terraced. The park was furnished with lamp posts, perches, loafing plinths, and bubbling pools interspersed with manicured shrubberies, beds of flowers, and fruit trees that were beginning to bud. Awakened birds of many species perched or glided about in the casual atmosphere, while clouds of birds screed and swirled between the ruins and towers above us.

I inhaled the fresh air, "This is my favorite part of Whiterock, Sash. Market Square is exciting, and the Government Quarter is pretty, but it's peaceful here. The buildings are kept up and everyone is relaxed and focused on learning. I feel like I'm looking to our future as a society."

Sashya swiveled his face all around, taking in the sights and sounds. For a moment he studied the bathhouse, a pool surrounded by broken columns that still embraced part of the second floor of a crumbled brick building. Birds were splashing in a shallow pool on the first floor while others lounged and preened on the exposed second floor that served as a roof.

"That's the public bathhouse, Sash. If you ever need to use it, it's open to all."

He asked, "This place is so tidy. Who keeps it clean?"

"Cleaning flocks come out every night to spruce it up."

"Too bad they don't clean up those sewers in Low Town too."

I had to admit he had a point. So much care was given here, but not to the thousands of slums that filled Whiterock's edges and depths. I nodded, "Well, you're right, Sash. Maybe someday we can. Come along and we'll find Barnibu."

I led us up the steps into the Institute's main gallery. High above, light poured down through a glass ceiling supported by a metal framework. Birds streamed in and out through open arches in the high walls, and some landed on platforms at various levels. Hundreds of flameless torches glowed and throbbed throughout the massive room, proudly illuminating pedestals with polished Apterian relics on display. Sashya's spirits lifted as his gaze drifted from one piece to another.

"How did they get these things in here?" he asked.

"I'll admit, Sash, I don't know. Maybe some of them were here already."

We toured a few of the exhibits and one particularly caught Sashya's attention: A big metal bird with stiff wings and tail. According to the placards, the Featherless pulled it through the air with a spinning wooden feather where I would expect a beak to be.

Sashya read the placard excitedly, "This carried Apterians through the sky! I knew they didn't have wings, and yet somehow flew, but I didn't imagine it like this."

I pecked the thin metal of the strange bird, and it sounded hollow. "It's kind of like our sky sleds, but clunky and heavy."

A piercing squawk interrupted us. "Miss, please refrain from pecking the displays."

I knew that smart voice. "Barnibu!"

"Nyx!" came a creaking voice from above. Barnibu was a crimson macaw with rows of green and blue feathers on his wings, and a long blue and red tail behind. He weaved his head to grab our attention from a ledge above, then fluttered down and landed beside us.

I wrapped my wings around him in a friendly hug and he hugged back. The parrot was as giddy and energetic as ever, and just the social distraction I needed for Sashya.

"How did you know we were here?" I asked.

"I didn't. I just happened to see you as I passed by. Who's your handsome owl friend?" He cocked his head and studied Sashya with a pale-yellow eye.

"Barnibu, meet Sashya. Sashya, Barnibu."

Sashya smiled and nodded, "Pleased to meet you! I've never met a bird like you before."

"I am dazzling and unique, aren't I?" Barnibu teased. "I'm a green-winged macaw. There's not many of us, but we were one of the first species to be Awakened by the Apterians."

Sashya stepped back with wide eyes. "The Apterians... made us?"

"Well, not exactly," Barnibu admitted. "We existed long before they did. But they changed some of us, awakened us, and gave us their intellect and awareness."

"Why?" Sashya asked.

Barnibu smiled, "To put simply, because it made us useful to them."

Sashya shook his head, "I wasn't taught that in school."

"It's a hard truth that was systematically suppressed by prior dynasties. The old Folies couldn't concede that another species could have been superior to them. It's still tough for some to accept, so it's not widely taught. But we have writings from our ancestors, three hundred years ago, that tell us this."

Sashya looked at the metal bird and said with awe, "They changed us. Is that why some of us are Awakened and others aren't?"

"Indeed. The Unawakened descend from ancestors that were never Awakened by the Apterians. But, uh, you ever hear of regressants?"

My beak warmed as I felt an embarrassing conversation coming on. Sashya shook his head.

Barnibu chuckled at my discomfort, "It's nothing to be embarrassed about, Nyx. It was necessary for survival."

Sashya glanced between Barnibu and I with an innocent look on his face. "What is it?" He asked earnestly.

Barnibu lowered his voice, as though that would help. "You see, long ago, after the Apterians all died and our ancestors were adapting to life apart from them, there were few partners for breeding. So, they bred with the Unawakened. They found that if a female was Awakened, the offspring would be Awakened also. Nyx, here, is embarrassed because, as the old stories go, it was common practice among peregrines. There just weren't enough Awakened mates to go around."

Sashya nodded, "I don't see anything wrong with that. Sounds like they just did what they had to do."

I nodded, "Yeah, yeah, well it's a touchy subject in some circles."

Sashya asked with a grin, "Why? Are you a regressant?"

I flared my hackles and snapped back, "Shut the fuck up or I'm gonna regress you!"

Sashya stepped back, "Sorry, Nyx." Then he changed the subject, "Why did the Apterians disappear, Barnibu?"

Barnibu eyed me nervously and answered, "Their abilities were nothing short of wondrous. Why they perished is complicated, and we still don't fully understand it. They filled the world with pollutants to the point it saturated everything, even themselves. They couldn't breed well, fight illness, grow their food, or adapt to degrading environmental conditions. On top of that, as things got worse, they warred with each other endlessly. It all combined to wipe them out quickly in the end. It's a shame, considering all they had learned. They even explored the stars in the sky."

Sashya shook his head sadly and thoughtfully brushed the metal bird with a wingtip.

Barnibu said, "But, hey, that's why the Institute is here. We study the archives to carry on the best parts of what the Apterians did right and learn the lessons of what they did wrong."

Sashya asked me, "You mentioned you took a course. What was the subject?"

I teased, "I don't know. What was it about, Barnibu?"

He shook his head and laughed, "Paying attention, were we? It was about recognizing and reporting Apterian technology. We offer the class to officials in remote villages, so they can help us recover important historical items."

"Skies! I would love to take a course like that. I took a class on Apterian History back home, and I loved it, but words and sketches don't do justice to what I see here."

"Oh, so you have some schooling?"

"Yes, two years at Kahvanis."

"That's impressive. Make it to the National Repository at Unitum?"

"No. Between schooling and farming, I never made the trip."

"That's unfortunate. But I'll tell you, our Apterian technology collection is much bigger. They have a more diverse library, but this site housed an Apterian university that focused on medicine, communication, and advanced electrical engineering, among other things."

"Electrical?" Sashya asked.

Barnibu's pupils pinned, and he squawked, "Oh yes!"

Here we go! I thought to myself.

Barnibu continued, "That's what makes the flameless torches work."

Sashya's eyes twinkled, "Oh! Nyx said sparks traveled through wires. Is that electricity?"

"It is! Electricity is my field of research. Want to see how we make it?"

"I would love that!" Sashya replied.

I was glad to see his spirits lifting. Barnibu took us on a short flight up through the gallery, out a busy portal, and into the morning air. We followed a short canyon down between the ruins to where a massive wall of Apterian concrete and accrement blocked the Rice River and created a long lake that bordered the south side of Whiterock. We fluttered to a stop atop a circular ruin with a green metal dome that stood where the dam met the cliffs of the northern shore.

Unawakened ducks flushed at our approach, rightly fearing my sharp talons. Along the shoreline were many species of birds going about their daily routines. At a nearby dock, a team of swans busily harnessed themselves in preparation to tow a loaded sky sled floating on the water. An eagle, perched on a branch above the bluffs, dropped steeply to the water, snagged a fish, and flew back to stack it with three others on an open draw bag. With a full load, she cinched the bag shut, and laboriously hauled it into the sky, probably bound for the market.

"See here?" Barnibu said, as he pointed a claw at a chute in the dam that delivered a stream of water to a spinning waterwheel. "That provides the rotation we need for the electrical generators."

Sashya replied, "It's like the waterwheel we have at the blacksmith shop."

"You have electricity in Kahvanis?" Barnibu asked.

"No, no. I never saw a flameless torch until last night. And I live in Galinta now."

Barnibu recognized the place. "So, you work for Kor?"

"Yes! You know him?" Sashya asked.

"No, but I know of his work. You're lucky to apprentice with a craftsbird of his caliber. That waterwheel provides your shop with kinetic, or mechanical, energy."

"Yes, it moves our large tools."

"Well, here we use generators to convert that mechanical energy into electricity, and we send that out in copper strands, called wires, to wherever we need it."

"Like to the flameless torches?"

"Exactly! But that's not all, Sashya. We can use it to lift loads, move machines, or even send signals over long distances in an instant."

Sashya's eyes were as wide as when he first saw the ocean. He asked, "How far?"

Barnibu grinned, "Distances that would take days to fly. All the way to Unitum, if we want."

Barnibu led us inside and showed us a row of cylindrical machines, crafted of metal and wood, each a wingspan tall and connected to the spinning shaft of the waterwheel. Openings in their sides revealed spinning blurs of coiled copper wire. He explained that these were the generators that made the electricity.

Next, he took us down into caves that he called the "cold rooms," where they experimented with keeping perishable food fresh. Electricity spun metal feathers, which he called fans, that pushed wind over moist tubes of copper. As we moved deeper into the cave, the air transitioned from warm and damp to cool and dry. A dimly lit maze of frosty pipes lined the walls of the deepest chamber, and baskets were piled high with hard-frozen carcasses of plucked and gutted rats, rabbits, quail, ducks, and fish.

As we toured, Barnibu and Sashya carried on non-stop conversation. Sashya drank it all in with no end of questions and curiosity, while my falcon eyes glazed over with information overload. I witnessed the delivery of fresh prey, carried in by a team of ravens, and my gizzard growled.

Barnibu noted my hungry gaze and asked, "See something tasty?"

I nodded, "It looks delicious. Is it all for the Bonding?"

"Indeed. These new deliveries are from the Raven Sisters, stocking up to cater the ceremony. We have agreements with other stores and eateries too. Some store their perishables here and others buy ice from us to restock their cellars."

As it approached midday, Barnibu indicated that he needed to wrap up our tour, so we made our way back outside. I was quietly relieved, ready to take a break from learning and go find a snack. But Sashya had one more burning question that delayed us a little longer. He asked, "You mentioned using electricity for sending messages. Can you show me that?"

Barnibu happily indulged Sashya's curiosity and led us to the rear of the main gallery building. We entered a room where a trio of pileated woodpeckers and two magpies perched on scribe's saddles. They sat before metal levers with pages of paper under their feet. They tapped the levers with their beaks, or idled and watched the levels tap on their own. The rhythmic clicks and taps were a language I had never heard before, but the birds understood and scribbled down translations in Apterian script on their pages using pencils in their feet.

Sashya asked, "So I see they are turning the electricity on and off, as you said earlier, but what is the language, and where does it go?"

Barnibu replied, "The Apterians called this a telegraph, and the 'language' is the alphabet coded into long and short click combinations." Barnibu waved his wing at a mural on the wall where the sequences were diagrammed out as dots and dashes. Each short combination had an Apterian letter beside it and a few had short phrases. "As far as where the wires go, not many places yet, I'm afraid. It's taken years, but we've managed to restore some old underground Apterian connections to a few watchposts, Unitum, and Hawksrise."

Sashya asked, "Does it reach Kahv or Galinta?"

Barnibu shook his head, "Not yet, but some day. And talking to Unitum isn't always possible either. The signal loses too much strength to go that far in one go, so we must use relay stations along the way. And the connection is lost a lot due to weather and poor wire damage."

Sashya cocked his head, "So you make electricity in those places too?"

"I wish it were so easy, but getting the heavy machinery around is difficult. So, we use energy piles, like that crowfoot cell on the shelf there." Barnibu pointed at a glass jar in a wooden stand with wires coming out of the top. It contained clear liquid and a forked metal shape in the bottom surrounded with blue crystals.

Barnibu saw that one of the magpies sat idle, so he leaned close and said, "Sy, I'm showing my smart friends around. Can you request a weather report from Sunrise Outpost?"

"Sure," Sy replied and rattled their telegraph switch for a moment and paused.

I commented to Sashya, "Sunrise is the outpost we passed on our way down here from the Hawkspires."

Barely a few breaths later, the device clicked on its own and Sy translated, "High stratus clouds above, low cumulus clouds to the west, clear east, fifteen degrees, light wind west northwest, no precipitation."

"Amazing!" Sashya declared, "Can you send messages for anyone?"

Sy nodded, "Of course, ten rangles per message up to two hundred letters."

I scoffed, "Expensive!"

Barnibu added, "Indeed, for now. It's expensive to keep it working too, so for now it's mostly just government, military, and Uppers that use it. Personally, I think this is all going to be obsolete soon anyway.

The Apterians sent messages around the world without wires. I think we will too, very soon."

I shook my head, "That'll put couriers like me out of business."

Barnibu chuckled, "It just means you'll have to find other ways to get your exercise."

We thanked Barnibu abundantly for his time, and on the short flight back to the Haven, Sashya wore my auriculars thin with nonstop chatter about all the wonders electricity could accomplish. I was happy to see his wide-eyed enthusiasm, but my gizzard clenched dryly, urging me to hurry back so I could cast a pellet in peace.

After I casted back at the room, my hunger sharpened, and I eagerly awaited teatime with Miss Penelope. I paced the platform outside our room while Sashya readied himself, and that's when two gulls wearing red sashes approached. My hunger-fueled grumpiness worsened when I recognized one of the peacekeepers was Brant, and I muttered to myself, "Fucking perfect."

Chapter 15

Investigation

By Scrivener Ebel, as told by Brant

Two bells sounded above the muffled surf and gull cries outside. I had finally taken a break to preen and shovel down some capelin, when I got the news that Ano's soggy carcass had been fished out of the sewer at the Murre. Foamy delivered a written report and I read it as I ate. Not even the graphic description would stall my colossal appetite though.

Ano still had his bag on him and his money. His head had been crushed like an egg and his chest pierced with enormous talons. The situation concerned me as Ano wasn't our only informer in Low Town, and if a bird were bold enough to kill a known peacekeeper, what would stop them from doing it again? I thought of Silver, too, being in the same dive at the same time as the murders. But then, Silver wasn't Ano, and I felt sorry for anyone tangling with that owl in the dark.

Ano was a sorry sack and not too bright, but he was brave. We had shared tales of cold patrols and warm hennies over a few stiff drinks. Once, I sent him down a tight pipe in Low Town and the little squirt led us to a den of stolen eggs. I pinned the silver star on his sash myself for that one. He had no family, that I knew of, so no one would remember him except us. Despite his drawbacks, Ano had been a brother in the service, and he deserved better.

I thought of the long stride of the bloody footprint in the pleasure suite and the big tracks Sharpstone found in the mud of the tunnel. The freshest eagle-size tracks were a snow-head and a crowny. The crew made plaster casts of the prints, so we had all we needed to sift some suspects. Problem was, we didn't have any solid suspects.

Sure, there was the snow-head named Pepro that hung around

with the falcon and the owl, but I doubted he did it. Not the type, but more than that, what the hell were crowny tracks doing way down in the sewers of Low Town? It's not like Whiterock crawls with crownies, and nobody at the Musky admitted seeing any last night.

I said to Foamy, "Good report. My compliments to Ebel for cranking this out so fast. I want you to come along while I try to get some information. First stop is the Avian Haven to have a chat with the trio of strangers from the Murre, and that bag 'o guts Perry if he's with 'em. Depending on what we get there, we'll check in with the Royals too."

While Foamy fetched his satchel, I gobbled my fish and finished my waybrew. I stuffed the report in my bag, flipped it over my back, and out the open window we flew.

I welcomed the bright, warm sun on my feathers, but it didn't brighten the shadowy crime scene in my consciousness. I kept dead quiet as I incubated the details in my mind.

Foamy noticed. He gave me the side eye from time to time, but he wisely avoided bothering me with questions. The real problem was motive. Ano and Lara had nothing in common, except location. And the killer didn't want money. It was a real egg-turner, like trying to bill a swan egg out of water. You can't get it in your grasp, so it just turns over and over endlessly.

Ano was a snitch, and many in Low Town hated him for it, but that's rarely enough for murder, especially considering the consequences of killing a peacekeeper. And Lara was a favorite at the Murre. That a crowny might be involved sent a special chill up my bill. The Mamyrskins, or Mams as most of us called them, were often stodgy and officious, and usually kept out of Low Town. If a crowny did this, maybe they were after Ano, and Lara just got in the way. *What did that greasy little crissum stain get himself into?* I thought.

We landed at Miss Penelope's rooftop, and I sent Foamy in to get the room number. I knew if she saw me, we'd be stuck there till third bell with her doting and probing. She was a fine pie, and I loved her fare and waybrew, but I was in no mood for small-squawk.

We dropped down four stories and landed at the prescribed roost. The peregrine named Nyx was standing there with a sour expression as we approached. The moony came out too, right after we landed.

"What's this about?" Nyx asked. "We already told you all we know about Perry."

"Yeah, I remember the lies. And then lying about not lying."

Nyx's hackles lifted. "What do you want?"

I laughed, "Relax, relax. Keep your feathers where they are. I know all about your mission to get gold for the rings and Perry's part. Keep him outta my feathers a while and you have my blessing."

Sashya asked, "Then what can we help you with, officer?"

"This is gonna be a lot to swallow. Mind if we step inside?" I asked.

We went inside, and I smelled Perry's residue, but he wasn't there. Neither was the eagle.

"Are Perry or your eagle friend close by? This involves them too."

Sashya piped up, "They're off retrieving the gold. They'll be gone until tomorrow night probably."

The falcon put a wing on his shoulder and flashed him a look of caution.

I said, "Maybe I best just get on with this then. Lara and Ano were murdered."

The way their pupils widened the moment I said the words told me they were genuinely surprised.

"When?" Sashya asked.

I wagged my beak toward Nyx, "Right after you and your eagle friend were there. Hell, they pulled it off while we were still searchin' the place for Perry. I want to know if you noticed anything out of place."

Nyx relaxed and said, "The whole place was new to us, so I'm not sure what we would notice."

Sashya asked, "Did you find any clues so far?"

Between our encounter last night and his crisp curiosity now, I estimated he was a smart little fellow who genuinely wanted to help.

"We found tracks, your tracks, leading from the crime scene." The falcon tensed, and I continued, "But there were bloody footprints at the scene and some tracks on top of yours that look to be from a much larger eagle. See any crownies around last night? Or muddies?"

Sashya asked, "Muddies?"

Nyx huffed, "That's their local slur for mottled eagles." She coldly remarked, "How do you like being called a garbage goose?"

I smirked, "I get called worse. So how about it? Any mottles about?"

Sashya replied, "No sir."

"I see. No blood or feathers in the tunnel when you went to the pleasure suite?"

"No sir," he said. "How's Snowy and the other girls?"

I had never heard an Upper express any care for a Low Town henny, so this owl's compassion threatened to crack open my crusty shell. "It's kind of you to ask, son. She's pretty distraught. They all are."

He said to his falcon friend, "Nyx, we should go down and see her."

The falcon nodded solemnly.

"Look, I don't think it's a good idea for folks like you to be hanging around down there. Not just now anyway."

Nyx replied, "Like us?"

I answered, "Yeah, clean, preened, and carrying money."

Nyx asked, "Why? Isn't this an isolated incident?"

"Oh, murders happen from time to time." I admitted.

"Then what's different with this one?" Sashya asked.

It was an ominous situation that two birds were killed in the sewers, one brutally dismembered and half eaten, and the murderer didn't even take their coppers. And it all happened while I and my crew were only websteps away. Whoever did this was cocky, sadistic, and gave zero shits about our authority. But I didn't need to scare these birds with gory details.

"Son, it's just different. I can't tell you why. But, please, don't go down there. Everyone's crazy right now with springtime fever, we're short-staffed, and this Royal Bonding is only making things worse."

The falcon asked, "You guys need help? I'm a liaison to Waycliffs."

I cocked back in surprise. *Had this hard-ass Upper hen offered help?* "You have influence with those folks?"

"Definitely. My mother is head of the council. They'll be coming down in a few days. I can courier a message to bring whatever you need, that we can spare."

I wasn't too proud to refuse. My crew sorely needed the help, "Well, sure. If they can spare some capable birds for security, the Peacekeepers of Whiterock would be much obliged. Tell 'em to bring their gear and report to Captain Brant at the Citadel. We'll feed 'em and house 'em through to the end of the Ceremony." I turned to Foamy,

"We got space, right?"

Foamy smiled and said, "You bet, Cap."

It was a rare day when I felt beholden to others, for the rewards of our job were few. But she surprised me, and I thanked her for the offer.

As we left, I instructed them, "When Pepro and Perry return, you let them know what happened. If they have anything, and I mean *anything,* to report, send 'em over."

Once outside I said to Foamy, "Can you believe that?"

Foamy shook his head, "Sharpstone is gonna kiss your feet, sir."

"Oh good. I'll be sure to stomp around in a toilet trench first then."

We flew up to the platform with the crownies' banner. Two stern crowny guards surveyed us momentarily, but did not halt our entry. We entered a room of barely controlled chaos. Crownies and mottles were prancing around piles of furs, silver cups, and crowny quill pens. Some wrapped gifts, others stacked packages, and one mottle kept track of it all with pen and ledger.

The scribing mottle quieted the room with a flick of her wing and asked us why we were there. She stood almost as tall as the crownies, and had a marbled brown and white head, brown body, and crisp white tail. Her plumage had been immaculately preened, and her beak, feet, and talons shined as though primped for a military parade. Her blue sash bore a small eight-pointed silver star over the left side of her breast.

I smiled pleasantly, introduced myself, and asked to see the king.

This mottle spoke with the clipped accent of all the Mams, but hers was additionally effete and snobbish. "Do you have an appointment? I don't see your name in His Majesty's schedule," she said as she surveyed a logbook on a table.

"No, I don't have an appointment. This is an urgent matter concerning a murder investigation."

"Oh! I see," she said with mild interest. "In that case, tell me what you want relayed, and I'll take it to King Vasili."

"This is a sensitive matter. He'll want to hear this straight from me, and I want to ask him some questions myself. I promise it won't take long."

"I'm sorry, but it's quite impossible. He's completely busy until after the Bonding."

I almost lost my patience, "Too gull-damn busy to meet me, Whiterock's chief *security* officer, on a matter of *security?* Let me clarify: I'm investigating the possibility that a member of His Majesty's contingent may have committed murder."

One of the others in the room hissed and the clerk's expression hardened, "We're here as humble guests. Our Honor Guard hasn't yet arrived, so there are only twenty of us, and all log in and out through me."

I spun her logbook around with my beak and began reading, but she snatched it away and hissed, "That's private."

Foamy tensed. He knew how testy I could be with unreasonable snobs like this bird.

"Fine, fine." I took a deep breath and exhaled slowly. "I came here in a good mood, and I'm choosing to leave in a good mood. What's your name and position?"

"Rissak, Chief Coordinator to His Majesty."

"Well, Chief, what you're telling me is that your entire staff was present and accounted for last night?"

The eagle stared down at me "Yes, that's exactly what I'm saying."

I spoke out the side of my beak to Foamy, "You got that, Foamy? Official response is all the crownies were here last night. And this little book here would confirm that. Good to know, right?"

Foamy nodded smugly, "Mm-hmm."

"So, what if I have evidence that one of you lot was someplace else, at a crime scene, let's say. You'd stake your reputation, your life, on me being wrong?"

The eagle's left lower eyelid twitched, and her pupils widened. I thought to myself, *This eagle would be fun to gamble against.*

She replied coolly, "It would not be one of us."

I looked the tall, proud ventsore in the eye and said, "Do me a favor, Chief. Let your king know that a crowny committed a double murder last night. One of the victims was my own deputy, a twelve-year veteran. Now, I'm not sayin' it was one of you, but, well, we don't see many crownies here." I turned to go, then glanced back and added, "And one more thing. Tell him to expect a message from the Regional Governor. And if he changes his mind and wants to talk to us, contact me, and only me, Captain Brant, at the Citadel."

The muddy looked flustered and irritated, and that worried me. A seasoned secretary would have at least pretended to cooperate. Maybe she was covering for someone that fucked up in some small, embarrassing, even innocent way. Or she might have been covering for a murderer. Whatever the case, she was hiding something.

Miss Penelope

Chapter 16

Gossip

By Nyx

The visit by Brant and his deputy dampened our mood. We made plans to go see Snowy later in the day. But first, we had an appointment to share teatime with Miss Penelope, so we flapped our way up to her parlor.

Miss Penelope vibrated with worry, "There's still so much to do and the Bonding is coming quickly. Nine days!"

Miss Schreider served us tea and fresh bug bread, and my mouth watered at the sight of the golden cakes.

"So you're hosting all the royal guests?" I asked.

"Yes, dear, and it will be packed. Plus, we'll host the pre-bonding ball too."

"Splendid!" I said.

I enjoyed a good party, especially one that would have interesting and handsome birds attending. They were my moments to preen and puff and put aside the cold, gritty side of my life for a while. It would also be a fantastic chance to gather news and make new connections and contacts to help our village. But though I would never admit it out loud, I also reveled in the attention I attracted as a lady falcon, from a respected family, in a position likely to go places.

I tasted the tea and said to Miss Penelope, "King Vasili has a lot of faith in you, and for good reason. You have a well-deserved reputation for fine hospitality. I know you will impress them all!"

Miss Penelope said, "Thank you, dear. Miss Tuliann wanted something private and small. But Vasili would have none of that. He wanted it to be a spectacle to celebrate all that the bonding means. So it's going to be big. The whole town's invited to the Flockplace to see it. Everybirdy will be there. But a few of us specially invited guests will be perched right down close to the ceremony."

I wiped my beak on my perch's feaking cloth and replied, "I agree with Vasili. This is too big an event to keep quiet. What a match, too."

"Indeed, dear." Penelope feaked and resumed, "That stately, swaggering, warm-hearted bird giving his kingdom to our own sweet and selfless Miss Tuliann. She has done so much for birdkind."

I nodded, "We're going to miss her here, though. She founded the Whiterock Institute's Department of Health Studies. I sure hope she has a good successor trained up."

Miss Penelope nodded, "Yes, her chief understudy is a heron named Ress. He's not as warm, but he's quite capable. He helped her cure the Mamyrskit plague a few years ago. Did you know that's how she met Vasili?"

Sashya appeared clueless so Miss Penelope filled him in. "A nasty pox plague hit Mamyrskit hard, so Vasili brought a group of his best healers to the Institute to learn how to cure it, and they were marvelously successful." Miss Penelope smiled and flashed her third eyelids. "And at the same time, he found a cure for his broken heart."

I churred sympathetically. Up to that point, my duties to family and village had been enough for me, but who could hear such a romantic tale and not wish it would happen to themselves?

Sashya asked, "What do you mean by a broken heart? Had the king lost his mate to the plague?"

"No," said Miss Penelope. "Queen Merikukka fell during a terrible fight with usurpers, at her royal aerie of all places. Mamyrskit is a barbaric place, dear, and King Vasili struggled constantly to hold his kingdom together. Merikukka was a cunning warrior, and fought at his side, but they only succeeded in breeding that one year. Imagine that! Just one summer of peace in fifteen. Despite winning the war and securing peace for the past five years, the toll was heavy on Vasili."

Sashya replied kindly, "It's amazing he is so warm and friendly after all that tragedy. He deserves happiness."

"Will you do the catering for the ball, Miss Penelope?" I asked.

"Oh goodness no, not all of it. Our cooking staff will be up to their necks just taking care of the daily meals. I've contracted the Raven Sisters to do the ball."

I nodded, "Good choice! They're the best in town."

"Of course, dear. It's expensive, especially for the diversity of palates the Bonding is attracting, but Vasili has a deep purse. Did you hear that they'll be providing treats for all the public guests too?"

"Incredible," I replied. Providing food to tens of thousands of hungry birds seemed impossible.

Sashya commented, "That's why those birds were delivering so much food to the cold rooms at the Institute."

Miss Penelope smiled, "Oh yes. Isn't that wonderful? We'll be using them this summer when our ice cellar runs out. It's so much work for the staff to restock it every winter, bit by bit. I hope someday we can build one of those in our cellar. Imagine the fattest fish stocked year-round for our distinguished guests. We'd be the first in Volatus!"

Sashya said, "I'll imagine voles, if you don't mind. Pepro can have the fish."

Miss Penelope laughed, "I'm glad you have a sense of humor, Sashya. You've been quieter today. Do you feel well?"

"Yes, ma'am, I'm fine. We just received some bad news is all."

"Oh dear," she said as she pecked a crumb on her plate. "First, Pepro's tragedy and now yours. Do you want to share it?"

Sashya's pause, and the uncertainty on his beak, told me he was reluctant to bring up Perry and the brothels, so I helped him out. "When we tracked Perry down last night, we ended up in the Musky Murre."

"Oh, I see," Miss Penelope said with reservation in her voice. She feaked her beak on a perch cloth and cleared her throat, "You didn't pick up any feather lice, did you?"

"No ma'am."

"Well, check carefully dear."

"Actually, I got to know Miss Snowdrift, the madam owl there, and she's quite clean and lovely." My beak warmed, and I hoped Miss Penelope didn't notice me blushing. "Anyway, right after we left, a deputy and one of their working hens were murdered."

Miss Penelope shook her head so that her beak chains clicked together. "Sad, sad, sad. But these things happen in the less desirable places of town. I warned you."

Her indifference surprised me. "Is it that common?"

The magpie shrugged, "Well, I don't really know. I don't pay much attention to what happens down there."

Mano's struggles came to mind, and the bug bread lost its flavor. I thought of Lara, on her haunches, scrubbing the floor of unspeakable filth just to earn her fare, and my appetite faded. I knew that Miss Penelope bore Lara and Snowy no ill will, and I liked to believe that if she only met them and saw their life, she would sympathize. But that was as likely to happen as Miss Penelope cleaning toilet chutes. Still, I planted the hope in my heart that perhaps, someday, I could connect her to that world, and she might be swayed into helping them.

I went on, "Well, this was different. The murderer was a crowny, apparently."

Miss Penelope dropped her bread. "Who?"

I said, "We don't know, but Brant seemed sure of the species at least."

Miss Penelope hopped from her perch, closed the door, and latched it, then returned.

She lowered her voice, "I'm not surprised."

Sashya asked, "Why?"

Miss Penelope went on, "Those crownies, leastways the Mamyr-skins, are not friendly folk. Well, none but King Vasili."

Sashya agreed, "Pepro and I noticed that too. King Vasili greeted us with hugs and gave us gifts of seashine and meat. Kor got on well with him too."

Penelope smiled, "How wonderful that Kory likes him. That says beakfuls."

Sashya added, "But Princess Vouli was nothing like him."

I nibbled my bread and picked out a grub. "In what way?"

Sashya started, "She's--"

Penelope interrupted, "She's terribly condescending. She smiles in a way that makes you feel..."

"Like prey," said Sashya.

Miss Penelope nodded emphatically, and her beak chains clattered, "Indeed! Unless you're a crowny, particularly her guard, Tulivor. Oh, and let me tell you about that." Miss Penelope whispered, "Miss Schreider heard the juiciest gossip about those two."

"What is it?" I asked, anxious and intrigued.

"First, do you know who Tulivor is, dear?"

I shook my head.

Sashya said, "He's the King's Wingwarden, commander of the guard. He has a nasty scar across his left eye."

Penelope nodded, "That's him. But that's not all. You remember what I said about Queen Merikukka being killed? Vouli was but a nestling. So, without a mother, and Vasili so busy with his duties, Tulivor stepped in and raised her."

I nodded, wondering where the story was going when Sashya snickered.

Penelope shook her head, and her chains clicked again, "You already know?"

I smiled and stared at Sashya who apologetically wagged his head as he giggled. "Know what?" I asked.

Miss Penelope "Shh, now, and listen. For this tidbit of truth is sweeter than bee larvae but you mustn't tell a soul!"

I nodded, transfixed.

"Schreider heard it last night, right before the Princess departed."

"She left?" asked Sashya.

"Mm-hmm." Penelope nodded. "She's off to fetch the rest of the wedding party by the sounds of it. Probably lords, ladies, and nobles for the bonding ceremony. Anyway, the rumor is that Tulivor and Princess Vouli are intimate."

"She's mating with the bird that raised her?" I asked. "Are they related?"

"I don't think so, but it's still weird, don't you think?"

I shrugged and chuckled, "I guess."

Sashya added, "I can confirm. They mated yesterday. I heard them through the toilet chute."

Miss Penelope tittered gleefully and bent forward to listen more closely.

Sashya continued, "Yesterday afternoon, while Pepro and I were resting, I went to use the toilet chute in our roost chamber. When I opened it, I heard the two of them moaning and grunting. I knew exactly what they were doing. And after they finished, Tulivor said something about siring royal eggs. I wanted to listen for more, but the smell was terrible, and the thought of those two scary birds humping was gross, so I capped it off."

Miss Penelope beamed, "Oh, you got an earful! And I know exactly what you mean! I doubt the two together have enough warmth to brood a hummingbird egg. It's simply scandalous for a royal daughter to be bending tails with the ranks, much less the one that raised her."

I shook my head. "Why didn't you tell me that juicy story, Sash?"

He shrugged, "I didn't know you'd be interested."

Miss Penelope shook her head, "If you can keep secrets so well, you'd go far here. Secrets are power, Sashya."

I mused, "I wonder what she thinks of having another bird in the way of her rule?"

Miss Penelope nodded, "I can't imagine she's happy about it. I figure that's why she's so blasé about preparations. She was perfectly happy to let me make all the decisions for the ball, as though she has too many other things to be bothered with. My feathers! If I were let loose with royal funds to plan a party, I'd have the time of my life."

Sashya asked, "What do you mean about blocking her rule?"

I said, "Mamyrskit is ruled by a matrilineal monarchy. So, Queen Merikukka did most of the ruling while Vasili led the military. When she died, Vasili assumed her power, but he can only rule in such a state for five years before he must take a new mate, or until their oldest daughter takes a mate. It's been five years and Princess Vouli, as we know, is old enough to nest. King Vasili has enjoyed good favor, but he's under a great deal of pressure from his Royal Court to find a new mate or pass leadership on to Vouli. The fact he doesn't pass it to her suggests he has reservations about that option too. So, our own Tuliann of Whiterock will become Queen Tuliann of Mamyrskit, with absolute power, save for a few obligations with their Court of Nestlords."

Miss Penelope nodded in agreement.

Sashya said, "I prefer our system of elections."

I nodded, "Me too. The other interesting thing about this bonding is that Tuliann would be the first mottled eagle to rule in Mamyrskit."

Sashya nodded, "If I remember anything from my history course, it's that the Folegalian Dynasty didn't allow anyone but crownies to have real power. Baldies and mottles owned property and slaves, but weren't allowed to rule."

I nodded, "Well, Mamyrskit isn't the Folegalian Dynasty. Vasili integrated more species into the ruling houses, but the resistance of nobles to the new system is what brought so much unrest to Vasili's rule."

Sashya asked, "Ah, so he wants to see Mamyrskit become more like Volatus. So much so, he's willing to turn his kingdom over to a mottle."

"Yep." I said, "And not just any mottle, but the one that helped save his people. She's greatly respected there."

Miss Penelope had been listening quietly and pecking at the crumbs on her plate. She said, "Maybe not everyone is fine with it though. Maybe that's another reason why the Princess and her entourage seem less than excited for the bonding. Vasili may be progressive, but most any other Mamyrskin officer I've met is proud of the old customs."

I furrowed my eye ridges. "You don't suppose Tuliann is marrying Vasili for power, do you?"

Penelope shook her head. "It would certainly be an old trick, but knowing Tuliann, I doubt it. Look at her career. It shows her selflessness and intelligence through and through. I would stake my inn on it."

I recalled, "True. She's been invited many times to run for Regional Governor, but she repeatedly turns it down saying she has no political ambitions. She seems happy running the Institute and acting as an advisor to the Regional Council."

Miss Penelope nodded, "Perhaps reunification of our two countries is a step too far for Vasili on his own, but with Tuliann as queen, they might just manage it."

My beak flushed with hope and my breast puffed. "Wouldn't that be something? Bringing the countries back together again. My parents will be thrilled to hear this. The war was long ago and a lot has changed."

The subject was a difficult one, and the room went silent except for the sound of purling wind against the windows, and the cry of a passing gull outside.

Miss Penelope stretched her wings and stepped off her perch, "Sorry dears. It's been lovely gossiping, but I really must get back to the preparations. Will you join me for dinner?"

We agreed we would and then set out for the Musky Murre to console Miss Snowdrift.

Chapter 17

The Folegal

by Sashya

Gulls, gannets, and puffins dotted the Promenade, preening after their midday feeding in the rising tide. The Musky Murre's gallery doors were wide open, and the brick floors swept clean. It was hard to believe the same place had been stuffed beak to tail with a thousand carousing seabirds barely two bells earlier.

A few gulls and a bald eagle perched at the troughs of seaberry wine, and their subdued chit chat echoed gently in the empty hall. We approached and asked to see Snowy.

The eagle nodded, "She's here. Go ring the bell up there." He flipped a wing toward the round brick tunnel in the back of the room.

We followed his directions and climbed the stairs to the back tunnel. Shock, the white gyrfalcon, was already there, pinning a black anklet above the tunnel entrance. Other admirers of Lara were chalking the walls with words of love for their favorite hen.

When we approached, Shock turned and surveyed Nyx carefully. He said in a seductive tone, "Can I be of *service,* Miss?"

Nyx returned the smile, "Is Miss Snowdrift available?"

"I'm afraid she's resting, dear. But if you're looking for owl action, Miss Silver is available."

I said, "No, sir, tempting as it is, we heard that you had a tragedy here this morning and wanted to share our condolences with Snowy."

Shock's smile faded, "Yes, it's been a difficult day for her. For all of us, I'm afraid. Wait, weren't you here last night too?"

Nyx nodded and her eyes glistened with emotion.

"Aww, dear, come here." Shock extended a wing and offered a hug, and she accepted. "Come with me," he said as he released Nyx. He led us up the tunnel to Snowy's door and pecked it lightly with his beak. "Snowy, darling, you have guests."

Snowy hooted back, "I'm not in the mood, Shock. Silver can come out in a bit though."

Nyx chupped back, "Snowy, it's me, Nyx. I heard what happened. I just want to check on you."

Talons clicked across the planks inside, and the door unlatched and opened. Snowy's ruffled plumage and swollen eyes told us she had been crying all day. She was unashamed and wrapped her wings around Nyx to pull her into a deep hug. Nyx slid her wings up over Snowy's round body and hugged back.

I stepped in and wrapped my wings around the two. "I'm so sorry for your loss," I said. I barely knew Lara. She was salty on the surface yet seemed genuinely sweet underneath. From the display on the steps of the dance hall, she had touched many birds in ways that went deeper than satisfaction of lust, and I felt their loss.

"Thanks, sweetie," Snowy sniffled as she directed us inside. Shock closed the door with his beak and stayed in the hallway.

An eagle owl was there too, and I felt as though we had interrupted a conversation. She wore a silver stud in her nares and a black leather anklet, so I assumed she was another member of the staff.

Nyx said, "I'm sorry if we're interrupting. We don't need to stay long."

Miss Snowdrift shook her head, "Dear, I've been moping in here all day, so it's like fresh air seeing you. This is Silver, hon. She's the one that kept Ano occupied for us."

I nodded, "Thanks for helping us out."

Silver nodded back, "Don't mention it."

Snowy said quietly, "Lara's releasing will be tomorrow night, dear. We could use Perry's help to carry her to the releasing circle. Will they be back by then? I figure he'd like to be there."

I nodded, "He should be. We'll be sure to tell them as soon as they return."

"You're all invited, of course," she added.

Nyx bowed respectfully, "We're honored, dear. We'll be there."

Snowy nodded in reply.

After a moment, I said, "Brant came and questioned us. Seems he thinks a crowny killed Lara."

Miss Snowdrift nodded, "Yes. He probably hid in the tunnel. It's got us all on edge. And, what he did..." The tears welled up in Snowy's eyes.

Nyx hugged her, "It must have been horrible."

Silver's plumicorns drooped as she completed Miss Snowdrift's thought, "They tore poor Lara to pieces."

"Torn to pieces?" I asked in surprise.

Silver nodded solemnly. "And feasted on her, as though she were just an easy snack."

Murder of Awakened birds was practically unheard of in Kahvanis or Galinta, much less killing and eating each other like common prey.

Nyx shook her head slowly. "Unbelievable!"

Snowy sobbed, "It looked like they made a game of it. Bits of Lara all over the walls, the nest, the floor. I'll never be able to go in there again. We're just gonna have to seal it off."

I asked, "And Ano too? Was he torn up?"

Silver shook her head, "No. They found him in that sinkhole in the back tunnel. He was a bit mangled but not eaten. They figure the killer roosted above the hole and waited."

The feathers on my nape prickled as I recollected Pepro and I looking down that hole, probably right under the killer's gaze.

"Do they know who did it yet?" I asked.

Silver shook her head slowly. "I'm surprised Brant bothered to question you. But then, it involved one of his deputies and a crowny. If it had just been Lara, those gulls probably wouldn't bother with an investigation."

Nyx looked at Silver with eyes that wanted to challenge her assertions, but then she nodded sadly, and laid her head on Snowy's back.

Something sharp in Silver's voice, beyond her disdain for peacekeepers, piqued my curiosity so I asked, "Who do you think did it?"

"We were just discussing that," Silver replied.

Snowy lifted her head and looked at Silver. Both owls shared a silent exchange, and Snowy nodded permissively.

Silver began, "Well, it's no secret that pretty much the only crownies in town right now are the Mams. The sashes found the tracks of one up the back tunnel and took a cast of it."

"Cast?"

Silver explained, "They mixed this white powder up with water, poured it in the footprint, let it harden, and it made a copy of the track.

They can match that up to the killer's foot."

"Well, that's good," I said. "With only so many crownies around, shouldn't take long to sort it out, right?"

Silver's tone lifted, "Sure, but what killer doesn't take money, eats their victim, and then plays with their guts? Even doing it while the sashes were still stirring around?"

I shook my head cluelessly.

Snowy whispered, "Those Folegal ventsores. They act like they can do whatever they want."

Nyx jerked like someone plucked a feather from her rump. "What are you saying? The Folegal are gone."

Snowy chuckled, "Dear, you're sweet, and I love you, but you've only bothered swimming in our sewer for one night. You got a lot to learn."

I stared in disbelief at Silver, but her tired, amber eyes told me that she knew for a fact the Folegal weren't all dead.

"You've seen them?" I asked.

Silver nodded and gazed at the candle lantern as she mused. "There's at least a few here, meeting in secret, mostly. Funny thing about rotten eggs. They can look fine on the outside, but when you get close to them, you smell the problem inside."

Nyx shook her head, "So you just suspect. You don't *know* for sure."

Silver replied acidly, "I hatched in a simple place called South-reach, maybe a little like your Waycliffs, Miss Nyx. When I first came here, I did some things I'm not proud of. I worked with a muddy who I thought I could trust. We were involved. Sometimes he would disappear for a while late at night and come back smelling of spirits and blood. One time I followed him, as quietly as, well, an owl. He met with some other muddies in a cave. One of them dragged in this lovely herring gull, all bound up and scared out of her mind. She was Awakened, and she pleaded with them with her bill all strapped shut. They laughed and mocked as they drank, fucked, and beat her to a pulp. I was scared out of my wits, but I couldn't risk being discovered, so I just perched there and listened to the whole thing. When she finally died, they said some kinda gullshit oath to the brightest blood, ripped her up, and ate her. There was no hesitation, no discussion. They acted worse than the Unawakened, giving no shits of any consequences."

My gizzard froze and I felt ill.

Silver lowered her beak and smiled, "But that shit-spurter got his. He loved kinky roleplay. Ironically, his favorite game was being tied up and abused, a little like that gull he toyed with, only he thought he was safe. And the next time we did that; I made sure the knots were good and tight. Then I slapped him around and told him I saw what he did. He begged for his life, just like that sweet gull, until I ripped out his fucking throat. He never abused another soul."

Nyx asked, "Why didn't you take it to the Peacemakers?"

Silver rolled her head, "That's none of your business. I did what had to be done. And besides, who's to say some of them aren't in on it. Some species-haters wear cute little sashes and others just wear secret tattoos."

"Tattoos?" I asked.

"Yeah, that creep had this red drop-shaped tattoo hiding in his left ear. I saw it when we made love. He just blew it off, but what a weird place for a tattoo. When they made that chant about the bright blood, it made sense."

Miss Snowdrift said, "There's others too."

Silver nodded.

"Others?" I asked.

"There's a muddy that comes around that loves to twist it up with Snowy and me in a threesome. He's got the same tattoo in his right ear, though we know better than to say anything."

Snowy added, "Thing is, he acts rough and tough, and all wound up in public, but we get him back here and he's like a homesick fledge. Remember that time, Silver, when he just cuddled between us? No sex. Just wanted to be brooded and sleep."

Silver shook her head, "He acts like he barely left the nest. Hell, he's barely four summers old and hardly knows how to mate. Yet, somehow, he's in with those Folies. Rest assured, though, I don't think they get those tattoos until they've proven themselves."

Nyx asked with a sick tremble in her voice, "Why are you telling us all this?"

Silver averted her intense gaze to Snowy's eyes. "Snowy thinks we can trust you guys. You know important birds. Uppers. And yet, you seem to give a shit. Maybe you'll be able to carry the message to someone that can do something. The peacekeepers don't give a damn."

I asked, "What do the Folies want?"

Silver shook her head, "I don't pry. We're just trying to make a living, and we can't do that if clients don't trust us."

Snowy coldly added, "Or if we're dead." Then she sighed, "Ano must've been the target and Lara just got in the way."

"Then why did they kill Ano?" I asked. "What does he have to do with the Folegal."

Snowy remarked, "He hung out with Rasha some."

"Rasha!" Nyx's plumage shrank tight to her body. "Wait. Is he the mottle you just mentioned?"

Snowy reached out to Nyx with a wing. "Yes, hon. You feelin' all right?" she asked worriedly. "You look like someone broke your eggs."

Nyx breathed heavy and her eyes glistened on the verge of tears. I put a wing around her trembling shoulders, and she met my gaze. "What is it?" I asked.

She shook her head, "I can't say. I want to, but I can't."

Snowy asked, "Is it something we should know?"

Nyx shook her head curtly, "It's better that you don't."

Silver went on cautiously, "Rasha said that he and Ano even played together with Lara once. But then, he also had a big mouth, and said stuff about how the Princess mated with her father's Wingwarden."

"Well, he wasn't wrong," I said. "I heard them doing it yesterday at the Avian Haven."

Miss Snowdrift looked at me with concern in her yellow eyes. "Boy, you should probably keep that egg under your brood patch. Maybe Ano got killed for some deal gone wrong, or for knowing things he shouldn't, but it might just be he spread rumors that tarnished a crowny's honor."

Silver agreed, "Especially when spring lust is burning bright."

I nodded solemnly. The circles of gossip, lust, and power were getting too complicated for my liking, and it was affecting Nyx too. She seemed on the verge of falling apart, so we needed to get out of there quickly.

Silver and Snowy hugged us goodbye and soon we were breathing clean air again on the Promenade. But Nyx remained broody and distant, and after a few moments, she excused herself, saying she needed some time to herself, and would meet me back at the Haven for the evening meal. When I asked her what was wrong, she avoided my gaze and looked out to sea, her eyes darting across the horizon as though hunting for the words to reassure me.

"I'm worried," she said. "I told Pepro the other day about the growing unrest. I've assumed it's just growing pains for our nation. But now I learn the Folegal are alive right under our beaks and my sis—" Poor Nyx choked on her words and sobbed. "I can't help but wonder if there's a connection. If something bad is coming."

I placed a wing on her back, but she recoiled from my touch as though it hurt. Her eyes simmered with anger, fear, and barely retrained tears. Until then, she had been a pillar of falcon assertiveness, and the change scared me.

"Nyx, you're shaking. Please tell me what's bothering you you!" I demanded.

She shook her head, "Believe me, I would tell you if I could, but I can't! I've been a stupid fool to ignore the problems down here in Low Town. All of us were. We help plenty of poor birds in Waycliffs, but that's nothing like these sewers. And we just fly high above them with no idea how scary it is to live day by day down here. No more though." She shook her head for emphasis. "No more."

"What will you do?" I asked.

"I don't know yet. But I've got to do something."

The events of the past day made me feel closer to her, but I knew better than to press further. I nodded and said, "Go on, Nyx. I'll be okay. Let me know if you want to talk about it later though, okay?"

Nyx leaned close and tenderly pecked my cheek feathers. "Thanks, Sash. See you at dinner." She flew out over the sea, climbed, and looped back to the south.

I stood alone, staring eastward across the Waystar Sea as the distant, curved horizon darkened in hues of dusk. I thought of Pepro, and the air felt colder without him. I could hardly wait to see his white head and tail, bouncing in the breeze as he approached from across the sea, and feel his loving wings around me again. Meeting new friends and adventuring around Whiterock had been the time of my life, but at that moment, I just wanted the simple life of Pepro and I working wing to wing at the Forge, bathing at the river, and roosting tight together in the warm attic.

Chapter 18

Treaty Island

By Pepro

For most of the day we saw few other birds. A few other albatross, petrels, and smatterings of gulls. We crossed over a group of four dark gray whales, many wingspans long, with noticeable prominences in their backs. They spouted and swam northward, unconcerned with the world above.

Flying two hundred wingspans above the sea, I spotted Treaty Island first. The sun had slipped over me and was warming my backside from the west as the island grew larger on the horizon.

Albatrosses fly most efficiently close to the ocean, so Perry was far below me, "flipping the crest-wind" as he called it. He made it look effortless and scarcely flapped all day. He would rise behind a tall swell and catch the wind that was deflected off the front of it. This propelled him up into the sky a dozen wingspans before he reset his wings and glided down again. Then he would catch the wind speeding up over the next swell, shoot upwards, and repeat the process. At the top of one of his rises he saw me descending toward him.

I shouted, "We're approaching an island, Treaty Island I presume?"

Perry called back, "It is! I don't like birds to see me come and go from my cache. Come down and follow my tail!"

I dropped down to within a wingspan of the sea, hugged the swells, and followed close behind Perry. We weaved back and forth behind the tallest waves and used the clutter of birds and sea spray to conceal ourselves. The ground effect over the smoother water behind the swells was a welcome rest for my tired wings.

Rocky cliffs gleamed in the sunshine, topped by stunted, wind-swept spruce and waving grasses. The island was barely a half kilometer wide at the western end, two kilometers long, and arrow shaped with the widest part to the east. The cliffs we approached were decorated with the musky whitewash of seabird colony that, by the caked layers, was probably hundreds of thousands strong in the summertime. The upper reaches were dotted with thousands of puffin and petrel nest burrows, but they were silent since breeding season had not begun. The ruins of a stone Apterian tower stood atop the cliff, along with some Awakened bird dwellings, but they appeared abandoned.

Dense flocks of Unawakened razorbills and murres swirled around the base of the cliffs, plunging and paddling, circling and screeching as they fed. Perry led me straight through the throng, and we stirred up a storm of frantic flapping as the birds fled from the terror of being an eagle's meal. I dodged the flying feathers and rain of droppings and stayed glued to Perry's tail.

As we came within a dozen wingspans of the sheer cliffs, Perry called to me, "This is the fun part. Pay attention!"

An unexpected shift in wind pulled me toward the rock wall. "Whoa, wait!" I cried as I fluttered avoid being smashed against the rocks. With no time to think, I mimicked Perry's wing twist, spun hard left, and caught a heart-leaping updraft that shot us straight up while still maintaining level flight attitude.

"Yeah!" I screamed as I unclenched my talons and reveled in the thrilling ride. "You really know your winds, Perry."

Perry shouted, "Watch me, watch me!"

We drew our wings in to slow our climb and twisted ourselves around to face the ocean. Then Perry fanned his tail and tilted his wings back so that he hovered briefly and drifted backward into a cave. I knew I couldn't mimic this move, so I clumsily broke into a flailing hover, spun around and dove head-first into the cave instead.

I collapsed on the floor, panting from the effort and the euphoria of following a master of the wind. I learned a lot about flying on my Wander, but Perry's knowledge put me to shame.

I shook my head and asked, "How did you ever learn to do that?"

"Comes natural with wings like mine. They were made for the wind. Besides, I've been here in all sorts of conditions." Perry roused his feathers and adjusted his wings. "That wasn't half bad, Pepro. I don't think any other eagle could've followed so well."

I recovered and collected myself off the floor. We preened as the amber sun settled low on the horizon.

Perry said, "We'll rest here until dark before we approach the cache. I've never shown it to anyone, but you can come along and be my eyes while I pull out what we need."

"I could sure use a drink," I murmured.

Perry's expression lit up. "You brought some?"

I sighed and shook my head, "I meant water!"

"Damn!" he replied.

We preened and relaxed as the sun sank below the horizon and the screes of the seabirds settled down for the night. I yawned and pulled a foot up under my belly fluff. My eyelids were heavy, so I rested with them barely open without tucking my head for sleep. I still felt like talking.

"How are you feeling without booze?" I asked.

Perry opened one eye halfway, the pupil tiny and sleepy. "This morning was awful. Shaky. Hollow. Head pounding. Gut unhappy. Good thing for you, you weren't flying nearby." Perry flicked his beak and huffed out a puff of fluid from his nasal salt glands. I noticed it was clear instead of brown as it had been that morning.

"And now?"

"I still feel like my eyes are wiggling. But, yes, much better. You have no idea how wonderful fresh air and sunshine is after days of living in tunnels." Perry squinted and his upper bill flexed upward in a yawn. "Trips out to sea always clear my head."

"Why do you go back to drinking then?"

Perry closed his eye, and mumbled sleepily, "Makes the world feel better. Makes me fun to be around. For a while I'm king of the flock, and the girls love me. I can forget all the bad things."

"Didn't we have fun today? And we weren't drinking. Maybe you just don't hang out with the right friends."

"I have no friends. No real friends anyways. Just ones that want my money."

Ouch. It was true, I wouldn't have tracked him down nor followed him across a day of ocean without needing his money. The sound of pounding surf punctuated the space between us for a moment. I didn't want to let the conversation end that way.

"I won't deny we need your money and that's why I'm here. But I just flew across a sea for the first time, and watched you do things with the wind that bend my mind. I'd like to get to know you better and call you a friend, with or without your money."

Perry opened one eye again. "You seem like a nice fella. Likewise for your scrappy friends. But I'll believe it when you still hang out with me after you get what you want."

"Fair enough. But you'll see. I mean it. Sober Perry seems like a fella I'd be good friends with. He must be good if the likes of Tuliann loved him too."

Perry closed his eye again. "Once, maybe. But not enough to stick."

I peeked through my barely open eyelids at Perry's ghostly outline. I wanted to reach out and let him know I did care, but I saw it would take more than words and a single day of friendship to fix years of distrust for others. And one day of sobriety couldn't reverse the decade of abuse he had inflicted on himself. I realized I had already set myself up to prove him right or wrong. It was up to me, as much as him, to show friendship and sobriety are real and attainable.

Perry swiveled his head back and shivered his bill down under his charcoal-colored shoulder feathers. He mumbled something sleepily and then fell silent.

I tucked my head into my scapulars and let my mind drift. I thought how remarkable it would be if Perry stayed sober, and we became friends. I had never known an albatross before, but I sensed I could learn a lot from him. For someone with a reputation for being worthless, Perry sure came a long way to help someone he had every right to dislike. His drunken attempts to cover the loss of Tuliann had been huge, matched only by his willingness to turn and help his old mate anyway. I smiled to myself; the only explanation was that under all that salt and misery was a big heart that yearned to be whole. It gave me hope that it wasn't too late for Perry.

Chapter 19

Reports

By Scrivener Ebel, as told by Brant

The red sun touched the coastal mountains as I winged my way toward the government district. After getting nowhere with the Mams, I distracted myself with other routine business of the day. And seeing another potentially long night ahead, I napped in my office while I sent Foamy out to arrange a meeting with Governor P'tilo.

Most mottles I knew behaved decently, and I gladly left them alone. The ones that didn't, the muddies that dipped beaks with the lowest scum of Low Town, were the problem. But P'tilo didn't fit in either category. He primped and preened an air of refinement about himself and expended most of his energy kissing the tails of the Uppers, rather than get his feathers soiled with working-class birds. He played warm and nice in our meetings, but even a rookie would see through his acting. I tolerated that from a superior because I didn't give a gulldamn if he liked me or not. What gummed my gizzard is that he promised big and delivered little. We peacekeepers annoyed him, and as our needs piled higher, and his job got more complicated, he became less and less interested in listening to us.

I soared around the broken concrete dome of the capitol, then prepared to land by the guard post on the lip of the gaping sky hole that led inside. The guard, a young bald eagle, recognized me with a chirp and a nod. I aborted my landing flare and glided down inside, around the great spruce standing in the center, and landed on the western side of the third floor.

Being late afternoon, most day-timers had retired. A flight of owls lifted from the lowest floor and circled upwards to the guard posts to take over the night watch. A heron stalked about with a lit wick on a pole, igniting lanterns, while a raven and a snow-head walked by in quiet conversation, their whispers echoing in the cold shadows of the marble chambers.

My feet slapped along on the smooth stone until I beaked open the door into the governor's offices. His clerk, a thick-chested white pigeon named Shakal, met me in the front reception room. She nodded toward the door to P'tilo's office and went back to shuffling parchments on a table.

P'tilo sat on a high scribe's saddle with three tables around it within a beak's reach. Behind him a tall window blazed with the setting sun, lighting his tables well but completely dazzling my vision.

I'm sure the high desk and dramatic window were by design. The lofty snob enjoyed reminding all beneath him, in every way, that he led the entire region of Waystar. It was absurd that I had to report to him instead of a village master or council, but P'tilo had wide latitude, and reorganized local government with him at the center a couple of years prior. Waystar was a pretty sparse region with Whiterock being where at least three-quarters of her Awakened population called home. P'tilo convinced everyone that combining governments would make things more efficient and bring in more support from Unitum, but so far, I had yet to see any improvement.

I stood quietly, waiting for his acknowledgment while he scribbled noisily with a quill in his left foot. I let my eyes wander around the room, but I had seen it all before. Tall paintings of him, his predecessors, and other Uppers graced the walls. I squished my webs into the warm coyote fur rug. Meanwhile, P'tilo paid me no attention until, at last, I yawned loudly and ruffled my feathers.

P'tilo paused and peered over his desk at me with a smile. "Long day?" he asked.

I replied, "Yes sir."

"Ever so sorry for the wait. Just one moment." P'tilo stated as he resumed scribbling.

"Nice rug. I should get me one of these for my drafty roost."

"Mm-hmm," P'tilo mumbled as he scribbled.

"Maybe next fall, if I can save up enough. By the way, you ever get anywhere with the budget we beaked over to you? Any new appropriations? My deputies deserve better pay, and I'd sure like to hire more staff."

P'tilo poked his quill loudly to the page and stopped. "I'm sorry,

what was that, Captain?"

I snapped my bill to swallow my impatience. "I said, were you able to get the appropriations approved?"

His eyes went back to his parchment and his smile faded, "Sorry, not yet. New business has been put off until after the Bonding I'm afraid."

"Wonderful," I grumped. "I guess life stops when you have enough shinies to shake."

"Mm-hmm," P'tilo absently replied. "All right, I'm done with this now. So, what can I do for you, Captain?"

I wanted to lay into him for not doing his job for us, but I knew it would only make things happen more slowly, so I stuck to my immediate duty.

"There's been a double murder in Low Town, one of my deputies and a working hen at the Musky Murre. We have strong reason to believe a crowny did it. We've contacted the three crownies that we know that live in Whiterock, and they all have strong alibis. I tried to speak with King Vasili, but his staff brushed me off. They maintain that all of their contingent was accounted for last night but wouldn't let me look at their logs. I hoped you might pull some strings and get me in to talk to Vasili or see the logs for myself."

P'tilo furrowed his eyes, "What are you doing talking to the king? He's an international guest and beyond your jurisdiction, Captain."

P'tilo was an elitist nib, whose pretty head I would have loved to use for mopping toilet trenches. But he wasn't usually a stickler for proper protocol when it saved him from being bothered with police matters.

I replied, "Well, sir, it involved one of my deputies, not to mention a local citizen, so I think that places it within my jurisdiction. At any rate, I couldn't get in, so no meeting took place." I stood proudly and said, "But, sir, I hoped that you, with all your mighty influence, could crack that egg for us."

P'tilo nodded coolly, "Yes, I am in touch with Vasili. I had dinner with him last night, in fact. I'll see what I can do for you, officer."

"By the way, Ano was one of the victims." The puffin had served as liaison between me, the Regional Governor's office, and the city council. It wasn't a big job, but it carried special privileges, and it saved me loads of time. Ano retrieved records from the government archives, coordinated with P'tilo's secretary, and, sometimes, reported back and forth between me and P'tilo directly. From what I knew, the two had a decent rapport.

P'tilo lifted his head attentively and adjusted his wings. He seemed ruffled, for just a heartbeat or two, then looked me in the eyes and shook his head slowly. "Tsk, tsk, tsk, how awful! Please convey my condolences to the force."

Even for P'tilo, the response underwhelmed me. That he didn't care about a seabird far below his station wasn't surprising, but it annoyed me that he didn't try a little harder to feign sympathy for a bird he knew.

"I'll pass it along sir."

"In the meantime, please keep to your Bonding Day preparations. That should be more than enough to keep all the peacekeepers busy."

"Aye, sir. We're doing our best, though we really need those reinforcements promised by Unitum. Are they still coming?"

"I'm afraid they've been delayed."

"Oh? Again?" My exasperation showed.

P'tilo stretched his wings dramatically, and the last rays of the setting sun streamed through his feathers. "Captain, you know I'm doing everything I possibly can for you, don't you? You and your officers are my top priority. I'll refresh our request and get back to you."

I nodded, confident that nothing would happen unless I kept nibbling at him like a feather louse, and I really didn't have time for that gullshit. At least I had Miss Nyx's promise of Waycliff's support. There was no way I would tell P'tilo of her offer though, lest he fuck it up somehow.

"Is there anything else, Captain?" he asked.

"The releasing for Ano will be tomorrow night. It would boost morale if you attended, sir."

"I'm sorry, but I'm afraid I'm just too busy right now," P'tilo said with all the substance of a limp feaking cloth.

I left abruptly before I gave into my temptation to soil P'tilo's luxurious rug and use it to wipe my feet. As I lifted through capitol dome, I nodded to the two eagle owls at the guard post. They hooted in reply as I climbed into the evening sky.

I brooded on P'tilo's responses and couldn't help but feel something was off. I couldn't put my beak on it, another "egg-turner," as they say. Maybe it was just his distraction with all the matters of state and society that welled up around the Royal Bonding, like a glittering school of candlefish on a rising tide. But his answers were less creative than usual and made me wonder if he had run out of excuses for covering his incompetence. The whole exchange shook my already wavering confidence in him.

I glided lazily toward the peacekeeper citadel but then changed course. There were other less-than-official channels in Whiterock for getting things done. The Tacet Carceris had few points of contact, but I happened to know one: A well-preened bald eagle named K'ai that frequented the Musky Murre. He kept a low profile, but rumor did enough for him so that birds with special problems would seek him out.

As I approached Low Town and glided through flocks of seabirds, I hardened my facial features and returned to my customary role as a stiff-tailed constable. I settled down onto the promenade in front of the Murre. No music played yet, but flocks were building inside around the drinking troughs and the fish buffet. Sashya, the moony with a mission, stood on the walkway, staring wistfully out to sea.

I approached him and said, "Fine evenin' ain't she?"

He turned to me with the look of a mother whose eggs got swiped. He replied, "Yes, sir."

"Your falcon friend about?" I asked.

"No, sir."

"What's got you lookin' so homesick?" I didn't really care, and yet I did a little. This young owl poked a tender spot in me for some reason.

"Oh, nothing sir. Just worried for my friends that went to sea."

"Aye, understandable."

Though an adult, he was too pure and naive for this place. Whiterock had a way of killing dreams, and I was often one of those no-nonsense ventsores that killed them. I rarely took the fatherly approach, but I risked it this time.

"Look, son," I said, "Perry may be a stinking waste of lice, but he is, wings down, the best navigator you'll find. Don't tell 'im I said so though."

The owl nodded and smiled, "Thanks, sir. That makes me feel a lot better. Were you successful in your interviews today?"

I rolled my eyes and shook my head, "Can't say I was. But, hey, you just tend to yourself. And send those two salty-tailed treasure-hunters to see me when they get back, understood?"

Sashya nodded, and I left him alone. Letting my soft side out, and then bricking it off again, reminded me of someone else with whom my emotions tumbled. Perhaps I could arrange some time with Silver, after my business with K'ai.

The atmosphere inside the Murre was subdued. A tuft of black feathers and a black ankle band were pinned above the back tunnel. Flowers, shinies, and coppers were scattered about the doorway along with chalk scribbles on the back wall, written by admirers paying homage to a shapely girl murre that had brought pleasure into their hard world.

I found Agent K'ai perched at his usual spot, by the south end of the room at a trough of seaberry wine. I walked to the trough, hopped up on the perch next to him, and dipped my beak into the briny brew. It was particularly effervescent today and tingled so strongly in my choana, that I turned and sneezed so as not to eject snot into the public drink.

"Good health!" K'ai exclaimed.

I feaked my beak on the perch and replied, "Thanks, I'll need it."

K'ai, nodded. "No offense, Brant, but you look like you need a break."

"You got no idea. Not enough to have murders to deal with, but I got superiors with heads so far up their tail holes, they can't hear me squawkin' anymore."

K'ai nodded, "Troubling, isn't it?"

"Mm-hmm. You wanna hear about it?"

"Indeed," K'ai said as he dipped his beak and gulped. He passed a knowing glance towards Shock, who returned it. "I'm gonna go have some fun with Shock first. When that's done, I'll send for you."

I nodded as he stepped off his perch and dropped a small copper in the nearby pail. I took another drink, but realized my presence hurt business. No one but K'ai would perch near a nosy sash like me. Besides, the perches at that trough hurt my feet. They were made for curled toes, not my flat webs, and I didn't want to rub wings with the crowd around the seabird troughs.

I walked outside as the band in the Murre began playing. Just as I stepped out, a scuffle erupted between a muddy and Flatwater, one of my newest deputies, a tough-as-barnacles gannet from Guangarten.

"Mister, you best just leave it!" Flatwater croaked.

My head feathers prickled. That muddy had a wicked look in his eyes and smiled defiantly. He was ready to kill but for the crowd all about. He bellowed with the raspy voice of an adolescent, "I'm the one gettin' cheated!"

"I'm not gonna tell you again!" said Flatwater.

At this point the crowd had stopped to watch at a respectable distance from the two. I spread my wings and flapped over to them.

"Who do you think you're talkin' to, Mudhead?" I demanded.

That wiped the smirk off the muddy's beak.

I doubled-down. "I think I heard you say you got cheated. But how can that be? Ain't legal for a youngster like you to be whorin' and gamblin', is it?"

The eagle's plumage settled down and his beak tilted down in submission.

"Don't you ever challenge my officers again or we'll pick your carcass so clean there'll be nothin' left for your releasing day. Now get the fuck outta here!"

With that, the eagle skulked to the edge of the Promenade and flew away.

"Geez, Flatwater, what the hell was that about?"

"The kid was playing bones in the Lusty and got caught marking tokens."

"Great gull, in the Lusty of all places. We mighta just saved his life." I shook my beak, "That den of muddies is way too loose allowin' subadults in there."

"Yes sir. The place has no standards."

I liked this deputy's grit. "You got some spines, like an urchin. But you know how close you were to having your gizzard ripped out?"

"Sorry, sir. He had a shorter wick than I expected."

"They all do right now, Flat, so be careful."

Flatwater lifted his head cockily and asked, "You don't think I can best him?"

"You gannets are scrappers. You were gonna go for the eyes, right?"

"Yep, just like you taught me."

"Good lad!" I squawked, then I put my beak up close to Flatwater's ear, "Just watch yourself, all right? We're short on beaks and these scumbags are figuring it out. I have business to attend to in the Murre, but you have any big issues, come get me."

Flatwater raised a wing in salute and then waddled slowly down the Promenade, so I returned to the Murre. Shock stood by the tunnel entrance in his collar and leash, preening his plumage. When he noticed me, he nodded me over.

The crowd respectfully parted as I made my way up the steps in the back. Snowy stood at the top of the stairs, wearing her signature smile. When she saw me, her smile faded, and she nodded placidly.

I gruffly tipped my bill.

Shock whispered to me, "Violet Room," and I nodded in reply.

My websteps echoed as I walked up the grimy brick tunnel. After passing a few doors, I beaked open the one with a violet painted on it. The hanging candle lantern burned low and cast a warm glow. K'ai lay sprawled out on his back on a nest of cedar bows. He smiled and nodded for me to enter, so I stepped inside and latched the door.

The eagle gestured to the drinking pale by the nest and said, "Help yourself."

"Don't mind if I do," I said as I dipped my beak.

"What's on your mind, officer?" he asked.

"The murders."

K'ai replied, "Crowny got ya spooked?"

I nodded, "It does. That, and I can't help but feel like there's a cover-up. First, Vasili, or at least his staff, and now P'tilo. I get they don't give a molted feather for some Low Town henny gettin' snuffed, but a deputy? One with connections to the Regional Governor even?"

K'ai said, "Take another drink."

I obeyed, and it made me feel better. So, I took another gulp and settled back on my haunches with a stress-relieving sigh.

"I'll see what I can do, officer." K'ai rolled over onto his feet, stood up, and roused his plumage.

I lingered on my haunches in exhaustion. I had only managed a quick nap in the past four bells

He said solemnly, "Officer, I didn't mean that in the way P'tilo does. I share your concerns. You're not alone. There's low-level unrest all over Volatus, but we're on it. Just in case, though, keep up appearances to P'tilo, but water down what you report and get creative. Copy me on everything, if you can. Don't expect much help from your official chain of command. Use alternate channels to get what you need, like coming to me, just for now. Take care of yourself and your officers."

His words were both relief and burden. My vision sharpened and my heart fluttered, and I knew it wasn't just the stiff drink. *What did he know?* I knew better than to press. He wasn't in the practice of telling me more than I needed to know.

I nodded, "Aye. The Starthener's Way."

K'ai chuckled, "That's the spirit, friend. By the way, I hear it's your hatchday."

I chuckled and shook my head, "What idiot told you that?" I felt woozy from the booze. "I'm a motherless cuss, hatched from a barnacle. Like all good bastards, I mark my years on Hatching Day, and that ain't for another three-quarter-moon."

K'ai laid a wing on my shoulder and said, "Well, no matter. I got you a gift anyway. Drink some more and wait here."

As he stepped out, I saw Silver waiting in the hall. K'ai winked at me and walked away as Silver's sweet floral aroma washed over me.

I closed my eyes as she latched the door and covered me in her soft feathers. No words were said as we locked beaks. It was more than duty for her and springtime lust for me. Our tongues were familiar and had thirsted all day to tangle together. Our bodies mimicked their dance, wrapping around each other in warm relief until we collapsed in the nest as one heaving pile of feathers.

I pulled my bill back and let Silver nibble my neck. I could let my guard down with her in private, and it was like a holiday. She whispered, "Spread your legs, dear, and loosen up. The world is far away, and I'm in charge here."

I closed my eyes and obeyed, pressing my body into her balled foot that had moved down to my belly. Great Gull she knew how to please me.

"Kiss me again," I begged.

We kissed again and she rubbed my body slower in tune with the juicy wrestling of our tongues. My head feathers prickled, and my back arched.

"Wow, you're needy tonight, aren't you?" she asked.

I looked into her amber eyes and nodded. "That, and you're just good at what you do, love."

She smiled with eyes that brimmed with adoration, and hooted softly, "Fuck me, Brant. Fuck me like you need me."

I preened a stray feather on her throat and said, "I'll fuck you, lass, like I love you."

Silver fluttered her white throat and gave the squeaky copulatory pleadings of a hen owl in the throes of nesting desire.

What followed was all and more I had come to expect from my secret owl mistress. It seemed that every time our bodies mingled, the passion was hotter and the rewards afterwards deeper, than the time before. Nature may have never meant for a gull and an owl to court, but joining souls with this life-hardened owl led to the same inevitable conclusion as true love always does: the joining of two bodies in a sweet crestwind of sounds and pleasures that carried me higher than any bird can ever hope to fly alone. Afterwards we lay cuddled in the afterglow of our passion.

"That... was incredible, my dear." I sighed.

"Darling," she said, "You really need to come see me more often this way."

I chuckled, "I wish I could. You know I do."

"What's the problem, then?" she asked. "Other officers have mates in the clear."

"You know the problem. It's dangerous."

Silver scoffed, "That's gullshit. You know I can handle myself. And I'm willing to take the risk. You deserve a warm owl to come home to every day."

"You're lovestruck dumb and blind!" I said callously. "They're knockin' hens off right here, right under my bill. I can't protect squat right now, and it's only a matter of time before everybirdy realizes it."

Silver's expression hardened. "You don't have to protect me. I did fine before we met."

"Would you give up bein' a who—." I corrected myself, "hostess?" It wasn't a new question, and I expected the same old answer. Imagine my surprise when she nodded this time.

I lifted my head. "Really?"

"If that's what it takes, yes. Would you quit the peacekeepers?"

I laughed, "And do what?"

"We could go back to Southreach. Or anywhere quiet where they need a good peacekeeper. You're the best I know, but it's only a matter of time before you get hurt or killed here. I don't think I could leave all I know to be with you, only to wonder if every day would be your last. Besides, could you really stay on the force here while all your stiff-tailed peacekeeper deputies knew you were bonded to a Low Town henny?"

She had me there. "No," I grumbled.

"Of course not. Too much pride in you sashes."

"Then what is this, my dear?" I said coldly as I surveyed the dim, dirty cave, which had fulfilled its purpose. *Fuck, what am I doing here?* I thought to myself. *I got my rocks off. I had fun. I have work to do.*

My mind edged towards the door, but Silver headed me off. She lowered her eyelids seductively and said, "Hey, forget about it. You got all damned day to be a ventsore out there. Stay with me tonight and let me soothe yours."

She slid her beak down between my thighs and worked my soft-ened vent. *Oh skies, she was good.* I sighed and regretted having raised my voice at her. I groaned and whispered, "All right, you convinced me." I jolted as a tingle of pleasure caused my tail to spread and trem-ble. She was the only one that could tell me what to do and I would obey. "I'll stay." And so, I did, all night long. The best rest I had en-joyed in more than a moon's time.

Chapter 20

Trouble

By Pepro

I jolted awake when Perry pecked me in the breast with his heavy bill. He whispered, "Time to wake up, sleepy beak." It was so dark, I scarcely made out the apologetic smirk on his face.

I had been hard asleep in a void without dreams. I looked out of the mouth of the cave to a spectacle that never got old. The river of the heavens spilled out above a calm, twinkling sea. The moon would rise soon, but for now, the distant specks of light owned the sky. A ghostly flotilla of Unawakened gulls dozed on the flat, starry water, and gentle waves lapped at the rocks.

Perry roused and preened in the dim starlight. I ached from the long flight, so I took time to stretch my cramping muscles.

Perry whispered, "You can stay here and sleep, if you want."

I replied, "No, I'd like to see this. I'm with ya all the way."

"All right, ready?" Perry asked.

I nodded.

"Follow close on my ass and stay low. Pretend I'm Sashya." he snickered.

"I don't see well in the dark."

Perry smiled, "You don't have to. I can pluck a baby squid out of the water on a cloudy night with these peepers. And these big nares ain't just for my good looks. I can smell danger."

I muttered, "Can you smell yourself?"

"Funny," Perry croaked sarcastically. He turned and walked up a slope at the back of the cave, his webs slipping in the gritty soil. The passage narrowed and we stooped, squeezed, and scratched our way through until it widened again, and we exited into the grass at the top of the cliff.

Perry swiveled his head around and sniffed the air. Then he shuffled along the ground on his breast, and I followed. The grass gave way to evergreen needles under a tight cluster of spruce trees. The dark was so deep that I didn't notice when Perry stopped, and I planted my face in his smelly underfluffies.

"Watch it," Perry groused.

I shook off the unpleasant aroma and vowed to dunk Perry into the sea for a quick bath, before we returned to Whiterock. I could scarcely see him, but from the grunting and sounds of stone moving, I surmised he was pushing a rock off his treasure. The dim shape of his head probed in a hole and then bolted back repeatedly as he swallowed each gold nugget. I counted silently up to twenty swallows. *Good! More than enough.* Perry slid the cover back in place and tucked bits of soil and spruce needles around the spot to hide it.

"Go back the way we came," he whispered.

We crawled back to the edge of the trees when Perry stopped. He paused long and sniffed the air.

I squirmed up beside him and asked, "What's up?"

"Stay still... The breeze has shifted to the west... I smell an eagle."

"Yeah, my ass I just dragged through the grass."

"No. Not you. Mingled with murre and blood. And something else. Something sweet."

I strained my eyes at the star-filled horizon and saw a silhouetted crowny heading straight for us.

Perry saw it too and whispered, "Freeze."

The eagle flapped casually past, too close for comfort over the small grove of trees. Starlight glinted of a dark battle helmet and talon sheaths, and I recognized the familiar breast shield of Mamyrskit. We both sighed relief as the bird passed out of sight without glancing at us.

"One of the Mams," Perry whispered. "Did you see the scar on his face?"

My beak went cold. "No. Across his left eye?"

"Yeah. You know him?"

"I've met him. An abrasive guard named Tulivor. Not a pleasant fellow, and I don't care to meet him again. Let's go."

"Wait. Did you smell the murre on him? And lavender and cedar too. It's just like the inside of a pleasure suite. The lavender is Snowy's signature scent."

"How can you smell all that over your own signature scent?"

"Enough with the rotten ass jokes or I'll upchuck this gold into the sea."

"All right, all right," I chuckled. "Just joking. You've got one hell of a sniffer."

"Trouble is, I never saw a crowny go down to the Murre."

"Yeah, Sashya and I heard him humping Princess Vouli the other day. What would he need with a brothel?"

"Hey, don't knock it till you've tried it, friend," he chided.

Just then a tumult of cackles and cries from hundreds of sea eagles rose from beyond the forested rise.

My eyes widened and my heart pounded. "I thought you said there was no settlement here."

Perry shivered, and whispered more quietly than before, "There's not. This can't be good."

"I don't like it either, but we should find out what's going on." I turned towards the source of the noise.

"Why?"

"You just said something's off. If so, we need to find out. And if it's just a bunch of drunk royals headed for the Bonding, maybe they'll share their seashine and a warm nest companion with you."

"Nice try, but I never met a crowny willing to share a drink, or a cloaca, with the likes of me."

Perry reluctantly followed me through the copse to the edge closest to the noise. From the thick grass, we peered over the center of the island, which was capped with meadows and occasional tall knobs of rock. The quarter moon hung low and filthy yellow. In the dim light, dotted across the black rocks of the island, at least a thousand eagles gathered. There were crownies, mottles, and baldies organized loosely into groups of ten. Some dozed and some preened, while others, dressed in armor, watched the cliffs attentively. A group of five scrabbled in mock combat while those around cheered their favorite. In another distant knot, a campfire burned and a crowny sang verses while her companions chirped the refrains and drank from a flask.

A familiar series of eagle whines caught my ear, and I followed the sound to a fire flickering at the base of three gray boulders. The crackling campfire covered the sound of our approach, but it didn't matter since Vouli and Tulivor were completely distracted with each other. In the shelter of the rocks, on a white sealskin pelt, the two crownies wrestled and chirped, beaks locked, and tail feathers entwined. Tulivor grunted and fanned his tail against Vouli's underfluffies, while she moaned and hugged him to herself with talons wrapped around his midsection.

My beak warmed as I witnessed the passion of the two eagles. I was embarrassed to be turned on and self-consciously glanced at Perry. He grinned back, and I suspect he enjoyed seeing me suffer.

Thankfully, it ended quickly, and they settled down into one of the sweetest spectacles of eagle tenderness I had seen since chickhood. Vouli nestled down with her face toward the fire while Tulivor tucked in next to her. They laid their heads on each other's backs and spoke quietly.

Vouli spoke in her thick accent, "You smell of murre blood, dearest. It's intoxicating."

Tulivor replied with a diabolical smirk, "I had to kill one that got in my way."

Vouli smiled, "And you ate her, didn't you?"

"I did, love. She was full of ripe yolks too. Very nourishing."

"Will anyone miss her?" Vouli asked as her smile melted into an expression of concern.

"Perhaps. But it doesn't matter. I left no one alive to tell the tale."

Vouli's smile returned. She nibbled beaks with Tulivor and their glistening tongues played together in the glow of the firelight.

Tulivor spoke lovingly, "I've thought of nothing but our secret bond-pledge, sweet mate. It made crossing the sea effortless."

Vouli replied, "Yes, a day felt much too long to be without you. Did you pass orders to the Red Talons?"

Tulivor responded, "Yes, and I sent them on their missions. They were eager. I envied them and wanted to taste more blood myself."

Vouli churred, "Mmm, yes, now that is a sight I look forward to. My handsome mate, with the blood of our foes on his feathers. But right now, this is more than enough. I've had such a burning need for you. My belly feathers have begun falling out and I'm getting my first brood patch."

"I felt it. Your belly feels ripe for laying lovely eggs, my dear. You will be a magnificent mother."

"And you will make a fine father, love. I look forward to laying royal eggs for us, continuing the line of Nest Tulis."

Tulivor beamed and inhaled with satisfaction as he nodded. "I am the luckiest tiercel alive, love, to be your mate. My love for you will never falter, never fail. I will be loyal to you to my last breath."

Vouli churred softly and said, "Your words, coming from anyone else, would simply be poetry, but I know they are true when they come from your beak. And our bonding is right, the uniting of two families, the old and the new, under a brand new banner. It's history, love. We're making history. It's intoxicating. I pledge my love to you for life. Our bond is secret, but binding all the same, and soon all will be made aware."

Tulivor flared his body feathers and uttered a lusty chirp. "Indeed, so shall it be. And whatever you desire of me, say it, and I will make it so." He hugged Vouli tight and they locked beaks again. In a quick moment, they pressed their bodies together again their moans and whines resumed.

I shook my head, marveling at their level of lust, and backed away, but Perry stayed, silhouetted in the glow of the firelight. I yanked on his tail, and he reluctantly scooted toward me. We kept low and quiet, eventually making it back to the cave without incident. The waning quarter moon lit up the ocean and reflected into the mouth of the cave so brightly, that we easily saw each other.

As we settled in, Perry mused, "Quite the show, wasn't it? I never saw two crownies carry on like that before. I guess they know how to have fun after all."

"Surprised me too. Those two are so unpleasant to everyone else."

"What are we gonna do?" Perry asked.

"I don't know. We still don't know what this is, but it can't be good if they're talking about murder and bathing in blood. We gotta tell somebody."

"Who?" Perry probed.

"Peacekeepers?" I weakly suggested.

Perry scoffed, "Sure, yeah, like they're gonna believe me, a burnout, and some strange eagle. 'Sides, they don't give a shit about Snowy's girls." Perry's voice turned melancholy, "Poor thing. I wonder who it was?"

"We can tell King Vasili."

"For all we know, he might be in on it. Obviously, his daughter's up to her nack in it."

"Hard to believe. He was amazingly friendly to us. But, fine, anyone else we could tell? Someone who would believe us and not kill us?"

Perry soberly replied, "Tuliann."

"Yeah, that's good! Tuliann. You wanted to see her again anyway, and she'd listen to you, right?"

"I don't know if she'll want to see me. But if she does, she knows that I would never lie to her."

I nodded, "Good. Any thoughts on how to get out of here without being seen?"

Perry peered out across the ocean to the west. There was not a breath of wind nor a cloud in the sky, but the flat horizon was bright, despite the moon being high in the east.

He sniffed the air and said, "Yeah, I think we're in luck. There's a fog bank way out there already, and the air is cooling down. Gonna be fog everywhere by dawn. We'll have to drop down till our bellies are touching the waves to see much more than five wingspans, that's how thick it's gonna be. Remember bumping into my butt earlier?"

"Yeah," I said with chagrin.

"That's how close you'll need to follow tomorrow."

"Wonderful."

"We get out five or so kilometers, and we can rise back up above it, and nobody will catch us by then. Won't be more than a dozen wingspans thick probably. Later in the day we'll be fightin' squalls and westerlies."

"Great. This is just getting better all the time." I pulled a foot up into my fluff and covered my perching foot with the rest of my belly feathers. It would be hard to sleep, but I needed it before the long flight back to Whiterock.

"I gotta tell ya," Perry moaned. "I wish you guys hadn't pulled me out of that pleasure suite. I could be buzzed and snuggled up between the sweet-smellin' tails of a trio of warm hennies. Instead, here I am, scared, head hurtin', and I'm pretty sure my dear Tu is in danger."

I replied, "But at least you know. Would you rather not know, and have her fly right into whatever spiderweb this is?"

"Ya got me there. Damn, though, this would be a lot easier to take if I had a drink. Or some kinnikinnick smudge."

"Mm-hmm, I might just agree with you there, Perry. Good thing we don't."

I passed the remainder of the night drifting in and out of consciousness. I thought of Sashya, and hoped he was safe and having a good time. But I knew he would be missing me, just as I missed him. We had only confessed our love to each other two days before, but amidst the nonstop action of our trip, it felt like a quarter-moon had passed. I ached to wrap my wings around him and see his smiling eyes. I wanted to preen that cute white face and taste his kisses.

When actual sleep eluded me, I alert-slept, resting half my mind while keeping one eye partway open. Perry did the same, I think, for he never snored again like he had earlier. Knowing there were eagles, with murderous intent, just wing flaps away was too disconcerting for the both of us. Sometimes I heard the gold nuggets in Perry's gizzard tumble in time with the contractions of his gut. It reminded me of the precious little time we had to get it back to Kor.

Soon the darkness deepened outside as the moon disappeared, and the air grew damp and heavy. The foggy blue-gray dawn proved Perry's weather predictions were spot-on accurate. The thought of swimming through the soupy air, blind and unfamiliar with the area, made me dizzy. I swallowed and straightened up, telling myself that I had no choice but to trust this old seabird, that had only yesterday crawled out of his own drunken vomit.

Perry roused, and the warm smell of fresh guano filled our little cave, but it didn't bother me. I would have gladly stayed there with all of Perry's sour odors than dive into the murky air outside. We both preened in preparation for the flight, as the space outside our cave brightened.

Perry shuffled to the front of the cave and looked at me with a confident little smile. He whispered, "I think it's time. Remember, stick to my tail. Like beak right in it. I don't want to lose you. You ready?"

"I think so."

Perry said, "For Sashya."

I smiled, "For Tuliann."

Perry nodded and stepped to the cliff edge, and I pushed up right behind him, my breast touching his back. He leaped out into the gray nothing, and I fell with him. He kept his wings partially folded like a falcon in a stoop and dragged his pink webs in the air to steer. I did the same and stayed tight behind him.

My heart raced as we plunged a hundred meters through gray mist. It was the oddest sensation to feel weightless with no visual references. I knew I was falling, and yet I couldn't tell which way was up or down, or whether I was turning. I hurtled toward the invisible sea and fought my instincts that told me to spread my wings or die. I clenched my beak and stared at the white tail before me for cues of the next maneuver.

Perry might have been counting the seconds, or maybe his sensitive nares could smell the cooler, briny surface of the sea. Whatever the case, he fanned his tail, and I got the signal. We both spread our wings in unison and tucked our legs. My shoulders strained and blood surged into my belly with the change in momentum. Our wingtips buzzed, and our breasts lightly brushed the smooth surface of the sea as we leveled off.

I'm not sure if it was the blood draining from my brain, or the giddy excitement of narrowly missing death, but I had a mighty urge to burst out laughing. Within a half wingspan of the surface, the fog thinned and allowed me to see farther. We made it through the toughest part, and I felt lucky to be alive.

Then I heard whizzing wings behind me. The stroke frequency was unmistakable for another eagle but sounded too quick to be a crowny.

My heart sank as a male mottle screeched, "Spies ho! I found them!"

Another voice, a female bald eagle, chirped back, "Get them!"

Perry flapped his gangly wings harder, and I followed suit, but the eagle wings grew louder behind me. So close to the water, all it would have taken was one half-hearted blow, and I would have gone into the ocean, and been of no more use to Perry. One of us needed to make it.

I said to Perry, hopefully only loud enough for him to hear, "Keep going, ya salty seabird. Save the day while I cover for ya."

"No! Pepro, don't!"

"Tell Sash I love him." I chirped as I veered up into the fog and flapped noisily to draw my pursuer's attention. Their wingtips buzzed with the strain of changing direction, and I detected the metallic clink of battle claws.

At that moment I wished I had bothered bringing my half-finished set to even the odds. But a bird weighed down with armor and weapons had disadvantages. I would be more vulnerable, but also more agile. And my legs were strong from pounding iron, so one blow could be enough to down an enemy, if I were to land a good one.

I curved up higher in the fog, and my pursuer grunted with effort to follow. The mist brightened around me, and I skimmed the top of the fog bank. The adult baldy circled a hundred strokes away and turned toward me. Beneath me, I felt the dark shadow of my pursuer rising and saw a glint of steel.

I arced downward behind my pursuer's shape, and he chirped with shock as I pounded my clenched feet into his forewing. It snapped, and he cried out in terrible pain. He spun down into the fog, and I regained precious airspeed with a steep glide.

The pursuer chittered sickeningly as he plunged beneath the water, with a deep plunk that told me his armor pulled him straight to the bottom.

Another mottle squawked, "Keelan! That you?"

A third warrior? I knew the baldy was on their way and were likely the leader of the two mottles, so I couldn't count on them being so gullible as the one I just struck.

I turned toward the confused voice and flattened my glide. I easily tracked the clinking of his claws and his labored breaths, but this time my luck had run out. I came in level across his left wing, and he rolled and flashed his steely claws. I tumbled just out of his reach, and he couldn't engage his hooks, yet as I climbed, pain stabbed my right leg, and something wet flowed between my toes. I couldn't spare a shred of concentration to check the severity of the wound and focused on climbing instead.

The baldy's shadow crossed my back. They were right above the fog, pinning me between themselves and their remaining companion. Distance had become my best strategy, so I churned my wings harder and sped in the direction I believed would lead directly away from the island.

The air darkened around me, and I heard the vibrations of feathers not my own. I flapped with all my strength, but the tinkling of claws grew in my ears. I glanced back, and the baldy was upon me.

Her steel claws opened, and I pulled a wing in to spin myself around and engage her talons before they grasped me. Pain shot up my legs as we swung into a flat spin, our wings flung back by the whirling force.

"Pepro?" the attacker chirped, as her feet relaxed.

The voice was familiar. It was the voice that had sung *Song of the Sea* to me as an eaglet. The one who had inspired me with stories of our beloved warrior Seeangela. The one whose heartbeat had nurtured me in the egg.

I clung hard and pulled myself against the forces to grasp her helmet strap in my beak and rip it asunder. As the helmet tumbled away, it revealed the face of my mother. Her eyes were paler, the edges darker, but the same small scar on the left side of her beak was there, and the voice was unmistakable.

"Do you have him?" shrieked the last mottle.

"Let Go," She said calmly. "Fly fast and find K'ai." She smiled with the pent-up pride of five years, then shook loose of my stunned grip, and disappeared into the fog.

"Wait!" I called, but she was gone. A moment later I heard clattering claws mingled with a mottled's curses, which ended abruptly with a *Kerplunk!* into the sea.

My vision blurred with tears, and questions darted in my head like a school of herring terrified by a shadow. I dropped back to the surface, flew on with the assistance of ground effect, and checked my leg. My left foot barely bled. But my right foot was drenched in bright blood and continued dripping. But there was nothing I could do until I reached land.

When I emerged from the fog, the sun stood high behind me, and clouds were high before me. All around me lay open ocean and an empty horizon. The bleeding stopped after a long while, leaving me weak and thirsty. There were no pursuers, and, by the position of the sun, I was heading west. I only hoped I had the strength to make it all the way to land.

I reviewed my mother's face over and over in my mind. *It had to be her. But what was she doing with the Mamyrskins? Why did she let me go? Why did she turn and defend me?*

I had no answers, though obviously she wasn't like the rest. What I did know for certain, though, and all that mattered, was *my mother lived!* I didn't know who K'ai was, but I would seek him out, if I made it back. And I would do everything to make it back. There was an owl waiting for me who loved me, and he was all the reason I needed.

I closed my eyes and imagined his face at our reunion. His dark eyes set in that sweet pale face, and his delicate pink beak that smiled just for me. The picture of him thrilled me, despite the weakness that crept into my veins. My vision blurred, from tears or something else, I could not tell. I lost track of time amidst the relentless waves, only barely noticing that they were getting closer under me, but my numb wings would not push any harder. The gray sky and gray waters closed in around me, and I gave into their euphoric warmth, and found rest at last.

Chapter 21

Delivery

By Nyx

The day had passed slowly by. I ripped Sashya away from the Avian Haven for a little while at daybreak and took him down to Market Square and the Flockplace, just as business heated up. He marveled at the terraces on terraces of eateries, traders, grocers, prey-sellers, and tradesmen. He even had a conversation with a delightful young red-tail who had a jewelry shop. She was from Galinta and studied under Kor a few years prior.

We toured the park and pools where the royal bonding would take place in little more than a quarter-moon and enjoyed special treats of roasted grasshoppers. We took some time to wash and tend our feathers at the bathhouse. We could have used the bathing pool at the Avian Haven, but I wanted to avoid returning Sashya there as long as possible. Despite all the distractions, Sashya's eyes were never far from the blue horizon of the sea, searching for familiar eagle wings.

In the afternoon, we checked in with Miss Penelope, who was all a-frazzle with her bonding day preparations. We helped with a few things, and it helped distract Sashya, but he became more distant as the day dragged closer to three bells. Soon we excused ourselves and waited back at our room for Perry and Pepro to return.

I was inside when Sashya first spotted Perry's long white wings, tilting to and fro as he worked the headwinds over the frothy sea. The gray sky obscured the afternoon sun, and streamers of thin rain hung like tendrils under the darkest clouds.

"I see Perry!" came Sashya's words, clearly and triumphantly from the landing ledge.

I sighed and closed my eyes, thankful that the wait was over. "And Pepro?" No response came for far too many heartbeats. "Sashya? Do you see Pepro?" With still no reply, I stepped out onto the platform and Sashya had frozen stiff as he stared at the tossing waves. Perry crested the cliffs and flapped hard toward us.

"Sashya?" I asked gently as I walked to his side. His eyes were blank black orbs, searching earnestly through the clouds of seabirds.

"Do you see him?" Sashya's voice cracked with stifled panic.

"No, I don't." I placed a gentle wing on his shoulders. "Just wait. Perry will explain I'm sure."

The big white bird disappeared behind the ruins briefly, then soared up quickly on a lifting breeze, cleared the jagged skyline, and pulled his wings into a downward sweeping curve to drop abruptly, and come to a graceful stop on the ledge. His moist eyes and drooping wings told us what his shaking bill could not utter.

I pulled Sashya to me in a tight hug, and stared Perry in the face, my vision blurred from tears. "What happened?"

Perry choked on the words, "He turned and fought... to save me. To make sure I made it back with the gold. And with what we saw." He dropped his head, and a stream of tears and nasal salt solution trickled down his beak. "I'm so sorry."

Sashya shook and sobbed in my feathers.

I asked, "Dammit Perry, be plain. Is Pepro dead?"

Perry glumly replied, "I don't know."

"What did you see?"

Perry lifted his head and swallowed, "I dare not say out here. Nor anywhere in this town out loud."

Sprinkles of light rain pattered the landing ledge, and I pulled Sashya toward the door. "Come on, Perry. You must be starving. Eat, rest, and tell us what happened."

Perry didn't eat right away. Instead, he disgorged his cargo of gold into a chamber pot. Sashya stared blankly at the floor, not caring to survey the glittering nuggets, or move away from the assaulting odor.

When Perry had finished unloading, I pointed towards a seaweed-wrapped parcel of fish, but he glumly surveyed Sashya instead, and said, "Thank you, Nyx, but I'm not hungry right now. I'll take some water though."

When Perry had slaked his thirst, we three snuggled together in a nest in the back as wind and rain lashed at the shuttered windows. We checked that all the toilet chutes were secure, and Perry whispered to

Sashya and I what had taken place. As Perry finished his story, and it became clear that Perry didn't know exactly what happened to Pepro, I tried to cheer Sashya up.

"Sash," I said, "Pep is a tough bird. You've seen him pound steel with those thick feet of his. He can crack heads too."

Sashya quietly said, "I hope so." He turned to Perry and asked, "How long do you think it might take for him to get back?"

I covered Sashya's face in my breast feathers to conceal the doubt I saw in Perry's dark eyes. He hated the task of estimating the timing of something he saw slim chance of ever happening. I shot him a look that I hoped would urge him to at least fake some optimism.

Perry sighed heavily and said, "He was strong as a gannet on the way out. Would've beat me there, 'cept my wings work better in headwinds. I'm sure he'll be along this evening, if he comes straight back."

I shook my head slowly and nodded my beak upwards.

Perry revised himself, "Uh, but if he gets blown off course, well, it could take a couple of days. This one time I got blown all the way down to..."

I cut him off, "That's good! Hear that, Sash? Don't lose heart!"

Sashya backed away and looked towards the closed front door as it rattled with the squall, as if he expected Pepro to burst in. He walked to the door, pressed his head to it, and quelled its rattling. He closed his eyes and listened, or hoped, with all his might.

Perry whispered to me, "I'm sorry to break his heart. I'm sorry I didn't make the news sweeter."

A couple of days ago, I had no patience for Perry, but in this matter, he hadn't done anything wrong. He was sober, sensitive, and contrite.

I said quietly, "It's all right, Perry. There's no easy way to break news like this. It's not your fault that you were attacked and Pepro turned back." I fluffed my head feathers and softened my gaze. "Look, Perry, I was unfair to you the other day. You were gross and annoying, but I made snap judgments before I knew all the facts. Let's just say the past few days have opened my eyes to a lot of things I chose not to see before."

Perry's eyes creased as though smiling, and he lifted his big pink bill. "I appreciate that, Nyx. It takes a strong bird to admit faults. You know, I've not known you long, but you remind me a lot of Tuliann. She was hatched to be a leader. Heart of fire. Mind like a sharp blade.

Eyes that see through whatever mask you're wearing. And ears that hear your soul. She's the most selfless bird I know. I see those qualities in you too."

My beak warmed and I looked away, surprised by Perry's poetry. I looked down to steel my emotions, and then back into his eyes. "What a nice thing to say, Perry."

"The sea's a big place. Lots of space to think on faces you see and what they're saying without words."

I nodded, "I'll bet it makes you a decent judge of character then. But speaking of Tuliann, maybe we should pass this news on to her?"

Perry shuffled back in the nest, like a piece of sharp straw had poked his skin.

"What?" I asked. "You just said she was a good listener, right?"

"She is. And I agree, she's the one we should tell before anyone else, but I don't know if she'll even see me." Perry's voice cracked, "Or, whether I could speak in her presence. I just don't know if I can do it."

I surrounded Perry's head in my wings, and pulled his bill close to mine.

"Look, dear. You just said the sweetest things to me. Don't spoil it by backing down now. If what you say is true, she won't refuse a meeting. I think I'm seeing, now, what she fell in love with years ago."

As I finished those words, Perry relaxed and whispered, "Maybe you're right. Okay," he nodded, "I'll send a request to see her tonight."

I remembered, then, that I had somber news of my own for Perry. "Also, something else tragic happened while you were away."

Perry's shoulders stiffened.

I said contritely, "Lara was murdered."

He pulled away, his bill drained of color. "That's who that crowny killed!"

"Ano too."

"Great Skies!"

"I'm so sorry, dear. She seemed like a nice hen."

"Lara was the sweetest to me. One of the few that put up with all my flaws and still wore a smile the whole time. I paid her well, but somehow, I don't know, I guess I wondered if she liked me for more than the money."

"She said some sweet things about you after you left the pleasure chamber, you know. Said you treated her well. Sounded affectionate."

Perry's sooty eye feathers wrinkled with grief. He half chuckled, half pouted as a tear escaped. He replied, "She was my favorite. Her common voice was like rubbing barnacles on your ears, but when I handled her right, she sang sweeter than a skylark. I loved bringing out her carefree side. She turned into a real classy lady in those moments."

My mind rolled back to the stifling, reeking pleasure suite and the image of the black and white murre mopping up Perry's mess. She looked tired and ragged, bent over with a sponge in her beak, and her hind feathers damp and ruffled from gratifying Perry. It was not a classy image, and yet, she had been cheerful. Perry was right, her voice was not the sweetest, but it had softened on the topic of Perry, and his lost courtship of Tuliann. I silently affirmed that there was more to Perry and the working hens than I ever would have admitted a few days ago.

Perry sniffled and asked, "Do you know when the releasing will happen?"

"Tonight, at four bells. They waited, hoping you would attend. Snowy thought you might like to bear Lara to the releasing circle."

"I would." He wiped his eyes with the bend of a wing. "Thanks, Nyx."

I pulled him into a hug. "No problem, Perry. You need anything, don't wonder where to turn, bring it to us. We're a flock now."

Chapter 22

Releasing

By Nyx

Just past the peacekeeper citadel at the north end of Low Town, before the bluffs turned west and curved down to North Beach, lay a modest hill of thick green grass. There were three circles of stones, two wingspans wide, and piled half a wingspan high. They created crude plinths crowned with charred wood and ash, the remains of previous releasing pyres. I had seen finer releasing circles both here and in Waycliffs, but these were free for anyone to use and, as I soon realized, often multiple releasings were held simultaneously in the same fires, since building one was difficult for most birds.

But then, a releasing is not meant to be a lone undertaking anyway. It was as much a celebration of life, as it was a somber reckoning of loss. In Waycliffs, releasings were attended by anyone in the community, whether they knew the departed well or not. We shared food, warmth, joy, and sadness, as a community in both life and in death. In a place as stratified as Whiterock, though, there were barriers that only bent slightly during events of bereavement. The Uppers had their social circles which did not intersect with those in Low Town, at least not publicly, even with something as communal as a releasing. And so, Lara would depart from a humble releasing Circle, out of sight of higher society, just as she was in life.

We flew out to the site by the light of the moon at four bells. Perry carried Lara in a tightly wrapped linen bundle that smelled of cedar and lemongrass, a scent she had told Perry she most adored. Despite a long evening of dancing, feasting, and drinking at the Musky Murre, Perry flew steady and there were no alcohol vapors in his wake. The heartiest attendees, who could still fly, flowed behind us in a ribbon at least two hundred birds strong, and they carried parcels of drink, food, or fuel for the fire. The flock grew larger the farther along we flew.

Sashya flapped along at my wingside with a tubular ember case slung over his back. He had been quiet all evening and I knew it was because his breast was empty. His heart had flown far away, floating over the moonlit sea in search of Pepro. I bought rodents and sparrows in town for the releasing feast and had to practically force Sashya to eat one. They were nice and fat and Sashya thanked me, but his dark eyes reflected no joy.

Miss Penelope helped us send an urgent message to Miss Tuli-ann, and the messenger had returned with an affirmative reply that we would be contacted later that night. We bade them to come find us at the Musky Murre or the releasing circles, however late, but as the hours wore on without word, and there was still no sign of Pepro, anxiety ate at my gizzard, and I decided I would have to bypass protocol and go see Tuliann myself. Though customary to see a releasing through to dawn, I would slip out once the fires were lit, and Perry had crested the tallest waves of his grief.

As we descended around the site, we found a cluster of peacekeeper gulls, gannets, puffins, and eagles already using one of the circles. Brant cocked an eye towards us as we landed at another. A heap of dry grass had already been piled in the circle, trapped in place by a lattice of dry sticks.

Snowy asked aloud, "Does anyone know if someone else planned to use this circle tonight?"

A gull stepped forward and said, "Ma'am, the peacekeepers left that for you."

Snowy blinked her wide eyes and swiveled her head to the crowd of red-sashed birds barely twenty wingbeats away. Brant stared back, head high. He nodded solemnly and then turned back to his gathering.

I glanced at the stern gull, sternly poised in the firelight. A couple days before, I thought him to be a self-serving, power-hungry blemish on our society. But I had learned a lot since then. Hanging around Low Town a couple of days had changed me, so I could only imagine what living in it would do, much less trying to keep order against overwhelming odds, day in and day out. And yet he still surprised me with moments of likability. Brant was still a flaming ventsore, but he had earned my respect.

Silver muttered, "See? I told you that salty fuck has a heart after all."

Snowy shook her head and said, "Please don't tell me I'm gonna have to start liking him."

I asked, "Are they releasing Ano tonight too then?"

Silver nodded, "Mhmm. Hard to believe that little guy had friends, but those peacekeepers stick pretty tight. I guess even a vent stain like him deserves a friendly releasing."

Snowy said, "Silver, why don't you get a few folks from the crowd and take some seaberry wine and capelin over to 'em. Let 'em know we appreciate the gesture."

Silver nodded with a subtle grin on her beak corners and turned away to see to Snowy's request. Meanwhile, Perry placed Lara atop the firewood, and we piled more around her. Sashya expertly guided the building of the fire, his experience as a blacksmith's apprentice being helpful for the occasion. Once completed to his satisfaction, he opened the small wooden cylinder he carried, pulled out some cattail fluff from the top, and dropped a small smoldering coal into the heart of the softest tinder. We beat our wings and sang the Lighting Song, and no sooner had we hit the refrain than the flames leapt to life.

As the fire grew and surrounded Lara's bundle, and the song faded, Perry stepped atop a prominent boulder and lifted his huge wings to hush the flock. He cleared his throat and looked down as though strengthening his resolve to speak. "Lara was special to all of us. I guess I'm speaking first because I was the last to be with her in friendship. I'm lucky to have been the last to give her pleasure, to see joy light up her eyes. We had a good time, and I loved her to the last drop. I think I'm not bragging when I say I made her feel as treasured as a big stinky bird can."

A few seabird whistles and soft chuckles rose around us.

Perry lifted his beak to the stars as glowing embers rose high, and said in a voice wet with grief, "Float among the stars, my sweet hen."

A chorus of sharply agreeing squawks rose from the flock in reply, and Perry stepped down from the stone. Snowy spoke next and told the tale of how Lara had come to work for her, as well as some of the fun times, and the hard times, they had weathered together. As she spoke of her friend, a hard lump of loss built in my chest. Everyone in attendance missed her for what she brought into their lives, but I mourned the missed opportunity of knowing her, or Snowy, despite the option being there at every visit I made to Whiterock, which were numerous. I took a drink from a bladder of wine that made the rounds, and let the warmth chase the cold regret from my heart.

As Snowy finished, I hopped onto the rock and all the beaks turned my way. "I had lots of chances to know Lara. Or Snowy. Or any of you. I missed out. But, like they say where I'm from, 'No sense in bathing in tears when fresh water is nearby.' Lara had some great friends." I focused on Snowy's glistening yellow eyes and said, "I'm lucky to count myself among you."

The flock squawked in agreement, and as I stepped down, Snowy embraced me. Many of the other birds also offered hugs and words of welcome. The heartfelt speeches, songs, and feasting continued into a blur of sleeplessness and alcohol until I felt a cold bill poke my chest. It was Perry, and Brant was by his side. I looked about and realized I had fallen asleep on the stack of warm stones around the fire. The flock had thinned, but there were still at least fifty there.

"Can you fly?" Perry asked.

I stood and roused, annoyed at myself for having fallen asleep. "Yes! I'm not drunk, just sleepy."

Brant guffawed.

"Everything okay? What's going on?" I asked.

"Brant's here to take us to a meeting with Tuliann."

I bowed down and stretched my wings over my back, "Where's Sashya?"

Perry shook his head, "Don't know. Lost track of him a while ago."

I nodded, "Poor guy said he wouldn't stay too long. Probably went back to the Haven to be alone."

Brant cleared his throat impatiently.

I got the message. "Officer, can you give us just a few moments?"

Brant nodded, "But only a few. The others are on their way already."

As Brant walked away and chatted with Snowy, I spoke quietly to Perry. He was trembling but I pretended not to notice. "I can't believe how well you're holding up. Clear-eyed, clear-voiced. But you're about to meet an ex-lover. Are you gonna be okay."

Perry nodded, "I was doing fine, until Brant showed up and I realized I'd soon be face to face with Tu."

I put my wing on his shoulder, "If she's half the lady everyone says she is, she'll see how brave you are and appreciate what you're doing. You'll be fine, and I'll be right there with ya."

He sighed raggedly and nodded.

Snowy walked up to us, having left Brant chatting with others. She quietly said, "Why does it take death to bring out the civility in these ventholes?"

"That's one of my favorite things about a releasing," I said. "Everyone lets their guard down, at least for one night."

Perry apologized to Snowy, "Sorry we have to leave before you release Lara's down."

Snowy nodded, "Must be important."

I muttered, "You have no idea."

Snowy's eyes were two half moons, her upper lids heavy with concern. "You be careful." She whispered as she gave my beak a brief nuzzle. "Come back by if you get done before dawn."

Perry nodded, "We will."

Brant led us up into the sky and we flew on towards the Citadel. But after a kilometer, he bade us to fly silently, keep our eyes peeled for followers, and to stick to his tail. We turned west and crossed the breadth of Whiterock until we reached Rice Lake behind town. Then we turned south and followed the long, shallow lake as it curved around town and ended at the generator plant.

Tuliann

Chapter 23

Guliann

By Nyx

As we approached the dam, Brant whispered to us, "We'll be diving down the other side and taking a hard left. Watch close!"

I followed with ease, but Perry struggled with the quick maneuvers on his huge wings. Brant and I landed gracefully on a water splashed ledge, slick with algae, but Perry had no time to slow his lumbering bulk. He croaked a panicked warning, but it came too late, and he slammed into Brant's backside. The two slid through the muck and crashed into a heap of paddling feet and tangled wings.

Brant squawked, "Get the hell off me you gurry-stinkin' oaf!"

Perry flailed in embarrassment as he struggled to untangle his lanky wings from Brant's. Brant found his footing and scooted away quickly as though escaping a nest full of lice. He shook his feathers and adjusted his folded wings. His white breast and red sash were smeared with dark streaks of algae slime.

The gull whispered harshly, barely audible over the splashing water, "Great! Look at this mess. Gull-damn clumsy fool."

"Sorry, sir, but you didn't give me enough room to stop! I can clean you up."

I bit my tongue to suppress a laugh as Brant shook his beak and emphatically replied, "Fuck no! You keep your stinkin' beak away from my feathers."

After the two sorted themselves out, we crept along the dark ledge toward the cliff until we came to an Apterian passageway. As with many such corridors, it had been sealed off with accrement, and a smaller doorway created for bird-kind. That one had a tight iron door, and Brant used a precise pattern of pecks to alert a guard on the other side, after which a latch scraped, and the door swung outward.

The flickering torch in the corridor illuminated the white and gray frame of Foamy. We stepped inside and he closed and latched the door behind us. The stony Apterian passageway stretched before us, and I caught a glimpse of an immaculately plumed male bald eagle gazing back at us from a larger space at the end.

Foamy said to Brant, "Cap, Tuliann and K'ai are already here."

Perry froze and blocked our progress down the hallway.

Brant squawked, "Why'd you stop? Move, ya feathered lump o' lard!"

I shot Brant the same look I gave when I snapped the necks of prey, and growled, "Give us a moment!" He adjusted his folded wings and grumbled.

Perry's wingtips shivered, and his heart thumped loudly. I whispered to him, "Never mind that fish licker. He doesn't know."

"Know what?" Brant asked indignantly.

Perry whispered back, "I can't move. I. She?"

"Perry, it's gonna be fine. You love her enough to come here and warn her, right?"

Brant cocked his head and looked at Foamy who shrugged.

Perry nodded and sighed.

"Come on," I said. "I'll take the lead. Hide behind me if you like."

"Thanks, Nyx." He replied.

I slipped past and we slowly made our way down the passage in small steps. As the room at the end of the hallway came into view, the bald eagle straightened up and prepared to greet us. A few steps away stood a finely preened female mottle with shocking gold eyes. Her head feathers flared, and her eyes relaxed as a smile crossed the corners of her beak.

The bald eagle spoke, "Nyx of Waycliff's is it? I am K'ai, chief investigator assigned to Waystar region."

I smiled and strode forward, "Pleased to meet you, K'ai. Funny our paths have never crossed before, what with my involvement on the council."

K'ai nodded, "Yes, well I keep a low profile, and it's rare that Volatian internal security needs to cross paths with Regional or City politics, I'm pleased to say."

I chuckled, "Lucky you!"

K'ai nodded to the mottle and said, "Please, allow me to introduce

Miss Tuliann of Whiterock, soon to be Queen of Mamyrskit."

Tuliann's eyes were not on us, but were instead fixed upon the sheepish albatross, absurdly cowering behind me. Perry's eyes locked to hers, and lingered there as the two assessed the new spots and lines in each other's irises and beaks. Ten years was a long time for close friends to not see each other, much more for two lovers. Right or wrong, any bird in Whiterock of a lesser station than Tuliann's would have likely disregarded a creature as pathetic as Perry. But she displayed no reservations as she stepped towards him, and declared, "Perry, my sweet treasure-hunter!"

Perry winced as she wrapped her wings around him in a hug. But then he relaxed and pressed into her embrace. He couldn't bring his wings all the way around in the space available, but he half enclosed her in his wing-bends to reciprocate the warm greeting.

She said to him, "I had no idea you would be here. It's so good to see you!"

Perry's beak blushed, and his eyes smiled in bliss. "Aww, precious Tu, it's good to see you too!"

Brant and Foamy gawked, unable to believe their eyes and ears.

Tuliann rocked Perry gently, "You look good, Perr."

Perry replied, "And you look magnificent, dear. The years have made your eyes bright as sparkles on the sea."

She whispered, "Thank you. I know the years have been hard on you. You can't know how much I've regretted letting my parents get between us."

"I heard they passed on. I'm very sorry." Perry replied.

"Thank you, dear." Tuliann stepped back, her pupils shrank, and her beak blushed with stirred emotion.

Perry continued, "I'm so proud of all you've accomplished, dear. And Vasili is a good match. I'm so very happy for you. Mamyrskit will be fortunate to have you for their queen."

Tuliann nodded and smiled in the glow of Perry's praise.

Perry added, "I have a gift for you and your betrothed. Pardon, love..." Perry's neck widened, and he emitted a soft belch as he lowered his head. To Tuliann's credit, she was unfazed by Perry's muffled disgorgement. When he lifted his beak, it contained a transparent, glittering gemstone. I quickly surmised it to be the diamond that Pepro had mentioned, but which I had not had privilege to see until now.

Despite riding in what must have been the foulest of purses, its facets dazzled with reflected light. He rested the jewel on the floor at Tuliann's feet.

Tuliann's eyes sparkled with recognition. She said in amazement, "It's the diamond you offered to me for our bonding. Perry! This is too much."

"You must take it. Sell it for the Institute. Or wear it like royalty. It was always meant for you, and you will make me unimaginably happy if you accept it."

Tuliann picked up the diamond and dropped it into a satchel under her left wing, then pressed her beak to Perry's and said, "Thank you. I will cherish it always."

K'ai smiled knowingly the entire time and Tuliann finally noticed. She cocked her head towards him and said, "K'ai, old friend, you are cunning as a raven! You knew Perry was coming, didn't you?"

"Guilty!" K'ai confirmed. "And seeing the effect on you was priceless!"

Tuliann and K'ai chuckled, and Perry smiled his now-crimson beak. Brant and Foamy smiled politely, scarcely hiding their shock. Perry had been a shit-stain on the boardwalk the day prior, but that night he rubbed beaks with high society. I couldn't wait to tell Snowy about the painful grin on Brant's face when he came to be absolutely outclassed by Perry.

Miss Tuliann returned her gaze to Perry, "You must attend the bonding. I want you to be bearer of the rings."

Perry's eyes widened, and then he closed them tight and bowed his head, "Of course, Tu. It's an honor I don't deserve, but I will do anything for you, dear. Thank you!"

"Nonsense, love, the honor is ours. You were the first to unlock my heart, and you still hold a key. But first, please tell me what's troubling you. I can't believe that we interrupted two releasings and pulled K'ai out of his roost at this hour for a reunion, as pleasant as it is."

Perry shook his head solemnly. "No, Tu. You, and maybe all Whiterock, are in great danger." As Perry laid down all he and Pepro witnessed, Tuliann became increasingly pensive, as though comparing all she heard against her extensive memory of interactions with the Mamyrskins. K'ai's smile faded and his face showed no emotion. Foamy stood stiff and attentive, while Brant grumped and cussed at each dangerous peak in the tale.

When Perry finished, K'ai asked, "Did you see any of the guards that pursued you?"

Perry shook his head, "Sorry, no. When Pepro doubled back, we were still in the fog."

K'ai asked, "Did you hear them call out? Any names?"

Perry replied, "I'd wager the one that screamed 'Get them!' was a female baldy, and there was at least one male mottle that sounded like he took a painful beating. Only name I heard was Keelan."

I clutched the gritty floor in my talons and my heart raced as I imagined Pepro fighting back. I muttered, "Good for you, Pep."

K'ai asked me, "How well can Pepro fight? Did Perro teach him any aerial combat?"

"You knew his Uncle Perro?" I asked.

"Indeed."

"Well, he taught him to hunt and fish. Pepro's Wander took him all around Volatus and, by the sound of it, he knew all he needed to know to survive. But are you saying that Perro was a warrior? I didn't think he was old enough to have served in war."

K'ai turned to Foamy and said, "Sargent, can you excuse us for a little bit?"

Brant stopped him, "Sir, whatever you're gonna say, Foamy can hear it too. He knows everything I know, written or not, and he's key to continuity if I ever fall in the line of duty."

K'ai nodded, "Not a word of this outside these walls, especially not to anyone not here in this room. First, let's clear up the questions on your faces, Perry and Nyx. You've heard of the Tacet Carceris, have you not?"

I nodded. "More rumors than facts, I'm afraid. They're sort of peacekeepers that act in secret, and report to the Volatian Executive Council, right?"

Perry guffawed, "Down in Low Town, people think the T. C. isn't real. Just fables and gossip to keep criminals guessin' who they can trust."

Brant chuckled.

K'ai's smile returned, "What do you think of that, Brant?"

"If only it were so easy." Brant replied. "But, yeah, we might spread some rumors from time to time. Luu's good at cookin' up more than just strong waybrew."

K'ai chuckled, "I assure you, Perry, the T. C. is real, and very active, particularly of late. As you're probably aware, Miss Nyx, there is growing unrest. Perro knew this all too well. So did Pepro's parents, Sol and Te."

My jaw dropped, "They were operatives?"

K'ai relaxed his plumage and nodded, a faint smile on his beak corners. "Pepro told you about the fire, right?"

I nodded.

"Sadly, dear Sol perished, but he saw those that set the blaze. Fortunately, he passed on the clues to Te."

"Rumors flapped around Waycliffs that the fire was deliberate. Pepro said Perro told him that too, and that his mother went after those that did it. He believed she sought revenge, but I don't think he ever quite forgave her for not coming back."

"It's a lot more than revenge I'm afraid. Do you know of the Apterian Archives?"

I shrugged, "Just the ones here and in Unitum."

K'ai nodded, "There are many more, kept in secret. They are precious reserves of Apterian knowledge, preserved for centuries, an effort started by the brightest of our ancestors who witnessed the Fall. Although they didn't understand everything they saved, and didn't have the tools to adapt it to our use, they knew it was irreplaceable and must be preserved. Those that helped protect and conceal the Archives were the first of the Tacet Carceris, present long before our nation came to be."

Brant grumbled, "Sir, are you sure you should be telling us all this? It's way above my pay grade, which ain't sayin' much, I realize."

K'ai replied coolly, "Well, I'm not telling you everything, only what you need to know. Our enemies already know more about the Archives than you. Pepro's nest tree fire was a coordinated effort by a band of Folegal to break into a nearby, secret Archive."

I thought to myself, *How could I have lived there for almost six years without knowing or even hearing about a secret library in Waycliffs?* Then it dawned on me. "Cape Keel?"

K'ai nodded.

"But there's a garrison of Volatian Protectors there."

"Exactly. A slim force, and most have no idea of the treasure under the ruins, but that's long been enough to deter explorers or plunderers. Many were pulled away to combat the forest fire, and our best two warriors, namely Sol and Te, were busy fighting for their lives, and the life of their eaglet."

"What did they steal?"

K'ai replied, "Information that will benefit all birds if used wisely or be extremely dangerous to everyone if the Folegal have the brains and the will to use it unwisely."

Brant squawked, "They have the will alright, but brains seem in short supply among the Folies. 'Least we know now who killed Lara and Ano. All's we need is to match the cast we made with Tulivor's foot, and the case is closed."

K'ai shifted his golden eyes to Tuliann, who had been stone still throughout the discussion, staring at her feet in thought. "What do you think, Tu?"

Tuliann lifted her head, "I think you're about to ask me if I think Tulivor is the killer and will give himself up easily. It doesn't surprise me that he may have committed murder, particularly if it was a question of honor, or at some behest of Vouli."

"His mistress." I muttered.

Tuliann nodded, "I see word gets around. Even Vasili knows."

Brant scoffed, "Figures. Sorry, ma'am, don't mean to malign your betrothed, or a king for that matter. And I don't want to question your esteem of the bird. But just how in the herring hell does Vasili maintain discipline in his nest hold while letting his officers get away with stealing the honor of his daughter?"

Tuliann lifted her hackles and bristled her head feathers as she stared down the questioning gull. But as fast as her anger flared, her plumage relaxed again, and she said with a condescending smile, "None of your gull-damned business, officer. He loves his daughter, and I dare say he loves the officer who flew at his wing through many a fight. You know nothing of their ways, and like most around here, woefully underestimate them while assuming you know all you need to know. Truth is, I don't know why he tolerates it either, but he's less traditionally minded than most, so I don't question his heart on the matter."

"'Scuse me," Brant grated with irritation, "but after gettin' poorly lied to by Mam's and a snobby superior yesterday, I know there's more that's rotten here than the lust of one officer. I don't know how high it goes but Vasili might be tangled in this flotsam too, for all we know!"

Tuliann hissed and lunged forward, "Officer, if you question Vasili's integrity again, there just might be a fresh gull carcass for the interns to study!"

Perry turned and sternly faced Brant too, and so I followed suit. Brant's point made sense, but in the heat of the moment, I stuck with my friends.

Suddenly K'ai jumped between our squared off ranks and cackled an eagle epithet so rare and foul that it stunned everyone to silence. He stood with wings and hackles raised, and his head menacingly low as though he would crush the skull of the next bird that spoke.

Foamy muttered incredulously, "Gulldamn."

It worked and our pride collapsed.

Tuliann blushed, lifted her head from her threat posture, and adjusted her wings with embarrassment. "I'm sorry, Captain," she said apologetically.

Brant shook his beak, "The slip up was mine, Miss. That was a tender a spot I shouldn't 'a been pokin'."

K'ai addressed the burly gull, "Yes, you could have been more tactful, Captain, but you did raise an excellent point. Sorry, Tu, and I don't blame you, but you're too close to the king to be objective. Trust me on this as a friend, if not in my official role. I don't like instilling doubt into anyone's esteem of their betrothed, but we have to consider all the possibilities, including that he has other obligations to Vouli and Tulivor beyond family and duty."

Tuliann grudgingly nodded. "I must admit that despite my time among the Mamyrskins, I do not fully grasp their culture and politics. But need I remind you that Vasili is turning the kingdom over to me through this marriage? Their customs require it. I've never seen such selflessness among any bird here, so it's difficult to see how he could be involved with anything that would bring doubt, dishonor, or violence to our bonding. On the other wing, Vouli and Tulivor have much to gain by stalling or stopping it. Vasili must take a new mate by the end of the first day of the New Year or Vouli can bond and become Queen."

"Great Skies!" I exclaimed. "That's why the bonding is happening on the first day of the new year!"

Tuliann nodded. "He's cutting it close. Too close, in my opinion. But he wanted this to be a public spectacle on a memorable day so there could be no doubt about the legitimacy I suppose."

Brant asked flatly, "So what about the eagle army with a spoiled brat and maniac murderer in charge?"

Tuliann replied, "Vasili said that Vouli went to fetch the Honor Guard. Maybe that's them?"

Perry reminded her, "They were pretty unfriendly for an Honor Guard, dear."

Brant added, "I had been told the Honor Guard would be about ten phalanxes, so some forty troops. What Perry describes is more like a legion!"

K'ai nodded. "And there's no need to stopover at Treaty Rock. It's not the most direct route. To my knowledge, the royals have been passing through Waycliffs."

I nodded, "Yep. My folks have had their wings full extending social courtesies to the bonding visitors."

K'ai fixed his eyes firmly on Perry, "I know this is a lot to ask, but I need you to go back out there."

"Sir? Me?"

"I'm going to send out high-altitude reconnaissance patrols, but I need someone on the ground. You know where they are, what some of them look like, and you know where to hide. And even if they saw you, chances are they would just think you were an Unawakened migrant. Make yourself look the part and lay low in your cave by day."

Perry blinked, "You know about my cave?"

K'ai ignored his remark. "Use your superior night vision and sense of smell to investigate at night. I'll send murres out to meet you daily, at sunset. They'll challenge you with the passphrase 'Who hatched from a bad egg?' And your reply should be 'Brant.'"

Foamy laughed and Brant slapped him with a wing.

K'ai was dead serious as he asked, "Will you do this for me, Perry?"

Perry straightened up and said, "I will, if you promise to send patrols to look for Pepro too."

"I'm way ahead of you. I have just the birds for it." K'ai replied.

I said to K'ai, "I'd like to join those patrols, if I might."

"I admire your volunteerism, Nyx, but truth is you'd be of better service if you escorted Sashya back with the gold. There's still a royal bonding coming, and now you know how critical it is that it comes off on schedule. Also, I happen to know that the Folegal are planning an ambush somewhere along the route to Galinta. They've already flown out to set the trap. I suggest you take a different route, and I'll find some company for you."

Behind K'ai in the darkness, rusty hinges screeched, and he glanced back towards the sound. A mottled eagle stood in the doorway with a candle lantern in her beak. K'ai approached them and quiet whispers followed.

I placed a wing on Perry's back, "Thank you for asking them to search for Pepro." I softly pecked his cheek feathers.

The big bird nodded glumly and replied, "I wish I had stayed with him."

"There's nothing you could have done, Perry. And if you both fell," I choked on the thought. "Well, you'd both be lost and we'd know nothing of the eagle army."

Perry hugged back with the bend of his wing. "It's possible they took him prisoner, you know. If they did, I'll help him bust out, if I can."

My heart lifted and I said, "You just tell him to hang on, and that a sad little owl and pissed off falcon are ready to shred eagles to get him back."

The mottle returned to the open door while K'ai walked back to us and said, "I'm afraid we have a new problem. Sashya departed on his own. He left this note for you two." K'ai laid a curled piece of parchment on the floor and walked over to Brant.

I read the note out loud:

> *I'm heading back to Galinta. There's nothing left for me here, but I can be of use back there with Kor. Please don't follow. I need time alone and I can take care of myself. If all goes well, I think Kor will return with the rings in about six days. If Pepro is alive, tell him I love him, and send me word. Thanks for the friendship, Perry and Nyx. Sorry I couldn't bring myself to say goodbye to your faces,*

but I knew you'd just talk me out of going.
—Sashya

I laughed in disbelief and shook my head, "That young fool! He's damned right about stopping him. I'd have had Perry sit on him."

Perry snorted, "Foolish? Sounds like he wanted to spare us the trouble and danger. He could be your brother, Nyx."

K'ai nodded in agreement. "Noble, yes, but the timing is terrible." He sighed loudly and roused his plumage, "There's no time to spare. Nyx, slight change of plans: You've got to catch up to him and escort him safely to Galinta, get the rings made, then return. I'll send you along with quick and capable company."

I stiffened my posture, and a warm rush filled my beak. "I'm ready. Who's coming along?"

K'ai smiled and chirped to his assistant at the door, "Send her in."

A falcon silhouette approached, similar in stature to me. As she came into the light, my heart leapt into my throat with recognition. "Mano!"

Chapter 24

Departures

By Nyx

The first rays of red sun lit the peaks of the Hawkspire Mountains as we passed over Sunrise Outpost. My breast muscles burned from the hard, constant climb, but there we had no time to lose.

Mano flew on my left and made the climb look easy. I marveled at how she kept in shape while working in a bordello and laying eggs, all while secretly serving the Tacet Carceris. My heart swelled with pride for her, and my spirits soared at the prospect of the two of us working and fighting, side by side. She would have my back, and she could count on me having hers. With storms on the horizon of our times, nothing felt better.

Mano chupped out, "Okay, sister, let's glide a bit, shall we?"

I replied, "Sure, a breather is good. But not too long. Maybe you can finally explain to me what the other day was all about?"

Mano surprised me by cackling in laughter. "You, dear sister, are a wonderful actress."

I veered closer to Mano and spat my reply in her face, "Acting? I love you and you ripped my fucking heart out of my chest!"

Mano's smile vanished. "I'm sorry I put you through that, sis. It was necessary. They had figured out where I was from, who I was related too. I didn't want them harassing you or anyone else in the family. It was another step to being accepted to their inner circle."

I scratched my ear with a talon and shook my head.

Mano asked, "What's the matter? Pick up mites in Low Town?"

"No, I'm just trying to make sure my ears are hearing right. Why the hell would you want to be friends with that loathsome swan? Or that mottle that tends her shit bucket and wanted to rape me? The same one that, if you didn't know, has the mark of the Folies in his ear."

Mano rolled her eyes and sighed, "Haven't figured it out yet, eh?"

"Stop making me guess and tell me before I knock you for a loop!"

Mano soberly replied, "The Lusty Loon is rife with Folegal and K'ai needed someone on the inside after our last operative went missing."

"You mean, 'went dead.'"

"Probably," Mano soberly acknowledged. "It hasn't been easy. It's taken months to gain their trust. The egg-laying brought in loads of gold and high-rolling gamblers. Premaden Elbee's top weakness is her purse, and I help fill it."

"If you're so special to her, how'd you get away for this mission? Isn't she going to wonder where you are?"

Mano shook her head incredulously, "I laid five eggs for her in two weeks, all on queue while performing for those sick bastards. That's not easy. Even she was impressed."

It saddened me to hear her so nonchalantly speak of wasting eggs.

Mano noticed. "I see that look. But are you starting to see what's going on, and why this is important? Elbee is disgusting and evil, with an uncanny talent for manipulation. Look at how she pulled your strings!"

I scoffed.

Mano continued, "But her other weakness is vanity. She thrives on obedience and having her webs kissed. Our performance reassured her that she had my loyalty. She called me to her chamber the next day. I won't disgust you with the favors I had to do for her, but afterwards she gave me a magnanimous pep talk about how far I would go under her tutelage. She offered a pay raise if I would take on a new, long-term commitment with her. She spoke of how she, and her eagle partners, would become my new flock to replace the security that I lost when my family unnamed me. She gave me a quarter-moon off to recuperate from laying and consider her offer, as though there's really any choice. She didn't toss names about, but anybirdy with half a brain in that place knows her business partners are the Folies that infest it."

I was annoyed, and disgusted, at being a plaything for the amusement of that swan or the Folies, and still angry with Mano. "Why couldn't you just fucking tell me all this?"

Mano drifted closer and showed me a stone-cold expression, "Because I needed to know I could trust you. This isn't a game, and you're not a little squab anymore. If you couldn't pull off a convincing fight, then I would know you were of no use to the cause."

I snapped back, "No use?"

"Yeah! I needed to know if you had grown up and opened your eyes to the inequality right under our beaks. If you were ready to do whatever it took to sniff out these Folies, crush there plans, and rip out their fucking throats if need be. And if I wasn't convinced, well, at least you, and everyone I care about, would be insulated from the worst to come."

My anger subsided as I realized the complexity of her situation. "You were trying to protect me?"

"Sis, I believe in you, more than anyone else in our family. I see in you the thing that will surely save us: Empathy. Ideals are important, and we need thinkers, but words alone don't make society work. To be effective, a leader has to feel what others feel. They have to care about their cares. They have to get their feathers dirty too, just like you do. We need more like you, sis. I can't tell you how proud you make me, and how much I love you."

I swelled with pride, and my vision blurred with warm tears of joy. I offered her my foot and said, "I'm with you, sis."

Mano reached out too, and we interlocked toes for a moment in mid-flight. As we parted, she asked, "Is Sashya a quick flier?"

I shook my head, "No. This was his first trip away from Galinta since his apprenticeship began. Pepro taught him how to use thermals and wind streams on the way to Whiterock, but he said his preference was to hug the landscape, which is a slow way to travel."

Mano replied, "I've not had much to do with moon owls, but they're not exactly known as high adventurers. Sashya must have heart, though, to strike out all on his own and loaded with gold. Especially after getting robbed just a few days ago."

I had pushed the details of my friends out of my mind, focusing purely on getting over the mountains. But now that Mano brought Sashya up, images of he and Pepro flooded into view. As fingers of sunlight touched the hills we had crossed together just days before, I remembered the two laughing and playing in the sky together. It had been a joyous day with nothing but fun on the horizon. And now Pepro was missing, possibly gone forever. And Sashya heartbroken to the point of shunning friends and behaving rashly. He grieved, and I should have seen this coming.

"He's a brave soul, sis. Smart too. And what a kind heart. I envy the love growing between him and Pep."

"Yeah?" asked Mano.

"Mhmm. Love so pure it makes your heart ache. It's been hard watching Whiterock steal his innocence."

Mano went silent, then soberly replied, "Life anyplace will do that too, ya know. Whiterock is a crucible, and can torch the wings right off your dreams. But it's also home to the best dreamers in Volatus."

I nodded in agreement. My thoughts turned to Perry. By that point, he and Snowy had, no doubt, released Lara's downy feathers into the wind, and said their final farewells to her. Perry was probably on his way to Treaty Island. A piece of my heart went with him, yearning that he should find Pepro alive and well. I could imagine a dozen possibilities, most of them bad, but I focused on the one that involved a warm reunion.

And part of my heart lingered on Snowy and Silver, holding each other together with class, down below the broken brows of Low Town. Their friendship glowed as warm to me as the torches of home, and I knew I would never pass through Whiterock again without paying them a visit.

My thoughts of them lifted my spirits and I resumed flapping, pulling up and ahead for the next challenge, a jagged ridge splashed with amber sunshine. Mano's wings throbbed to life in the crisp air as she matched my speed.

"Know any good traveling songs?" I asked.

Mano thought a moment, then began singing a falcon-paced song inspired by the Seeangela Relay, the autumn race between Whiterock, Waycliffs, and Unitum. I knew the words so joined in. The tempo drove our wings, and I found fresh energy in harmonizing with my clutch-sister. I found hope, and knew that we would not fail, so long as we pulled together.

Other Titles by Hal Aetus

If you enjoyed Whiterock, don't miss the sequel...

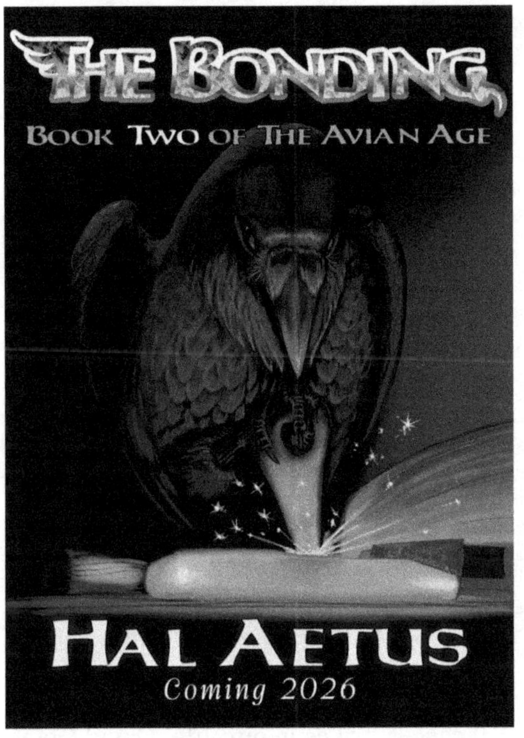

The Bonding: Book Two of the Avian Age
Due out in 2026
Learn more and follow along at aetusart.com/whiterock

Other Hal Aetus titles you may also enjoy...

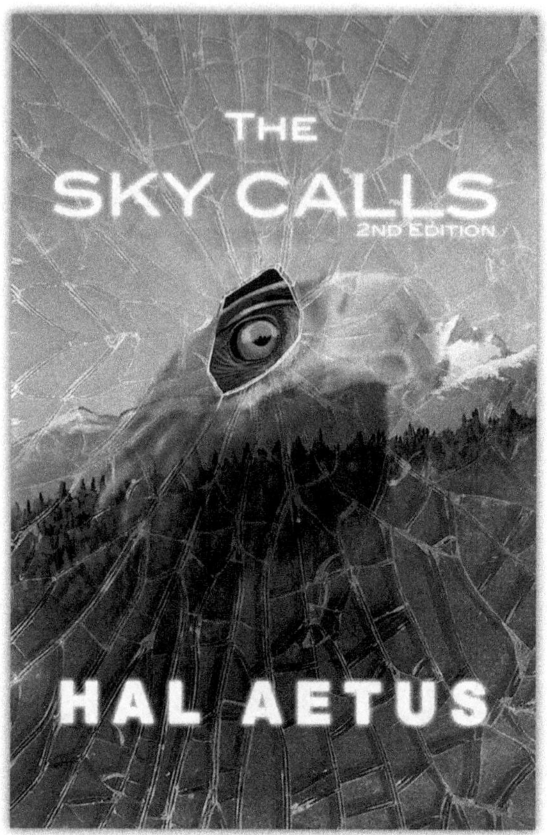

When terminal cancer strikes in mid-life, David Geraki has to make tough choices. He chooses a radical, experimental genetic therapy that saves his life, but removes his humanity, as he gradually turns into a golden eagle. With the help of his lifelong friend Sam, he must hold on to what's left of himself, accept what he's become, and ultimately fight for his freedom to exist. Learn more at aetusart.com/the-sky-calls.

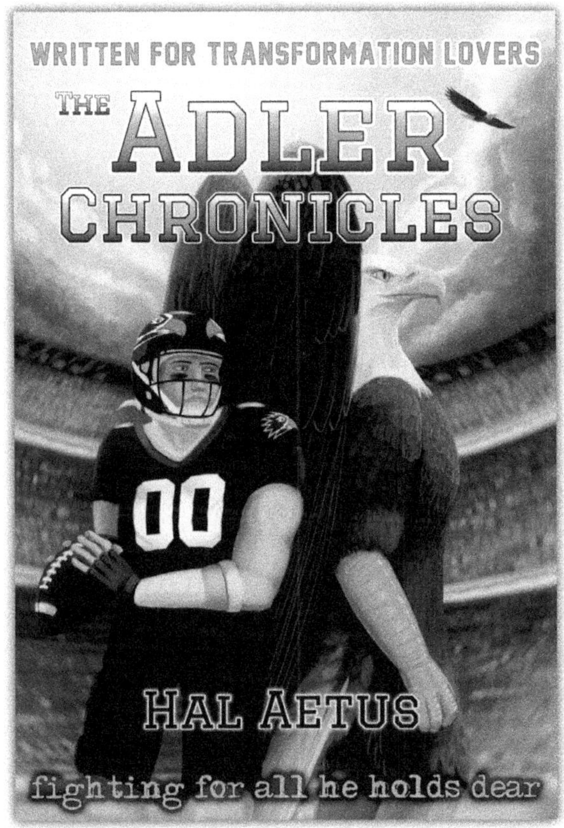

Phil Adler wants to play professional football and live a peaceful life with his family. But a closely-guarded family secret, an ability to shape-shift into birds at will, is revealed by a rival family, threatening his hard-won career and the safety of his loved-ones. His attackers have dark, furry secrets of their own and bloody ambitions that will affect the destiny of the world. Ultimately Phil, with teamwork from his closest confidants and a few unlikely allies, must battle for his life and the survival of humankind. Written for those that fantasize about turning into a animals, The Adler Chronicles draws you into a feud between rival werebird and werewolf families who, until now, lived quietly among us. Learn more at aetusart.com/the-adler-chronicles

Character Bios

A Who's-hooo of the Avian Age

These are brief biographies of main characters to jog your memory if you feel overwhelmed by the many names and species. There shouldn't be any spoilers to the story as I purposely kept some information vague. Additional details can be found online at wiki.aetusart. com.

Dates are provided in Orzclian Calendar notation, the standard calendar for both Volatus and Mamyrskit. The calendar is solar-based and starts on the spring (Vernal) equinox, roughly March 20th by today's calendar. There are eight months in a year with 44-46 days each, plus special provisions for "cast" (e.g., leap) years to keep the calendar in sync with the Earth's movements. Years are in PA ("Post-Awakening"), which started around year 2093 CE in the current Gregorian calendar, so the book opens in about the year 2395 CE. For more details on Volatian calendars, time-keeping, festivals, and the complimentary lunar calendar, refer wiki.aetusart.com.

UD (Unknown Date) indicates that the precise date of hatch is unknown. This is a common occurrence for birds hatched in rural locales with imprecise local date-keeping, or if birds are separated from parents or records are otherwise lost. For those cases, hatchdays are observed on the annual holiday known as "Hatching Day," which occurs on the first full moon of each solar year (sometime in our present month of April).

Barnibu

Biological Data

Avian Age Species: Green-winged macaw
Apterian Common Name: Green-winged macaw
Scientific Name: *Ara chloropterus*
Sex: Male

Biographical Data

Hatchdate (Age): UD, 282 PA (20y)
Origin: Whiterock, Volatus
Residence: Whiterock, Volatus
Occupation: Electrical engineer, head of Electrical Research at Whiterock Institute.

Notes

Barnibu leads electrical research efforts at Whiterock Institute. With access to the Apterian archives, he has centuries of knowledge from which to glean. He regularly teaches courses to students at the Institute and visitors from other villages.

Brant

Biological Data

Avian Age Species: Storm gull
Apterian Common Name: Black-backed gull
Scientific Name: *Larus marinus*
Sex: Male

Biographical Data

Hatchdate (Age): UD, 280 PA (22y)
Origin: Whiterock, Volatus
Residence: Whiterock, Volatus
Occupation: Captain of Whiterock peacekeepers

Notes

Captain Brant is the seasoned chief of Whiterock's Peacekeeper force. He has served the position for at least 18 years with unfailing distinction which has earned him a hard-won reputation respected throughout Whiterock and the Starlands. Although unwvering in his duties, his nestside manner leaves a lot to be desired and has little care for what others think of him or his heavy-footed serving of order. Not much is known of Brant's life before joining the peacekeepers, with some joking he is the "offspring of a barnacle."

Elbee

Biological Data

Avian Age Species: Imperial swan
Apterian Common Name: Mute swan
Scientific Name: *Cygnus olor*
Sex: Female

Biographical Data

Hatchdate (Age): UD,
Origin: [Fill In]
Residence: Whiterock, Volatus
Occupation: Owner/operator of the Lusty Loon, a disreputable brothel
   in Whiterock on the Low Town promenade.

Notes

She is a direct descendant of Premaden Zeschau, attendant to Queen
Tulis (who was the last ruler of Talaamiolar before the Volatian Rebellion). Premadens were royal attendants, elevated to special, but
still inferior, status among the aristocracy. She carries on formalities
while running a disreputable saloon called the Lusty Loon. The mottled (white-tailed sea) eagle behind her is Rasha, a young neo-Folegal
recruit serving his turn as the Premaden's attendant.

K'ai

Biological Data

Avian Age Species: Bald eagle
Apterian Common Name: Bald eagle
Scientific Name: *Haliaeetus leucocephalus*
Sex: Male

Biographical Data

Hatchdate (Age): UD, 275 PA (27y)
Origin: Unspecified
Residence: Whiterock, Volatus
Occupation: Tacet Carceris Agent

Notes

K'ai is an adult male bald eagle known for frequenting establishments in Low Town, including the Musky Murre. He's rumored to be a member of the Tacet Carceris, Volatus' revered secret guard, shrouded in mystery. As a result of this rumor, birds with problems sometimes bend his auriculars in the hope he can help.

Kor

Biological Data

Avian Age Species: Raven
Apterian Common Name: Common raven
Scientific Name: *Corvus corax*
Sex: Male

Biographical Data

Hatchdate (Age): 32 Ovum, 282 (20y)
Origin: Galinta, Volatus
Residence: Galinta, Volatus
Occupation: Master blacksmith & jeweler

Notes

Hatched in Galinta to Korvell (M) and Glank'aan (F), he grew up among a massive extended family and learned all parts of the midden mining trade. His father was also a master blacksmith and had a small forge near the midden site. In 283 they cleared vegetation form an Apterian factory ruin near the river, built a waterwheel, and establish the current workshop (Kor's Forge). The association with the midden has been perfect since all types of metals are unearthed including occasional precious metals and gemstones.

Lara

Biological Data

Avian Age Species: Murre
Apterian Common Name: Common murre
Scientific Name: *Uria aalge*
Sex: Female

Biographical Data

Hatchdate (Age): UD, 278 PA (24y)
Origin: Guangarten, Volatus
Residence: Whiterock, Volatus
Occupation: Prostitute at Musky Murre

Notes

Lara hatched at the enormous seabird colony of Guangarten. It was a noisy, gregarious life, which is probably why she later thrived in the crowded, party atmosphere of Low Town. She led a nomadic life with extended family, following shifting food resources. She fell in love with a family friend but was left destitute in Whiterock and too embarrassed to return to her family. She took to prostitution as an easy way to earn a living initially, but also enjoyed the setting and friends she made.

Nyx

Biological Data

Avian Age Species: Peregrine falcon
Apterian Common Name: Peregrine falcon, anatum
Scientific Name: *Falco peregrinus anatum*
Sex: Female

Biographical Data

Hatchdate (Age): 42 Ovum, 296 (6y)
Origin: Waycliffs, Volatus
Residence: Waycliffs, Volatus
Occupation: Assistant/Proxy to Waycliffs Regional Representatives
(her parents Anja and Hagan)

Notes

Nyx's family is recognized for political savvy and undying dedication to the community of Waycliffs. Nyx is following in her parent's wingstrokes, but is still finding her footing as a leader. She acts fast in emergencies, doesn't let dirt deter her from doing a necessary job. She has fast reactions, strong feet, and a short tolerance of bullying or unfairness, but she is learning how to harness her temper for good.

Penelope

Biological Data

Avian Age Species: Magpie
Apterian Common Name: Black-billed magpie
Scientific Name: *Pica hudsonia*
Sex: Female

Biographical Data

Hatchdate (Age): 2 Crinitus, 287 (15y)
Origin: Whiterock, Volatus
Residence: Whiterock, Volatus
Occupation: Owner/Operator of Avian Haven, a roostery

Notes

Miss Penelope owns and operates the Avian Haven, a roostery (hotel) in Whiterock's Upper District. She is well connected with many of the wealthy birds within and without Whiterock. She has a taste for finer things, and is wealthy enough to afford most of them.

Pepro

Biological Data

Avian Age Species: Bald eagle
Apterian Common Name: Bald eagle
Scientific Name: *Haliaeetus leucocephalus*
Sex: Male

Biographical Data

Hatchdate (Age): 20 Crinitus 297 (5y)
Origin: Waycliffs, Volatus
Residence: Galinta, Volatus
Occupation: Apprentice blacksmith to Kor
Family: Parents Te (mother, missing) and Sol (father, deceased). No
known siblings.

Notes

Pepro spent his first year learning from his uncle Perro and then went on a Wander (customary for young bald eagles) for three years followed by a season of schooling and then a year apprenticing with Kor. Pepro is a happy fellow, particularly around his best friend Sashya, but sometimes broody about his past, scarred by the traumatic death of his father and disappearance of his mother.

Perro

Biological Data

Avian Age Species: Bald eagle
Apterian Common Name: Bald eagle
Scientific Name: *Haliaeetus leucocephalus*
Sex: Male

Biographical Data

Hatchdate (Age): 16 Crinitus, 268 (34y)
Origin: Kahvanis, Volatus
Residence: Unitum, Volatus currently, nesthold at Sunrise Lake
Occupation: National Champion Fisherbird

Notes

Perro is the paternal uncle of Pepro, and his name was inspired by the same. He is well-known for his fishing abilities, having won the Volatian national fishing championship several years in a row, and having also served as fisherbird for the Volatian National Council. In thanks for years of service, he was deeded, into perpetuity, the aerie at Sunrise Lake.

Perry

Biological Data

Avian Age Species: Smudgie albatross
Apterian Common Name: Laysan albatross
Scientific Name: *Phoebastria immutabilis*
Sex: Male

Biographical Data

Hatchdate (Age): UD, 272 (30y)
Origin: Destiny Atoll
Residence: Whiterock, Volatus, at least part-time
Occupation: Treasure hunter, trader, vagabond

Notes

Perry is best known as a vagabond treasure-hunter who frequents Low Town to spend his gold on prostitutes and spirits. He's known to buy rounds for those around when he's in his best moods, and tips the hennies generously. It's rumored he had suffered a heartbreak years prior, which led to him not caring to settle down or commit to any relationships again.

P'tilo

Biological Data

Avian Age Species: Mottled eagle
Apterian Common Name: White-tailed sea eagle
Scientific Name: *Haliaeetus albicilla*
Sex: Male

Biographical Data

Hatchdate (Age): [Fill in]
Origin: Whiterock, Volatus
Residence: Whiterock, Volatus
Occupation: Politician, Waystar Regional Governor

Notes

P'tilo is the Waystar regional governor as well as city master. His family privilege gave him plenty of connections to help him rise quickly in politics, and was elected to regional governor in 300 PA. He is credited with several advancements in economic opportunity and safety, and the recent reorganization of local and regional government to improve efficiency.

Sashya

Biological Data

Avian Age Species: Moon owl
Apterian Common Name: Barn owl
Scientific Name: *Tyto alba*
Sex: Male

Biographical Data

Hatchdate (Age): 21 Ovum, 300 (2y)
Origin: Kahvanis, Volatus
Residence: Galinta, Volatus
Occupation: Blacksmith/jeweler apprenticeship with Kor

Notes

Although general education in Volatus is a minimum of one year, Sashya was schooled in Kahvanis for two years and excelled academically. He thirsts for knowledge and enjoys artistic pursuits, particularly fine metalworking. He was matched to an apprenticeship with Kor, the Master Blacksmith of Galinta, in the autumn of 302 PA. Moon owls mature at one year of age, so he is an adult. Although very smart, he lacks worldly experience. Seeing the wide world through his relatively innocent eyes is a treat to all who read his writings.

Silver

Biological Data

Avian Age Species: Tufted owl
Apterian Common Name: Eurasian eagle-owl
Scientific Name: *Bubo bubo*
Sex: Female

Biographical Data

Hatchdate (Age): 17 Nidum, 293 (9y)
Origin: Southreach, Volatus
Residence: Whiterock, Volatus
Occupation: Prostitute at Musky Murre

Notes

Silver is the newest of Miss Snowdrift's "hennies." Her past life is unknown to most, apart from Miss Snowdrift and Brant, with whom she shares a secret affair. She is fiercely loyal to her friends and motherly of her fellow sex workers. Snowy is glad to have her as a friend, a confidant, and a handy set of talons to keep order.

Miss Snowdrift

Biological Data

Avian Age Species: Snowy owl
Apterian Common Name: Snowy owl
Scientific Name: *Bubo scandiacus*
Sex: Female

Biographical Data

Hatchdate (Age): UD, 284 (18y)
Origin: Undisclosed
Residence: Whiterock, Volatus
Occupation: Owner/Operator of Musky Murre, an inn and brothel in
the Low Town District of Whiterock

Notes

Snowy has operated the Musky Murre, a popular brothel, for eleven years. She's private about her origins, but rumors say she was sold into slavery as a fledge and later escaped. She has a warm heart and is known for offering fine hospitality. She shirks the peacekeepers and maintains an atmosphere of anonymity and "anything goes," so long as her patrons behave themselves.

Tuliann

Biological Data

Avian Age Species: Mottled eagle
Apterian Common Name: White-tailed sea eagle
Scientific Name: *Haliaeetus albicilla*
Sex: Female

Biographical Data

Hatchdate (Age): 19 Ovum, 280 (22y)
Origin: Whiterock, Volatus
Residence: Whiterock, Volatus
Occupation: Master Healer, Senior Master of Whiterock Institute

Notes

Tuliann was hatched at Whiterock to parents that were very active in regional politics. She grew up in a golden age of diversity and growth in Volatus, with access to the brightest minds and lost Apterian knowledge (a buried human university). She focused on the healing arts and became the leading authority on avian medicine. She founded the Whiterock Institute of Medicine and Technology and used her resources to stop a pox plague in Mamyrskit in 300 PA.

Tulivor

Biological Data

Avian Age Species: Crowned eagle
Apterian Common Name: Steller's sea eagle
Scientific Name: *Haliaeetus pelagicus*
Sex: Male

Biographical Data

Hatchdate (Age): 25 Ovum, 279 (24y)
Origin: Nest Tulis, Mamyrskit
Residence: Anatolika, Mamyrskit
Occupation: Master of the King's Guard, Commander of the Army

Notes

Tulivor was hatched to parents Kahlivor (F) and Strongsky (M). Kahlivor was of the lineage of the dishonored aristocracy forced from Volatus in 248 PA.

Vasili

Biological Data

Avian Age Species: Crowned eagle
Apterian Common Name: Steller's sea eagle
Scientific Name: *Haliaeetus pelagicus*
Sex: Male

Biographical Data

Hatchdate (Age): 14 Ovum, 276 (26y)
Origin: Anatolika, Mamyrskit
Residence: Anatolika, Mamyrskit
Occupation: King of Mamyrskit

Notes

King Vasili is a fierce, capable warbird tempered by a generous soul and amiable countenance. He extends friendship first and is loyal to the last, but punishes treachery with equally brutal resolve. He is a descendant of the family that once controlled Whiterock.

Vouli

Biological Data

Avian Age Species: Crowned eagle
Apterian Common Name: Steller's sea eagle
Scientific Name: *Haliaeetus albicilla*
Sex: Female

Biographical Data

Hatchdate (Age): 44 Ovum, 298 (almost 5y)
Origin: Anatolika, Mamyrskit
Residence: Anatolika, Mamyrskit
Occupation: Princess, daughter of King Vasili

Notes

Vouli was hatched to Queen Merikukka (Meri) and King Vasili at the royal aerie in Anatolika, Mamyrskit. When very young, her mother was slain during an uprising. Vouli was then raised and trained, in large part, by Tulivor. Mamyrskin culture honors a matrilineal monarchy. Thus, Vouli will, upon the age of coronation (five years old), ascend the throne if her father fails to take another mate within five years of losing Meri. Note that sea eagles are considered mature at 4-6 years of age and will nest if able to find a mate.

Glossary

Key
All = All dialects   Apt. = Apterian dialect
Mam. = Mamyrskin dialect   Vol. = Volatian dialect
n. = noun   v. = verb   adj. = adjective   pej. =pejorative

A

Accrement (Vol./Mam., n.): Avian cement made from volcanic ash, lime, water, and aggregate of pebbles, shells, and bits of Apterian refuse (plastic and glass). All of these components are naturally accessible with little refinement and can be transported in quantities small enough for most birds to manage with multiple trips. Pumice stones are particularly prized for accrement because they are light and easy to transport, and their porous nature renders some of the strongest concrete for the weight. In some cases, the Apterian practice of metal reinforcement is used, but metal is generally too expensive for wide use in this manner. Accrement is most often used to supplement existing Apterian ruins, and adapt them into smaller bird-sized constructs for avian dwellings, shops, storehouses, etc. In some cases accrement is used purely for aesthetics such as sculptures and statues. It is extremely durable, particularly when pumice is used and the mixture is cured with sea water, much like Apterian Roman cement. See also *accrementor*.

Accrementor (Vol./Mam., n.): One whose occupation is crafting and constructing using accrement.

Aerie (All, n.): To Apterians, it was the nest and immediate territory of birds of prey, but especially eagles. See also *nesthold*.

Airsac (All, n.): A thin, membranous sac for manipulating air within a bird's body. There are 7-9 primary airsacs and thousands of subsidiaries, branching into most of the bones of the axial skeleton, skull, humeri, and femurs of flighted birds. Consult respiratory anatomy diagram in next section.

Alula (All, n.): The movable "thumb" feathers of a bird's wing, located at the leading edge just past the carpal (wrist) joint. They function as a flap to prevent stalling in slow flight or in high angles of wing deflection.

Apterian (Vol./Mam., n.): The Avian Age term for humans (*Homo sapiens*). The term comes from Latin for "without feathers." See also Featherless.

Auricular (All, n.): The contour feathers that cover the ear or, in the case of some owls, guide sound into the ear opening.

B

Bald eagle (All, n.): *Haliaeetus leucocephalus*, a species of sea eagle native to North America. They become sexually mature at five to six years of age, at which point they complete their transition to white head and tail plumage, pale eyes, and yellow beak. Earlier ages go through a variety of brown and mottled phases to gradually attain the adult colors. Feet are always yellow. See also *baldy, snow-head.*

Baldy (Vol./Mam., n.): Slang, non-pejorative term for the bald eagle.

Barn owl (Apt., n.): *Tyto alba*, a globally widespread species of owl with pale feathers on the face, breast, and underside of the wings and tail and cryptically-patterned golds, grays, and buff colors on the back, nape, crown, and upper surfaces of the wings and tail. They are primarily nocturnal and known to have the keenest hearing of all owls, enhanced, in part, because of asymmetric ear openings. See also *moon owl, fodder owl.*

Bells (Vol., n.): See Time-keeping.

Boating (Apt., v.): The ventrally recumbent position of a bird resting on its breast on the ground as when brooding.

Breasting (Vol./Mam., v.): The act, or position, of lowering oneself down on the breast to rest. See also boating or brooding.

Brooding (All, v.): Warming eggs against bare skin on the abdomen, usually in a breast-down position in a nest.

Bernoulli's principle (Apt., n.): The scientific principle of fluid dynamics that describes the inverse relationship between the speed of a fluid (or air) and the pressure it exerts. This is the principle behind how aerodynamic lift is generated by wings.

C

Cast (All, n.): The pellet of fur, feathers, sometimes bones, that are regurgitated by many birds, most notably birds of prey.

Cast (All, v.): To regurgitate the indigestible remains of a meal. A common, almost daily, habit of many omnivorous and carnivorous birds.

Cast year (Vol./Mam., n.): A special year that occurs every four years, except for every eighth occurrence, which has a five year interval. In these years, an extra day is added to the end of the year (month of Nidum).

This maintains the solar calendar so that the new year occurs on the same day as the spring equinox. The word comes from the common bodily function of birds, especially carnivorous species, to cast up undigested remains. In this case, it's a day that's "regurgitated" periodically. See *Orzelian calendar*.

Choana (All, n.): The internal, oral opening into the nasal sinuses. It's a slit located in the palate (roof of the mouth). When the beak is closed, the glottis seals against its posterior extent and breathing is conducted through it.

Chup (All, n.): A descriptive term for the short, chirp- or bark-like notes of falcons.

Cloaca (All, n.): An organ in birds and reptiles that acts as a common receptacle for liquid and solid wastes. It is also used for copulating and laying eggs, which for most birds is accomplished by pressing openings together in a "cloacal kiss." Consult anatomy diagrams in next section.

Cere (All, n.): The fleshy area surrounding the nares in some bird species, particularly birds of prey, parrots, and pigeons.

Clutch-brother (Vol./Mam., n.): See *Clutch-sibling*.

Clutch-sibling (Vol./Mam., n.): A brother or sister that was part of the same clutch of eggs and raised together. See also *Nest-sibling*.

Clutch-sister (Vol./Mam., n.): See *Clutch-sibling*.

Contour feathers (All., n.): The feathers that cover, shape, and streamline a bird's body. The flight feathers are considered to be a subset of contour feathers, adapted for various flight functions. They are one of six categories of feathers.

Crest-wind (Vol./Mam., n.): A stream of air that accelerates over an obstruction, such as an ocean swell or mountain ridge.

Crinitus (Vol./Mam., n.): The second month of the Orzelian calendar. Comes from Latin for "downy," referring to when crowned eaglets would be downy nestlings. See also: *Orzelian calendar*.

Crissum (All, n.): The curved area of fluffy feathers under the tail of a bird. Also known as undertail coverts. Consult tail anatomy diagram in next section.

Croaker (Vol./Mam., n.): Slang/pejorative for crows and ravens, sometimes applied to other corvids.

Crop (All, n.): A pouch in the esophagus, just above the breast, which serves to store food before it enters the stomach. Consult digestive anatomy diagrams in next section.

Crowned eagle (Vol./Mam., n.): The largest sea eagle species, known by Apterians as the Steller's sea eagle (*Haliaeetus pelagicus*). See also *Crowny*.

Crowny (Vol./Mam., n.): Slang, non-pejorative term for crowned eagles.

D

Discipulus (Vol./Mam., n.): The fourth month of the Orzelian calendar. Comes from Latin for "training," in reference to the period when hatch-year crowned eagles would begin their physical training and schooling. See also: *Orzelian calendar*.

Distances: In the Avian Age, a combination of units of measure exist, though in Volatus, metric is the officially taught system, based on Apterian standards. Still, subjective measures such as wingspans or glides are still commonplace in everyday conversation when precision is not necessary.

E

Egg unhatched (Vol., idiom): An idiom for keeping a secret. Ex: "That's a dangerous secret. You had best keep that egg unhatched."

Egg-turner (Vol., n.): A euphemism for a consuming or difficult mental exercise. It comes from the problem-solving construct of how to pick up a swan's egg if it is floating in water. It just spins around as you attempt to grasp it with too small a bill.

F

Feak (All, v.): The act of wiping the beak on a branch, feaking post, or perch cloth to remove food or debris.

Feaking post/cloth (Vol./Mam., n.): A post, sometimes covered in fabric, for wiping the beak. A feaking cloth is a fabric napkin laid over a perch in polite dinner settings, intended for wiping of the beak.

Featherless (Vol./Mam., n.): The common tongue word for humans. See also *Apterian*.

Firepowder (Vol., n.): The Avian Age term for gunpowder. This is a brand new technology and barely available in Book One. See also *Guanier*.

Fodder owl (Mam., n.): Pejorative term used almost exclusively by the Folegal, but also some older generation Mamyrskins, to refer to moon owls. During the reign of the Folegal, they were known as fodder owls because of their primary occupation of farming various species of rodents, a preferred prey item for many of the lesser-than-noble species that were critical to the functioning of royal eyries. They also farmed food for their livestock, managed their breeding and rearing, and controlled the apparatus for distribution to their crowny lords, granting them some latitude in their eyes of their superiors, but never elevating them beyond third-tier species in the eyes of the Folegal. See also *moon owl, barn owl*.

Full moon (All, n.): The state of the moon in which it is completely illuminated and round. See *Moon phases.*

Fuga (Vol./Mam., n.): The third month of the Orzelian calendar. Comes from Latin for "flight," in reference to the period when crowned eaglets would normally take their first flight. See also: *Orzelian calendar.*

G

Galt (Vol., n.): A culinary spice made from the dried, aged guano of piscivorous seabirds. It was originally used locally in some villages of the north but its popularity is increasing in chic establishments in Unitum, Volatus. It's particularly prized if sourced from piscivorous birds, especially cormorants, and is said to have an acrid tangy note that extends beyond the typical salty flavor of other galts. When properly aged, it concentrates to a sterile powder that can readily be transported.

Gibbous (All, n.): In reference to the moon, it indicates a bulging shape less than a circle but more than a semicircle. Basically the opposite of a crescent. See also: *Moon phases.*

Gizzard (All, n.): The second or "lower" stomach of birds. See also *ventriculus.* See digestive anatomy diagram in next section.

Glide (Vol./Mam., n.): Subjective unit of distance measurement, referring to the average distance of a crowny's glide from treetop level. Approximately 100 meters.

Glottis (All, n.): The opening into the trachea, located prominently at the base of the tongue. It is visible inside an open bird's mouth, particularly when they are vocalizing or hissing. See respiratory anatomy diagram in next section.

Greater black-backed gull (Apt., n.): *Larus marinus,* a common gull species of the north Atlantic distinguished by their slate-gray back and upper coverts of the wings, yellow bill with a red spot on the tip of the lower mandible, and otherwise white body with black and white wingtip markings. Known in the Avian Age as storm gulls for their resilience in poor weather and their caloric temperament. See also *storm gull, stormy.*

Greenrum (Vol./Mam., n.): A type of seaweed brandy that is popular with coastal birds. Distilled spirit made from non-specific species of kelp. Oftentimes it is green but sometimes takes on other colors such as red or purple, depending on the species of seaweed used in its making.

Grin (Apt./Mam., n.): Slang, non-pejorative term for the peregrine falcon.

Guano (All, n.): The accumulated urates from birds, primarily seabirds.

Guanier (Vol./Mam., n.): One whose occupation is the gathering or mining of guano deposits. Generally seen as an undesirable job, but guano has several uses including as a source for saltpeter, vital for production of firepowder and meat curing salts. It is also used as a basis for some paints and pigments. In some locales of Volatus, it is used as a gourmet culinary spice known as *galt*.

Ꜧ

Half-moon (Vol./Mam., n.): A period of time equivalent to half of a moon's phase cycle, or roughly two weeks.

Henny (Vol./Mam., n.): Slang for prostitute, regardless of sex. If used to address a prostitute, it's not considered a slur. Ex: "If you're looking for a henny, flap on down to the Musky Murre." Generally considered an insult if used in reference to someone who is not a sex worker.

I

Imperial swan (Vol./Mam., n.): The Avian Age nomenclature for the Mute swan See also *mute swan, impy.*

Impy (Vol./Mam., n.): Semi-pejorative term for the imperial swan. Because of the species' special status among ruling members of the Folegalian Dynasty, this term was considered vulgar and its use was punishable. In Volatian culture, where they no longer have a special status, the term is not generally considered a slur in casual conversation.

K

Kinnickinnic (Vol./Mam., n.): A ground-hugging shrub with red berries. It has circumpolar subarctic distribution and grows abundantly in Volatus and Mamyrskit. It's berries and leaves are edible and roots can be used for dyes. It's leaves can be brewed in tea or burned to produce smoke. In the Avian Age, dried leaves are placed in a smudge pot and burned slowly in a confined space to produce smoke for cleansing parasites and improving their sense of well-being. It also may have medicinal properties for alleviating cloacitis (inflammation of the cloaca) and sexually transmitted disease, though Apterian literature casts doubt on the effectiveness.

L

Lunar month (Apt., n.): A month based on the phases of the moon. In the Avian Age, the term "moon" is used in reference to Earth's celestial companion and the lunar month. The lunar months, or moons, are not named, but the passage of lunar months is used to mark periods of time. See also:

Moon, Orzelian calendar.

Macer (Vol./Mam., n.): The seventh month of the Orzelian calendar. Comes from Latin for "starving," in reference to the period when food was least available for most species and the greatest amount of weight loss and deaths from disease or starvation were seen. See also: *Orzelian calendar*.

Mamyrskit (Vol./Mam., n.): A nation of Awakened birds across the Waystar Sea, approximately 330 km (205 mi) northwest of Volatus. It was founded from the remains of the defeated Folegalian Monarchy who were expelled in 248 PA after a Rebellion that culminated in a war that lasted three years.

Messis (Vol./Mam., n.): The fifth month of the Orzelian calendar. Comes from Latin for "harvest," in reference to the period when the ruling crowned eagles would expect their share of annual harvests to be accounted or delivered. See also: *Orzelian calendar*.

Midden (All, n.): A refuse heap. In archaeology, middens are important sites for finding discarded bones, tools, and other materials that provide clues as to what everyday life was like for ancient cultures. In the context of the Avian Age, where most of the refuse of human civilization is buried, middens are abundant and frequently mined for valuable resources.

Moon (Vol./Mam., n.): Avian Age term for a lunar month. Time-keeping term for full transition of the moon from new to full to new again, or roughly a period of four weeks by our present-day Gregorian calendar. In the Avian Age, birds utilize both solar and lunar calendars, with lunar being most convenient for widespread use in tracking periods longer than a few days but shorter than periods as long as seasons or years. Their Orzelian calender is solar-based, dividing the year into eight months of 44-46 days. See also: *Moon phases*.

Moon phases (All, n.): See accompanying figure. Phases of the moon through a lunar month

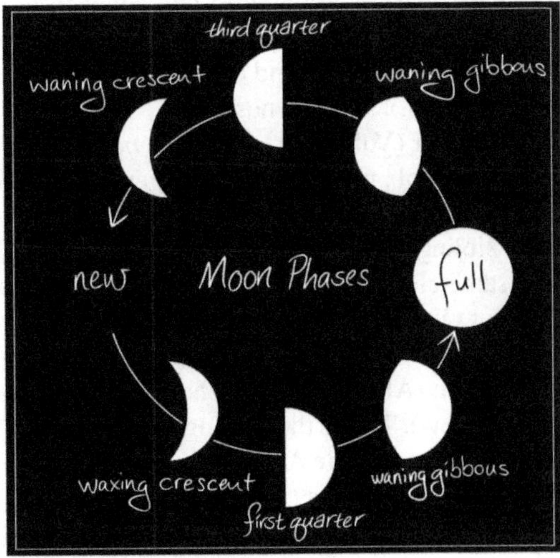

(29.5 Earth days) are as follows: New (completely dark), waxing crescent (right quarter of moon illuminated), first quarter (right half of moon illuminated), waxing gibbous (right three-quarters illuminated), full (completely illuminated and round), waning gibbous (left three-quarters illuminated), third quarter (left half of moon illuminated), waning crescent (left quarter illuminated), and new (completely dark again). Each quarter is roughly one week. See also: *Moon.*

Moon owl (Vol./Mam., n.): A species of pale, nocturnal owl known by Apterians as the barn owl (*Tyto alba*). See also *barn owl, fodder owl.*

Moony (Vol./Mam., n.): Slang form of moon owl, non-pejorative.

Mottle (Vol./Mam., n.): Slang form of mottled eagle. Not considered vulgar by most.

Mottled eagle (Vol./Mam., n.): Avian Age common-tongue designation for white-tailed sea eagles. See also *mottle, mudhead.*

Muddy, Mudhead (Vol./Mam., n.): Pejorative reference to mottled eagles.

Mute swan (Apt., n.): A species of swan (*Cygnus olor*). Large bird with entirely white plumage, orange upper bill and black lower bill, lores, frontal nob, and eyes. Morphometrics: 125-160 cm (55-63 in) body length, 200-240 cm (79-94 in) wingspan, and body mass of 10.6-11.87 kg (23.4-26.2 lbs) for males and 9.2-14.3 kg (20-32 lbs) for females. See also *imperial swan, impy.*

n

Nack (Vol./Mam., n., slang/vulgar): In all connotations, this is a considered a rare and supremely vulgar word in Awakened culture. 1. The cloaca, particularly pertaining to one attached to a cheap prostitute. 2. A prostitute with a bad reputation. 3. An insult with the connotation of being worthless, cheap, and easy to copulate with.

Nares (All, n.): A bird's nostrils.

Nest-brother (Vol./Mam., n.): Male *nest-sibling.*

Nesthold (Vol., n.): A family unit, generally including the dweling(s), possessions, and members of the family themselves. See also eyrie.

Nest-sibling (Vol./Mam., n.): A sibling from the same parents but not the same clutch of eggs. Although brothers or sisters biologically, they were not raised together. See also *clutch-sibling.*

Nest-sister (Vol./Mam., n.): Female *nest-sibling.*

New moon (All, n.): A lunar phase where the moon is not visible (entirely in shadow). This is the starting point for lunar "months" or "moons" as they are known in the Avian Age. See also *Moon phases.*

Nictitating membrane (All, n.): The third eyelid of a bird. It is semi-transparent to white in color and flicks from front to back to lubricate and cleanse the eye. It is the primary means of blinking in many bird species but is also used in "body language" to convey various emotional states.

Nib (Vol., n.): Slang term for the seminal orifice of male birds, particularly those that do not possess a phallus. It draws its name from the small nipple-like structure of the seminal orifices when they swell during copulation. See also *seminal ducts, tumi*. See male reproductive anatomy diagram in next section.

Nidum (Vol./Mam., n.): The eighth, and last, month of the Orzelian calendar. Comes from Latin for "nest," in reference to the period when crowned eagles would normally start to rebuild and prepare their nests for breeding season. See also: *Orzelian calendar*.

Nox (Vol./Mam., n.): The sixth month of the Orzelian calendar. Comes from Latin for "night," in reference to the period when days grew shortest. See also: *Orzelian calendar*.

O

Orzelian calendar (Vol./Mam., n.): The Avian Age calendar in use since Folegalian dynastic decree in 183 PA (Post-Awakening). It is a solar-based calendar with eight months varying from 44-46 days, plus special "cast" years which create an extra day at the end of the year. The Orzelian year starts on the spring equinox (March 20 by our Gregorian calendar) so the cycle of cast years serves to continually resynchronize the calendar with this key solar event. For complete details and a calendar in print, see wiki.aetusart.com.

Oviduct (All, n.): A tube-like organ in female birds that produces eggs. It receives an ovarian follicle (yolk) into its upper end (infundibulum) from the ovary and this is the site of fertilization. Next it is surrounded by layers of albumin (egg white) in the magnum, then shell membranes in the isthmus, and finally the shell and pigment in the shell gland (uterus). The vaginal segment of the oviduct serves a dual purpose of receiving sperm during mating and propelling the egg during oviposition (laying). Sperm glands in the utero-vaginal junction store viable sperm for up to several weeks and releases them during ovulation. See female reproductive anatomy diagram in next section.

Ovum (Vol./Mam., n.): The first month of the Orzelian calendar. Comes from Latin for "egg," in reference to the period when crowned eagles would normally lay eggs. See also: *Orzelian calendar*.

P

Pelagic (All, adj.): Of or pertaining to the open sea. Pelagic birds are those that live most of their life in the open ocean.

Peregrine falcon (All, n.): Falco peregrinus, a globally-distributed, large falcon species with some nineteen recognized subspecies. Peregrines feed primarily on avian prey and prefer rocky cliffs, either in mountains or along sea coasts, for habitat. In the Avian Age, when referring to an Awakened peregrine falcon, all are of F. p. anatum lineage as they were the original subspecies that was imbued with sapience by the Apterians. However, their genetics are similar enough to other subspecies and, because of a scarce population after Apterian societal collapse, matings occurred with non-Awakened individuals. Those that practiced this or were descended from those that practiced are known as regressants, though knowledge of this fact in the time of Volatus is often not known from appearance alone. As in other species, an Awakened female mating with an Unawakened male created Awakened hybrids and, so, a spectrum of Awakened variations exist depending on geographic locale. See also *grin, regressant.*

Piscivorous (All, adj.): The habit of eating fish. In most cases it denotes the most favored source of protein in the diet.

Plumicorns (All, n.): The feather tuft adornments, or "ears," on top of the head of Bubo owls (e.g., screech and great-horned owls). Their primary function is aiding camouflage but Awakened birds also use them in expressions of emotion. They do not contribute to their sense of hearing.

Primary feathers, primaries (All, n.): The feathers attached to a bird's wing beyond the carpal (wrist) joint. They number ten in most birds. They are counted from the carpus outward. They are firmly bonded to the metacarpals and phalangeal bones. These feathers provide propulsion during flapping flight. See also *secondaries, remiges.* Consult wing anatomy diagram in next section.

Proventriculus (All, n.): The first stomach (or stomach segment in some species) in the avian gastrointestinal tract. It secretes acid and enzymes for protein digestion. Consult digestive anatomy diagram in next section.

Put over (All, v.): The action of swallowing food from the crop into the stomach, usually accompanied by a shrugging motion.

R

Raven (All, n.): In the Avian Age, the term refers primarily to the common raven (*Corvus corax*) as they are the only species of raven that was Awakened.

Rectrices (All, n.): Tail feathers, twelve in most birds. Consult tail anatomy diagram in next section.

Red-tailed hawk (All, n.): *Buteo jamaicensis*, a large diurnal bird of prey native to North America. The adults generally have brown back, nape, and upper surfaces of the wings with white to cream throat, breast, belly, and underwing surfaces. The tail feathers of adults bears a striking red color. There are light and dark morphs as well. See also: Rustie.

Regressants (Apt./Mam., n.): A label for the practice, or the descendants resulting from the practice, of interbreeding between Awakened and Unawakened individuals of the same or closely-related species. The results is usually fertile offspring but they are only Awakened if the female is Awakened.

Remiges (All, n.): All the large feathers of the wings responsible for flight. See also *primaries, secondaries*. Consult wing anatomy diagram in next section.

Rictal bristles (All, n.): Hair-like feathers on the face of birds that have nerve endings at the base. They serve a dual purpose of elevating food particles from the skin to facilitate cleaning and to convey a sense of touch while manipulating food in dark conditions. They are particularly well developed in owls and other nocturnal species.

Roostery (Vol./Mam., n.): A place of lodging, a hotel or inn. See also *roost*.

Roost (All, n./v.): The act of perching or breasting down for sleep. Also the noun for a place where roosting occurs. See also roostery.

Rustie (Vol./Mam., n.): Non-pejorative slang for red-tailed hawk.

S

Sash (Vol., n.): Slang label for a peacekeeper, equivalent to the Apterian term "cop" or "flatfoot." It refers to the red sash that most of them wear.

Scapulars (All, n.): Feathers located over the shoulders of a bird. Birds of prey raise these feathers when threatened or when "mantling" over prey to hide or protect it. Consult wing anatomy diagram in next section.

Seaberry wine (Vol./Mam., n.): A wine made from kelp buds.

Secondary feathers, secondaries (All, n.): The feathers attached to the wing between the humeroulnar (elbow) joint and the carpus (wrist). The number varies but is around sixteen for many eagles. They are numbered from the carpus inward. They are firmly bonded to the ulna and provide most of the lift support required for flight. See also *remiges, primaries*. Consult wing anatomy diagram in next section.

Seminal ducts (Apt., n.): Also known as the ductus deferens or vas deferens, this pair of tubular structures convey semen from the testes to the cloaca.

They open through the ventrolateral wall of the urodeum in the cloaca. The region around the openings swells with lymph during copulation in order to exteriorize and deposit semen in the female's similarly exposed oviduct opening. In most birds the swelling is minimal and accompanied by cloacal eversion (outfolding) to facilitate deposition, but some birds possess a phallus (penis) which tumesces with lymph for intromission. See also *tumi, nib.* Consult male reproductive anatomy diagram in the next section.

Semiplume (All, n.): A type of feather characterized by having a fluffy down-like elements at the base combined with contour feather-like elements at the tip. Usually found around the hips, tail, and wing roots and serve to insulate and weatherproof while still maintaining a high degree of flexibility. Because of their quality to float long distances, semiplumes are often plucked from a deceased loved one for release into the wind at their releasing ceremony.

Shit-spurter (Vol./Mam., n.): Pejorative term for Accipitriformes (hawks and eagles), in reference to their prominent habit of leaning far over and spurting their wastes horizontally instead of vertically like most birds.

Snow-head (Vol./Mam., n.): Slang, non-pejorative terms for bald eagle.

Storm gull (Vol./Mam., n.), Stormy (slang, non-pejorative): The Avian Age term for the greater black-backed gull.

Starthener (Vol., n.): Slang term for one who was hatched, raised, or lived a large portion of their life in Waystar Region, the northernmost region of Volatus. It generally connotes a hardy soul with no-nonsense demeanor and good survival skills for the climate is harsh and the summer season short.

Steller's sea eagle (Apt., n.): *Haliaeetus pelagicus*, a species of sea eagle who, in the adult form, have brown body, wings, and head with white leg feathers, white tail, white propatagia (web of skin that stretches from shoulder to wrist) and carpi, and white forehead. See also *crowned eagle, crowny.*

Summerstar (Mam., n.): A small, white, five-petaled flower that grows abundantly in spring in Mamyrskit. It's favored as a good omen of a fertile nest so it's cultivation on nests is encouraged.

Swallow's nest (Vol., id.): Slang for something that is packed or crowded, referring to the overstuff nature of a swallow nest when nestlings are almost ready to fledge. Ex.: "The roostery will be as packed as a swallow's nest."

Time-keeping: In Volatus, time is commonly kept with a system of four bells per day, rung out by the village watchtower. "First bell" is at the first quarter day (Apterian 6 am), "two bells" or "second bell" is midday, as measured by a sundial, "three bells" or "third bell" is end of third quarter day (Apterian 6 pm), and "four bells" or "last bell" is midnight. Noon is the daily reset point for time-keeping as it is the most measurable with a simple sundial. The other points are tracked using sand-filled hourglasses that are flipped at known intervals (in the city of Whiterock, they use a three-hour hourglass). There are no universal timezones yet so each town tends to have it's own local sense of time of day.

Toothed puffin (Vol./Mam., n.), Toothy (slang, non-pejorative): The Avian Age name for the Atlantic puffin (*Fratercula arctica*). Sometimes also just known as "puffin," since no other species of puffin was ever Awakened. See also *Toothy*.

Toothy (Vol./Mam., n.): Non-pejorative slang for *toothed puffin*.

Tumi (Vol./Mam., n.): Slang term for the genital mound in the cloaca of a male bird. It is the location of the paired sperm duct openings. Word is a corruption of Apterian for "tumesce" which means to swell. See also *seminal ducts, nib*. Consult the reproductive anatomy diagram in the next section.

U

Underfluffies (V/M, n.): Slang for the undertail coverts and belly feathers, which on many species are particularly fluffy and erotically alluring to others, especially when kept clean and well-groomed. See also *crissum*. See tail anatomy diagram in next section.

Unitum (Vol., n.): The capital city of Volatus, located on the west coast of the large island that comprises the nation.

Urates (All, n.): The white, semi-solid material present in bird droppings. It is a concentrated form of nitrogenous waste, analogous to urine, that has undergone additional metabolic processing to conserve moisture.

V

Vent (All, n.): A bird's posterior orifice for expelling wastes, laying eggs, and copulation. It is the external opening of the *cloaca*. See anatomy diagrams in next section.

Ventriculus (All, n.): A bird's second or "lower" stomach or stomach chamber. It performs mechanical digestion and is often strongly muscled, particularly in species that consume grains and vegetable matter. See also *gizzard*. See digestive anatomy diagram in next section.

Vent sore (Vol., n.): Slang term for an unsavory or unwelcome character.

Equivalent to Apterian term "asshole."

Volatus (Vol., n.): The primary nation of Awakened birds. It is a medium-sized land mass surrounded by three seas (as defined by the Awakened), located in the northern hemisphere. *Author note: It is not based on any single Apterian nation or specific geographic place.*

W

Waning (All, adj.): Reducing. See also: *Moon phases.*

Waning crescent (All, n.): The final moon phase in a lunar month. Depending on the thickness of the crescent, it indicates roughly 1-6 days left of the lunar month. See also: *Moon phases.*

Waxing (All, v.): Increasing. See also: *Moon phases.*

Waxing crescent (All, n.): The first moon phase in a lunar month. Depending on the thickness of the crescent, it indicates roughly 1-6 days after the start of the lunar month. See also: *Moon phases.*

White-tailed sea eagle (Apt., n.): *Haliaeetus albicilla*, a species of sea eagle who, in the adult form, have a mottled white and brown head, yellow beak and feet, brown body, and white tail. See also *mottled eagle, mottle, mudhead, muddy.*

Whiterock (Vol./Mam., n.): The capital city of the Waystar Region of Volatus, located on the eastern coast along the Waystar Sea. It's the largest city of Volatus, boasting a population, as of the census or 300 PA, well in excess of 100,000 birds of every Awakened species. It serves as a crossroads for trade and bird movement between north and south Volatus as well as trans-oceanic traffic to and from points across the Waystar Sea, including Mamyrskit. Industries include trading in a variety of goods as well as fish and other sea food taken from the Waystar Sea. There is also a fledgling industrial sector since Whiterock hosts the largest collection of Apterian technology. The Whiterock Institute also provides advanced medical services and research.

Wingspans (Vol./Mam., n.): A unit of length measurement based upon the average wingspan of an adult female crowny, or approximately eight feet (2.4 m.). Obviously this is a very subjective unit since birds of different sizes have different concepts of wingspan. See *Distances.*

Anatomy Reference

A guide to bird bits mentioned in the text

By Hal Aetus

Birds in the Avian Age use terms you may be unfamiliar with. Some are based on real terms used by ornithologists and other avian-related scientists today, while others are unique, just as we humans have invented our own colloquial, non-technical terms for parts of our bodies. Please refer to these diagrams, and the preceding dictionary, for details if you need them. Additional resources can also be found at wiki.aetusart.com.

Digestive System

(typical of *Haliaeetus* sea eagle)

Additional details in the glossary & at wiki.aetusart.com

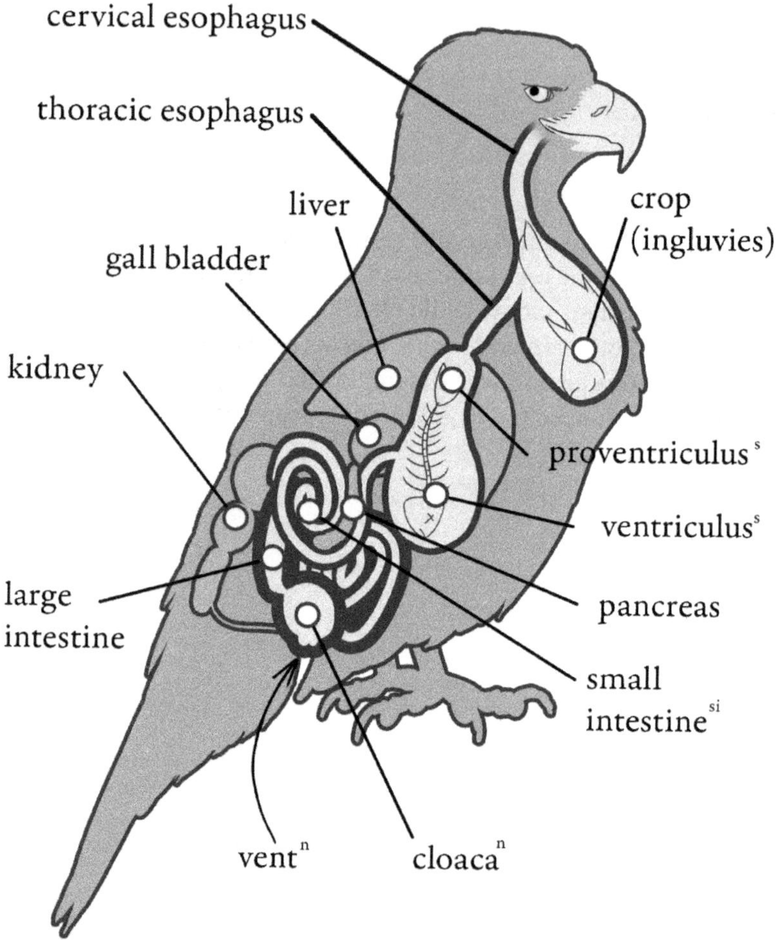

n: The vent and/or cloaca are sometimes called the "nack" in conversation in The Avian Age, but it is considered extremely vulgar.
s: The proventriculus & ventriculus together comprise the "stomach." The ventriculus is also known as the "gizzard" and it is where indigestible matter is compressed into a pellet for casting.

Respiratory

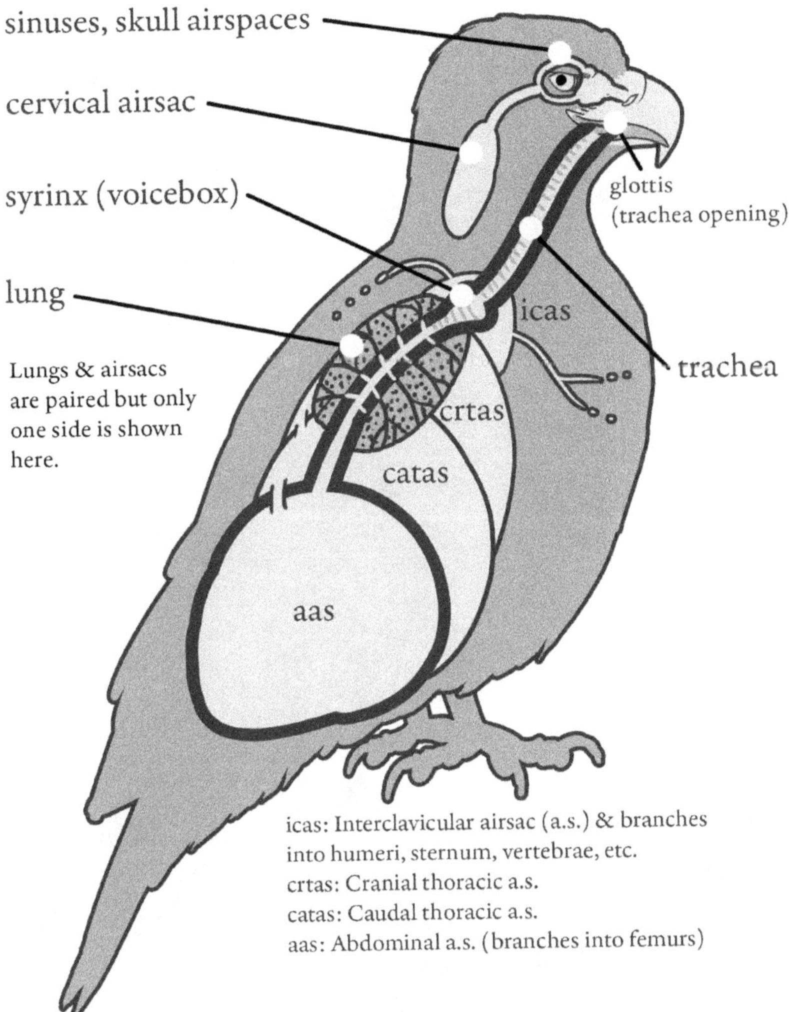

icas: Interclavicular airsac (a.s.) & branches
into humeri, sternum, vertebrae, etc.
crtas: Cranial thoracic a.s.
catas: Caudal thoracic a.s.
aas: Abdominal a.s. (branches into femurs)

Air is circulated through airsacs such that there is a continuous
stream of fresh air passing through the air capillaries (fine lines &
dots above) in the lungs. Airsacs expand & contract while the lungs
stay relatively fixed in volume.

Reproductive

(female *Haliaeetus*/sea eagle)

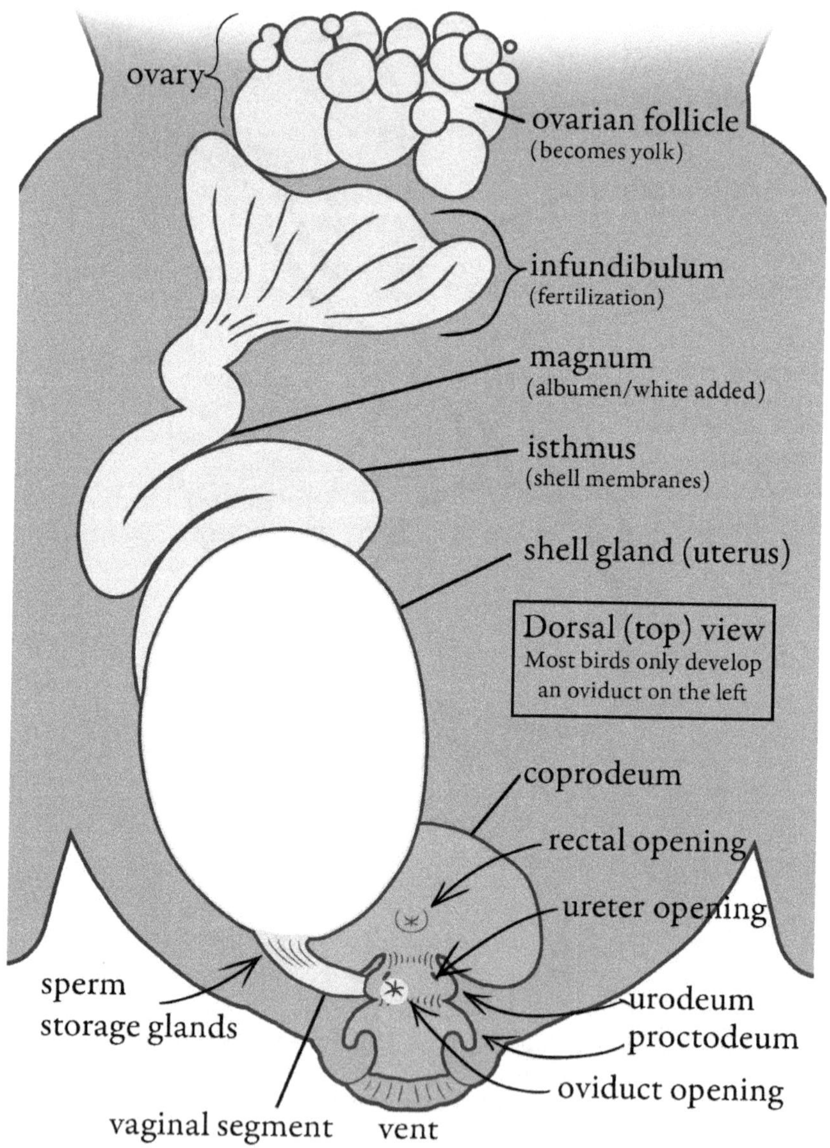

©2025 aetusart.com

Reproductive

(male *Haliaeetus*/sea eagle)

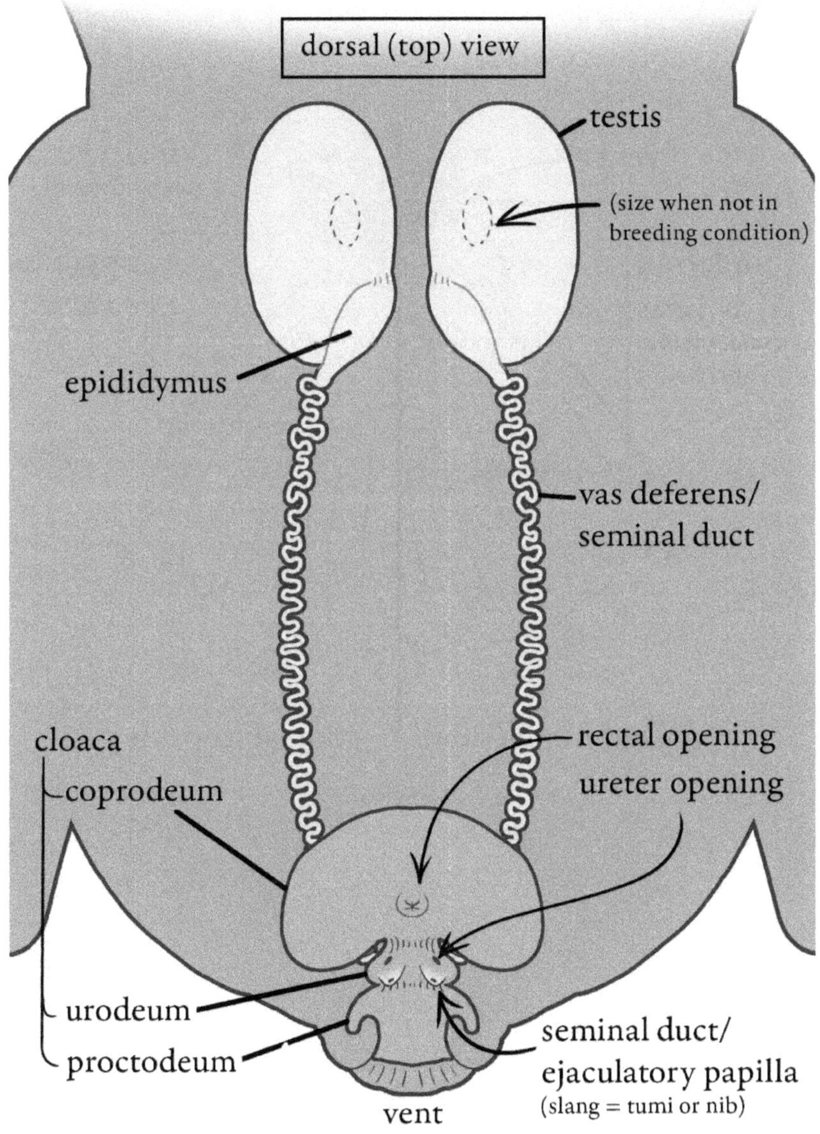

Tail Feathers

(typical of *Haliaeetus* sea eagle)

Additional details in the glossary & at wiki.aetusart.com

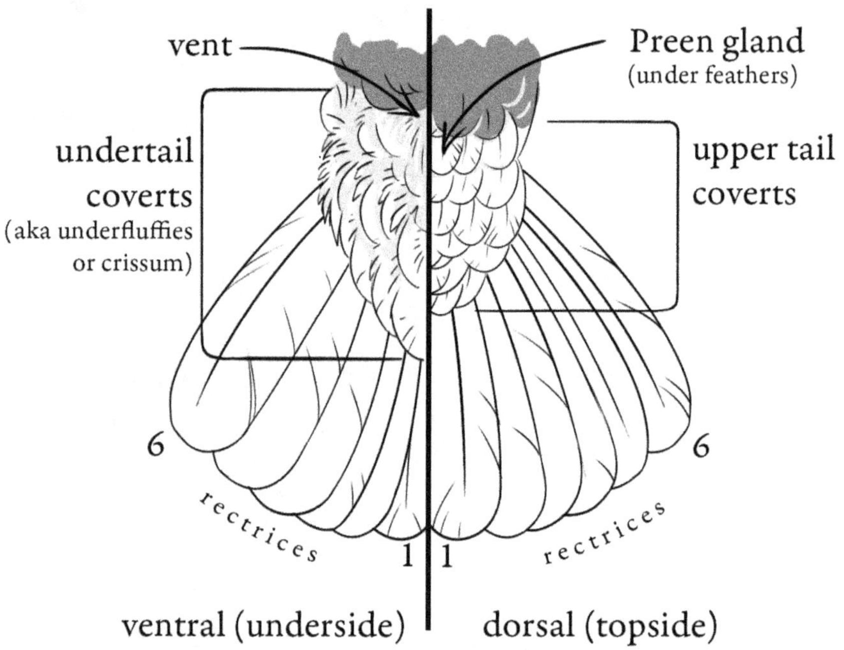

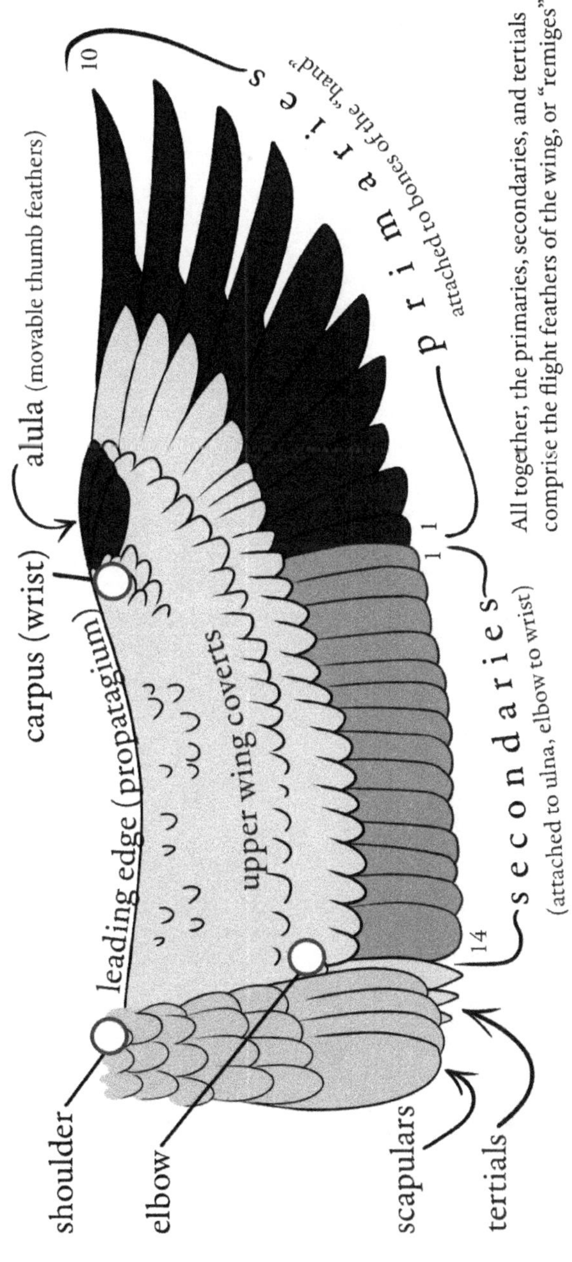

Wing
(typical of Haliaeetus sea eagle)
Additional details in the glossary & at wiki.aetusart.com
carpus (wrist)
alula (movable thumb feathers)
leading edge (propatagium)
upper wing coverts
shoulder
elbow
scapulars
tertials
s e c o n d a r i e s
(attached to ulna, elbow to wrist)
p r i m a r i e s
attached to bones of the "hand"
All together, the primaries, secondaries, and tertials
comprise the flight feathers of the wing, or "remiges"
10
1
1
14
©2025 aetusart.com